Infernal Machines

John Hornor Jacobs

This edition first published in Great Britain in 2018 by Gollancz

First published in Great Britain in 2017 by Gollancz
an imprint of the Orion Publishing Group Ltd
Carmelite House, 50 Victoria Embankment
London EC4Y 0DZ

An Hachette UK Company

1 3 5 7 9 10 8 6 4 2

Copyright © John Hornor Jacobs 2017

A CIP catalogue record for this book is
available from the British Library.

ISBN 978 0 575 12427 1

Typeset at The Spartan Press Ltd,
Lymington, Hants

Printed and bound by CPI Group (UK) Ltd,
Croydon, CR0 4YY

MIX
Paper from
responsible sources
FSC® C104740

www.johnhornorjacobs.com
www.orionbooks.co.uk
www.gollancz.co.uk

Si vis pacem, para bellum

If you want peace, prepare for war

PART ONE

I can show you what is left. The ruins of Harbour Town, in Occidentalia. Of Rume, the Immortal City, herself, if you wanted to walk among those charred stones, if you wanted to see what the machines of war, the machinations of man, and what Hellfire can wreak. And, maybe, someday, when you are ready, we will take you so you can learn. And by learning, rule. – Dveng Ilys

It is the stillness of the mountain lake you must find within you so that at the moment the moon rises, its face is mirrored in the waters. Then action is equal. The still will always master the restless.

– Sun Huáng, The Sword of Jiang

ONE

Kill Their Horses

'Ia-damn it,' Fisk said. 'Ia-damn it all to Hell.' His horse, the new one, had froth working out from under the saddle-blanket and champed the bit furiously in her mouth. Fisk wore a pinched expression – he was irked. Like most men accustomed to the rigours of the Hardscrabble, he liked to do the chasing. Not be chased.

'They're what, a half day behind? This godsdamned place has a million hidey-holes we can bolt to,' I said, sweeping my arm to take in the cracked and sundered expanse of the eastern reaches of the Hardscrabble. The bright, brittle sky became hazy at the edges this late in the summer, and the heat was on us something fierce. Bess barked and coughed occasionally, due to the burns on her rump from the titanic blast of Hellfire that had destroyed Harbour Town.

And now the Hardscrabble, and soon the rest of Occidentalia, would be lousy with Medierans. Like the ones pursuing us – Beleth and his new moustachioed friends.

'Half day, yes,' Fisk said. 'Maybe more. But he had some *daemon*-gripped stretchers with him, leaping this way and that. If he sets those damned dogs on us, we'll be in a spot.'

'We can't keep this pace forever,' I said. 'We don't have enough water and we're too far from anywhere or anyone who might give us succour. We could make for the Bitter Spring, maybe.'

Fisk thought for a long while.

'We'll rest the horses for a bit, over there, in the shadow of those rocks. Then we'll push hard on to the Long Slide, and wait.'

'You're getting sly in your old age, Fisk,' said I. 'An ambush?'

'That's about all we can do, unless we discover that half-century of legionnaires toddling about the Hardscrabble.'

'Don't hold your breath,' I said.

We rested the horses in the shade of a crag of sundered rock as the sun rose. I stripped Bess of tack and saddle and tended her wound as best I could – water, maguey sap slathered on her arse, and kind words. She blew hot air through her nose and nipped at my britches with yellow-green teeth, her stubbly mane bristling. Fisk tended his own mount and we gave them what water we could, though there was scant to spare.

The brutal sun rose in the sky and the shadow where we rested the mounts narrowed and shrank so that we ended up pressed against the rock face, moving to stay out of hammer-blow light. Weariness passed over me, and the injuries and insults all over my body pricked memories – burns on my hands, ears, and back of my neck recalled the incandescent flame of Harbour Town's destruction; the throbbing knot on my scalp where he sapped me, Beleth and his *daemon*-gripped stretchers; my abraded wrists, where they bound me – Gynth, the *vaettir*, fighting, saving me; my hunger and thirst, the taproom of militarised *dvergar*. Beyond that, and before, I could not recall then. I passed a hand over my stubbled head where the hair was almost burned away.

Everything had gone to Hell. And my old carcass was just a mirror of it.

Not much shadow, by then. Even the horses seemed to feel the growing tension as pursuit neared.

'This is Ia-damned ridiculous,' Fisk said, finally, his boots on the line where rock-shadow met brilliant Hardscrabble. 'Let's go.'

Bess and Fisk's mount weren't ready to move in the heat of the day, but our urgency swayed them, though Bess hawed something fierce. I loved Bess dearly, but she was still wilful, like any beast, or offspring, possessed of abnormal intelligence where parents simply want for a docile and accepting child.

When I had her tacked out, I took the saddle and she chuffed hot air and chucked her head – in annoyance or agitation from the chase, I could not tell. Her smarts were hard to fathom.

We lit out, taking it easy. Taking it easy, urgently. No canter, but alternating between trotting and walking, over the Hardscrabble. It was a matter of hours before the Long Slide hove into view and then a matter of hours more before the ascent was well made.

'You thinking what I'm thinking?' I asked Fisk as we took the rise.

'We wait here for them, there's no other approach except up the Long Slide for miles around.' He looked back behind him, over his horse's rump. Far in the heat-warped distance, something moved on the horizon. Horses, maybe. 'We kill as many as we can. If he's got *daemon*-gripped with him, kill them first and then, once it's just us . . .' He paused, thinking. 'Just us men, well, we know what to do then.'

I assumed he meant more killing. 'We need water. We can't hold out pinned down here for days on end.'

Fisk nodded. 'If it comes to that, then, you'll ride on to the Bitter Spring. But it won't come to that.' He looked at me closely. 'You let the stretchers and the *daemon*-gripped get right on top of us, Shoe. Close enough for a kiss,' he said, pulling his carbine and checking the rounds. He thumbed each one's warding, checking the integrity. He'd restocked his supply in Harbour Town – possibly the work of Samantha or one of her junior engineers. Some paltry

5

comfort there, that she was here with us now, even if it was solely through her handiwork.

I laid out my six-guns and began unloading and reloading them.

Almost to himself, Fisk said, 'Yes. You kill the stretchers and *daemon*-gripped, my friend. And I'll kill their horses.'

TWO

A Thousand Tomorrowless Days

THE HARDSCRABBLE: THE tawny gold of the dirt from which sprang the *dvergar* and *vaettir*, emerged from some fathomless, impossible origin; the countless skeins of bramblewrack veining through the gulleys and mountainside, the impassable breaks and soars of gambel and ash and keening pine, traced now with the passage of native creatures – shoal auroch and turkey buzzard and lickerfish suspended in eternal movement, to rise and fall, to eat and be eaten, in a steady progression of a thousand tomorrowless days; now comes the tread of man, first the Medieran boots flickering across the Hardscrabble plains, then Northmen for a year or day, for a blinking moment, and then again Medieran for years following the mapless miles of the Occidentalia wildernesses; blood, the piping-hot blood of the creatures hunted and harvested by man, *dvergar*, and *vaettir* alike, spilling into the dust to be joined by the blood of Medieran and Ruman and Northmen, watered with blood, drenched in the hot stuff, at the clawed hands of *vaettir*, and the swords and guns of men. Dispossessed, too, the land: the dwarves held it, and the stretchers hunted it, ravenous ghosts, not knowing the bounty and treasure they had and with the coming of the Ruman, Hellfire in one hand and whiskey in the other, they lost it; dispossessed of land and identity too, not knowing where to belong and only realising it maybe when the Rumans

7

– when *we* – gave them something to fight against. Dispossessed of home and hearth, but never the *vaettir*, never the stretcher, the genius loci, the leaping lord. It is he that is the possessor of the land, and the West, and while he might die, he will never relent of it or be dispossessed.

Unlike me.

We sail to Rume.

I have no home but where Fisk is, and he is lost to me.

Juvenus, pale-faced and sweating, entered our stateroom after a polite knock. He'd put on his suit and even worn a tie, though we'd become inured to the sight of the man sweating in shirtsleeves. The Nous Sea grew high with towering swells and the weather had turned cold, but the innards of the *Malphas* were always hot. Hellish hot.

I greeted him as Lupina fed young Fiscelion and Carnelia stretched, sore from her *armatura*.

'Miss Livia,' the captain said. Behind him stood two lascars bearing carbines and frightened, taut expressions. He cleared his throat and scratched at his arm. The bare white of a fresh bandage peeked from the cuff.

'How may I help you?' I asked. I pointed at his wrist. 'You come to me freshly bandaged, and not by my hand, so I assume you have had use of a Quotidian and have received a message and that it bodes ill for us.'

'I am here,' he said, clearing his throat and tugging down his cuff to cover the bandage, 'to relieve you of your Quotidian device, Madame. By order of Tamberlaine himself.' He looked uncomfortable and his voice pitched toward nervousness, rather than villainy.

'And what reason did he give?' Carnelia said, straightening. She had sweat plastering her hair to her neck and was dressed in the loose, flowing garb that Sun Huáng had insisted they – lost

Secundus, Tenebrae, and her – train in. Carnelia placed her hand on the *jian* that she'd negligently sat upon the dresser. The two lascars shifted their weight.

'He is Emperor and our Great Father,' Juvenus said. The words were rote, and came from him like stones falling from one's mouth. 'He need not explain himself to me.'

'I am of as noble blood as he,' Carnelia said. 'Cornelians can trace our history back to the gods, just as Tamberlaine can.'

Juvenus lowered his head. The muscles popped and worked in his cheek. 'I am sorry, Livia, Carnelia. I am sorry. You are to be placed under guard until we reach Rume. This is his command.'

'Is Tenebrae also to be placed under guard?' I asked.

Juvenus paused. 'No, he is not.'

'I see. We are to be corralled home to become pawns on the knightboard of Tamberlaine once more.' I went and took Fiscelion from Lupina and kissed his fat cheek. He cooed. 'Are we to be confined below decks?'

'No, Madame,' Juvenus said. He gestured to the lascars standing behind him, white-knuckling their carbines. 'You will have an escort should you want to venture about.'

'Guards, you mean,' I said.

'Escorts. You remain my guest and will receive all due honour and civility that the *Malphas* and I have to offer,' Juvenus said. 'I am sorry it has come to this.'

'You are sorry,' I said, thinking of how the folk of the Hard-scrabble used that word. 'I have never seen someone as sorry.'

Juvenus, bowing his head, said, 'Please send me a message if you have any needs and I will make sure they are addressed.'

'Wonderful,' said I, though I can only imagine that my tone belied my words. 'Thank you. You may go,' I said, waving a hand toward the passageway behind him.

He stood there a long while, looking agitated and sheepish.

Eventually he screwed his courage up to say, 'But you have not turned over your Quotidian. I cannot leave until you do.'

Handing Fiscelion to Carnelia, I retrieved the argent-warded box. It smelled of sulphur and blood and woodsmoke and when I handed it to Juvenus, I felt heavier rather than lighter because of it.

When Juvenus was gone, Carnelia began cursing and clenching her fists – maybe because she felt some great furore at being controlled once more by the patriarchs of Rume, or maybe because she knew that by forcing us to return to Rume, Juvenus consigned Fiscelion to be bereft of a father. I did not know. Lupina watched implacably, sucking her teeth.

'Sissy,' said I. 'We must come to an accord.'

'What? And let them do this to us again? Let us be corralled like beasts? I think not,' Carnelia said. Her neck was flushed red, as if the anger in her belly grew and moved through her like fallowfires across the shoal grasses.

I approached her and lowering my voice, said, 'I do not know if they will stoop to eavesdropping on us, but I say to you now I will *not* submit. *We* will not submit to Tamberlaine. I will not remain in Rume. The Emperor has said I am divorced, but I am not *here*.' I struck my breast with a fingertip. 'And I will get back to Fisk and Occidentalia.'

'I will stay with you, sissy, unto the ends of the earth,' Carnelia said.

I embraced her then, which was made awkward by Fiscelion being held between us, and he squawked and made infantile coos and gurgling noises.

'Oh, sissy, how you have changed,' I said, looking at her. There were lines at the corners of her eyes, and a fierceness in her disposition that was marked and new. She had always been fierce and wild – but before, it was the fierce outrage of uselessness, the restlessness of chattel. But now she was like me, dispossessed, divided from a home, her fierceness had meaning and usefulness. And she had her *jian*, her talon. And her wits, which had never been inconsequential, but the pettiness had fallen away and left something altogether remarkable.

She smiled, but it did not touch her eyes. 'And what of this accord?'

'We must wait and watch for a time to escape. I doubt we will be allowed off ship at the Ætheopicum port when they take on fresh water, wine, and supplies. And so, we will find ourselves at the Ostia pier before the Ides to be returned to the society of our father and the rest of Rume.' I touched her hand. 'We will appear entirely content with our situation until the moment we must move. We will dote and exclaim over our father, as he dotes and exclaims over Fiscelion, and do whatever Juvenus asks with absolute aplomb and grace.'

'That's a fucking bitter role,' Carnelia said. 'Where's the fun in playing nice? I would spit in their faces. Or,' Carnelia said, wetting her finger in her mouth and then drawing circles in the air with it as if it were a sword, 'Better, prick them with my sword.'

She smiled, and it was not wicked, but avid and predatory.

'Yes,' I said. 'I know you would. I hope you will not have to.'

Carnelia was quiet for a long while, thinking of it. Fiscelion reached up and played with her hair with fat, pink hands, and gurgled.

'We must raise no suspicions of our intent,' I said. 'And be compliant.'

'And mendacious.'

'Yes, mendacious. Yes, coy. Yes, docile, if we are to have a chance,' I said.

'Too much of my life have I been so,' Carnelia said. 'I do not want to be so again.'

'Would it ease the chafe of having to be so to know you will be working toward that break?'

'A little,' Carnelia said, and wandered over to the settee, where her hand found the *jian*'s hilt as if of its own accord.

'Can you do it?'

She thought for a while. 'Livia, once you denounced Rume and parentage and everything else in front of our father, and tossed it all into his teeth. I watched you then with a little girl's grubby heart, only thinking of my own pleasure and ease. But when you said those words, something stirred in me that I didn't know was part of my make-up. And I was jealous and envious and terrified for you all at once.'

'I remember,' I said.

'It has taken me a long while to get to that place myself. Gnaeus is gone. Secundus is gone. I would renounce all, like you, without home and without destiny except that which I make and I will not give that up lightly.'

'So, you will be compliant until it is time to not comply?'

Carnelia withdrew her sword and held it up so that it caught the *daemonlight*.

'I will,' she said, looking at the blade and turning it this way and that to catch the light as she once might have a mirror.

Writing becomes habit. Over the long months separated from Fisk, I've become used to taking down a history of my events of the day, my thoughts. And now the Quotidian has been taken from me, it is to myself I write, instead of my love. Indulgent. Indulgent but necessary. A much less bloody endeavour altogether, and I have not yet decided if that is a good or bad thing. Sometimes, when I write, it is like whispering my secrets into the great Occulus of the Cælian, the eye of Rume peering toward the heavens, the hushed voices of its visitors echoing strangely. Other times, it is like a cough, a reflexive exhalation – all my love, my hate, my worries, my concern for Fiscelion the Younger – all exhorted in a mad rush of words that I pen down.

There are nights, though. There are nights when young Fiscelion snuggles with Carnelia or Lupina in our stateroom, and on numb feet I go onto the deck and stand on the prow, in the shadow of the swivel guns, the salted air heavy and cold, the *Malphas* rising and falling on the swells as the lascar guards watch me silently, gripping their carbines. I ignore them as best I can. I would scream but for the observers and the accord Carnelia and I made. Off in the distance Rume awaits, and there's no turning away from it. No amount of bribery or wheedling could change Juvenus from this course.

At times, Carnelia joins me on deck, under the stars, with her *jian*, and she makes the arcane moments, the tracery of air, the turnings and jumpings of Sun Huáng's swordplay until she is slathered in sweat and panting. Once Tenebrae appeared on deck, a wooden gladius in hand, as if to join Carnelia, but the look she gave him was so frightful he paused and then went back below decks.

We both have our *armatura* of grief.

THREE

Time Enough And Bullets

THE DAY GREW long, and we found a vantage at the peak of the Long Slide, where Beleth, the Medierans, and the *daemon*-gripped thralls they had in tow would have to approach. The Long Slide is a curious tilt of solid rock, and has been so for aeons; a stone raft two miles long, tilting up in the dirt waters of the Hardscrabble's eastern reaches and bordered by mapless leagues of impassable and impenetrable gulleys. Even the most agile of *vaettir* would have trouble making their way through the scrawls of deep fissures and eroded passageways, choked with bramblewrack and ruin. At the peak of the Long Slide, a slurry of boulders and a worn, thousand-year-old switchback trail threads its way down and away from the tilted rock plane. There was nowhere to hide on the face of it, and it was in full view of the summit for a mile or more.

The perfect spot for an ambush.

'They'll wait until night,' Fisk said, leaning against a rock and pulling the dusty brim of his grey hat over his grey eyes. I watched the Long Slide, searching the far end where stone met dust. 'And you won't have any trouble seeing them, with your—' He waggled two fingers in a V at my eyes. '*Dvergar* nighteyes, or dim sight, or whatever you want to call it. But I should make sure I nap beforehand. When I open my eyes it will be dark and I might not have your vision, but it'll be good enough to kill the engineer and

14

his Ia-damned followers,' he said and then, with no more fuss or talk of it, he gave his hat a second tug, settled back further into the rock and sand, and promptly fell asleep.

You take rest when and where you can find it, in the Hardscrabble.

Shadows grew long, drawing east as the sun fell across the western vault of sky. I kept watch on the foot of the Long Slide, letting my mind drift off, trying to stay away from brooding about recent events and the current situation, with no success, and found myself considering Gynth, the *vaettir* who saved me. He'd been a strange one, and it niggled at me that I knew not if he were alive, or dead. It takes an enormous amount of damage – traumatic bodily damage – to kill a *vaettir*, and while he'd been deep in the shite, torn to bloody ribbons when I last saw him, I never saw him cease to breathe or give up whatever spirit that propelled him, be it fierce will or some other inscrutable working of the stretcher heart.

But I'd be lying if I said I hoped he was dead.

And from there my mind emptied, finally, and I found that unfettered ease that comes with staring for long periods, mindlessly, at the big wide world underneath the big unbroken Hardscrabble sky, bruising now pink to purple to the deepest blue, the billions of pinpricks of stars spraying across the heavens. In the distance, coyotes yipped and called. Fisk snored with light chuffing sounds under his hat.

And there, in the distance, smoke. I marked it, imagined I smelled it, though that was near impossible since it was miles away. There lay the ruinous husk of Harbour Town; the charred bodies of thousands of men, women, children, *dvergar* and human alike. Countless tonnes of goods, timber, wickerwares, fish, goat, shoal auroch, sage and gambelnut, honeycomb and garum. All gone, all blown to vapour – the integument of their corpus destroyed, rendered to char, reduced to ash and now that carbonite stuff spread to the winds of the Illvatch to spread over the Hardscrabble as a caul. Weeping would not do. Nor remorse. No emotion seated in the heart but lust for vengeance would suffice.

I kept watch, closely, waiting until it was full dark before nudging Fisk with my boot.

His head came up, and he pushed his hat back, as if he'd been waiting for that touch all along. And perhaps he had been.

'They've set a camp and built a fire,' I said, pointing in the direction of a new sliver of smoke. They were burning bramblewrack, or some other thin combustible. Charcoal, maybe, which they'd toted along with them inside saddlebags or rucksacks.

'They'll not stay at it. It's a ruse to draw our eyes away, and they'll be coming,' he said, and spat downwind toward where the smoke rose. 'They won't wait until dawn.'

'No,' I said, considering. 'You're right.'

'They might have a native with them who could've anticipated our use of the Long Slide,' he said. 'Someone that knows this country. Or, maybe one of the *daemon*-gripped could answer questions, if that's the way the engineer's summoning works. If so, they'll know this is an ambush.' He put his hand on the carbine, worked the action, and checked the chamber.

'Let's hope they lack foresight.'

Fisk nodded. 'Shoe, we've got to be patient, and wait. We have to let their Hellborn pets get as close to us as possible and make sure they're dead, and hope they show themselves on horseback.'

'We've been over this, pard,' I said. 'I know the plan. I drop the stretchers, then whatever *daemon*-gripped men are on us, you'll kill their horses.'

Fisk nodded, once more, and pursed his lips and turned to face the Long Slide.

It was in the small hours of the morning when they made their move. Two shadows, creeping up over either edge of the Long Slide, up from the gulleys. They remained low, crouched and walking on all fours like a lizard or other creature – but faster, moving with a speed born of infernal desire. The big one, the *vaettir*, scurried up the face of the Long Slide in the weak illumination, its head turning on gimbaled pivot, scenting the air like a hunting hound. Some sort of ichor oozed from its jagged mouth, blood maybe, the wet stuff catching starlight, my *dvergar* vision catching its glint. The smaller one – a *daemon*-gripped man – followed, tracing the northern edge of the Slide.

Fisk patted my arm to draw my attention and inclined his head toward the possessed man. Plans change with the situation. No horses in sight. It took just his nod to indicate intention. I was to take the possessed man, and he would meet the stretcher. I nodded my agreement and eased down from the view we had and softly made my way around the boulders and up a higher path, until I was perched upon a pile of stones high enough to regain vantage. After a moment I found the man again, and he was much closer and had picked up devilish speed.

The *daemon*-gripped stretcher was almost upon Fisk. He'd reached the base of the boulder slurry that capped the Long Slide and had craned his leering face upwards, toward where my partner waited, eyes sharp glints of broken glass. The thing was dressed in frontiersmen clothing, new, short at the sleeves and the cuffs. The undersized human garb gave it a strange, otherworldly appearance, like a lanky man dressed in children's clothes, and the half-light of stars washed it clean of all colour. He looked as if he smelled like corpseflowers, but I guessed Fisk – and maybe I – would know soon enough.

The stretcher scrabbled up the boulder, vaulting higher than a steamboat's top stack, and found purchase on another slab of rock some fifty feet shy of the crest of the Long Slide where we waited. From the corner of my eye I noticed movement from Fisk;

he stooped, snatched up a large rock and threw it toward me, but down-slope. It fell with a short, sharp clatter, and the stretcher's head whipped about, gaze fixing on the area where the sound came from, while the *daemon*-gripped man scuttled like a crab toward it.

My breath caught. Down-slope, horses with riders stepped into the open and onto the Long Slide. There were three, moving slowly.

Fisk held up his hand to me, gesturing to hold.

The riders walked onto the Slope, leisurely. It occurred to me that they might not, after all, know we were there and were simply following our trail.

All the better.

The possessed man and *vaettir* came together where the rock had fallen and turned to look toward us, again reminding me of Hellish dogs of war. Fisk snatched up another rock and let it fly, beyond and behind them, but they only turned their heads to glance down-slope and then gazed back up at us. They began to move.

Motion congealed to slowness, my breath came short and fast in my chest. Screams. From the possessed stretcher, or the *daemon*-gripped man, or from me, I could not tell you with any veracity now. The creatures moved like wind over the shoal grasses, up and over the lip of the crest and were suddenly between Fisk and myself, and moving fast.

But, in some vagary of fate, neither of the creatures noticed Fisk; their cold, fervent gazes fell upon me and they raced forward.

I sighted the *vaettir*'s chest with my carbine and fired, filling the air with a booming report, despair, and brimstone. I whipped the carbine around, levering another round into the chamber, then fired again. The stretcher pitched forward and then the *daemon*-gripped man was upon me.

He hit me like a bull auroch, bellowing. I fell backward with him on top of me, slamming me into the ground. All the breath whooshed out of me in a great heave, and I could not find air.

The man's hands ripped at my chest and I felt the carbine spin away, then there was a hot explosion of pain as black gnashing teeth bit where my neck met my shoulder, furrowing toward the vital sanguiducts below my skin. Reflexively I pulled in my chin, like a turtle ducking its head into its shell, but the infernal man's teeth tore through my shirt and into the meat of my shoulder.

The pain was excruciating and I cannot recall now what desperate sounds I might have made, but I can recall clearly the Hellish grunting the *daemon*-gripped man made, whipping and fretting his head, fast and vicious. There was a separation and his face pulled away, mouth full of a gob of my flesh, a spray of blood in the air.

I fumbled toward his face with my hands, catching his stubbled cheek and following the contour to sink my thumb into the socket of his eye. *Dvergar* are many things, but our hands are made for industry and rough work. I was knuckle-deep in the man's face before he gathered whatever infernal wits he had – I know not what a man with such a rider upon his soul has in the way of reasoning. Was he a creature purely of instinct, divorced from higher thought, except for what impetus that Beleth gave him?

With my thumb sunk in the socket, I jerked the possessed head to the side, slamming it into a boulder – once, twice – impacting with deep meaty sounds. My other hand fumbled to my gunbelt and drew Hellfire. The mind splits, awareness separates: the sound of distant drums, the reports of a carbine, echoing away into the night; the tug and fret of my hand, knuckled deep in a man's eye socket, smashing skull to rock; the trigger, cold, the pistol unsteady in my hand.

I stilled. The barrel came to rest on the man's chest. I pulled the trigger. The six-gun jerked in my hand in an eruption of smoke and noise and his body fell away.

I lay there breathing for longer than I care to admit.

Pulling myself up, I saw Fisk at the crest of the Long Slide, his attention down-slope.

I wiped the gore on my trouser leg and looked down at my spattered clothes. Fastidiousness is as useless in gunplay as it is in the Hardscrabble. As I joined Fisk, he said, 'Put a couple more notches on that gunbelt, friend.'

He glanced at me when I said nothing.

'There's three dead horses halfway down the Slide. The idiots rode Hellbent for leather up-slope when they heard the gunshots.' He shook his head and allowed a grim smile to flash across his features. 'They're hiding behind the carcasses.'

I made my way over to Bess, who chuffed and stood nervously, agitated by the scent of Hellfire and blood hanging about me in stinking streamers. I dug out a clean handkerchief from her saddlebag. Having no cacique, I wadded the cloth into my freely-flowing wound in my shoulder, collected my carbine, and went to rejoin Fisk.

We stood breathing in the pre-morning light, waiting for the sun to rise. I peeked my head over the boulder to look where the dead horses lay, and the bright sound of a rifle came skittering across the stony distance between us and the fallen horses as a whistling sounded overhead, the bullet passing inches from my skull.

'Not a bad shot, that one,' Fisk said.

'He didn't get me,' I said.

'Nor did those *daemon*-gripped. You're fearsome, Shoestring.'

I checked the bleeding of my shoulder. 'Don't feel so fearsome.'

'Neither does the bear or badger,' he said, dipping his fingers into his shirt pocket and fishing out a hand-rolled cigarette.

'Real easy to be fearsome when you're toting Hellfire,' I said, and peered over the crest again, then ducked my head before the rifle report could sound. A little explosion of rock and debris came from overhead where the bullet hit a boulder.

We waited, watching, checking over the crest in turns. Right at dawn, one of the fallen riders, the one closest to the southern edge of the Long Slide, stood and ran in a stooped, lumbering fashion toward the falloff where the gulley began.

Fisk shot him and he fell. He moaned once and then remained still.

The sun peeked over the rim of the world and the gunmetal grey peaks of the Eldvatch, the Smokeys. Colour rose up from the dirt like a fog, first tawny, then ochre, the ferric dirt streaked with light yellow and red.

'Let's heat it up a bit,' Fisk said, once the sun was fully risen and the visibility had improved. He popped up, sighted his carbine, fired, and ducked back, underneath the lip of rock. He began counting down from twenty, before doing it again.

On his sixth or seventh shot, I glanced over with him, and saw the blood spattering the rock face of the Long Slide. He was shooting the corpse of one of their horses, over and over again. Whoever was hiding behind it was due for a wet, sticky morning.

When Fisk's gunbelt was half empty, he cupped his hand to his mouth and yelled, 'We got your pets, Beleth! But you probably already know that!' The sound floated out over the sun-baked Hardscrabble. The temperature was rising. 'Throw out your Hellfire and stand up with your hands on your head and we'll have a nice chat.'

Silence far below, but my ears pricked and I swore there was some discussion going on down there.

'We've got water for days and I can just keep shooting your dead horse,' Fisk hollered. He sent an unsmiling wink my way with the lie. 'At some point, one of my bullets will find you. Come out!'

'If we do, what assurances do we have that we'll go unharmed?'

'You have my word!' Fisk bellowed.

'Would you swear on the life of your wife? Your child?'

Fisk's face contorted, and his mouth pursed as if he tasted something sour. He waited too long. So I yelled, 'Yes!'

There was another long silence while the trapped men conversed down-slope.

Beleth's voice rang out. 'I think not, Mister Ilys! And look there, on the horizon.'

I lifted my gaze past the dead horses where the loathed engineer hid. Across the now bright and burning Hardscrabble an ochre plume of dust billowed up from hooves.

'We are the vanguard, Mister Fisk. More horsemen follow behind,' Beleth called. As he did, his companion popped up and fired, making us duck.

'Is he speaking truth, Shoe? My eyes cannot see that far in the glare.'

'There are riders approaching,' I said.

Fisk rose again and levered and fired, his cloud of brimstone mirroring the one in the distance. One, two, three shots, each one slapping into the downed horse. Even from this distance, I could tell the rounds were making a gory mess of the horse's innards. The men hiding there would be painted red.

'I think maybe I'll keep making soup of that horsemeat, Mister Beleth!' Fisk cried. 'One of my shots will find you.'

He fired again.

'We got to run, partner,' I said. 'Nothing for it.'

'I can kill that man, now,' Fisk said, face tight and angry.

'Had you time enough and bullets, you could,' I said, soft. 'But we've got to go. They're two, maybe three hours off, if we're lucky. We can reach the Bitter Spring before them, and plan another ambush, maybe. But if we stay here, we'll be outgunned.'

His eyes narrowed and he rose, fired at the horse once more.

The viscous gore oozed from the creature in a slick that curled around the mound of its great belly – it had fallen backward when it died, leaving its underside facing us. The mess of it made me cringe. Shame that such noble creatures had to die, and in such an ignominious fashion, to preserve our meagre lives.

'Save your bullets,' I said, then turned and went to Bess and pulled myself into the saddle.

After a moment, Fisk followed to his own horse.

FOUR

Comfort In Blued-steel And Wood

FATHER WAS DRUNK and wearing his silver bear leg when he greeted us at the Ostia wharf. It was an inebriation he'd been developing, working at it like a man at a labour he loved dearly, I could tell: wine in the morning, beers at lunch, and onto the harder stuff by nightfall for days, if not weeks. His belly was drum-head taut, his hair a clotted, greasy mess, his eyes rheumy. He wore his *toga minima*, the black one, the loose fabric drawn over his head in mourning for our brother and his son, Secundus. It seemed Tamberlaine, Juvenus, Tenebrae – or another of the Emperor's agents – had filled him in on the details of our journey and its sorry end.

'Let me see him! Let me see my grandson!' he cried as we appeared on the deck of the *Malphas*.

To each side of him were praetorians holding carbines and gladii in their sheaths, war-aprons unbloodied and neat, their blue uniforms and phalerae immaculate. The day was cold, and bare, and everything was brown – the pier, the muddy water pouring down from the Ruman hills out of the mouth of the filthy Tever River. A misty rain fell upon us and Fiscelion cried as the cold air and dampness infested his bedclothes. A mechanised swing-stage unfurled itself from the *Malphas* and we disembarked as a flurry of stevedores, shoremen, and porters replaced us on board to gather our belongings and trundle them down to waiting wagons.

Tenebrae disappeared quickly, though not before giving our father a terse greeting. As he left, he paused to look at me, and I could not help but think there was some tense unsaid thing between him and myself. He opened his mouth as if he wished to speak and then closed it and left our presence.

Father took Fiscelion and made inane, cooing noises to him. 'He has the Cornelian complexion,' he announced, and waggled the baby's chubby hand. Fiscelion didn't enjoy that, and began the prelude to outright crying. 'And something about the eyes, I think,' Father said.

'Will we show him to his grandfather?' I asked, observing Father closely.

'You are, presently,' he said, looking into Fiscelion's face.

'No,' I said, shaking my head. 'Carnelia and I are the daughters of Tamberlaine, now. Thanks to the damned diplomatic mission that killed our brother. Did you know of this? Have you been informed of the events and the Emperor's manipulations?'

He opened his mouth, shut it. The muscles in his stubbled cheek tightened, a tic began beneath his eye.

Once Fiscelion began to cry, he handed him back to me. He blinked rapidly as if seeing us for the first time. Awkwardly, he embraced first me, and then Carnelia.

' 'Nelia, you've put on weight,' Father said, glancing over us. 'It's quite becoming. It seems a long sea journey flatters you. Sad that it will be your last.'

'Ah, so we are to remain here?' Carnelia said.

'Yes,' he said, wiping his hands on the hem of his *toga minima*, as if to rid himself of the grime of handling an infant. 'Tamberlaine has arranged marriages for both of you that will occur before midwinter.'

25

I nodded my understanding, if not acceptance, and glanced at Carnelia, who met my gaze.

'Before you say anything,' Father said, 'I too liked Fisk. He is an able man and I was happy for you to remain wedded to him. But the political wind has shifted and there is no denying our Great Father.'

I said nothing.

'Hate me if you will, but it is out of my control,' he said and slumped his shoulders.

All of life, a diminution. Maybe all size is relative. The world grows large and he remains the same – small and withered and drunk. Dispossessed.

But there he stood, dishevelled, like some crossroads prophet preaching for bread in the morning, through the day for alms, and begging for a cup of wine at the end of it.

'And me?' Carnelia asked. 'Who am I to wed?' She did a little hop of excitement and smiled. For a moment, it was easy to believe that she was the same frivolous sister, full of mischief and snark. Except her smile did not touch her eyes.

'You will wed Brenus Galvanius Caelo, senator and legate of the Latinum Fifth. He's quite the rising star.'

Carnelia clapped and kissed Father and he gave the vacuous, half-placating, half-annoyed expression that marked most of his dealings with Carnelia, or at least had in the past.

'And for me?' I asked.

'Messala Corvinus has been widowed and his dealings in the North have quite pleased Tamberlaine, and so in addition to a governorship, he will take you as wife.'

Corvinus was Father's age, though still hale and virile. His wife had been a beauty, pale and translucent as aged vellum beaten thin, and I couldn't imagine what death might have surprised her. I had known the man since I was a child.

I bowed my head in acceptance. 'There is nothing I can do but accept.'

'That's right,' Father said. 'I'm glad you see the sense of your situation. I feared you might—'

'You feared I might what, Tata?' I asked, raising my eyebrow.

'Rebel. You have never really taken to being told what to do.'

I patted his arm, kissed his stubbled cheek. *You have no Ia-damned idea, Father.*

'You look terrible,' I said. 'How much have you been drinking?'

He scrutinised me for a moment with glazed eyes. 'Enough to wash away the shitstorm of the debacle in Far Tchinee. They've fallen into civil war. And these praetorians would be marching you to the Spire to be tossed to your deaths had not you succeeded by failing. Kithai is no longer a player on the knightboard. They have fallen to their own internal pressures.' He pursed his lips and then spat into the waters. 'But Tamberlaine punished me anyway and stripped me of my governorship in Occidentalia.' He was silent and his gaze moved across my features, maybe searching me for the ghost of my brother's visage. 'Enough to forget, for a moment, that all my sons are dead.'

'I'm sorry, Father,' Carnelia said. 'For the loss of our brother. And that we are all that is left to you. He died protecting us.'

Our father fell silent and bowed his head, thinking. After a moment, he said, 'And the body?'

'Packed in a cask of oil.' I pointed to the stevedores moving our chests and baggage, and the large cask where our brother's body was stored.

'I would look upon him before burial,' Father said.

And I thought, *I'm sorry, Secundus, but I will not be the one to bury you.*

'Sun Huáng tells me that the oil acts as a preservative, but the flesh becomes soft, and he will only just resemble our brother and your son. It has been two months since his death,' I said.

'I would still see him,' he replied, and turning, walked back to the carriage, limping, his false bear leg stumping against the planks of the pier.

After an exchanged look, Carnelia and I joined him.

It began to rain, as if night wore the storm as a gown, trailing streamers of droplets as it came, and darkness followed as its handmaid. Father did not speak during the ride but looked out at the rain-slicked cobbles of Rume's streets, the myriad paths marching up the Cælian, the dull, unlit faces of villas and insulae passing silent as sentinels as we progressed. The deluge made a percussive, atonal patter on the carriage rooftop and conversation was impossible.

The villa was sombre when we arrived, and Fuqua – Father's manumitted head of household – stood on the doorstep with a powerful mirrored *daemonlight* lantern in one hand and a concerned expression upon his face. He bowed to Father as our Cornelian patriarch passed inside, wordlessly. I had never seen Father act this way and part of me wanted to comfort him, but the harder, incalcitrant core of me could not: he had help orchestrate our brother's demise, either by outright collusion or lack of spine. Either way, I could not assuage whatever grief or guilt churned in him. Nor in myself.

Fuqua greeted Carnelia and me by name and acknowledged Lupina, who bore Fiscelion upon her breast. The head of household peered at the boy and held a hand up when Lupina made to enter the Cornelian villa, as if he were a guard requesting a bribe or toll. A smile split Lupina's wide, genial face, and she pulled the swaddling away from Fiscelion's face and for a moment Fuqua made googly faces and ridiculous noises in the doorway. Fiscelion gurgled and cooed.

Glancing into the villa, and then to me, Fuqua said from the corner of his mouth in a casual yet hushed tone, 'Your father's been in terrible shape since he heard the news of Secundus via those bloody contraptions. I only heard of his response to Gnaeus' sad end second-hand, but I was witness to his devastation at *this* loss. The only thing that has allowed him to—' He gave another look to the interior of the building, as if fearing to be overheard '—keep his *shite* together has been the knowledge that this little lad was coming home, and the fear of Tamberlaine himself.'

Fiscelion grabbed Fuqua's finger and Fuqua waggled it, making idiotic faces. 'That's right, that's right, little master. Who's the chubbiest little man? The chubbiest maxiumus? Who is?'

'Thank you, Fuqua,' Carnelia said. 'For the telling. We will not forget.'

A procession of expressions promenaded across his face. He was a Cornelian man, through and through. Rumour had it that after forty years of slavery under Father's hand he asked to remain a slave, when Father offered him his manumission. Freedom was forced upon him, a horse field-shy and reluctant to leave the barn.

'You will be brought before Tamberlaine tomorrow,' he said. It came out in a rush.

'What?' Carnelia spat. 'I will not.'

I placed my hand on her arm, stilling her.

'It will be interesting, I think, to hear our Great Father's take on our house's misfortune,' I said.

'And *his* part to play in it,' Carnelia said.

Fuqua's expression became worried. 'I am just a servant and know nothing of these things.' He turned to go inside. 'I should not have spoken.'

Carnelia, moving in an easy, gliding movement, interposed

herself in front of Fuqua. It was like oil, the way she moved. 'Thank you, Fuqua, for your candour. We truly are in your debt.'

'It is nothing,' he said. 'Your father will drink. In his study. I have prepared cold dinners and clear wine for you in your rooms. It waits for you now.'

Carnelia held her place for a moment, until it drew out until the stretching point, and then moved aside. Fuqua scurried past her.

Once he was gone, Carnelia said, 'He keeps the purse. We will have to visit him.' Her expression was grim. 'Later.'

'Yes,' I said. 'But he will not be harmed.'

Carnelia opened her hands. 'We'll see. If it's between his life and our freedom—' Carnelia made a little twisting gesture with her hand, as if she was snapping a dove's neck.

'No harm.'

Carnelia made no response and turned from me to enter our ancestral home.

We had unpacked and supped on the meats and cheeses, bread and olives, that Fuqua had provided. Lupina poured us wine – fine, rich Ruman wine, the only consolation for being back in this Ia-forsaken city. Fiscelion slumbered in a crib that Father (or more likely Fuqua) had had the forethought to procure for us.

From my weathered travel chest I withdrew the sawn-off shotgun that I'd carried over half the known world, and its sweat-stained bandolier. Its grip was hand-sweet and welcome. Would that I had a pistol or carbine for more range, but all in all, this gun took the form of comfort in blued-steel and wood and Hellfire.

Fifteen shells gleamed on the chamois cloth I'd placed on the bed's coverlet. Only fifteen Hellfire shells to get me to Occidentalia unless I could find an engineer. I picked up each one and wiped the casing clean, checking the wardings for scratches or marring. Somewhere, a world away, my husband might be doing the same.

I hoped he was not in such dire straits as me and, like me, had his most boon companion at his side – Mister Ilys. Shoestring.

I can allow this sentiment here, where Carnelia, and Lupina, cannot see it – I am powerfully afraid. Afraid for myself, afraid for my child and husband, and afraid for my loved ones.

Carnelia noticed what I was doing and came over. She placed her *jian* on the bed and then went to her chest and withdrew a gunbelt.

'Where did you get that?' I asked. Guns are expensive and ammunition even more so.

Carnelia flushed. 'Do you remember that cavalry praefect in New Damnation? The handsome one?'

'No.'

'He was a regular at our hotel. I came to know him some, while Father and Gnaeus were whoring at Pauline's,' she said.

'I remember Pauline's. I had to retrieve them one night when Marcellus' legatus came calling.'

'Well,' she said. 'From him.'

'Surely he did not give it to you.'

'Not exactly,' Carnelia said. When I looked at her closely, she said, 'I don't know why I took it. But I did. It's a wild, frightening country there.'

'The question is, *how* did you steal it?' I asked.

Carnelia blushed even deeper. 'I'm always getting into things that don't belong to me.'

That answers that.

'Or are those things getting into you,' I said. 'Ia's bones, sissy, the only thing that saved you from being tried in an open court for thievery was your father's name and position!'

'I'm not proud of myself, Livia,' she said, and the blush was gone. 'But I have it still. Would you rather me package the Ia-damned thing up and send it back to Praefect Bullus?'

'Bullus?'

31

'Family name,' she said. Her face took on the coy look she usually reserved for Father.

'Never mind.'

Carnelia oiled the pistol and checked the rounds, of which she had but twelve. She sniffed, looking down at where the two weapons and their ammunition lay spread across the chamois cloth. 'Thank the gods for my *jian*, sissy, for we are desperate shy on Hellfire.'

'We will make do with what we have. And we'll have Fuqua take us to Father's office.'

'He will balk,' she said.

'And we will convince him otherwise.'

The hour was late though we had not yet reached the middle of the night. Lupina watched us from a chair, where she was brushing and oiling our high-boots – the broken-in ones we purchased at an outfitter in Novorum when I first set foot in Occidentalia. Other bits of our darker clothing – oilcoats and undergarments, wool skirts and winter tunics, socks and rain cloaks, rain hats and night raiments – lay stacked around her. From somewhere, she had found three rucksacks and organised our clothes into small stacks.

'I am not so much worried about Fuqua, if you'll beg my pardon,' Lupina said, 'but making all *this* fit into those.' She gestured with blunt hands at the rucksacks. 'And have you still be able to lift them.' She frowned.

'Pack but one change of clothes. We will make do with that. Should all go well this night, we will have money enough to buy more,' I said.

A knock came at the door. Lupina moved fast, snatching up the rucksacks and tossing them underneath the bed as Carnelia pulled the coverlet over the guns.

Lupina went to the door and cracked it. 'Master?' she said, in a deferential tone.

A phlegmy cough sounded, and my father's voice said, 'I would bid my grandson good night.'

I joined Lupina. 'Father, he is asleep, as should you be. If he wakes now he will be cranky.'

'Oh,' Father said, crestfallen. His hair was unkempt, as were his clothes. The smell of whiskey poured off him like smoke from an incense-heavy brazier. 'I just wanted—'

He stopped for a moment, looking lost. 'I just wanted to see the boy. To hold him, maybe.'

'One moment, Tata,' I said.

I looked back into our room, holding the door so Father could not see inside. Carnelia had moved piles of clothes onto the bed to cover the guns. She looked at me with a questioning expression.

'All right, Tata, you may see him. But—' I held up a finger. 'In the future, you'll need to keep your visits to Fiscelion within acceptable hours.'

He nodded his head. 'I remember when you were just a babe. How you'd keep your mother up all night. I saw no harm in the time, tonight.'

'Fiscelion takes far more after his father, then,' I said. 'He sleeps a' night like a little man. Come in.'

Father entered and peered about, squinting. It was dim in Carnelia and my adjoining rooms, the *daemonlights* banked low.

'It's a blasted mess in here,' he said, and tottered over to the chair that Lupina had occupied only moments before. 'Lupina, you've grown lax in my daughter's service.'

'Yes, Mister Cornelius.' She ducked her head in the servile way that many slaves and servants have to keep away over-long scrutiny. It was an act, I knew. Women are always forced to pretend.

'Do you have whiskey? No?' He looked about, frustrated. 'Wine, then,' he said and held out his hand. Lupina poured him a glass and placed the glass in it.

I went to the crib and picked up little Fiscelion, softly. His baby breath came as little chuffs of sweet air. 'You can hold my child or that wine, but not both,' I said.

Father looked torn for a moment. He tossed back the wine, handed the glass back to Lupina, and then extended his arms for Fiscelion. I gave the child to him, gingerly.

Father brought him to his chest and looked into his sleeping face.

'He is chubby, is he not?'

'Yes. A plumper,' Carnelia said. 'You should've seen Livia's expression when he first latched onto her teats.' She covered her own breasts as if protecting them. 'O Fortuna!' She laughed and I couldn't tell if that was an act or not. Something about my breastfeeding always amused her.

Father fell silent. Lupina busied herself around the room. Carnelia poured herself another glass of wine, but I noticed she watered it heavily. I looked upon my father, possibly for the last time.

Tears began to well and then flow down his stubbled chin. One fat drop hung on the tip of his nose for a moment and then fell, plopping on Fiscelion's face. He stirred, woke, and began making the mewling preamble to a good cry, seeing Father's strange, male face so close to his. Sensing this, Father handed him to me and stood, his tears still standing plainly on his face.

Never a man to be embarrassed – as a noble of Rume, he let his emotions war across his features unabashed – he said, in a voice thick with alcohol and some emotion, 'I am glad he is home. Oh, what a man he will make. I will show him all of Rume. I will show him all of Gall and Tuetons and the Northlands—'

'Yes, Father, but not tonight,' I said. 'It is time for a feeding and then all of us to bed. The hour is late.'

'Right. Of course.' He looked around and patted his clothes, as if forgetting something. 'Ah,' he said, and bending, withdrew a small clever flask that was part of his false leg. The leg I'd cut from him.

Only Father could take dismemberment and turn it into a way to always have a drink available.

He unscrewed the flask's silver cap, and turning it up to his mouth, found it empty.

'It seems that well is dry,' I said. The phrase – such a Hardscrabble turn of words – gave me a quick pang of yearning for Fisk.

'Yes,' he said, and turning, began to leave.

'Wait, Father,' I said. I kissed him on the cheek. Carnelia, too, came close and kissed him.

He looked confused. 'What did I do to deserve such lovely affections?'

'Nothing,' I said. 'Everything.'

'We love you, Father,' Carnelia said. 'Please remember that.'

'Of course!' he said, and swayed some. 'How could I forget?'

He stumped off, looking for whiskey.

We waited.

After the villa settled around us, the soft sounds of footsteps and washbasins filling and emptying faded away, slaves and servants banking lanterns and stoking fires and filling decanters ceased, and the final hush of night settled on the Cornelian villa like a blanket. We left Lupina watching Fiscelion. Fully dressed in dark, outrider garb, we crept from our chambers on cat paws and made our way to Fuqua's quarters, downstairs, near the library. Carnelia held her sword in hand, sheathed, like an elderly gentleman who carries a cane for fashion's sake, but does not need it.

In Rume, no slave or servant may lock a door within his master's house. There is a distinct law prohibiting this after the Terracina

35

Revolt of 2501, and it's one I've always found antiquated and ridiculous. Should the patriarch come round at night and fix the shutters and close and bar the front gate? Should he lock the cupboards and all the entryways? Most of Rume ignored this antiquated law. But Fuqua was a Cornelian man, through and through.

At his room, I pushed the door open. There was no lock.

He was sitting at his desk. The space was well lit, and he looked up from his writing as if he was expecting something.

'Will you take the boy with you?' he asked.

'What?' I said, too startled to say anything else.

'Will you leave Fiscelion here, when you go?' Fuqua asked.

'No,' I said, somewhat taken aback. The idea had never occurred to me. 'He goes where I go.'

He looked a bit disappointed at the news. 'I don't want to know where that might be,' he said. He pointed to a money purse on his desk. 'There is all the money in the house, less our operating costs until we can make a withdrawal from the College of Investment and Indemnity. It's a tidy sum, over a hundred silver and many gold denarii.'

I picked up the purse. It was very heavy. With it, we could get to Occidentalia.

'How did you know?' I asked.

Fuqua glanced at Carnelia, who stood holding her sword, silently. A curiously soft expression was on her face.

'I have watched you both grow, if not since children, since you were young women. You are your father's children. Never in my time here, serving your family, have I seen either of you ever do a thing that you did not acquiesce to,' he said, spreading his hands in explanation. 'I had to take but one look at your faces to know.'

'Are we that obvious?' I asked.

'At least to me,' he said. He stood and came around the table, holding keys. 'There are horses in the stable – I readied them myself. Now, I fear you must go. But before you do, you must—'

Carnelia, holding her *jian* in a strange reverse grip, smashed the hilt into Fuqua's face and he collapsed to the floor. She snatched up the keys.

'Why did you do that?' I asked. 'He might have had more to say—'

'I spared him the anxious waiting. I am not cruel, and he knew it was coming. If we left him unharmed—'

'Father would crucify him,' I said, putting it together. I had not thought this endeavour all the way through, it seemed.

Carnelia checked his breathing. 'He'll live.' The side of his face had swollen horrendously in the few moments he'd been unconscious. 'And have a cracker of a headache when he wakes.' She looked down on him. 'Thank you, Fuqua,' she said.

Lupina was ready when we returned to the room. She had Fiscelion in a curious fabric sling hugging her chest. At her belted waist, a cleaver and small cudgel. I took up my rucksack, and Carnelia took hers. I checked my sawn-off, in its holster on my thigh.

'We will have to go out of the window as we used to when we were girls, sissy,' Carnelia said. 'Risking the guards at the doors is too much.'

'Of course.' I turned to Lupina. 'Do we need to lower Fiscelion—'

Lupina moved to the open window, hopped up on the stone casement, and said, 'I've scaled the Eldvatch with a child sucking at my breast. This is nothing.' She disappeared outside.

We followed, clinging to the wet Finder's Rose that covered the rear side of the villa. When we were girls, we would sneak away so often and with such determination to see the Covinian boys who lived close-by, going in and out down the wall's growth, that it had a strip of roots bare of leaf running from the ground to our window. The house cook then, Drusillia, would complain about the lack of capers for her tunny, though the wall still provided ample – the house slaves and servants loved their two wild Cornelian girls. And their capers.

The horses were saddled – including a small pony for Lupina, who mounted and rode with no trouble at all – and we took them into the street without bothering to put cloth on their hooves – that would have been a sure sign of skulduggery, if there was any. The rain muffled our horse's footfalls and our cloaks, drawn over our heads, hid our identity from view. But it was with great restraint that we walked out onto the Cælian and down into the cobbled streets toward the Mithranalian Gate.

We passed the desolate Mezzo Market, empty at the late hour, though there were chickens clucking nearby and a few shadowed figures slumped in watchful repose under oilcloth tarps, guarding wares.

Past tenements and shanties to the great, grotesque Tever, muddy and gurgling and swift, flowing west toward Ostia and the sea. Through the rain-slicked financial district and counting houses on the Macean Hill, and to the suburbs of industry on the edges of Rume.

The city was dark and still. The grey, rain-threaded skies made a pregnant hush that filled the streets. It was a Rume I never knew and one, now that I was leaving it forever, I might have wanted to know better.

We made our way, quietly, softly down alleys and past crossroad colleges. The few *vigiles* and praefects that noted us did not ask for our identities and we did not offer them. They moved with the desperation of the wet with a warm, dry place waiting for them.

The Mithranalian Gate was in view when a man stepped into the road, directly in front of us.

'Where do you think you're going?' Tenebrae said.

FIVE

The *Vaettir* Need Hellfire

NIGHT HAD FALLEN and Bess was sucking wind hard by the time we reached the Bitter Spring. I'd put her to the spur – something I'd never done with any vigour before – and she took great umbrage to it, bucking and hawing. The situation made it necessary, but that hurt me. She'd been called my wife in jest by Andrae, and that had rankled, but I loved the beast and hated Beleth all the more for forcing my urgency upon her.

The Bitter Spring was a sulphurous, if fresh, upwelling of water from the sundered Hardscrabble, situated in a warren of eroded gulleys. Some time in the dim recesses of history, more water flowed from it and made smooth the gulley walls that, if one travelled them, could open up on canyons or disappear into the earth in caves with mouths like the gullets of giants.

The water smoked and stank of rotten eggs. Nothing is easy in the Hardscrabble. We had to fill the only skillet I'd managed to keep since the destruction of Harbour Town and let it cool before being able to drink. Cool, the water was yellow and gritty. The horses drank first, slowly, so slowly, tonguing the pan when the water was gone. When they stopped foaming and heaving, we took our share of the rank stuff. It tasted terrible, but it eased our terrible thirst and refreshed us. I filled our canteens and waterbags and then continued to fill the skillet for our mounts until they were sated.

Fisk opened his Quotidian and let blood and fed it to the infernal thing. It steamed and hissed and gave off a charnel stench, yet did not write down any words when he placed the parchment beneath it.

I have never seen Fisk as enraged as he was then. He screeched, as if he was a *vaettir* howling at the sky, and kicked the dust, bowling over the device and spilling the remains of his blood onto the dirt.

'It could be anything,' I said.

He did not respond, but stood panting, staring into the myriad gulleys that snaked away from the Bitter Spring.

'She has Fiscelion. Just a babe. Did she not say that feeding him was tiring and she needed to keep up her strength?' I rolled tabac in a paper and lit it. 'She is safe. She is well, my friend.'

Those sentiments went unremarked upon. Fisk drew his pistol.

'Now, pard, you don't need to—'

'Shut up, Shoe,' he said. His shoulders tightened and he stilled. 'We got company.'

I hopped up and drew my six-gun. I had let my mouth get away with me, once again.

'How did they get here so fast? It's nigh on impossible,' I said.

'It isn't Beleth, or his Medieran horsemen,' Fisk said.

In the dark I could make out many figures moving in the gulleys. Small figures. 'And it ain't *vaettir*, because they don't move like—'

A voice rang out in the dark. 'On the contrary, *dimidius*, we are *vaettir*,' rang out a woman's voice from the darkness.

They came forward, weapons out. It was *dvergar*, my kin, bearing arms – guns, knives, swords, cleavers, scythes. And at their head was the hard-bitten, wrinkled old woman from the Harbour Town meeting. The mean-spirited one who didn't have much trust for me, and looked upon my person with the aspect of a matron at market, having found a tomato that has gone rotten.

'Matve Praeverta,' I said. 'I am glad to see you made it out of Harbour Town alive.'

'No you're not, *dimidius*.' Like in Harbour Town, she used the Ruman word as an insult – a thing of halves. 'Throw down your guns and we won't kill you where you stand.'

'That's not going to happen,' Fisk said, and fired. A larger *dvergar*, one who carried Hellfire, yelped and his gun went flying. 'I'll put one in his eye next, grandmother.'

Praeverta's expression did not change – her dour, craggy face remained immobile. But she stopped and gestured for her companions to do so as well. *Dvergar* live long lives, and Praeverta could remember Occidentalia before the Rumans and Medierans came to take the land. But it's a Ruman custom to believe that with age life is less precious because of the lack of it remaining. My kin know that even with our long lives, the last years are the most precious, and we do not wish to give them up easily. Not without a fight. She would not hazard herself – or her party – unless desperate.

'It looks like there are eleven of you,' I said. 'And it just happens that that is how many bullets Fisk and I have left. So why don't we all take a step back and calm down.'

Praeverta sneered, but took two steps back. 'We need water. We're here to drink, the same as you.'

'Send someone forward to retrieve it,' Fisk said. 'I'll not shoot them unless they make a hostile move.'

Praeverta chucked her head and two figures came forward. They were *vanmer*, the fair, blond *dvergar* that are rare and considered beautiful or hideous, depending on whether you value the differences in people or hate them. They both were missing hair and had burns, like myself, on the backs of their hands and necks. Refugees from the Harbour Town conflagration.

Behind us, Fisk's horse nickered. I watched as a sly expression creased the crags of Praeverta's face.

'Inbhir!' she called. 'The horse!'

A gun boomed, followed by a high-pitched falling scream. Then silence.

Praeverta, who held a short hand-scythe, hooked it into her belt and said to her people, 'Put up your weapons, and go butcher that thing. We'll have a fire and meal before morning.'

Fisk began cursing, long and steady. Praeverta laughed. 'Keep your weapons, Ruman. You're with us now.'

Bess hawed in the darkness and I worried they would kill her too, but they did not.

'There are men, many men, with guns and blades and Hellish companions on their way here now,' Fisk said, grinding his teeth. 'And you've reduced me to walking.'

'To keep you from running. Hard being taken down a notch, is it, big man?' said a rough-voiced *dvergar* man, busying himself with a small pail at the Bitter Spring. 'There are great changes on the wind, and the smell of brimstone,' he said.

'Catch Hands,' Praeverta said, 'help with the horse, the Ilyani won't know muzzle from arse.' She turned to me, ignoring Fisk. 'Keep your friend on a leash and we'll get along just fine. Now. About these men following you. Why are you on the run, *dimidius*? I could tell from the first time I saw you that you were a man of no place and unwanted. But why? Have you turned against the foreigners, too?'

I spoke to her in *dvergar*, 'I am of the West and this is my home. My blood offends you, yet it is of this place as much as yours.'

'Don't dirty your mouth with our speech. You are half-Ruman and serve them. Why do these men chase you?'

'The man chasing us does so because we have injured him, and his endeavours, greatly. He was the one who destroyed Harbour Town,' I said.

Praeverta squinted at me and pursed her lips. She might've been a handsome woman once – she had strong cheekbones and still lustrous, if greying, hair. She was fit, if bowed some by years, and had clever hands. But her mouth was cruel.

'You're lying to me. About what, I don't know.' And on that score, she was correct. I could not tell her about the *daemon* hand that Fisk held, and I feared that her horse-butchers would find it themselves.

Fisk must've had the same thought because he scooped up the Quotidian, returning it to its warded case and then went to his fallen mount. 'Hold there, hold on. Have you never butchered a shoal auroch?' He pulled his longknife. 'I'll do it, or you'll cut my tack and bloody my gear.'

Praeverta had watched him closely, I noticed. 'These Rumans with their infernal machines. And you ride with them.' She shook her head before I could respond. 'Let us circle back, *dimidius*. How could one man have destroyed Harbour Town, hmmm?' she said.

I said nothing.

'What? A stretcher taken your tongue?' Praeverta chuckled. She squatted down on her hams and removed a small steel flask and took a sip. 'No. I think not.' She looked at me a long while. 'These infernal machines,' she said again, softly.

Something in her demeanour changed and she stood up.

'*Vaettir!*' she called. 'Brothers and Sisters of the Mountain. Let us eat this flesh the Rumans have so willingly provided. Then we shall plan and make ready an ambush. One of the Ruman engineers rides to us, following these sad souls.' She gestured to Fisk and me.

Turning in a circle and speaking loud for us all, an exultant look suffused her weathered face.

'We shall catch this man and bring him to Neruda,' she said, raising her hands in a victorious gesture. 'We shall capture this engineer, for the *vaettir* need Hellfire!'

A sculptor. A man very much like me, a child of halves. Neruda, the man of the West, father of the *vaettir* and leader of the *dvergar*.

SIX

Not Entirely Honourable

TENEBRAE REMAINED MOTIONLESS, framed in the alley, the Mithrandian Gate looming in the rain-misted distance, behind him. The moment drew out, elastic.

Carnelia moved. She was off her mount almost faster than I could see and her *jian* was out and flashing. Tenebrae, not one to be caught off guard, drew a pistol in one hand and a gladius in the other and assumed a defensive stance.

Their swords met with a bright sound, ringing out in the night, cutting through the sound of the rain. Carnelia lunged, but Tenebrae moved off her centre-line and swung his six-gun like a bludgeon. Carnelia wasn't there any more, having followed her forward momentum with a roll that seemed almost animalistic in its fluidity. She popped up and turned, her cloak swirling around her.

Their swords met again as she came forward, clanging twice so fast it was hard to discern the separate sounds, and Carnelia's foot lashed out and caught Tenebrae hard on the thigh as he was stepping forward. His foot slipped on the rain-slicked cobbles and he went tumbling at an angle, away from her.

But he was a trained praetorian, having spent years at *armatura* and war-play, if not war itself, and he was back on his feet before Carnelia could press her advantage.

A strange grin came across his face. 'Sun Huáng would never have given you a sword had you not merited it,' he said, his voice not angry; if there was any emotion there, it was sadness. 'How Secundus wished that it had been him.'

Carnelia dashed forward, again. A flashing feint, a crosswise strike, a pointed lunge. Tenebrae danced backward and out of the way. The blows that came near, he caught on his blade and would twist, redirecting, so that her sword would whip around, as if he had used the power of Carnelia's strikes to rebound against her. He was not over-matched, yet he was wary.

Like her wit, Carnelia's sword was vicious.

She attacked in a breathless rush, feinting, slicing, and probing Tenebrae's defences. He stopped talking and pursed his lips in concentration, his blond hair plastered to his face. I slipped from my horse and withdrew my sawn-off.

Tenebrae pressed against her. Carnelia was fast, but he was strong, and his sword was heavier. He came forward, using both his sword and gun, batting the *jian* to the side and lashing forward with the muzzle of his pistol, catching Carnelia in the side. Had he fired at that moment, much of the alleyway would have been covered with my sister's insides. She twisted away, hissing.

But then, I was near. I levelled the shotgun at Tenebrae's chest and he stopped his forward movement and raised his hands. 'Enough,' I said. 'This noise will draw guards, and had you wanted to arrest us, you would have been accompanied. Why are you here and what do you want?'

Tenebrae lowered his weapons. 'I guessed you would run – what Tamberlaine has planned for you both would not sit well with you.'

'Does all of Rume know we're fleeing?' Carnelia asked, exasperated, sword point still firmly levelled at Tenebrae's heart.

I shook my head. 'That matters not. You did not answer my question, Mister Tenebrae. What do you want?'

'I will come with you,' he said.

Carnelia gave a snort of derision. 'You're Tamberlaine's man, from crown to crotch. Sissy, he'll only betray us and turn us over.'

'I am sworn to the Emperor, the protection of his body and heirs, as are all praetorians,' Tenebrae said.

I glanced at Lupina, who sat stolidly on the pony, one hand holding her oil-cloak over Fiscelion, keeping him dry from the rain. The sound of crossing swords must soothe him, for he remained quiet.

'His heirs,' I said.

'Yes,' Tenebrae said, and he too looked toward Lupina. 'I loved your brother. He was . . .'

Tenebrae stopped and he swallowed uncomfortably. 'He was my true soul and that is not an occurrence I can forget or slough off lightly. I would help preserve his memory. His family.'

'You betrayed us to the August Ones. You sold us!' Carnelia said, furious. She stepped forward, raising her sword.

'No!' he said, and his voice was desolate. 'I did not know the contents of the message! Tamberlaine did not trust me with it!'

'Nevertheless,' I said. 'We cannot trust you and we cannot ride with you. So what are we to do?'

'You need me.'

Carnelia made a disgusted sound.

'Harbour Town is no more, blown away on infernal winds. It burns still.'

'So?' I said.

'If Harbour Town can burn, Rume can burn as well. It takes but innocence, blood, and a hand willing to commit such a heinous crime. The gates are barred. Every person is searched. Trade has stalled.' Tenebrae took a great breath. 'You are noble and were

46

not subject to customs and have only been in the Immortal City for hours. But things are desperate. People fear for their safety. This rebel engineer, this Beleth, if he can destroy a city, then we are all at risk.'

'Why are you telling us this?' What he said made sense. I feared and waited for what else he might reveal.

'You cannot pass the Mithranalian Gate without a dispensation from the College of Trade or the Emperor himself.'

'And you have such a dispensation?' I said.

'No, I do not,' he said.

'So how is it you think you can help us?' Carnelia asked.

'I cannot get you through the gate,' Tenebrae said. He holstered his pistol and sheathed his gladius. 'But I can get you under it.'

We followed Tenebrae through the alleys. He led his horse and we rode, north and away from the Mithranalian Gate.

'How can we trust him, sissy?' Carnelia said, from the corner of her mouth.

'How can we trust anyone? You just put your faith in whatever connection you feel, you hope your decision isn't shite,' I said. 'Do you believe him about the gates and Rume's fearfulness?'

'Yes,' Carnelia said. 'It is a sore blow. Beleth wielded almost godlike destruction against us. Would that I had killed the man back on the *Cornelian*.'

'I have wished the same thing,' I said. 'We will remain wary and watchful, but what other choice do we have? We must leave Rume and the night is growing long. I would be miles away before the sun rises.'

Carnelia nodded, tight-lipped.

Tenebrae led us to a stable. There was a small sign with a gold-enamelled signet of crossed gladii framed in laurels. Below that, a

47

stylised bull with a dog biting at its neck and a scorpion stinging its testicles.

This answered some questions.

'So, the praetorians are aligned to Mithras, is that it? How do the priests of Ia feel about this?' I asked Tenebrae as we dismounted.

'The priests of Ia content themselves with sweet boys and Gallish whores and the contemplation of the food served at the final father's triclinium and allow the praetorians to do as they will, as long as we remain true to our earthly Father,' Tenebrae responded. He pulled open a large stall and, gesturing as if welcoming us all to his home, he said. 'Here we are. Dismount and bring your packs. There will be horses on the other side.'

Carnelia clutched her sword and said, 'How do we know you're not leading us into a trap?'

Tenebrae shook his head in disappointment. 'I could've called for guards a dozen times over. Would you just get over yourself for a moment and *think*. I am risking everything for you and all I'm getting in return is stupid Ia-damned questions.'

Carnelia blanched and fell silent. They were similar, those two – mercurial and sharp, but heedless and mouthy. Had he been inclined toward females, they might have made each other happy. And miserable. And happy again.

But that was not to be.

We untacked the horses, and the weight of both our rucksacks and the saddles and gear was tremendous.

Lupina bore her pack without complaint – and Fiscelion, too, who began to make sounds of discomfort.

'Quick,' Tenebrae said. 'Before the lad begins to bawl.' He went to the back of the stable and, pressing one of the planks, opened a door that swung inward. 'It's steep for the first fifty or so paces, and then it levels out.' The passageway revealed was old, made by hands hundreds of generations past. The fitted stones ran away into the darkness, shining with moisture. A cold wind blew from the open mouth, and the smell of mould and rotten things came with it. 'The praetorians have always been more than guards to the Emperor,' Tenebrae said. He pulled a small mirrored *daemonlight* from his cloak and held it up, illuminating the darkness. 'We were clandestine, once. And not entirely honourable.'

Carnelia barked out a muffled laugh.

'Aye, you think me treacherous. But I swear to you I am not. I loved your brother as much as I love myself. I would gladly return him to you and take his place.'

'Fat lot of good that does us now,' Carnelia said.

'Sissy. Listen to the man for once and put aside this childish rancour,' I said. 'Do you truly think he colluded with Tamberlaine?'

There was a long silence broken only by our footfalls on the slick stones and Fiscelion's intermittent vocalisations of discomfort. He would cry soon.

'No,' Carnelia said. It was reluctant. She had always been slow to admit wrong and despite all the changes within her since leaving the Hardscrabble, one can never deny one's own nature.

'Then stop this childishness and focus on our task. We must *leave*. If we are not miles away by morning, I fear we will *never* leave Rume,' I said.

Carnelia said nothing. Tenebrae spoke: 'Where will we go? They will be watching the ports, once they know you're gone.'

'North and east, I think. To the sunken city of Nexia on the tongue of the Nous Sea. Tamberlaine will expect us to go to Ostia, or south to Cambria or Pintus, to find passage. They are mendacious, but direct in their mendacity. We shall be circuitous,' I said. The flagstones of the passage were treacherous and with my rucksack and saddle, both my legs and arms ached with the exertion. The walls dripped now, and the ambient light from the

49

doorway was gone – only Tenebrae's *daemonlight* provided any illumination.

It was a relief, then, when Fiscelion began to cry in earnest. Our little party stopped then, and Lupina dropped her burden and began to unsling the child.

'Will he be heard above?' Carnelia asked. Her tone had changed, and she was tentative.

I could not see it, but I did sense it in his voice – a smile. He said, 'No, as long as the lad is not too vociferous. On the *Malphas*, his wailing would seep into every room through the bulkheads. It was a hard journey—'

'You should—' Carnelia said with anger and then stopped herself.

'His britches are soiled,' Lupina said. 'Little man, we're going to clean you right up. Yes we are,' she said in a singsong voice. She lay him on the hollow underside of the saddle and changed his nappy with deft hands. It was cold there and he squalled and squirmed. The soiled cloth she tied tightly and left on the ground. 'Will he take the teat, you think, ma'am?'

'He would, but let us save that until both of us need it more,' I said.

We took back up our packs and saddles and continued on.

In the darkness, we came upon a grate, thick steel bands inset in stone. Tenebrae withdrew a key and inserted it into a recessed stone enclosure. It unlocked with a loud click that echoed strangely off the stones.

'When Ia came to us, the worship of Mithras was outlawed for a time. Soldiers have always loved the bull god, and that has never changed. Ia is Father, but Mithras, in his mystery, is succour and friend. We had to hide our rituals and tauroctonys, and so The Skein was created, a maze beneath this part of the city where we could celebrate our warlike god without fear of condemnation or persecution.'

'That is why we entered through the stable! The tauroctony!' Carnela was excited, and all her rancour at Tenebrae gone. Emotions passed over her like wind over shoal grasses. 'To bring in the bulls!'

Tenebrae smiled again. 'Yes. And they would come here,' he said. 'Follow me.'

The maze opened before us. There were many doorways and passages with very little indication or demarcation as to the difference between any one or another. But Tenebrae led us on, confidently and swiftly. We passed through small, dripping chambers reeking of rotten meat, and other sections that seemed dry and sandy and smelled of tallow. One room was full of casks – of ale, wine, oil, fish-pickle, salt-pork and more I could not tell. Eventually, we came to another grate with a lock. Tenebrae withdrew his key once more – as he took it from his tunic I caught a glimpse of the stylised bull-head that crowned it – and, using it, gave us passage beyond.

'It is not far now,' Tenebrae said. 'We go down more. Your feet will get wet, I'm afraid.' He looked at the ceiling. Moisture beaded and dripped here. 'Ack, I hope this damned rain hasn't flooded the culvert,' he said, and moved on before I could question him about it.

The passage sloped downward and water began lapping and splashing at every footfall. Soon we were up to our knees. And after twenty more paces, our waists.

'Give me that saddle,' Tenebrae said to Lupina. He took it and bent over. 'Climb up, Madame. Climb up. Today you have a fairer mount than you've had before, I should think.' He pulled his cloak to the side and bent over.

Lupina moved Fiscelion's sling around to one side so that my child was nestled under her arm rather than her bosom. The sling was quite an ingenious contraption and spoke highly of the cleverness of *dvergar*, I should say. Had Lupina not been there, I would have been at a loss for what to do in the situation. I thanked the gods – Ia, Mithras, the Mater, Pater Dis – that fate had brought this indomitable little woman to me, and that I had had the sense to fight to keep her near me before our ill-fated journey to Kithai.

Once Lupina had her arms around Tenebrae's neck and was secure, he hefted high her saddle and waded into the rising water, full force. My arms were of lead, and I was growing weak from the exertions of the night, but I managed to lift my saddle above my head and follow him into the frigid water.

We pushed on. All feeling left my legs and my heart hammered in my chest like a smith at an anvil. My breaths came in short, sharp inhalations. But we kept moving.

Fiscelion began to cry, softly at first, but louder and louder as time went on.

I wanted to cry out, to drop the saddle and take him in my arms. Why was he with Lupina and not me? I could not say, then.

He screamed and whined. It pitched up and down. He wanted to feed. He was wet. He was cold. He was in distemper.

Water now at my breasts and my breath coming in heaves. The water pushed against me: a current here. A current in these dark waters. I lost my footing and went down, under water. Silence except for the expansive hush of liquid filling my ears. The shock of icy cold. My saddle slipped from my grasp and I knew not where it was but I was glad it was gone.

I felt strong hands and a powerful heave.

'Ia-dammit, sissy. You're like a fatted cow. Get up and come!' Carnelia said, dragging me through the water. My clothes, lead-heavy. Stones tied around my neck, fitted to me like a gown of rocks.

I was insensible in the dark. I could not feel except to know my body shook, my teeth clattered. I smelled only must and mould, and the minerals in the water. The rhythm of breathing gave measure to my world.

And then it grew shallower and a light came from in front of us. Carnelia released my arm and pushed ahead.

We came out into the pre-dawn light, sodden, with a squalling child, in the shadow of the great wall of Rume.

Tenebrae let Lupina down on the ground. 'Quiet the child and follow! Swiftly! A half mile and we'll find horses. And horse blankets,' he said, and the urgency in his voice was unmistakable. He glanced up to where the wall of Rume met sky and, finding no guards looking down, said again, 'Come!'

We followed.

SEVEN

Are You Out Of Your Ia-Damned Mind?

Thirteen was our number, and I couldn't tell if that was a good sign or bad.

The *dvergar* busied themselves cooking the horse, and drinking the stinking water of the Bitter Spring and refilling their stocks, as could be expected. They made much ado of Bess and stripped and re-organised her packs to stow their gear. Bess, during the process, cast me agonised looks and hawed, showing her teeth and gums. But she did not buck. They ran blunt hands over her sides and spoke to her in soft tones, cooing in *dvergar* tongue.

A woman washed and tended my neck, where the *daemon-gripped* had bitten. I grimaced, and managed, myself, not to buck.

Not counting Fisk and myself, there were seven men and four women in the *dvergar* group and all seemed, if not battle hardened, then unfazed by the current situation. Such are my kin: they take chance and fortune as it comes and spend not much time in bemoaning or exulting in fate. I know not if that is a trick of racial demeanour or physical heritage, or neither. But it is true. We are survivors, my kind.

Inbhir, the bruiser that Praeverta called 'Catch Hands,' stayed busy, trotting up and down gulleys and into cave mouths, searching the area for points of defence, and points of opportunity. The one called Vrinthi took stock of weapons – our meagre supply – and found himself face to face with Fisk when he began inventory-ing *our* weapons. It was not an easy exchange, the dwarf facing the dour man, and neither came from it feeling good about the experience.

'The number of your guns?' Vrinthi asked.

'Three,' said Fisk. 'The carbine is here.' He was reclining against his saddle, smoking a cigarette. We had been awake for almost two score hours, since we'd caught naps a good day's ride from the ruin of Harbour Town, and weariness, at this point, was overcoming us. Fisk patted the sweat-stained leather, and pulled off the blanket, revealing the haft of the rifle. 'You can take it for use against the Medierans, and its ammunition. There should be quite a few rounds in the magazine. I will expect it returned.'

Vrinthi nodded sombrely. 'And your other weapons?'

'None of your concern. Take the carbine and let me rest.'

'I need to make count of *all* ammunition so that it can be distributed for best coverage and usage,' Vrinthi said. He had the dogged aspect of a man that takes his job very seriously, because failing to do so would not only break him, it would leave him devoid of meaning.

'You'll just have to trust that I will make good use of my ammu-nition and move along, friend,' Fisk said.

Vrinthi frowned and reached down as if to unclasp Fisk's gun belt. Fisk's hand flashed and he had the barrel of his six-gun pressed into the dwarf's eye socket. He rose.

'Little friend, you've mistaken me for someone who gives one damn if you live or die. But let me assure you, if I hear one more word issue from your idiot mouth regarding my weapons, I will waste one of my rounds and put it right here,' Fisk said, jabbing the gun barrel into the ocular cavity. Vrinthi cried out in pain. 'And afterwards, you won't even be able to adjust your tally.'

'Vrinthi!' Praeverta said. 'Come away. They are not of us.'

'Yes, Matve!' Vrinthi said immediately, placing his hand over his eye. Fisk pulled the carbine and offered it to him, stock first. The dwarf took it and moved away.

Once the *dvergar* had moved away, Fisk sank back down against his saddle. I sat near him. Weariness washed over me from the days on the run.

'How soon, do you think, before they get here?' I asked, looking up into the night sky. From where we sat near the Bitter Spring, the smooth rock faces of the adjoining gulleys framed the heavens in a rough X shape. Stars pricked the dark.

'Few hours, maybe. Dawn, likely. They can't travel fast at night, and they don't know the land. If their *daemon*-gripped can smell, like they look like they can, they may be here before that, but it's unlikely.'

'Lina,' Praeverta called. 'What is the situation? How many and how far?'

A dark-haired young *dvergar* woman came toward Praeverta and said, 'I'll need to get some distance away, but I will check.' There was something familiar about her – her face, her skin, her demeanour and carriage all seemed like I had seen her before. Maybe back in Harbour Town, at the *vaettir* meeting hall.

'Yes,' Praeverta said. 'Let us move away, and get to ground where you can hear what you can hear.' They walked away, down one of the gulleys, away from the rest of us and the Bitter Spring. Not understanding fully what I was doing, or why, I followed.

Away from the cook fire, my eyes adjusted to the dark and it was easy to follow the women. They had found a switchback path that climbed on the ledge of one of the dead-end canyons and it was there I came upon them. Praeverta looked at me silently, as I drew near. The one she called Lina lay upon the ground, her face pressed to the bare stone of the earth.

Breathless, she listened and we remained silent. Off in the

56

darkness came a single screech, from what sort of creature I couldn't tell. Stretcher, cat, coyote, man, raptor – it could have been any, or none at all.

Eventually, the younger *dvergar* woman rose and dusted herself off. 'There are over fifteen riders, and they are at least two hours away. Maybe more.'

'So, dawn then, or later,' Praeverta said.

'Yes. But there's something more,' Lina said. 'There are runners. But it's strange. One is—'

'A *vaettir*?' I asked. My voice sounded loud even to me in the stillness. The women turned to consider me.

'Yes,' Lina said. 'One of the runners is large, and terribly fast. A stretcher. But the other runners, they are fast as well. There's something unnatural about them,' she said, puzzlement furrowing her brow.

'They are fast,' I said. 'And unnatural. They are the engineer's pets.'

Praeverta looked confused and Lina cocked her head.

'This engineer you want so badly – he's not the kind of engineer made for filling Hellfire shells with *imps* and lesser *daemons*. No. He's after bigger things. And where he puts his devils is far worse than a rifle shell.'

Praeverta's eyes grew large and she said, 'Men?'

'And worse. His *daemon*-gripped are terrible to behold.'

'We heard rumour of this, but I did not believe it,' the old woman said.

'Believe it. Or not. You're about to witness it first-hand.'

'And how do we deal with these *daemon*-gripped?' Lina asked.

'Like anything. You shoot them. You stab them. The problem is getting them to slow down long enough for you to put enough metal in them to die.' I shook my head. 'Silver helps.'

'We have very little of that,' Lina said. She looked at me with a curious, penetrating stare, as if evaluating me for some task that I was not aware of, and again I had the niggling sensation – the memory almost – that we had met before.

'I think the best course is to let Fisk and me deal with the stretcher and *daemon*-gripped, and your people deal with the Medieran riders.'

'And the engineer?' Praeverta asked.

'He will not hazard himself. He never hazards himself. He prizes his own comfort and the integrity of his skin more than anything else. To reach Beleth,' I said, rubbing my lip and saying it almost to myself, 'We'll have to go through them. Be ready for the chase if we live through the vanguard.'

Praeverta lifted her chin. The skin of her neck was loose, and it stretched out with the movement. It wasn't pride, nor disdain; it was the eye. My grandmam had it. My mother, too. The one-eyed stare. Fixed in half their gaze, as if by halving it, it became distilled, more focused, making the open one more perceptive. I laughed when she did it. It was such a *dvergar* thing.

'Yes, Matve. Yes, ma'am,' I said, ducking my head. Ducking my head at nothing.

For a moment I thought she might smile, but instead her jaw locked and something in her calcified against me.

'You are a buffoon and an idiot. That we have fallen so low to have our fortunes shackled to you. Where will you and the human stand?' she asked.

'I imagine we'll take cover in a couple of the gulleys leading to the Bitter Spring. If we perch up here, the stretcher and his pet will sniff us right off.'

'And my *vaettir*? Where will they be?' she asked.

'We're clever, we *dvergar*,' I said, knowing that would irk her, claiming kinship. 'And mountainsides are our business from old. Set a guard on high, one guard.' I pointed at a lower fold in the land, creased by pathways, smooth and ancient, water-worn. 'Let that one guard give signal when they approach so that your people – your *vaettir* – can scramble up the gulley walls and do as much violence upon their persons as they can manage. Set ropes for climbing and gather stones for throwing. Sharpen your scythes and daggers. Dig holes to break their horses' legs and stretch hemp at rider height to knock them from saddles. Fight as we *dvergar* were born to fight. With cunning and ferociousness.'

The younger woman nodded. But Praeverta did not thaw. The old woman sniffed and gave the barest inclination of her head.

But she heard. Turning, she walked away without any farewell – not that I expected any – and worked her way back down the switchback path. I watched her go. Lina remained with me, as Praeverta walked away.

Finally, she said, 'I thought you'd be taller.'

'What?' I said.

'Taller. The way they always told it was you were a beast, a half-man brute, and taller,' Lina said.

'What are you talking about?' I asked.

'I'm talking about Tapestry. And my grandmother, Illina. The woman whose name I bear.' She stood and brushed off her dungarees and adjusted her longknife in its scabbard. 'And I'm talking about *you*, grandfather,' she said.

There was not much room for thought, then, and so much to do. Lina – or Illina, I should say, but I couldn't think of her as such, since all my memories with that name were bound up with love and lust and loss – fended herself from any more of my questions and set to preparing defences against the oncoming riders, and I was left stunned, tottering about.

'What in perdition is wrong with you, Shoe?' Fisk asked. 'You been into the cacique?'

'Family reunion,' I said.

My partner whistled. 'Ia-damn.' He chuckled. 'Hope it wasn't some bastard you got on someone you shouldn't have.'

'No,' I said. '*Dvergar* only have bastards when Rumans are around. She's my granddaughter.'

Ignoring the jab at Rumans, Fisk peered about, as if looking to spot Lina in the dim, timeless half-light of morning. 'The fast one, the sharp girl?' he asked.

'That's the one.'

'She's pretty, pard. And acute,' he said. For Fisk, this was high praise.

'She is of me, but a me that was so long ago,' I said. 'My wife. The devourer's disease. We had children but they were grown and I left because I was young then and stupid. And tainted.'

'Tainted?' Fisk said. 'How is that?'

'I share some of your blood, partner. Severus Speke was my father, a centurion of the First Occidentalia. He had eagle phalerae and a gladius and a Hellfire rifle and he took up with my mother during the push west through the Smokeys to the Hardscrabble. I wasn't born long after.'

Fisk looked at me for a long while. 'Parentage is a dicey business,' he said. 'They stand like mountains when you are young, and diminish with each year until you are on an eye-line with their peak, a long slide from idol to idiot.'

'Would that I had cacique,' I said, 'I would drain it to the dregs.'

'Bah. That's horseshit,' he said. 'Afterwards, maybe. And she knew you?'

'It seems I am short, and do not measure up to the old stories.'

'No one does.' Fisk laughed. Inbhir and the one they called Ringold looked at him strangely. 'And we're all short,' Fisk said. His smile died. 'None of us stand more than three hands high, in our graves.'

We took our places. Praeverta's *vaettir* made ready hemp and knife and Hellfire, what they had. Their guard, the fair *vanmer* Ilyani girl, scurried up a smooth gulley wall and perched herself where she could see any approach. The fire was stoked with bramble and any other combustibles, while Bess was led away to hide in a cave mouth. She hawed but did not buck.

The cross of sky lightened, sweet to the eye and striated with clouds, and fingers of light painted the *dvergar* faces, normally dark, in rosy, refulgent hues.

A clatter of rocks. A hiss and fall of sediment. A coyote's call. The signal.

The *dvergar* climbed high, strong hands digging into the stone gulley-sides. A hooting sound. A screech.

Down the gulley they came loping, half-devils, half-men. There were three of them. Their mouths black maws, their eyes empty, they ran on hands and feet in mockery of human form. Fire was in them and they imitated it as they ran, eating away the distance like a flame consuming hair.

Silhouettes of *dvergar* peeked over canyon lip. Rocks raised high. I lifted my hand in an angry fist.

Wait.

Behind them, it came. Towering. Fast as nightmare and shadow.

The *vaettir*. The bloody stretcher, *daemon*-gripped. It ran, feet churning like furious steamer paddles, like the beating of hummingbird wings. It arced down the gulley, running along the wall.

Gynth.

It was my friend, the *vaettir* that saved me, saved me three times, once in the Hardscrabble, once on the *Gemina*, and once in Harbour Town.

He was nude, now, and streaked in crimson as he ran. But it was him. Head full of teeth, hands hard and flexing. Dick flopping with every footfall. I wouldn't back him in the Passasuego Beauty Day Parade any more, that's for sure.

He leapt up and landed on the rim of the gulley above, looking down at us. His gaze fixed on me, and Fisk at my side.

'There!' Gynth screamed in the common tongue. 'There they are! Kill them and bring me the hand. *Kān*! *Kān*!'

The bedevilled men raced down the gullet of the canyon toward us.

'Now,' I yelled. The *dvergar* above let fly their rocks and they came raining down with a tremendous clatter.

A *daemon*-gripped man collapsed, head stoved in, and another dropped, back crushed.

Gynth peered about with dreadful malevolence and, leaping across the gulley, snatched up the poor *vanmer* girl who had stood watch, shook her like a rag doll, and cast her down. He was closer now and the morning's light fell full upon him; I could see the scorch marks and bloody intaglios carved upon his flesh. I had seen it before.

The other half-devil shot forward, faster than I would've thought possible. Fisk's pistol boomed, smoke billowed. Hellfire's despair and fear filled us. The last *daemon*-gripped man pitched forward like a marionette with its strings cut.

At the sound of Fisk's gunshot, horses whinnied and screamed and the sound of their hooves came thunderous, echoing strangely down the length of the gulley. More gunshots and smoke. The *dvergar* – they that had guns – began firing.

'Leave the *vaettir* to me,' I told Fisk. 'Do not shoot him.'

'Are you out of your Ia-damned mind?' Fisk said.

I pulled the knife – the silver one – from my boot. 'Possibly.'

I was out and near the fire as fast as my feet could take me. I lost my hat and my head stood bare beneath the stretcher.

'I've got that Ia-damned *daemon* hand, you son of a bitch. Come and take it,' I said, and ran down the gulley, away from the fire. Gynth followed. Despite the din of gunplay and the clatter of falling rocks, I could hear the *vaettir*'s footfalls as he came forward, each one distinct, the flurry of them. I ducked under one of the hemp clotheslines Praeverta's men had set out, and kept hauling.

A cessation of footsteps. I glanced back. The stretcher had leapt up and over the trap and came down right behind me.

I drew my six-gun and turned, one hand holding the silver blade, the other out and firing.

But Gynth was too fast for me. His hand lanced out and raked my forearm from nook to fingertip, ripping through cuff and shirt and leaving bloody furrows in the flesh. My pistol spun away.

Gynth pounced, snatching me up in big hands and falling forward so that I was pinned underneath him.

'Mister Ilys.' The voice came from that crooked, toothsome mouth. It wasn't Gynth but I had figured that already. 'So good to see you again.'

'I see you got yourself a new suit,' I said.

'Yessss,' Beleth said. The mouth cracked into a wide smile. 'We caught this one up in a net, after you killed my horse. I liked that horse. But I think I like this one,' he patted his belly with a long, clawed hand, 'even better. He fits me so well, it will be hard to go back to my own.' The glee that informed the stretcher's features disappeared. 'Enough of this. I will reduce you to scraps of flesh if you—'

A bright ululation, a screech. From a woman's mouth this time, and in imitation of a *vaettir*. Lina fell upon Beleth's back, plunging a knife into the meat of his shoulder. For an instant, he twitched and loosened his grip upon me.

It was enough. For I am old, and I will not give up this life so easy. I writhed in his clutch. I squirmed and fretted, jerking my head upwards. It caught his chin, the anvil jaw of the *vaettir* he rode, and threw its head back.

I held up the knife in one smoking hand. The silver ate at my *dvergar* flesh – the flesh that bore such kinship with the elf – and I put it up to Beleth's face, before his eyes.

'This is the blade that killed Agrippina and put the Crimson Man back in his cage,' I said. 'And it will be the one that will find you.'

The stretcher that Beleth wore bucked wildly and Lina went flying. I held on, one arm cupped around the thing's neck as if we were lovers. I brought the knife across with all my strength. Not across the stretcher's neck, not searching for those milk-blue sanguiducts there. On the intaglioed ruin of its chest.

I cut the *genius loci* glyph. I cut it deep.

The creature stiffened, its eyes rolling back in its head. His body went slack and I rolled away.

In the distance I heard gunfire and the clatter of rocks. Lina moaned. Horses screamed.

The *vaettir* opened its eyes and sat up. It looked around. Its gaze fell upon me.

'*Gynth*,' it said, and the mouth full of teeth cracked into a smile.

EIGHT

We're Going to Steal It

TENEBRAE WAS AS good as his word and at another stable with the markings of a bull, we found horses and blankets. Lupina changed her clothes and I changed mine – though the ones in my rucksack were damp as well. Lupina warmed Fiscelion and I gave the darling a teat to feed while Carnelia rubbed us down with the horse-cloth.

'Escape with an infant is problematic,' Tenebrae said. 'But he *is* a remarkably sturdy little fellow.' He looked down on the beatific face of my child and smiled. 'He looks like Secundus.'

'A bit,' I said. I did not bother to draw the blanket over my exposed breast. Our bodies root us, our bodies are what they are. We are born into pain, and our bodies tether us to it, but it does not have to be so, always. That part of us that cannot die, that incorruptible part that connects Fisk to me and me to my son – that does not have to live in pain.

And Tenebrae was not the sort of man to quail at the sight of a woman's breast. 'Too early to know how he will look as a man.'

We tarried only the briefest time, long enough to warm ourselves and sate Fiscelion. And then we were back ahorse – Carnelia and I doubling on horseback, since I had lost my saddle in our passage beneath the Mithranalian Gate – passing through farmland, past hamlets and villages that clung to the walls of Rume like ticks on a wild dog's belly. Past tenement houses and shanties and dust-filled graveyards of broken chairs and stoves and spokeless wagon wheels – the remains of industry unceremoniously trucked outside the walls and beyond the hills of Rume into the country to moulder out of sight of the greater population.

A mechanised baggage-train, *daemon*-driven, cut through the countryside, parallel to the Via Miasma that followed the Tever. The machine vomited black smoke from its stacks, and it whisked down the train to finally rise up to join the clouds hanging low and heavy. The rain fell on our party, and none save Fiscelion remained dry.

The Tever flowed shit-brown and wide there, swift and swollen with the deluge. Trees and submerged sodden things were carried downstream, turning sluggishly with the quickening current.

'There is a ferry here, near Rezzo. Some fifteen miles distant,' Tenebrae said. 'Let us hurry.'

'Rezzo? Where the College of Engineers keeps its headquarters?' Carnelia asked.

'The same,' Tenebrae said. 'Tamberlaine declared that all engineer work be done there, now, for fear of the fate of Harbour Town.'

'A sensible precaution,' I said. Tamberlaine was a meddling and manipulative man, but his rule of Rume and her territories was, as always, ruthlessly and eminently practical. It was even hard remaining outraged at his treatment of us, the Cornelian brood. It was like being angry at a snake for its venom, or a bear for its strength – it was his nature and we all, eventually, succumb to our own natures. I think what gives us pain in life is not recognising our natures and having to deny them.

I would be with my husband, and safe. I would provide a good home to my son and see him happy. I would make the world safe for him. Is that my nature? Or is it simply what I wish for?

Rezzo loomed in the distance. It was an industrial town, situated some twenty miles north of Rume on the Tever, and was the doorway to the mountains in the north and the nexus of all the highways leading to Nexia on the Nous, or Gall beyond.

I had never been to Rezzo. My life as a daughter of a Cornelian kept me from the more industrious and, I might say, dirtier parts of our land. Growing up, we visited Cumae, Cimbri, l'Umo Usca, and beyond, on the shores of the Occidens and the tip of our great sea – the play places of patriarchs and their overstuffed, alabaster wives and children.

But I knew of it. It was full of carpentry shops and wheelwrights – the most famous of which was the Sator Rotas workshop, of course. It teemed with stonemasons and fresco artists, plasterers and mortar men and shipbuilders shielded from the storms of the Occidens by thirty miles of land. And there were engineers. Many schools of engineering and official buildings related to that function – silver brokers and warehousers, cohort barracks that held the legionnaires who protected the silver pigs stacked high in their warded warehouses, and the apprentices and servants, the great throng of slaves that serviced those who serviced Rume.

An ugly town, squatting on the Tever's shore. Pillars of smoke poured from it and baggage trains ran to it to add their dust to the city's.

It was mid-morning when we came to it.

'They will have discovered we're gone by now,' Carnelia said. There was tension in her voice and hearing it, I felt it in myself, thrumming. Anxious.

'The question is, will Father drag his feet to notify Tamberlaine?' I said.

'He won't if he doesn't want to be crucified,' Tenebrae said. Lupina harrumphed. As one of our company who had experienced living under the shadow of crucifixion, she did not like hearing it bandied about. But Tenebrae was not exaggerating in this case.

'So, Tamberlaine will know soon, if not already. And he'll have his generals blooding themselves into Quotidians before afternoon,' I said.

'That's the shape of it,' Tenebrae said. 'He is a busy man, though, and I understand he's entertaining some Bedoun mathematicians and emissaries, so it is possible he could defer meeting with your father.' He bit his lower lip. 'Unless your father is forceful.'

'That will depend on how he feels this morning. Hopefully he drank himself into insensibility last night,' I said. 'Nevertheless. We must be away from here, shortly. We cannot risk being identified.'

I spurred my horse onward.

Rezzo had no walls, no gates to impede the flow of traffic and deliveries. Trains huffed into the great yards where twenty locomotives could stand abreast so men could de-crate their goods – casks of pork, grain, gravel, lime, wood, and the raw stuff of Ruman creation. Nearby, the port bustled with seagulls wheeling overhead in the dreary sky, calling over the piers. For an instant, I remembered the marvel of the little lóng dragons that held court on the arteries of air above Jiang City and the wharf Bund. Sun Huáng's wise and pained face. Min, his arrogant but beautiful daughter. So far away. So long ago, now.

The ferry-house was a simple affair; it cost a copper sestertius to cross and two for each horse. We paid the ferryman and he bade us wait for the next arrival. We stood on the pier, away from the other waiting passengers, their mules and horses, their wagons and carriages. There was a great commotion across the river from us, where many lascars and what appeared to be legionnaires gathered around a sleek black ship that was currently up on trucks but appeared to be being lowered into the Tever.

'That's an evil little craft,' Tenebrae said as it entered the dun-coloured water of the Tever. 'Two shrouded swivels, but a fifth of the size of the *Malphas*.'

A trickle of black smoke emanated from the ship's stack that was placed, curiously, near its aft.

'And *daemon*-driven,' I said.

'Yes,' he said, and fell silent.

I stood for a long while, watching the ship and the lascars and the stevedores loading things onto it. Our ferry came and we led the horses on. The thick, low-slung ferry-boat itself was *daemon*-driven, engine room nestled right behind the pilot's roost. Wagons trundled on, and horses nickered at the boat's shifting below them. Lascars came around and placed chocks under wagon and carriage wheels, and in a moment we were on our way.

The ferry thrummed, shivering, and moved into the currents of the Tever. The shipyards grew larger in our sights. The black, wicked little ship we observed came clearer – it was only the size of a locomotive itself, and had a deck, albeit a small one, and port-holes in the side. Where there normally would be a smokestack, there was a cluster of metal rods summited by a strange, finned device. Its deck guns were shrouded in greased oilcloth and bound extremely tightly – in my experience on the *Malphas* I had seen these protective contraptions, but they were only in use when the seas were high and the lascars did not want to spend hours oiling guns doused in salt water. Officious men stood about, none with the deadly look of legionnaires, nor with the distracted and ana-lytical postures of men who summon *daemons*. These were bean counters, administrators, and one held a clipboard as provisions were being loaded on the ship. It sat curiously low in the waters.

'Well, that's settled then,' I said.

'What's that, sissy?' Carnelia said.

'We're not going to Nexia.'

'What?' Carnelia asked. Lupina turned and raised an eyebrow.

'That ship,' I said, pointing. 'We are going to steal it.'

NINE

I Hope He Lives A Long Life, Full Of Misery

Fisk came barrelling down the gulley toward us, guns out. The din of Hellfire ripped through the night behind him and I heard voices raised and screams in Medieran.

I stepped between Fisk and Gynth and held up my hands. 'Hold on, pard. Hold on.'

Fisk ignored me, moving to the side. 'No, I think not. Step away from the stretcher.'

I shook my head. 'This is Gynth. This is the one. He was being controlled by Beleth. And Beleth is near.' I sensed, rather than saw, Gynth rising to his feet. Fisk's gaze followed, and his guns, rising above my head. 'Look at his chest. There was a *genius loci* glyph there. I cut it and he was released.' I turned, and in *dvergar*, said, 'Can you lead us now to Beleth? He is near.'

Gynth blinked and then slowly nodded. 'Yes,' he said. 'Yes. To the cursed one I can lead you.'

Turning, I saw Fisk's stunned face.

'He can and will but we have to go now. Beleth will have already begun to run.'

Down the gulley, *dvergar* shouting and the clatter of more falling stones and Hellfire. There was hooting and screeches, mostly from *dvergar* throats, unless I was mistaken.

Fisk watched Gynth for a long time, unnamed emotions fretting

70

under the surface. He was like the Big Rill, cold and steel-blue and placid on the surface, but urgent with hidden whorls and eddies and currents underneath. But I reckon we're all like that, to an extent.

He looked from the stretcher to me and back again. He holstered his gun.

I do not know what battles were won then, in the territories of Fisk's heart. He'd had a family once and *vaettir* had taken that from him. But that pain was locked somewhere away, at least for now, and he nodded once at the big creature standing behind me.

'All right then, Ia damn my soul to perdition,' he said. 'Let's get that son of a bitch.'

I went to where Lina was looking around, dazed. A runnel of blood traced its way down her face from under her hairline.

'Come on, Lina,' I said, raising her up. When she was standing, she pulled herself away and made a shooing gesture with her hands. 'I can walk. And you have an appointment,' she said.

Gynth had this expression like a great hound waiting for his master's lead. I made a chopping motion back toward the fire.

'Let's go,' I said.

'It was a rout,' Fisk said as we ran back to where the fire burned by the Bitter Spring. The sandstone walls had taken on a bright, tawny colour with the rising sun and it was warmer now. 'Those Medierans didn't know what hit them.'

'Let's hope they did not kill all the horses,' I said.

Praeverta's Vaettir looked dumbstruck by the sight of a real *vaettir* in their own midst. I held up my hands and hollered, 'Do not shoot! Do not! He is *gynth*!'

Gynth, for his part, was doing a passable job at not looking like he was going to kill everyone. He had his mouth shut, for a start, and all of those jagged teeth tucked away. His hands weren't too bloody, though his chest, where both Beleth and I cut him, was. His cock, however, was still on full display.

Praeverta whistled as she looked at him. 'This was one of them *daemon*-gripped, then.'

'Yes,' I said. 'Possessed by Beleth. He is close. Did you kill all the horses, Matve?'

The old lady snorted. 'No, though we still might. Killing can work up a hunger.' She did not smile when she said it.

'Gynth can lead us to him, but we must go now, quickly. His connection severed, Beleth will run. He is not a man that is willing to fight when odds are turned against him.'

'Inbhir,' Praeverta called. 'Bring them, quick.'

Inbhir led three horses to us. All were foaming and could use watering but we had time enough for that later, I hoped. Inbhir himself mounted one, and Fisk and I took the others.

Gynth bounded away and we followed.

Out of the gulleys, it was hard to keep pace with Gynth. The way he moved was powerful and full of deadly grace, all at once. Like watching a mountain lion hunt. Haunches bunching and flexing, launching him into the air and then coming down on powerful quick legs – two paces – and then vaulting again into the air. Hands out, fingers splayed, arcing through the air. Strange to have him running *with* us, rather than around or at us. All of my experience with stretchers out here in the Hardscrabble had been moments of terror and fear, save those with Gynth himself, and even those were frightful. Except then.

We would have to find the *vaettir* some trousers, though. I think Praeverta got flustered at the sight of him.

Gynth leapt up a rise and perched there, like some predatory bird, surveying the land. One great arm lanced out, pointing. And he was off again. We rode hard to keep up. The horses were failing, sucking wind. Foam slathered their haunches and came from under their saddle blankets. The Medieran mounts were fine creatures, noble lines and sleek bodies, but bred for speed and not endurance. The Hardscrabble requires stamina, and these foreign-born horses just did not have it. Gynth disappeared, ducking out of sight, beyond a low ridge. The horses fell into a canter. And then a walk, and no amount of prodding could make them hasten.

There was a gunshot, and it echoed strangely, beating at the air. Sound does weird things out here, bouncing off rock and ridge, and comes back to your ears warbling and indistinct, or louder than it should be. And there's no telling as to the whys and wherefores.

There was yelling, then, and it was in a human voice.

We came up the rise, and over it, slowly. Below lay a horse, grunting and struggling to rise. Its foreleg was broken. It would be screaming soon. There, near it, was Gynth. And scrabbling away from him on all fours, Beleth. He wore a suit, but it was dusty. The most pleasant thing about the man was the look of terror on his face. He would stand, tentatively, and Gynth would knock him down, smacking his head with a massive hand, sending the man sprawling.

Up Beleth rose, and down he went, knocked into the dust. If I had had one of Wasler's infernographs to immortalise this, to fix this in ink, I would have gladly given all my worldly possessions to have it. It would be an heirloom for my family.

We approached, and Beleth hopped up again. Gynth feinted like he would strike again, and Beleth threw himself to the ground to avoid it.

'Mister Beleth,' I said, clucking. 'How nice it is to see you again, and in such a marvellous state.' Pleasure can make me wordy, and glib. It's a failing, I know.

'Can you take hold of him, er . . .' Fisk said, addressing Gynth. Gynth, who at this point had only spoken *dvergar* to me, moved to do Fisk's bidding.

'Gynth, partner. That's what he seems to answer to,' I said. Fisk waved me away.

Gynth snatched up Beleth in much the same way he had done the *vanmer* girl on watch, when Beleth wore him. He gave him a little shake and Beleth yelped in pain, kicking his legs.

I dismounted, alongside Inbhir who was uncoiling some hemp rope.

'Today is your lucky day, Mister Beleth,' said Fisk. 'All the gods of heaven and earth, old and new, would smile upon us if we killed you now. I have never relished killing a man – and I've killed many – but I think I would enjoy killing *you*.'

Beleth said, 'I have information. I have information that Cornelius and the Emperor will want to hear.' He did not mess around, this shitebird of a petty man. He went right to the matter.

'I'm sure you do,' Fisk said. 'Information you'll use to barter for your life, such as it is. Hold him still, big one,' Fisk said to Gynth.

Taking the rope from Inbhir, Fisk trussed the engineer tightly, starting with his feet. He tied off one hand and cinched it to the knot between his legs and then, as if he were about to gut a hog, Fisk whipped out his longknife and cut a length of rope and gagged the engineer. 'You're gonna need that, I'm afraid, Mister Beleth, for what comes next.'

Before Inbhir could react, Fisk began sawing at Beleth, who squirmed frantically in his bindings. In moments he was holding Beleth's severed hand. His own were red with blood.

He tossed the hand away, in the dust, for the creatures of the Hardscrabble to consume. He took off Beleth's gag.

'There you are, Mister Beleth,' Fisk said, voice absolutely inflectionless. 'I would hear you whine.'

The engineer sobbed now, and cursed in a mewling, pained voice. Fisk punched him in the face, then, on a whim it seemed.

Fisk removed the engineer's belt and cinched it on the stump. He looked at it. 'Clean work, there.'

'You son of a—' Beleth said. 'You son of a whore.'

'Small price to pay for Harbour Town. But you'll not be doing any glyphs or wards until you've learned to use your other hand,' Fisk said.

'Praeverta will be furious,' Inbhir said. 'We need that engineer.'

'I could give two shites what you or your old lady want.' He put his boot on Beleth's chest and pushed him down, fully flat on the ground, and spat on him. 'This man killed everyone in Harbour Town, save a few. Men, women. Children. Children that will never grow up, now. I hope he lives a long life, full of misery.'

Inbhir frowned and looked worried. Fisk patted Gynth on the shoulder and the *vaettir* took Beleth in his hands and slung him over his shoulder like a Brawley stevedore slinging a rucksack. Beleth cried out then.

'I would see him miserable. And in fact,' Fisk said, 'I plan on seeing to it myself.'

TEN

Waken This *Daemon* And Set Him To Turning Screws

IT WAS A simple plan.

'Too simple,' Tenebrae said, shaking his head. 'There's no way it will work.'

'Its strength lies in its simplicity,' I said. 'And we are running out of time. Any moment, the garrison might mobilise and the streets flood with legionnaires searching for three women and an infant. If we do not act now, we might as well ride on to Nexia.'

Carnelia narrowed her eyes. 'Tell me, Shadow,' she said, using Sun Huáng's pet name for Tenebrae. 'How worried is Tamberlaine, and his agents, about Harbour Town?'

'After we arrived at the Ostia wharf, I did not have an audience with him. I was debriefed by his head secretary and spymaster about what happened in Kithai and on the journey back.' Tenebrae rubbed his jaw and thought. The ferry drew nearer to the far shore and Fiscelion stirred in my arms. We had only minutes to decide our course of action. 'After that, I came to watch your villa. But Tamberlaine's man did tell me of the winds that are blowing now. And the security of Rume is foremost in Tamberlaine's mind, and it is his policy to protect Rume at all costs. That policy has been disseminated throughout the legions.'

'So it might work,' Carnelia said. 'We have guns, we have blades. And it is not that large a ship.'

He nodded, but looked doubtful.

'Fortune favours the bold,' I said. 'But I would not ask you to hazard yourself if you do not feel it is possible. It is audacious. It has risk.' I looked at Fiscelion. 'And that is where I quail. For his sake, if not my own. But there is no guarantee that we will escape should we decide to travel on to Nexia. This seems the best course.' I thought for a long while. 'If there is any danger, we will surrender. For Fiscelion's sake. And our own. But until that moment—'

'We shall play it to the hilt,' Carnelia said. 'There is no Fuqua on that ship, sissy. There are only people who would keep us from our freedom and take Fiscelion back to Father and Tamberlaine.'

'I know,' I said.

'And are you ready to do what we must?' Carnelia said. Her face was intense, and her eyes bright. Looking upon her, she was like a person I had never known, never met.

Tenebrae nodded, lips tight.

'And you, Lupina? Would you do this?' Carnelia asked.

Lupina approached me and lifted the blanket and peered at my son. She held out her arms and took the boy. 'This is not my land. And it is not this child's, though he was born to it. He should be in the West, with his father and you, under the big sky. Things that get in the way of what should be—' She raised her shoulders and let them fall. It was a simple gesture, a blunt one. *Their fate is sealed and I have no issue with that.*

'And so you are with us?' I asked.

'Of course. Let me hold him for a while, before you bind my wrists,' Lupina said.

After the ferry was tied off and fixed to the wharf the stevedores and pier-urchins clustered about, unlimbering planks and placing them so that the horses and wagons could disembark. Seagulls wheeled and cried in the blustery wind, and the rain softened into a cold drizzle. Bells clanged and fishwives called and cursed. The panoply of waterlife spilled over the drear banks of the Tever. We left quickly, and made our way away from the pier, stopping in an alley near the shipyards.

Quickly, we bound Carnelia's and Lupina's wrists and stripped them of their cloaks. They looked appropriately bedraggled by the time the ferry, loaded again with another passel of horses and passengers, pushed back out into the waters of the Tever.

Tenebrae brought from his coat a leather cylinder that contained his orders and the seal of his rank – Primus Praetorian. It would take some reading to discover the papers were related to our trip to Kithai, but he kept them at hand. He pinned the crossed gladii and shield badge upon his cloak, the symbol of the Emperor's guard. He ran his fingers through his damp hair and drew himself up, gathering gravitas and authority about him like a cloak. He was a fine-looking man and impressive to behold – chiselled features, muscular build, shocking blue eyes. The very image of a Ruman officer.

'All right,' he said, and the way he said it, the infinitesimal quaver in his voice, indicated to me that he was as frightened as I was. I had never really warmed to the man – during our trip to Kithai his allegiance had been suspect, and his relationship with my brother, if not troublesome, gave cause for speculation as to his motives.

Tenebrae. A man alienated from the possibilities of divergent realities – everything in him and about him found confirmation of his own beliefs. Until Secundus died, maybe. Now, the great rasp of the world had knocked off his certainty's edges and angles, Secundus' parting gift to us, to make this man doubt himself. I loved them both – the one we carried back in a cask of fine oil, and the one standing here before me – all the better for it. But with that quaver, that hint of fear and humanity, something in me loosened to him. All reservations went away, and I placed my trust in this man. My gun and my courage would have to help him see this through.

'Let us go,' I said. 'Ready?'

Carnelia, hair bedraggled and water streaming down her face, nodded.

'You can get your gun? Your sword, sissy?' I asked.

'Yes,' she said, impatiently. 'My hands are not bound securely, my pistol is hidden but within reach. Shadow has my *jian* covered with yon cloak. Let us be on with this.'

Beauty does not trip down the long staircase of generations, nor does strength and grace. It glides. Impatience, from my father, had found a merry dance it could do in Carnelia, as it had in Gnaeus, to his own end. And like Gnaeus, the prospect of violence only made her antsier.

'Remember our brothers, sissy. Gnaeus and Secundus,' I said, and looked at her closely. As if I could impregnate her with caution simply through my gaze.

'Never shall I forget them. One the buffoon, the other a beloved pawn,' Carnelia said, the words twisting her face painfully. 'I will be careful, sister. I can feel my *Qi* brimming. I will not die today.'

I put my hand on Tenebrae's shoulder to indicate my readiness and squeezed. He drew his pistol, adjusted his swordbelt and gestured for Carnelia and Lupina to advance in front of him.

We marched down to the shipyard. Lascars, porters, stevedores and wharfmen took notice of our approach, some coiling hemp, others knocking cork into the bungholes of casks. Two legion-naires, standing near an office door, smoking cigarettes, perked up as we drew near.

Before they could ask for identification, Tenebrae withdrew the leather message cylinder containing his orders and, holding it over his head, said in a loud voice, 'Take me to the commander of this ship, by order of the Emperor!'

'He is on the *Typhon,* sir, preparing to cast off,' said one of the legionnaires.

Tenebrae nodded and then surveyed the shipyards. A dumpy portmaster and his servant peeked their heads out of the door, eyes wide.

'These two are enemies of the state and enemies of our Great Father. I have taken them into custody.'

'A woman? And her—' The legionnaire peered at Lupina. 'Dwarf servant.' He seemed puzzled.

'Take me to the captain, sir, and I will explain it there,' Tenebrae said, holstering his pistol. 'And guard these two. Tamberlaine will want them questioned closely.'

The legionnaires marched us to the ship without asking to see Tenebrae's orders, training their carbines on Carnelia and Lupina. Once we neared the *Typhon* the soldiers called to the two lascars on deck for permission to board. The lascars looked at Tenebrae's stern countenance, his 'prisoners' in tow, and bade us board.

We did. It truly was a small ship – one shrouded swivel at the rear, right below the stack – a curiously tall, narrow, and fluted thing, with an intricate vent on the crown – and a second swivel at the fore. There was a small station in front of the stack, where a man could stand, braced by a steel bulwark and railing, with some levers and wheels – a modified pilot's roost. Between the fore and aft was a deck the size of a contubernium's tent, fifteen by fifteen paces, and a runner that traced the perimeter of the bulwark. There were two entrances to below – one on either side, fore and aft, of what passed as the deck. What was alarming was how much of the vessel was of steel. Black, painted steel. Surely it was too heavy to float, even for such a small ship? Even more curious was its level in the muddy waters of the Tever – its draught must have been minuscule.

One of the lascars went below deck and returned shortly with the first officer, who was pulling on his broadcloth jacket. A tall, lanky man with thinning hair, hard jaw, and a long nose.

'What's this, now? Prisoners? This isn't a transport vessel, man!' The man scowled at the lascar who had fetched him, but his alert gaze fixed upon Tenebrae and his brow furrowed.

Tenebrae gave a sharp fist to chest salute and stated his rank once more.

The first officer waved his hand, dismissing it. 'And why are you here, Mister Praetorian?'

'Our agents got word of these enemies of the state and we took them into custody. I need to speak with your commander. It is a matter of utmost urgency,' Tenebrae said.

'I'll need a little more to work on than that, sir. And who is this?' The first officer looked dubious at best, suspicious at worst.

'I am Livia Cornelius of the House Cornelius, sir, and I was the agent that discovered these traitors,' I said, in my haughtiest voice. 'I would invite you to lead us to your commander immediately. Time is of the essence. We must take them to the Emperor.' There is no subordinate officer that can take being dressed down by a woman and keep his dignity intact – capitulation or refutation are his only recourse and I was wagering that this man, by the look of him, would capitulate. Now to wave the olive branch. I lowered my voice. 'Surely you have heard what happened in Occidentalia? In Harbour Town?' I held out Fiscelion. 'Why do you think this vile summoner would have an infant? What do you think this abominable piece of filth intended to do with this child?'

The first officer's face froze: he was a man who, when confronted with horror, or events out of his control, took careful stock of himself. Gave nothing away.

He pursed his lips. 'Follow me. You two,' he said to the lascars. 'Stay here, and make ready to cast off.'

We followed him below deck, through the curious round metal door with the circular locking mechanism at the centre of it and down into a main room, cramped and tight, with a lascar making notations upon a ledger, and a man sitting in a centre chair, looking at us curiously as we entered. Unlike the first officer, he was older, and shaggy with a beard and a full head of wild hair. His countenance was logy, full of slumber. I had met him before; where, I did not know – at some family or state function.

'What is the meaning of this, sir?' he said to Tenebrae. Tenebrae saluted again, the Imperial salute, and restated his name and rank. 'And why have you brought these ... people to me?'

I spoke, introducing myself. 'Captain—'

'Titus Curius, of the Regulus family. And this is my first officer, Spurius Albinus.' He pointed at Fiscelion. 'I know of you, Madame Cornelius, and I have heard of your family's recent fortunes. Both their ups, and downs.' He arched an eyebrow. 'Why have you brought an infant on board the *Typhon*?'

'Captain Regulus, as I was investigating some discrepancies in our family interests here in Rezzo—'

'Interests? Commercial interests?' Senatorial participation in commerce and industry was prohibited by law, the Lex Claudia, until the last two centuries, when those laws were stripped away due to the burgeoning and wealthy equite class – the senators, and Emperor Salvanius, too, wanted to partake personally of the wealth coming from the new utilisation of infernal combustion and the coin generated from this new industrial age. Yet there was still a stigma when a senatorial family engaged in commerce. Operating a business, rather than investment, was not only frowned upon, it was a source of rumour and speculation. Rume takes its name from rumour; snark is its handmaid; gossip its currency.

'We have some interest in some granaries and import business here, along with a silver smelt,' I lied. It was easy. I'd listened close to Father's clients – when I was a girl, I'd ensconce myself in Tata's office with a stylus and parchment and draw pictures of horses or caricatures of my father's clients. I knew he was a patron to those with businesses in this area, the Viducus clan in particular, and if called on the lie, I could bluff convincingly. I hoped. 'Which leads us to this woman.'

Regulus looked at Carnelia. 'What of her?' He looked discomposed. Our story was moving fast enough for him not to look at any part too closely.

'She was a senior scrivener and accountant at the smelt, except her tallies had been turning up short. After some investigation, we found her with this— This Occidentalian indigine.' I did my best to scowl. 'In their possession, engineering charts and summoner's notes.'

'What has this to do with the *Typhon*?' Regulus asked. I nearly rolled my eyes.

'Have you not heard of the events of Harbour Town?' Tenebrae asked.

'Yes,' he said. 'Dreadful stuff, that. Dreadful.'

'Have not your praefecti or navarchs debriefed you on those events?' Tenebrae asked.

'Of course!' Regulus said, a little bluster entering his voice. He sat upright. 'What are you saying here?'

'We are saying, sir, that an engineer with the motive, silver, and an infant or other suitable sacrifice can wipe even our eternal city from the face of the earth,' I said.

'And these,' he said, halting. 'They were—'

'Medieran agents.'

He stood, colour running from his face. 'Ia's grace, save me.'

'We need transport, now, to Rume. Quickly. This woman must be questioned by Tamberlaine's agents.'

Albinus looked doubtful. He said, 'If you have her and her collaborators in custody, why would—'

'Because, First Officer,' I said, raising my eyebrow, 'she might not be working alone. And there are other infants in this world.'

Regulus strode to the steps that led to the *Typhon*'s deck and bellowed, 'You dullards! Cast off, immediately.' He turned back to us. 'The pier at Xirtia, I would imagine, would be quickest to the Imperial Palace.'

'Yes,' Tenebrae said. 'With all due haste.'

Above deck came the light sound of the ringing of a bell and a soft shift in the balance within the main room. The *Typhon* was away.

'You,' First Officer Albinus said to one of the lascars. 'Rouse Ysmay and get him to stoke the *daemon*.'

'Mister Albinus, if you'd take the pilot's chair.' Albinus ducked his head in deference and settled into a chair with an odd-handled contraption that hung from the boat's ceiling. Inside it looked to be mirrored glass. He placed his face to the device as if he were peering through a fence or narrow window and said, clearly, 'We are away from shore. Where is that engineer?'

A lascar came in with a wan, pale blond fellow in tow. He wore worker's clothing, dungarees soot-stained and dirty with an ill-fitting tunic and a variety of wrenches, pliers, awls, calipers, and other instruments of both summoning and mechanical manipulation.

'Mister Ysmay,' Captain Regulus said. 'Let's waken this *daemon* and set him to turning screws, shall we?'

'Yes,' Ysmay said, looking curiously at first Carnelia and Lupina, and then Tenebrae and myself. For their part, our 'prisoners' were doing a fine job acting the part. Both were sodden and bedraggled, dripping through the grating that passed for a floor. It was becoming apparent that this room was what, in other ships, would be considered the pilot's roost. It was hard to fathom how this could be, below deck, but the device that Albinus peered through gave some indication – and I recalled the intricate device at the apex of what I thought was the stack. There was some correlation there.

The forward side of this command centre was covered in gauges and gewgaws, levers and handles, and another swivel chair with a peering device like Albinus', matched on the aft side of the space. I had to assume these chairs controlled the deck guns at fore and aft of the ship. It was all contained here.

'How big of a crew does she require?' I said. 'It's a marvellous vessel.'

'She's no frigate,' Regulus said, preening with false modesty. 'She's what the praefecti are calling a Cormorant Class Scout Ship.'

'She is lovely. But her crew?' I asked.

'That's the beauty of her. Everything is what Mister Ysmay calls—'

'Automated, Captain,' Ysmay said, turning a lever at the fore. He tapped a gauge with the back of a finger and then cranked a handle. The craft shuddered and then thrummed slightly – the vibrations of the screws turning.

Tenebrae said, 'I would witness this from on deck. It's a wonderful craft.' He took three long strides and hopped up the stairs to the upper deck. Ysmay looked puzzled. His mind worked, puzzling us out. I did not think we had much time.

Albinus, his face still pressed to the sighting machine, swivelled in his seat and back again. He disengaged from the peering mechanism, twisted a large multi-handled wheel, and then pressed his face back to the ocular device.

'With its automation, the *Typhon* runs on a skeleton crew. Six lascars, myself and Mister Albinus. And the engineer. We are sleek. We are compact. And we are fast,' Captain Regulus said.

'I am so glad to hear it,' I said. I shifted Fiscelion in my grip, pushed back my cloak. My hand fell near my sawn-off.

Carnelia coughed, either feigned or real, I could not tell – she was drenched from rain – and something about the sound drew one of the lascar's attention. Lupina looked at me, wild-eyed, and without words I knew her fear was for Fiscelion.

One of the lascars shifted, looking alarmed. 'Captain,' he said. 'I don't know if these prisoners are—' He reached forward, placing a hand on Carnelia's shoulder and tugged, in order to turn her around to face him.

Her cloak dropped to the ground, revealing her unbound hands. Unbound hands that held a pistol.

The lascar gave a strangled cry. Echoed by other sailors. Carnelia shoved the pistol into the man's stomach. She cried, 'Everyone, remain still. I will ventilate him!' giving her best impression of my husband. It was such a Hardscrabble phrase.

At the edges of my vision, I perceived Albinus moving. Things spiralled out of control. Regulus fumbled at his waist, pawing at his sidearm.

It was all going to Hell, and I was not one to wait for its arrival.

I withdrew my shotgun and shot Captain Regulus in the face.

ELEVEN

I Woke In The Earth And Pulled Myself Up

'STUFF IT,' FISK said to Praeverta, as Gynth slung Beleth's trussed body to the ground near the Bitter Spring. We had replaced the gag. Fisk grabbed a still-smoking bit of wood and jammed it into the engineer's stump to cauterise the wound (or further torture him, I could not tell) and watched with a blank, abject stare as the engineer squirmed and writhed in his bindings. Gynth stood watching, big hands twitching.

Praeverta's cohort looked at Gynth curiously. Few had witnessed a *vaettir* up close – only the elders could remember a time when *dvergar* and *vaettir* co-existed, if not peacefully, then with far less bloodshed and some rudimentary trade. When I was young, my mam would tell tales of stretchers coming to our villages with carcasses and meat, and leaving with clothing and steel. Though there were other tales of them terrorising villages, stalking the inhabitants, and only leaving once some offering was made.

The *vaettir* are our native cousins – *gynth* – but on the whole, they are capricious, if not violent.

The *dvergar* matron moved to stand in front of Fisk. He brushed past her. 'What have you done, you bloody idiot?'

Fisk filled one of Praeverta's Vaettir's buckets with water and set it to cool, away from the spring. He removed the saddle from the horse he'd been riding and tacked it out with his own gear. The horse sucked down the cooling water in one, continuous draught.

'I shortened the engineer a hand, Madame,' he said. 'So that the whore's son cannot work his tricks.'

'Neruda had need of an engineer!' she said.

'And he'll get one,' Fisk said. 'One lacking a right hand.'

Praeverta cursed in my mother's tongue, voluminously and with much invention. Inbhir looked miserable when she finally turned her displeasure to him to ask if he could've stopped Fisk.

I said to her in *dvergar*, 'Leave Inbhir be, Matve. There was no stopping the human. This man—' I gestured to Fisk '—he is a stormfront.' *Ye ven drimma val*. There is no negotiating with the mountain, there is no bartering with the river, or the sea. They do as they will. *Dvergar* is elegant, and a simple phrase can contain multitudes.

She pursed her lips, thinking. 'And you, why do you spend your days in his company? Is there none of the mountain left in you?'

I took off my hat, the old beater, and spread my hands. 'You were so kind to me when we first met, to welcome home a long lost mountain's son. He, at least, has not denigrated me for my blood.'

'Pah. All Rumans prefer to view this world with their boot on our back.' Her look intensified. 'But that will not remain so.'

'I would not mind living in a world where Rume does not hold the reins. But I would not have wholesale bloodshed and death. I drank my fill of it. Look west.' I grabbed her arm and pulled her to the mouth of the gulley, where the western sky was visible. Her compatriots hopped up and followed, outraged I would lay hands on Matve Praeverta. She jerked her arm away. I pointed at the western sky. In the distance, a smear. Smoke caught by crosswinds and borne miles upon miles over the Hardscrabble. A thousand lives turned to ash. 'Harbour Town is in smoking ruins.

The heavens bear witness. Are the Medierans better masters? I have met Neruda. I do not think he would want this, either.'

'We want no masters,' Praeverta said. 'And don't sully his name in your mouth, *dimidius*. You are a creature of nothing, fighting for nothing, standing for nothing.'

She turned and walked away.

And that, I am afraid, left me speechless. I had always been on the outside, looking in, child of no nation that wanted me. Not Rume, not Dvergar. In my long years, only Illina, Fisk – and Livia – Gynth and the land had accepted me for what I am. The Hardscrabble shows no favourites and loves us all equally. It would hug you to its breast and never let you go. But to say my compass – the one that turned in the chambers of my heart – kept no bearing, found no true north, it rocked me back on my feet. Was it not enough to try to stay kind in a world that would grind you to dust? Was camaraderie and bravery, respect for fellow man and *dvergar*, enough in this monster of a world? To be measured as worthy by my people, must I break all bonds and take up arms against those who had welcomed me as much as I'd been welcomed anywhere? But she had it right: I was a child of no nation.

I wandered back through the gulleys, and found Bess chewing on some scrub-brush. The mule chucked her head at my approach and blew air. I rubbed her neck and checked her burns from Harbour Town. The flesh on her rump was bubbled but healing. I would wash her wounds, soon. It was said the Bitter Spring had healing properties – that the earth sloughed off part of itself in the giving up of the precious water and its essence imbued it. Or it could just be dirty water. But it was what we had to hand.

As I turned to lead Bess back, Lina said, 'So, Grandfather, tell me about this hand.'

She had followed me on cat feet and I had not heard her. 'What are you talking about?' I asked. I looked her up and down. She was bloodied some – though someone had bound her head, where she'd had the knock – and there was a nasty abrasion on her chin and her trousers were ripped, her knuckles bloody, and she limped as she approached. But on the whole, she was relatively unhurt from her encounter with Gynth when Beleth rode him. Most who tussle with *vaettir* (or engineers) fare far worse.

'The *vaettir*, when he was *daemon*-gripped, he said for those things to "bring him the hand".' She cocked her head, waiting.

She was very pretty, even with the injuries – clear, intelligent eyes, fair skin, lustrous hair. For a moment, I thought of Illina, my wife, so long ago. I had never forgotten her. But I had tried. The end had been so painful and the desolation it wreaked in me still smoked like the ruins of Harbour Town did now. She was the first to accept me, Severus Speke's half-human *dimidius*. She was the first to treat me as someone worth more than meat, worth more than the strength in hands and back. This is how the world views us, the *dvergar*, as either workers or things to consume, in their avaricious appetites.

'It is nothing, do not concern yourself with it,' I said, drawing her away. 'Let me look at you, child.'

'I am no child, old one,' she said. 'I am a woman, full-grown, and of marriageable age.'

I laughed. 'Of course you are, and you know me not at all. So you'll ignore me when I tell you that you should only marry who you want and when you're ready.'

A half-smile crept on her face, and she shook her head. 'You are wily, old one, and shuck off an ambush easily.' She put her index finger on my chest and pushed me, so that I rocked back on my heels. 'What is this hand the devils were after?'

I shook my head. 'It's nothing that concerns you and I would warn you to forget it and not speak of it again,' I said. Bess hawed in agreement.

'Fuck that, Grandfather,' she said, her eyes blazing. Here was a woman accustomed to meeting resistance from the world, and not accepting it. Never accepting it.

I moved my hand in a chopping motion. 'It does not concern you, child.'

Lina grimaced, making her face turn dark, shadows in the hollows of her eyes. She'd not seen much sleep, lately. None of us had. 'My oldest friend's corpse lies cooling by the spring, and you tell me it is not my concern. A city burns in the distance, full of the bodies of my kin, but that is not my concern.' Strange turn, her using Harbour Town on me in the exact way I'd used it on Praeverta. She jabbed her finger into my chest again, to punctuate the words. It hurt.

'There is a greater danger here than you know,' I said. 'And it's bound to the Ia-damned engineer.'

'What don't you want us to know?' she asked.

'I don't want you to know what I don't want you to know.'

'If I wanted horse-shite like that, I would've stayed with Mam and Pap,' she said.

I laughed. There was so much of Illina in her, it was frightening.

Fisk called from the mouth of the gulley. 'Shoe, you coming?'

I brushed past Lina and made my way to where Fisk stood.

'I could go to Praeverta,' she said.

I nodded and adjusted my hat on my head. 'You would get her killed, and everyone else here,' I said. She watched me go.

'What in the Hell was that all about?' Fisk asked.

'The *daemon* hand, pard,' I said. 'One of them was paying attention, at least, when Beleth came a'bounding through wearing the Gynth suit.' We came back to where someone had restoked the fire and begun cooking more of the horse.

'She's the one who's your long lost kin?' Fisk asked.

'Yes,' I said. 'Granddaughter.'

'Figures,' he said. 'You don't miss many tricks yourself.'

'She's threatening to go to Praeverta,' I said.

'Make sure your six-guns stay loaded, then,' he said.

'Hopefully they won't shoot any more horses out from under us,' I said, leading Bess to where she could get to a full bucket of spring water.

'They're taking us to Wickerware, by way of Dvergar-town,' he said. 'Hopefully we can rejoin Winfried there. She was injured when we were searching for Beleth, in the Smokeys. Buquo took a fall and she broke her arm. Big_horse, and not one suited for mountains.'

'You were checking on the new silverlode for Cornelius?' I asked.

'We'd had rumour of Beleth sniffing around, and worried he'd got wind of the silver.'

'Think he did?' That would be bad news.

'I don't know. If he did, he would've shared that information with his new Medieran partners,' he said. He rubbed his chin, thinking. 'I doubt they'll move on the Dvergar silverlode, even if they do know of it. Talavera is producing right now and has all the machinery and industry running. Getting the Dvergar-town silverlode to produce will take some time. The Medieran course is clear – push north, up the Big Rill, all the way to Passasuego. The third legion is gone in the destruction of Harbour Town. The sixth can move south – closer to home – and try to get the Dvergar silverlode to produce, or it can move to protect Talavera.'

'The world wars on silver,' I said. 'Will the new lode produce, do you think?'

'It's a rich one. The *dvergar* have control of it now, it's in a remote and rugged little valley they call the Grenthvar, but the Ruman legions will be moving south, most likely, as fast as possible to take over. The real problem is that Rume has soldiers, but no workforce to mine it,' he said, and looked around at the dwarves, tending to the remaining horses, refilling canteens and waterbags, taking stock of their supplies. Refugees, all. And we were of their number.

Praeverta sat cross-legged looking at Gynth, who had taken a seat and was holding a haunch of horsemeat, bloody, and taking big bites.

I sat down near him. Fisk squatted on his hams. Someone had brought the stretcher some trousers and he'd put them on.

He smiled at me, meat hanging in streamers from his teeth, and offered me the haunch. I did not think I could hold it. I waved it away.

'Will you stay with us, Gynth?' I asked in my mother's tongue.

He bobbed his great head, up and down. 'I know of no other place to go. Where else?' His command of *dvergar* was solid, if halting.

I took off my hat and scratched my head. 'I don't know. Do you have family? Other—' I gestured in the air, unsure what to refer to his kind as.

A puzzled look overcame his big, angular face. 'I am newborn. I woke in the earth and pulled myself up. And I found you.'

'You woke in the earth?' I remembered the first time I saw him. His clothes were tatters, and there was mould and the whiff of the grave about him.

'Yes,' he said in *dvergar*. 'In the earth, high upon the mountains.'

'And do you remember anything else?' I said. 'Anything before that?'

'Fire,' he said. 'I remember flames. And before that water. And hunger. Terrible hunger.'

'Hunger? For meat?' I asked.

He looked down for a moment, in one of those thousand yard stares. 'For . . . for life. For the green in the flower, the green in the grass. The wind. The shoal heart. But that was before sleep.'

Fisk said, 'What's he saying?' I told him. Fisk's brow furrowed. There was distaste there, writ in his features, for Gynth. I could sense the currents in him, after so long as partners, wanting to kill the stretcher. But he was Ruman, and I had to remind myself of that. Expedience and reason won out. He would stomach his distaste and endure the stretcher's company. And, I hope, my word went some way toward staying his hand, for Gynth had saved me, over and over again. In the creature, I felt, lay the secret of the *vaettir*, our cousins, and by puzzling out him, something of the rest of them might become clear. 'He's talking about what Livia wrote. The Autumn Lords.'

'She said they called it *Qi*,' I said. 'I don't even know how to pronounce that. But it's like... energy or life force or something.'

'Like blood, maybe. The essence. Maybe that's why stretchers always played games. Cat and mouse. They take energy from fear, maybe,' Fisk said.

'Like the *vorduluk* you Rumans are always going on about,' I said.

'Blood drinkers, yes.' He sucked his teeth. 'We all devour life, but there were so many times that the stretchers seemed to relish it,' he said. 'So, why is he so different?'

'No idea, pard,' I said. 'Livia wrote you that the Autumn Lords fell to a heavy trance. A great lethargy, almost like a drugged slumber. And only occasionally would they rouse themselves. To hunt. To take life.'

Fisk nodded, thoughtfully. 'They live long, long lives. Maybe they change.'

'Maybe they *were* changed,' I said.

We were silent for a long while and then both of us looked toward the engineer. He was sitting upright, gagged, his remaining hand tied to his feet. His stump oozed blood into the bandage some *dvergar* had applied. Inbhir sat nearby, guarding the engineer with the carbine Fisk had given him.

But it was Beleth's gaze that we noticed.

It was one of pure hate.

TWELVE

I May Not Have Been Wholly
Honest With You, Madame

Many things happened then, and all of them at once.
The sawn-off jerked in my hand. Smoke and the flash and
despair of Hellfire filled the small space of the navigational room
of the *Typhon*, and a gigantic boom shook us all. Regulus' head
exploded with a welter of blood and brain and shattered cranium.
A blood mist rose, I tasted it on my tongue. One of the lascars
screamed and his voice joined Fiscelion's.

Carnelia fired and more overwhelming sound and blood filled the
small space, leaving my head ringing. Wheeling, she shot another
lascar – another tremendous *boom* – and he fell. She twisted away
from the dying sailor's grasping hands, falling into the grasp of
the other lascar, who snatched up her hair and whirled her about,
one hand pawing for a gun at his belt. Albinus, already disengaged
from the peering device and wearing a horrified expression upon
his face, pulled his sidearm. With the remaining Hellfire shell in
my sawn-off, I shot him as well, this time in the chest. He rocketed
away from the muzzle flash and fell in a bloody heap upon Ysmay,
the engineer, who was screeching like a scalded dog.

My sister placed a hand on her head, holding her hair, and
lashed out with her boot at the lascar holding her. Her foot met
instep. He howled, releasing her. In a flash, Carnelia had booted
him between the legs, hard, so hard his body rose off the grated

floor, shoulders folding in over his stomach. He fell then, his legs turned traitorous and leeched of strength. Carnelia stomped on his neck and he ceased to move. Lupina pulled his gun from its holster. He never had a chance to cry out.

Tenebrae appeared at the base of the stairs, a naked gun in his hand, Carnelia's sword in the other. He tossed it to her and she snatched it out of the air and drew the blade.

'There are two more lascars down here,' Carnelia said to Tenebrae, looking around. She pointed with her pistol at an open metal door. 'At least, if what the first officer said could be trusted. What happened to the lascars above?'

Tenebrae grimaced. 'One down. The other jumped overboard.'

'So, they'll know about us soon enough,' I said. I popped the chamber of the sawn-off and replaced the shells. I snapped it shut with a *chunk*. Fiscelion was screaming now with the noise and the horror of it all. Lupina came and took him from me and began cooing. My ears rang. My mouth tasted of thick blood and not my own. I was struck, momentarily, by the dreadful absurdity of it all – the blood, the baby, the ship – all of it. I wanted to scream. I wanted to cry. I wanted to go back and raise the captain from the dead. I had crossed a line. I healed people before this, I tended wounds and sutured them and found ways to make them mend. But now, I was a killer – maybe not a remorseless one, but a killer all the same. I did not think when shooting Captain Regulus. I acted. And there were two more lascars to deal with.

We're born into pain, and we live our lives in it, and we visit pain upon others and ourselves. All to protect those we love. And we love ourselves and our children above all.

'Come out,' I yelled, into the confines of the ship. 'Come out, you lascar! You have my word you will live to see shore.'

Silence. The *Typhon* shifted, and a hollow clang sounded throughout the vessel.

'The ship,' I said, and approached Ysmay, who still lay half-buried under the first officer's body. Albinus was still alive, but gasping now, holding his stomach, where the sawn-off's buckshot had penetrated his body cavity and made a swamp of his innards. His mouth opened and closed, as if trying to voice some curse, but he did not have the wind for words. A spatter of blood traced his cheek. He looked at me, not with surprise, but with bald intention. He would see me dead. These were the last thoughts of his life. My doom.

He stilled. His chest ceased its rise and fall. His eyes dulled, his gaze fixed upon the ceiling, never to see again.

Ysmay cried.

'Get up, man,' I said, nudging the engineer with my weapon. 'Get up and make use of yourself and you will live.'

'What—' His voice was raw, ripped and torn from screaming. 'What do you want of me?'

'If you cannot steer this ship, then halt it,' I said. 'Now.'

Ysmay blinked in the *daemonlight* of the chamber. He remained still, panting, watching me.

'All right then,' I said, and thumbed back the hammer on the sawn-off.

'Wait,' Ysmay said. 'Wait.' He pushed himself off the floor and went and cranked some levers and knobs and the thrumming that had shivered the *Typhon* before lessened. He went to the peering mechanism that Albinus had occupied before and turned a crank on the column. The *Typhon* shifted and tilted, almost imperceptibly.

'I have the *Typhon*'s nose upstream and she's holding position,' Ysmay said, voice quavering.

I turned to Carnelia. 'The remaining lascars?'

She nodded.

'Gentlemen!' she called. 'Gentlemen, throw down your weapons

97

and come out. We will take you on deck and you will be able to swim for shore.'

'I swear to you by all the gods, both old and new, by Mithras and Ia,' Tenebrae said. 'We would not waste any more Hellfire, nor life. You are free to go, if only you throw down your weapons.'

'Should we keep them,' Carnelia said, out of the side of her mouth. 'To man the ship? We have only us and the engineer?'

'Would you guard them, non-stop?' I asked. 'Would we lock them up at night? I think not. There are five of us. One less than their full complement. We will manage.'

We fell silent. The carnage that I'd wreaked upon the ship was glaring, now. Captain Regulus' bowels had released in death, and the stench was awful. It was not just that I had ended their lives, it was that I had ended them so messily. Thankfully, the grated floor did not allow for pooling blood, or viscera.

Fiscelion quieted. Lupina had masticated dates and was feeding him like a bird.

Inside the ship, where the remaining lascars hid, there was hushed arguing. A gun clanged off the metal flooring. And then another.

'Approach, hands visible,' Tenebrae called.

The two lascars hesitantly came forward, hands out. 'Please, please,' the dark headed one was saying. He looked like a boy, any boy, from any family on the Cælian. Any street in Rume. His companion, a thickset, burly man, covered in hair, looked like a gorilla and just as eager to squeeze the life from us. I was reminded, by his glare, that it was our lives. Or theirs.

Tamberlaine would not take me, or my child.

I gestured with the sawn-off for the lascars to take the stairs. The youngest bounded up three, in a rush to get out of the aquatic charnel house.

'Slow down,' Tenebrae said. 'You get more than five paces ahead, and I'll have to put a hole in you.'

We followed behind, onto the wind-wracked deck. The Tever was muddy, the sky was grey. The breeze made the river's surface ripple, thousands of tiny whitecaps rushing toward the far shore. The smell from below gone. The *Typhon* stood in the current, holding steady.

The lascars went to the bulwark. The tow-headed one launched himself overboard and hit the surface with a muted splash. The other sailor looked at us closely, face twisted in rage and distaste.

'There's a special place in Hell for you,' he said. 'Betrayers. Traitors.'

Tenebrae tensed. 'I can send you along ahead of us, if you'd like. You can make sure they're waiting for us when we get there.'

The lascar flipped over, backward, into the water. Tenebrae went to the bulwark to watch them swim for shore. After a moment, he returned.

'Gods,' said he. 'What a mess.'

'Yes,' I said. 'And before we're done, there might be more messes. Now to take this ship away from here, quickly.'

He looked at me closely. 'It was necessary.'

'Are you asking me? Or telling?'

'I don't know,' he said.

'It was necessary,' I said. 'And I killed the captain and his officer. You will not take that sin upon yourself.'

'If killing is a sin, I've sullied myself well enough for torment before I met you Cornelians.' He shook his head. 'But it has never been those that did not deserve it.'

'It's a hard thing we have to do, to ensure our freedom. You are having second thoughts?'

He shook his head. 'I loved Secundus. Can you understand that?' He looked at me, imploring. But he was confused. In him things

99

warred, his ineffable sense of honour and loyalty and the dawning realisation of his new situation. And even he did not understand how that loyalty could have shifted from Tamberlaine and Rume to a dead man in a cask of oil. And that dead man's sister. And her son.

'It's done, whatever the case,' I said. I walked over to the bulwark and vomited the contents of my stomach over the side, adding to the Tever's miasmic and foetid swifts. My hands shook and I sank down to my knees.

Tenebrae, not knowing what to do, exactly, came and squatted near me. 'It is hard, your first killing,' he said. 'It's good to talk about it.'

'I have killed before,' I said, thinking of the *vaettir*, thinking of the battle at the Winter Palace of Kithai.

He touched my shoulder. 'It is not the same.'

'No,' I said. No, none of that violence had been close, or so personal. Regulus' head was there and then gone, and all that was left behind was stench and red mist.

How could I hold my son in these hands? How could I?

When the shaking ceased, I stood and smoothed my dress.

'It is done,' I said. 'We have the ship. Let us take it away from here.' I laughed. 'We *took the ship*.'

'Aye,' Tenebrae said. 'We have become pirates.'

Carnelia, Tenebrae, and Lupina cleaned up the bodies while I spoke with – interrogated, rather – the engineer Ysmay. It was, as Tenebrae and I had discussed, a messy business. They threw the bodies overboard as I directed Ysmay to give a quick rundown of the functions of the ship. He did not prove recalcitrant, but I had points of coercion.

'And these gauges here,' I said, pointing with the sawn-off. It was a good instrument of indication. The man's eyes followed the bores assiduously.

'Those regulate the steam pressure and flow.' He touched one. 'This one is important – once Typhon has fresh blood—'

'Typhon?'

'The *daemon* that turns these screws. Did you not know this?'

'Yes, of course,' I said. 'I just did not know that we had fallen so low that we named our ships after them. Or that they required blood.'

'Low?' He cocked his head and looked at me strangely. 'Rume propels itself on their power but cannot bear to hear their names? It is a weakness—'

I centred the bores of the shotgun back on the engineer. 'Mister Ysmay, we will have ample time for discussing Rume and her citizens' prejudices and peccadilloes in the coming months, but now—'

The look on his face spoke volumes. The vastness of the Occidens Seas filled him.

'But the *Typhon* is a littoral ship, a vessel for the coasts and bays. She's not to make journeys of—'

I waved the shotgun and he ceased making sound. 'Littoral or no, prepare yourself.' I touched the barrel lightly on his forehead. 'Here. And here.' Again, the lightest touch on his breast. Blued gunmetal kiss above the heart. I did not even wonder what person I had become.

'Now,' I said, once he had settled his discomfort at the realisation of where we were going. 'Turn the *Typhon* downstream. Carnelia, Tenebrae! Come. Watch his every move.' I tapped him again with the gun. 'And you, talk. Everything you do, tell us how you do it, as you do it.'

He blinked rapidly. Glanced about, as if something in the room could save him. He was smeared in blood, possibly some of

Albinus' faecal mire staining his trousers. His eyes fell upon the place where Regulus fell. And his eyes snapped back to me.

'This is, of course, the compass,' he began, reaching to place an unstable hand on a gauge. 'It indicates the direction of true north. And here.' He touched a small wooden and metal wheel within reach of the peering mechanism. 'This controls the rudder.'

'Yes,' I said, nodding. 'I can see that.'

'There are two screws, as she is a littoral and should one become damaged, the other can take the burden of propulsion.' He reached forward and tapped two levers, capped in wood, hand-sweet. 'These are the throttle for both of the screws. Pushed forward – like as to like, the thaumaturge's dream – they propel the boat forward. Pushed back, beyond this marking, they reverse the boat.'

'And this contraption, what is it?' Carnelia slapped the metal side of the handled peering mechanism.

'That is the mirrored occulus, or Miraculous, and allows us to steer. And,' he paused here, looking at me, and then back to Carnelia as if we would react to his name for the device, 'other functions that we can go into. But I think time is—'

'Yes,' Tenebrae said. 'We've been wallowing here in the brown long enough.' He wiped his hands on a bloody cloth. 'Downstream. Now, and swiftly.'

Ysmay took station at the Miraculous – it was a ridiculous name, an elision, and obviously a pet one – and pressed forward the throttle. 'I am giving her more steam, and now turning her downstream. All is clear.' He looked from the Miraculous to the throttle and back. He made a small adjustment in the rudder. 'The *Typhon*, she's very sensitive.' A note of pride there. A whiff of ownership. He was the architect of the vessel, he was her father. And if I knew anything about parentage, he would do everything in his power to protect his child.

'Mister Ysmay,' I said. 'It is a marvellous vessel you've created. How do the guns work?'

He removed his face from the Miraculous. His features were animated. 'The key to making things for the Ruman Fleet is that everything must be the same. No variations!' Enthusiastic. A beaming father. So simple a deceit, to play to one's strengths and loves. 'The swivels came later, after the design of the Miraculous,' he said.

'That name is so preposterous, it makes me want to slap you,' Carnelia said. 'It is a scope that allows peeping. It's a peep-o-scope.'

'Ia's ballsack,' Tenebrae said. 'That's idiotic.'

Ysmay remained silent for a moment, looking into the peep-oscope. The Miraculous. Whatever.

The *Typhon* shifted beneath us. There was movement in the waters and the pressure of acceleration, surging.

'Uh, shouldn't there be someone on deck? Just to make sure we're heading the right direction?' Tenebrae said.

'There's a station beneath the stack where you can see the front quarter, and it would be well if it was manned. It comes equipped with a vocal horn that directs sounds to this chamber via sympathetic vibrating *daemon*s. In case of issues – mis-navigation, obstacles, antagonistic vessels—' He raised his eyebrow here and I could not discern if it was in hopes that we would be killed or he'd have a chance to show off his wondrous vessel. 'It should be manned,' he repeated.

'I shall man it, then,' Tenebrae said. He bounded up and out of the navigational centre. In but a few moments, a hollow sound, buzzy, tinny, came. '*Hello, below. We make good speed downstream. On our right . . . our starboard side . . . now passes Rumina and the shanty town of Little Flamina.*'

Ysmay looked into the peering device and then picked up a horn

103

– connected by some sort of tube – and said, 'I see something in the Tever, now, ahead and to port.' He adjusted the peering scope. 'Maybe a rotted hull of ship? Maybe a downed tree?'

'It's but a discoloured bit of foam. Some detritus. Some flotsam,' Tenebrae said.

There was a bump and shifting. The hull of the *Typhon* echoed strangely.

'*My mistake,*' Tenebrae said, in the horn. '*That was some deadfall. It seems there is a knack to reading waters that I do not have, yet.*'

'And the guns, Mister Ysmay? How do they work?' I asked.

'Much the same as the Miraculous, but with some modifications. I would have to abandon this position to show you their usage. If they are to be put into use, they will need to be unshrouded.'

'That is no good,' I said. 'We must make speed.' And we are dreadful short of hands. Would that Fiscelion would sleep so Lupina could assist.

I drew Carnelia to the side and spoke in a hushed voice. 'At this point, even Tamberlaine knows of our escape. And soon, they'll know that we have taken the *Typhon*. We have no teeth. Uncover the swivels, figure out their design and usage. Can you do that? Ysmay said that it is mostly automated.'

Carnelia's eyes brightened. Excited at the prospect of the deck guns, colour flushed her – her sense of play made her lovely. And deadly.

She scrambled out of the command room to move on deck. I remained still, watching the engineer. After a few moments, Carnelia reappeared, smeared in black grease and bearing a great wad of evil-looking canvas – the gun shroud. She dropped it at the foot of the topside hatch and disappeared into the front of the ship. A metallic clang and curses sounded. 'I'm fine, have no worries for my sake!' she called.

'We were not,' I said, under my breath.

So I was left to watch the engineer, who turned knobs and peered into the Miraculous. He explained the markings on the rudder's wheel, and made note as we came to a sweep of the Tever where the *Typhon* would need to turn some thirty degrees. He beckoned me to look into the scope to see the river, the twist of currents.

'I think not, Mister Ysmay, until we have some company,' I said, shifting the shotgun in my grasp. 'I have no urge to hurt you, but can have no assurance that you would not bludgeon me given half the chance.'

His expression paled, his eyes searched, searched in a private corner where motivations hide. 'I-I wouldn't, I—'

I held up a hand. The blood on it had dried to mud-brown, like the Tever's waters. 'No need to explain, Mister Ysmay. No need.'

I continued to observe him – making minute adjustments at the helm, checking gauges, 'a good head of steam, ma'am', tweaking the throttle – until Lupina appeared. She approached me, giving glances toward Ysmay as he manned the helm.

'He is asleep, for the moment, which is well,' she said. 'Though I had to stuff him full of masticated dates before he would go down. The berths in this beast do very well as cribs, with enough swaddling. Each one has a rail.' She wiped her mouth. 'I could use a wash.'

'Wait until you see Carnelia.' I handed her my shotgun. 'No time, now. Keep an eye on Mister Ysmay while I see to my sister.' Lupina took the weapon and sat near the engineer on a metal stool at another station. The command of the *Typhon* was cleverly designed, and most of that, I had to assume, rested on Ysmay's shoulders – a consequence of his engineer's mind. The slick, calculating part of me made figures and levies and calculations of his worth, once we arrived in Hardscrabble. A clang and hollow thonk sounded on the *Typhon*'s metal hull.

If we arrive in Hardscrabble.

I followed where Carnelia had gone, stepping over the porthole openings that passed for entryways in this vessel – each one fixed with a thick metal door and curious levered locking mechanism – down the tight gullet of the *daemonlit* hallway, passing shut metal doors that led to chambers whose function and contents I knew not and would have to wait to discover, until I came to one that was wooden with steel bands and densely wrought with intaglios and skeins of silver warding, like blue veins on a god's skin.

I wrenched it open and passed through. Inside was a circular chamber packed tight and claustrophobic with what seemed like warded metal casks – until I realised that each container was a Hellfire round for an impossibly large gun. Each one was polished and gleaming, every inch warded deep. The room smelled of oil and the residue of brimstone and human sweat. It was hot in there. I put out a hand and touched one of the Hellfire shells; it was as warm as the flesh of beast or man.

Carnelia stood in the centre of the room, looking into another peering device, this one handleless. She was ringed in a copse of levers sprouting from the floor, each one terminating in a handle with a smaller releasing device integrated into the whole.

'How comes it?' I asked.

'It is impossibly simple. And impossibly complex.' She pointed to a vertical steel framework containing a stack of the massive Hellfire rounds, with cotton wadding between each munition. At the chamber's roof, the framework entered the undercarriage, ringed in a greased circle, of what must be the aft swivel gun. Runners of chain and pulleys ran beside the framework from the chamber's floor to ceiling. 'Pull that lever – and you really have to pull it, it requires such strength, I could not have managed it a year ago – and it pushes open a hatch and inserts one of the rounds into the maw of the gun. This I have done.' Indicating the peering device, she said, 'There are no handles like in the command centre to swivel the view about. It remains fixed to the bore of the gun with hash marks indicating, I must assume, distance. I was considering pulling one of these—'

There was a moment of indecisiveness on her face, which changed quickly to dissatisfaction. It was almost as if I could hear her thoughts whipping around in her head: *this is troublesome and makes me feel of no consequence. However, I am of consequence, gods damn me, what am I afraid of?*

Her hand stretched out and I said, 'Maybe we should bring Mister Ysmay—'

She pulled the lever.

For a moment, there were flames, billowing flames filling the universe, not just above and below, but stretching back in time immemorial to the beginnings of the earth and lancing forward to the far reaches of all our possible futures, where our children's children's children might have lived. There was only flame, black flame, noxious. Forever and always.

And then it was gone and we were gasping.

'I believe, sissy,' Carnelia said, 'we've just had a wee taste of Hell.' She took a large breath. 'It wasn't so bad, was it?'

I did not answer. If I had anything left in my stomach to retch up, I would have done so then.

Tenebrae appeared in the door to the room. 'Ia's great sack, what is going on? I almost shat myself.' Streaming rainwater and wild-eyed, he looked like he'd been goosed. In effect, he had.

'Just figuring out the deck gun, Shadow,' Carnelia said. 'Eggs. Omelettes. All that.' She waved a hand at him.

'Most omelettes don't require you to visit the netherworld to eat them,' he said.

'Only the really good ones do,' Carnelia said. She tapped a lever with one long finger. 'All right. So this one fires the beast.' Her hand strayed to another. 'What does this one do?'

'No—' Tenebrae lurched forward, hands out.

She pulled the lever. Gears clanked and strained. Metal groaned. The gun's Miraculous turned, as did the floor beneath her and the undercarriage above.

'Aha!' Carnelia said, and clapped her hands like she used to do when she was a girl and had discovered some choice bit of rumour, or made some embarrassingly snarky bit of sexual commentary or innuendo. 'This swivels the gun about.' She turned to us. 'I have this well in hand, you two. Resume your former activities.' She made shooing motions with her hands. 'Go.'

'You better have this figured out, and soon,' Tenebrae said. 'Because you just rang a great dinner bell for the sea-wolves of Rume.'

'Where are we?' I asked.

'We are between Rume and Ostia, heading fast downriver. Despite her draught and low-slung appearance, the *Typhon* is a formidable vessel, that's for sure. She could not take the *Malphas* in a battle, but she could outrun and outmanoeuvre her.'

'Wonderful,' I said. 'We should check on Mister Ysmay and Lupina.' I turned back to my sister. 'And you will fire no more?'

'I can make no promises, sissy,' Carnelia said. Before she could stop herself, a grin came to her face.

'I should not have phrased that as a question. Fire no more, until necessary. Understood?' I said.

'If you insist,' Carnelia said.

Tenebrae and I returned to the command room. Lupina glanced toward us, eyebrows raised. 'Carnelia woke the lad, I can hear him crying now.' The echoes of his wails bounced off the metal walls, amplified.

'I will take over here,' I said, taking the shotgun. I was somewhat dismayed at the logistics of babysitting the engineer, but there was no alternative other than watching him closely. 'Mister Tenebrae, back on the deck, please. If we are approaching the bay, we'll need your eyes on the sea. Ostia will have sent other ships against us, possibly, if they've moved fast enough.'

Tenebrae nodded and bounded back up and in moments the tinny sound of his voice came through the speaking device.

I faced Ysmay.

'Sir,' I began. 'It has been an eventful morning and I am quite sorry for the manner in which I had to commandeer this vessel.'

Ysmay did not remove his gaze from the Miraculous, but I could tell he was listening. 'We are coming to the Bay of Ostia, as you know. I need from you a promise.'

He finally turned from his labours to face me. 'What sort of promise?'

'In moments, we will be making steam into Ostian waters, and with every passing second we'll be further from shore. Surely you see your predicament.'

He looked puzzled. 'My predicament? My commanding officers murdered in cold blood? Being kidnapped and my ship taken hostage?' He said 'my ship' like I might say *my son*. Something in his tone told me he was more outraged regarding the treatment and commandeering of the *Typhon* than at the death of his officers.

'It was a necessity,' I said. 'I will do what I can to make amends to you, and shrive that sin – it is mine and mine alone. But until then, I need to you to understand your predica— your situation.' I paused. 'Have we left the Tever?'

'Yes,' he said, 'Just.'

'Increase speed, then,' I said. 'Are you a strong swimmer?'

'What?' he said.

'Are you a strong swimmer?'

'I cannot say. I haven't swum in a long while. When I was young—'

'Soon, we will be in the middle of a bay, far from shore. Even should you be able to abandon the helm and make your way topside without being stopped, if you flung yourself overboard, you would drown before reaching safety.'

He had a nice face. Soft around the edges, with downy blond hair framing it. His lips were, if not full and beautiful, at least expressive and intelligent, as were his blue eyes. His teeth were bad, yellowed, like a dog's. His hands were articulate and knobby. For such a slight figure, his hands looked powerful. I could smell nothing of the man except the Hellfire and blood he'd been witness to. The blood I had shed.

'I need you to understand that, from this point on, all of our eggs are in one basket. Our fortunes – yours, mine, and the rest of us – are joined. Whether you like it or not. I need your promise you will work toward our escape, now.'

'I can't—' Our gazes met and held and after a moment, he depressed the two throttle levers. The *Typhon* surged and thrummed, as if we found ourselves in the barrel-chest of a large cat, purring rhythmically.

'*Ia's table!*' Tenebrae called through the device. '*We churn the sea! We make great waves and leave destruction in our wake!*' He fell silent, for a moment. '*The speed is remarkable. I feel like we're about to come out of the water.*'

'Full speed, Mister Ysmay,' I said.

He pushed the throttle fully forward. The thrumming increased even more. Tenebrae whooped and called and made sounds of delighted terror.

'*Ship, off the port, approaching.*'

Ysmay picked up a funnel with a scalloped metal tube connecting it to a command-board with many gauges, knobs, and levers.

He handed it to me. 'Speak loud and the man on deck and the woman at the aft deck gun will hear you, and so will everyone else in the ship.'

'Why are you giving this to me?' I asked.

He looked at me like some dullard. 'Are you not in command?'

I felt the pulse of blood in my fingers, the beat of it in my throat, my temple. The prickle of sweat on my brow. Scaling blood upon my wrist, my fingers, my face.

'Mister Tenebrae, give Carnelia assistance in aiming the aft swivel, sir,' I barked into the funnel. It reverberated throughout the *Typhon*.

'*Aye, Livia. Carnelia, approaching vessel two points forward port beam,*' Tenebrae said.

'*What in the name of all Hell does that mean?*' Carnelia said. She must have found her own speaking device.

'*Find the front of the ship and to the left, Ia-dammit!*' Tenebrae shouted.

Ysmay turned the peering device and stopped. 'He is correct. Another ship approaches. Small, and slow, with no apparent guns.'

'Can we outrun it?' I asked.

'It's small. We could, possibly, just plough right through it. But definitely outrun it. Yes,' Ysmay said.

'Hold your fire, sissy,' I said into the speaker. 'Hold. We will leave it be and make for open sea.'

Ysmay nodded and turned back to the helm. He made adjustments and I could feel the invisible currents of speed pushing my body in near unfathomable ways.

The *Typhon* continued to surge, a strange rocking motion, as if we rode on the back of a great horse, cantering, rocking back and forth in the waves.

'*The vessel falls away,*' Tenebrae called. '*Diminishing in our port quarter but ... Ia's blood! Large ship. Four points broad of starboard bow! Carnelia. Turn the gun ... Turn the gun. Turn the gun. Carnelia, turn—*'

'*I heard you the first time, godsdammit,*' Carnelia growled. '*Turning!*'

Frightening, this metal carapace hurtling through the foam. No windows, racing blind, toward the open sea. A disconcerting, sightless exodus from Rume. Fiscelion wailing in his metal crib like a siren, rising and falling. Dimly, far off – like a rock falling to splash hollowly at the bottom of a well – a boom sounded. Invisible pressures hidden away behind metal walls. The *Typhon* rocked dramatically.

'*Bloody Hell,*' Tenebrae said. '*That was close. Carnelia, where is the—*'

A cessation of life. Hellfire blooming behind eyes. Despair. The crack and pomp of our gun.

Carnelia howled. '*Ia-damn me to all the Hells.*'

'*That startled them. They're turning!*' Tenebrae panted into the receiver. It hissed and whispered without voice – sea foam green and the wind of our speed. '*They're turning! More guns!*'

Another far-off boom, and the *Typhon* pitched precariously. I took a balancing step – styluses and charts and papers fell from counters and work spaces. Ysmay lurched and caught himself on the handles of the peering device.

Our deck gun boomed again, filling the *Typhon* with dismay and the reek of Hellfire. Fiscelion's shriek pitched higher and higher – so frantic I felt it was going to snap, like an overstretched hawser or metal wire, and he would fall silent, never to make a sound again. A murmur overlay the din, the thrum of the screws, turning, Lupina's faint voice, *there lad, there my good boy, there there, I'm with you, dumpling, there now.*

Another blast of our swivel, and a pounding, invisible head of despair. Carnelia's screeches reverberated off the metal walls.

'*You've hit the bastards!*' Tenebrae crowed. '*Ia-dammit, you've punched a hole in them!*'

For a long moment, nothing. Just the rise and fall of the *Typhon*, surging. '*They have taken no notice of the wound,*' Tenebrae said, his voice strangely calm. '*Hit them again, before—*'

There came a far-off crack, resounding, and the *Typhon* shivered and shifted violently in the water. For a time, I feared all was lost. Inside the command spray wetted my face from a riveted seam. Ysmay cursed.

'I may not have been wholly honest with you, Madame,' Ysmay said, scrambling to work gears.

'Are we breached?' I asked.

'No,' the engineer said. 'Possibly. But I doubt it. We would be drowned, if that were the case.'

'Do we have time for this?' I asked. Above, the *Typhon* shook again with a blast of Hellfire. After-images of infernal flame flashed behind my eyes.

'*A miss!*' Tenebrae called. Carnelia's cursing pinged off the metal hull. '*We are outpacing them. Three points off starboard charter. Another volley.*' No indication then if that was an imperative or informative exclamation – then a far-off hollow boom sounded again. The *Typhon* shifted in the waters. '*We are too fast for them! No time to take a bearing.*'

'How were you dishonest, Mister Ysmay?' I asked.

'A sin of omission,' he said. 'That is all. Call Mister Tenebrae down.'

'Why?' I said, my voice pitching upwards.

'Call him down. *Call him down!*' He had abandoned all sense of self, of dignity, of importance. He was in the trench, under fire. The enemy bearing down. The veneer of civilisation swept away. He dashed away from the controls. Leapt toward the hatch leading to the deck.

'Stop, sir! Stop,' I said, centring the shotgun on his chest. I thumbed back the hammer on the shotgun's barrels and placed my finger on the trigger. But he was out of sight, by then. I began to follow, but no sooner had I taken two steps, he was back, and Tenebrae followed him shortly after. They shut and turned the lock on the metal door.

'Mister Ysmay, return to your post. Now.' I have spent a life listening to men of command use their voices to great effect, cracking them like whips. It came to me without much consideration, or thought.

'The aft hatch,' Ysmay cried, racing back to the command centre. Tenebrae bounded past, sodden and hurried, droplets of salty water flying about. 'Fasten it tight.'

Tenebrae did as Ysmay said, whipping the locking mechanism down. The sounds of the sea were walled away. A hush fell upon us. I placed myself near the engineer and raised my voice again.

'What is this? What did you omit, sir?' I said. The man was terrified, battle-fear making him weak and panicked.

He turned to me. His throat worked painfully, swallowing.

'This,' he said, and pulled a lever. 'Prepare for descent.'

THIRTEEN

An Army That Carries The Crimson Hand
Before It Will Be Invincible

W E RODE EAST to the Smokeys until dark. Fisk packed a trussed Beleth on his horse's rump, as if the engineer was a sleeping roll, and touched his gun when Inbhir toddled around to question the particulars of Beleth's bindings, position, and general arrangement.

After Fisk had run him off, Praeverta herself appeared. Fisk already sat on his horse. The other *dvergar* – those that had mounts – watched from saddle. Those that didn't had already begun the long march east.

'That man is important,' Praeverta said, the corners of her mouth tugging down. I couldn't tell if that was her displeasure or a natural state. 'And you would never have captured him without our help.'

'And your party, had they run across him, would now have *daemon*s or worse riding you like ponies. Didn't you comprehend *that* when the *daemon*-gripped came barrelling through?' Fisk swept his hand across the Bitter Spring and the fresh graves in the Hardscrabble dirt. 'We both helped each other, so let's stop this cock-play. I have taken the man into my custody and that's where he will stay, until we get to Dvergar or wherever else the Hell your Mister Neruda is.' He glanced at me when he said Dvergar, referring to the town, not the race.

It was curious, that glance. He must be worried about the silverlode that he, and Winfried, had sussed out when I was in the hands of the Tempus Union.

'We should bypass Dvergar, then, and head toward Tapestry. And after that Wickerware, if what the *vanmer* at the moot told us was true. Neruda plans to take up our cause and rally there.'

'Maybe so, ma'am, but we'll head for Dvergar first.' He raised his hand when she opened her mouth. 'No, you can argue all you want and dicker, but Dvergar is on the way and you'll find no more water in the Hardscrabble until you reach the Eldvatch.' He shrugged and put his hand on his saddle-horn and shifted his weight, ready to ride. 'Makes no difference to me. That's where I'm headed. Follow if you want. Try to stop me, you'll regret it.' He rode out.

I followed, touching my hat and nodding at the old woman as I passed on Bess' back. Praeverta's curses followed me as I rode.

'We keep on as we were,' Fisk said, looking at Inbhir and the other *dvergar* struggling to maintain pace on horseback. Some remained behind to escort the walkers. 'Nothing has changed, except now we have Beleth. Isn't that right, sir?' Fisk said, slapping the engineer's arse. The man moaned in response.

'I despise the man as much as you, pard,' I said. 'But do you think he'll survive the ride trussed up like that?'

Fisk glanced at me, eyes narrowed. 'Maybe. Maybe not. I'm not too concerned, either way.'

'He's a trump card,' I said. 'And we'll want to be able to play him should we come face to face with Neruda.'

'We'll come face to face with Neruda, don't you worry.' Fisk spat – his spittle hit the Hardscrabble dirt and became an ochre bolus. 'Rume wars on silver. The Medierans have taken and destroyed Harbour Town. They'll be headed upriver to retake the Talavera silverlode at Passasuego. But they don't know about the lode in the mountains north of Dvergar. Cornelius, Marcellus, all the Rumans do, thanks to Winfried's and my recon of the place. It's possible the dwarves do, too, and have been sitting on that knowledge in hopes of getting their hands on an engineer like our friend here.'

Bess and Fisk's new roan trotted for a while. It was a pace most Hardscrabble horses could keep up for a long while, though Fisk rode a Medieran capture. I remained silent, stroking my beard with a free hand, mind working at what Fisk had said.

'So, all of Occidentalia will be looking to Dvergar, soon. Rume, Mediera. Neruda and his people,' I said.

'Maybe not the stretchers,' Fisk replied.

I looked far off in the distance, where Gynth bounded as vanguard. 'I wouldn't be too sure of that.'

The next morning we rode into the shortening western shadow of the Eldvatch Mountains, commonly referred to in the Hardscrabble as the Smokeys. Blue pines stood on the heights, ash and gambel on the flanks of the gunmetal-grey hillsides and peaks, and mist wreathed their summits, the clouds welling up like ravenous ghosts around the haunted, towering figures. We found a stream, hobbled the horses and set them to graze and drink, and built a fire, watching for Praeverta's company to catch up. We had pulled ahead slowly, inexorably, so they didn't ever feel the need to chase – and, truly, we were not running from them, but leading. They would follow us.

I caught two trout and rustled some sage and wild onion. Bess carried one last pan from the old days; I had dumped most of our gear after the *daemonic* burning of Harbour Town to ease the beast's pains – and maybe some of my own. She was a good girl, if cantankerous, and I did what I could for her in the silent hour before the *dvergar* reached us: tended her hooves, brushed canescent fur, washed her burns and applied salve to the bubbling skin there (and to my own, if I speak true – the back of my arms and neck were a Hellish wasteland of wrecked skin). We watched the sun set as I cooked the fish.

I minded after Beleth. Other than wounding and taunting him, Fisk did not want to touch, talk, or tend to the engineer.

I changed the dressing on his stump, and he squirmed with pain as I washed it in water. I had no cacique or whiskey to sterilise it, and I don't think I'd waste the liquor on him anyway. When I removed the hemp rope that served as a gag to give him water, he gulped at it hastily, coughed. His mouth was cracked and bloody, his eyes alert and shifting, taking in all the surroundings. He looked even thinner now than he had in the warehouse in Harbour Town – was it just five days ago? Six? Just six? The whole world had changed since then. A city stood in cinders and ruin, and the southern reaches of the Hardscrabble teemed with Medierans. A fleet stood on the Hardscrabble's southern shore. I could only imagine how and where the Medierans would dump their troops. But they would, and quickly, that was sure. As we fled the conflagration, the flotilla moved toward the shore, and it was massive. Rume was no longer the sole power in Occidentalia.

'Thank you, Mister Ilys. I require more water,' Beleth said.

I was tempted to put away the waterskin, since it was something he wanted, out of pure spite. But I tamped that urge away. I knew not what Neruda (or Praeverta) might do if this man died – but their followers were fierce in their devotion to them. Neruda, I could understand. He was a firebrand, a natural orator, and his words came with clarity and conviction – he wanted Occidentalia for the *dvergar*, the indigenous population. Praeverta's draw was one of determination and raw will – she would be obeyed, or she would see you dead. I gave the engineer more water.

He coughed, and sighed. 'I am hungry. The fish smells good.'

'It's gone,' I said. 'And the bones go on the fire.'

His eyes shifted in their sockets. Of old, he never looked at me when he spoke – I was beneath true notice, or consideration. But now his baleful glare slid over to me, and there was real menace in his gaze. He considered me for the first time and did not like what he saw.

'Here we are again, Mister Ilys,' Beleth said.

'My lot to administer to the one-handed. I would rather be kissing Agrippina than here with you, sir,' I said.

He smiled. 'A toothsome kiss, that would be, I think. And you'd not be wagging your tongue much at the end of it, I think.' He did not know the half of it.

I extended a finger and made it hard. We have thick skin and dense bones, we *dvergar*, even those of us whose blood isn't pure. I jabbed him in the sternum with my index. He gasped and sucked wind.

'That was just a wee poke, Mister Beleth. Save your breath for when you need it,' I said. I leaned in close and drew my silver blade. My hand still burned from when I threatened Beleth before, when he wore Gynth for his Sunday suit. But I held it tight and my fist smoked around the hilt, the silver eating into my flesh. His narrowed eyes fixed on it. 'I slew her when she wore the Crimson Man, engineer. Never think I won't send you to Hell to meet her.'

'The Crimson Man?' He looked toward Fisk, who had disappeared around a small copse of trees. 'It pulls at him, the *daemon* hand, and he'll have to use it eventually.' A smile crept upon his face. 'And Hell? The burning fields of home, Mister Ilys. I'd not be there long.'

'What do you mean, he'll have to use it eventually? Does it have some glamour or trick about it?' I asked. I lowered my blade and nestled it in his ribs. I thought of William Bless' *Our Heavenly War. Just a small prick, I'll give thee. But thou hast one already.*

'Now you are the one doing the Lingchi, it seems.' Beleth's glee grew, maybe in remembrance of his torturous exercise on Agrippina so long ago, or moved by something else. Something darker, if that was even possible.

He was different, now, than he'd been on the *Cornelian*. If he was anything, he'd become the promise of the creature he'd been at the Pynchon. A distillation. Before he was a rising man, new money and one of the avaricious breed. A man of industry. But now there was something fell about him, and old. His breath stank of putrescence. His glee was unholy, totally inhuman. He'd gone beyond the simple economy of mankind, into the invisible war, the fret and tug of the infernal, and all its unknown eddies and currents. It was a black tide, and it had sucked this husk of a man away, and what it coughed up on the shore afterward, no one could explain or comprehend.

I brought up the knife. The pain in my hand was excruciating. But so was the desire to shove the blade in Beleth's eye and tickle his brain with it. But I did not. It was not some spasm of conscience or morality. How exciting life would be if I could wander about the world, doing just as I wished, stabbing people in the eyes.

Not conscience. I just did not have the energy to deal with the Nerudian storm that would blow then, once he breathed his last. It was pure selfishness that I spared him.

'The full attention of Mediera and Rume are here, on these blue mountains,' Beleth said. 'They will come to take possession of the silver. Yes, I knew of it before your indiscreet conversations with Mister Fiscelion. They will come with Hellfire to make war on each other. And an army that carries the Crimson Hand before it will be invincible.'

I thought back to Hot Springs, when Croesus' men tried to hang Fisk, who wore the hand around his neck. That town ended in flames, and the fire that burned through Fisk nearly consumed him.

Fisk had caused the bully-boys of Hot Springs' guns to fail – all the *imps* and *daemonic* presences within its awareness had been in its command. How would it play out if he who wore the *daemon* hand had an army at his back? He could neuter any force that came against him.

There was a sound, the nicker of a horse, a cough. Praeverta appeared by a tree, and bedraggled *dvergar* followed after her. She cocked an eyebrow at me, squatting so near Beleth, conversing. She came nearer. I moved to replace the engineer's gag and he laughed.

'No,' Praeverta said. 'Stay your hand, *dimidius*. I would speak to the man.'

'He's got nothing to say but lies and mockery, Matve,' I said.

'No, Mister Ilys! I would talk to her. Hello, grandmother,' he said. 'My bindings are tight and I've not yet had supper.'

Praeverta looked at two of her companions – Drugan, and the one they called the Wee Garrotte (nicknames seemed a pastime with this group) – in response they rummaged about in their gunnysacks and produced some hard tack and jerked auroch, then tossed it into Beleth's lap.

He sat there with this strange look upon his face. He was withered, yes, since I first knew him, and the weight loss seemed to have changed his once stolid and unremarkable looks into something more sinister. The glee, and wicked amusement, at everything we did was grating. Fisk had shortened the man a hand but he would not cease his mockery.

'Grandmother, you seem interested in me. What would you like to know?' Beleth asked.

'Can you make guns? Can you fill rounds with Hellfire?' she asked.

'Of course. We learn this as apprentices.' He smiled. 'And I can teach you how. Have you tinkers? Have you metalsmiths and engravers? It has been my experience that the tinker *dvergar*—'

Praeverta's face clouded. 'Do not speak that way about us. We are not tinkers. Or diggers. We are *dvergar*.' She had no problem calling me *dimidius*, but in this case, I agreed with her.

False consternation washed over Beleth. 'Pardon me, grandmother. And did I not hear you say that you are *vaettir*? I imagine you'll not want me to call you stretchers either, and it wouldn't fit anyway, because nothing about you seems stretched.'

'Except my patience,' Praeverta said. 'I have what I need to know.' She looked at me. 'Feed him and gag him when you're done.'

'And I thought we had come to an understanding!' Beleth said, the mirth apparent in his voice. 'We are fast friends, are we not, granny?'

Praeverta shifted her rucksack and moved away, toward where her company built a fire.

'Mister Ilys, please be so kind as to place the food in my mouth,' Beleth said, voice pitching toward saccharine.

I picked up the jerked auroch, took a bite, and replaced the gag.

FOURTEEN

They Called Us The Bloodless

THE *TYPHON* THRUMMED, but all else was hushed. Even Fiscelion had fallen silent.

Carnelia burst into the command, wild-eyed. 'Have we gone underwater? Are we sinking?' she asked. 'The gun whipped about and faced the stern. I thought we were done for.'

A spray of water came from above, where the peering device met the command centre's ceiling. 'No, not yet.' His voice seemed worried. 'She's been banged up,' Ysmay said, pulling his gaze from the Miraculous and glancing about, noting the various leaks. 'And it's possible we've lost the aft swivel, since it wasn't shrouded and secure at descent. But yes, the *Typhon* is a new kind of ship, I dare say. She is submersible.'

The implications of that began sinking in, figuratively and literally. Above the thrumming of the *daemon*-driven screws there was a susurration, the hiss of water slipping across the hull at great speed. Inside, the sprays of water hissed from rivets and seams loosened from the shelling.

Tenebrae laughed. 'I would not have believed it if you told me one of the old gods had come and rescued us from our pursuers' guns.'

'Believe it,' Ysmay said. 'Though we cannot stay down long. Maybe an hour, at most. It has to do with the air.' He shrugged.

'We will suffocate, even breathing this air, unless we surface and open the hatches.'

'But even an hour! That is prodigal,' I said. 'How deep are we?'

'The top of this device broaches the surface,' Ysmay replied, patting the cylinder of the peering mechanism. 'So twenty feet. Enough so that very little of our vessel is visible. I dare say our pursuers think us scuttled and sinking, thrice-damned.'

We remained silent for a while, until Carnelia said, 'I saw port-holes! I want to see!'

Ysmay said, 'They are forward. Beyond the front deck gun, in the captain's and first lieutenant's quarters.'

'Can you see anything?' Carnelia asked.

'A benthic view, to be sure. At this speed, you will not see much. But at slower speeds and nearer to shore—'

'You said the *Typhon* is a littoral, Mister Ysmay,' I said. 'Will she withstand open sea?'

'I do not think my response will matter much, Madame,' he replied. 'With all respect. For you will take her where you want her to go, will you not?'

'Not if you tell me it is a sure death if we do,' I said. 'I would not kill us all.'

He paused. I watched the thoughts turning like engineer's gears behind his eyes, millstones grinding. 'We will most likely die,' he said.

I blinked. 'You are unsure. Keep this course and we'll surface within the hour. Where is our pursuit? Can you see?'

He swivelled about, turning the device toward the aft. 'They have slowed. Most likely looking for debris where we "sank".'

I chewed my lip. 'Continue as we are. Carnelia, Tenebrae, find out what amount of food stores we have. Mister Ysmay, is there anything else we'll need for a long journey?'

'Fresh water, for the engine, for us. The lascars had not yet refilled the water tanks at Rezzo, though I think there are rations aboard.' He looked infinitely weary for a moment, and rubbed his face with an unsteady hand. 'The *Typhon* has only a complement of nine, including lascars and officers, and so there will not be much food since she is, as you mentioned, a littoral, and not meant for long journeys without port. I designed her with a mind to patrolling the shores and bays around Rume.'

'Yet she is able to submerge,' I said.

'Obviously,' he responded, a touch of irritation creeping into his voice. 'But—'

'Should we be at open sea, and in a storm, could we not submerge, or at least prepare to? Would that not make us unsinkable?'

'It is not that, Madame. There are certain stressors on a ship, especially in high swells, that never come into play in coastal hugging vessels. I do not know if the *Typhon* will withstand them, should she be in the thick. That nature of engineering does not fall within her purpose.'

'I am repurposing her, Mister Ysmay,' I said. I patted his arm, and he shied away from my touch, a look of horror coming over him. Still bloody, flaking brown, that hand. What could I do? I was a murderess, and his response was understandable. 'Take heart that at the end of this journey, you will be released to do what you will, and in the interim, you'll know the strength of your craft, and your design.'

He turned back to the navigation of the *Typhon*.

Lupina appeared again in the command room, absent Fiscelion. 'I think he likes the sound,' she said. 'Once we went below, he gurgled and fell asleep on my breast. He's forward, now.'

'I need to check on him,' I said. And, playing tag, I handed her my sawn-off; no words needed to be spoken there. She found a spot, out of the way, and watched Ysmay at his navigation, the weapon held loosely in her strong, capable hands. Ia bless the fortune that sent Lupina to me.

I went forward, through the rounded doorways, and into the swivel chamber where Carnelia had been stationed only moments before. The gunnery controls faced the stern of the ship. A goodly amount of water – salty and cold – showered from the seam of the greased runners where the gun turned. Some of it fell upon the shells, some onto the grated floor to fall below into whatever sluiceway might be there.

Tenebrae stood at the far door. 'That is not good,' he said, looking toward the roof of the chamber, from where the water emanated. 'We need to resurface and deal with it soon. I have been watching it for a few moments and the flow has not increased.' He gestured, and turned. 'We have that, at least. Things aren't becoming worse, every moment. Your son is this way.'

Stepping through, I followed Tenebrae. We came to a brace of four doors, two on each side, and the end of the short hall. Through the first door on the right, a small chamber with a single bunk, a small desk, chest, and shelf full of books and rolled parchment – navigational maps, I assumed. On the bed, Fiscelion slumbered in a sprawl of blankets. On his back, he slept with pure abandon, legs at different angles, chubby arms open wide. Hands grasping at unseen things in his private dreamworld. Thankfully, the bunk had a rail around which Lupina had bundled clothes and a blanket in a makeshift wall to keep him from falling onto the floor. Above the desk, a porthole. Beyond it, blue-green sea and thousands of bubbles, whipping by. I could see no discernible features out in the benthic dark, no fish, no seaweed, no bladderwrack – nothing but dim water. The murmur of sea slipping by, louder now. And the hint of speed. Once, when I was a girl, I swam out into the Salonica surf, Mother watching from the shore, slaves clustered about, and dived as deep as I could. Father had put Mother aside by then, and I didn't know where I belonged. Dispossessed. In the green deep, lungs expanding, I opened my eyes and they burned. I stretched for the surface to find the burliest slaves racing into the foam to get me. The flash of perception there, below, was cool and dim.

'It might offer a view, were we not going full-bore for open sea,' Tenebrae said, hushed, trying not to wake the baby.

I gestured for him to follow me into the hall. 'What of food,' I asked, changing the subject. 'Did you find any?'

'Some. Dry goods. Casks of salt-pork. Beans. Potatoes. A crate of limes. Rum. Wine for the officers. Standard fare. I'll show you.' He gestured to the door facing the captain's room – now shared by Fiscelion, Lupina and me. 'This seems to be the engineer's berth. Full of strange things. And here,' he said, gesturing to the right, most forward door, 'is the mess.'

'And the last?' I asked.

'Lascar bunks,' he said. 'Just four, so I think they'd alternate use, which seems like a horror to civilians, but I can tell you, having trained with them as a praetorian, by the time you hit the mattress you're so tired, you couldn't care who had just vacated it. Or that it's still warm.'

'Fascinating,' I said, lying. 'The quantity of the food?'

'Look for yourself,' Tenebrae said, pushing open the door.

I entered. There are many things in my life to that moment that had prepared me for our situation – the company of military men – almost all of my male counterparts, to a man; the society of commanders and those of high rank; the wealth required to have a lifelong familiarity with Hellfire; passing comfort with the machinery surrounding infernal combustion. Those are just a few. But none of it prepared me for such a simple task as taking inventory of food supplies.

The mess was a larger chamber than the captain's berth, and

there was a table that could fit five men – two on each side and one on the end – with still enough room for the cook to prepare food and to serve. On the far wall, many swaying pots, skillets, framed above a stove and oven crafted of steel, it seemed, and built into the very fabric of the *Typhon* itself, with many runnels of tubing and pipes running away from it and disappearing into the ceiling and the wall in what looked like watertight fixtures.

'There's the larder,' Tenebrae said, pointing. It was close in the mess, and as I moved to the opening of the pantry I banged my head against one of the pots hanging there and caught it before it clattered to the floor. The floors were painted in some thick naval tint – sea green – and did not have grates and a mysterious subflooring feet, or an armspan, below. But, having seen the piping running away from the stove, I had an idea, now, why other parts of the ship had the grate flooring.

I stood there, head throbbing where the cast iron skillet had almost brained me. For a moment, the metal walls pressed in, everything too close for thought. The *Typhon,* the cocoon of sea. I felt as if I couldn't get a breath of air. I was covered in blood, I was absent of remorse. What had I become?

It's the small meaningless moments that can kill you.

I looked in the larder. There were boxes and cans and crates and casks, full of all the things Tenebrae had mentioned. Dried herbs hung in bundles from the ceiling. It was fragrant and earthy, this room under the sea.

'I have no idea what I'm looking at, here. This seems like enough food for a cohort. I have no way to judge, since I've never cooked one thing in my life. But Lupina will know,' I said.

Tenebrae murmured assent. 'All right. I trust you'll give her your instructions, since she looks like she wants to chop my feet off every time I look at her.'

'She does, probably,' I said. Turning, I gestured aft. 'We should check the engineer's quarters and then engineering itself, but not without Ysmay.'

'And that means surfacing,' Tenebrae said.

I nodded.

We returned to the command centre but not before peeking in on Fiscelion, to make sure he still slept. Ysmay stood at the navigation controls, still peering into the steering device, and Lupina watched him, the sawn-off held loosely in her hands. Ysmay's body was taut as a drumhead, his shoulders hitched high. He jerked about when we entered, wild-eyed. The enormity of the situation had begun to sink in and he was becoming agitated. But I had no time for hysteria or histrionics.

'Mister Ysmay, what is our status?'

'We are out of sight of the shore, Madame, and heading toward open sea. As ordered,' he said. His tone was of nervous deference.

'And the pursuing ship?' I asked.

'Far behind. I cannot spot her,' he said.

'Then let us come to the surface and slow our speed so that we can take stock of the damage. And speak,' I said. I turned to Tenebrae and murmured in his ear, 'If there's rum, let's make sure Ysmay has a belly full before we rest. I would have him genial and sodden rather than tense and brooding, if that makes any sense,' I said.

'It does,' he said, turning away. 'I will take care of that, sir.' He stopped. 'Pardon me. I meant ma'am.' He turned back and looked at me closely. 'How would you like us to address you?'

'Whatever do you mean?'

' "The hand that slays the captain takes the tiller; at the helm of every ship there steers a killer",' Tenebrae said. Not in the singsong voice of someone reciting Bless' best known lines, but in utter seriousness.

'*Our Heavenly War* is too fanciful for my tastes. And if that line was true, every navarch would be a mutineer.' I shook my head. 'But I take your point. You can simply call me Livia.' Like it or not, I had assumed command and Tenebrae was not going to gainsay that.

'Of course,' he said, bowing his head.

'I am glad you are here, Shadow,' said I, using his nickname, something I rarely did. I had no explanation for that particular reticence; it was something that Secundus and Carnelia – both students of Sun Huáng – had called him and there was a part of their relationship that was opaque to those outside it. It wasn't exclusive, per se, but like the language of lovers, inward looking.

He put his hand on my shoulder. 'I am too. You'll need me in the coming days. And, I think, we'll all need you. You are a natural.'

'A natural what?' I said.

'Leader.' He withdrew a small silver flask from his leggings, raised it, and shook it. 'I will get the rum.'

He disappeared. The ship shifted and the thrumming decreased. I had, for a moment, almost forgotten it. It had been what? Two hours since I had killed Albinus and Regulus? Already I'd grown accustomed to the shiver and hum of the *Typhon*.

I took my sawn-off from Lupina and bid her look after Fiscelion. She seemed relieved to do so. I have no doubt that Lupina would spit a man on a knife if he made even the most veiled threats against her own, but she might not like it and would rather be cooking, and dandling babes. But what about me? I will kill for Fiscelion. At times it seems that Lupina is his real mother and I'm just some crazed harridan dragging him around the world, half-drowned, bathed in blood. I hope he never knows what I've done for him, or what I've done to him.

I turned back to Ysmay. 'Sir, show me what you just did, so that in the future I will know.'

Ysmay looked alarmed. And then resigned. He began explaining the navigation mechanism in detail, as we surfaced. Tenebrae gave me a meaningful look and patted his hip when he returned.

Once I felt I had a solid grasp of it, I said, 'Will the *Typhon* be at risk if we leave the navigation for a moment and you show us engineering?'

Ysmay paused and despite himself, his eyes brightened. 'No, she'll keep going in the direction we point her. It's rather clever, if I say so myself – I designed the navigation so that – through counterweights and springs – the rudder will keep a direction and adjust if it is blown off course. When you lock in a course here—' he tapped the edge of the compass, where there was a small warded contraption, '—the *daemon* there has a sympathetic bond with another *imp*, there, in the console, and they work, always, to be together. So the ship will correct course without—'

'Human intervention,' I said. 'That is very clever, Mister Ysmay. Indeed, this ship is fantastically inventive. You are to be commended. Set it to keep course, please, at a speed that isn't outrageous. I would see what I can of the *daemon* that spurs this ship on.'

He ducked his head in deference, placed his hand upon the warded box affixed to the compass and rudder, and winced. When he drew his hand away, I saw where the silver needle had pricked him, its tip glistening with fresh blood. It dripped down the needle and collected in a tiny reservoir where it blackened and smoked. The stink of sulphur bloomed, like spores from a ruptured mushroom. Hellfire.

The infernal device made a whirring noise, soft as insect wings, and glowed. 'She'll keep true course now, for an hour or so, at least,' Ysmay said, and sucked his finger.

We moved toward the stern, an area of the *Typhon* where none of us had ventured yet. Ysmay twisted the circular locking mechanism and swung open the door, revealing another swivel gun control room. We found no leakage and, according to Ysmay, all appeared well. Beyond that was a munitions storage where there was a small stock of carbines and Hellfire rounds to go with them, in addition to the larger swivel rounds packed in straw and cotton-filled crates. The walls of this chamber were warded heavily, built into the metal of the floor, walls, ceiling, and hinged steel doors. We moved on.

The next door was even more intricately warded, the engravings more dense, more intricate. It was hot here, and stank of ozone and brimstone. There was what appeared, almost, to be a ball centred in the room, surrounded by piping and a long tank. More warding, steam hissing and jetting in places.

'This is the devil Typhon's cage. I'm sorry you cannot witness him, for he is tremendous,' Ysmay said.

'I'm not,' I said. The heaviness that comes with the infernal settled upon us like a pall. I felt the throbbing presence of the *daemon*, bound in its silver warded cage, pouring off energy. A trapped dynamo sloughing heat to excite water into steam to turn the *Typhon*'s screws.

'This is the engine room, where we get the power and behind it, the motor room, through that door, where the power is turned into motion.'

'Does he require blood?' Tenebrae asked.

'Yes,' Ysmay said. 'But only in the summoning. Or the banishing. Far more for the banishing.'

'Why do you have to give blood to some regularly, and not to others?' I asked. It was something that had niggled at me, ever since the *Valdrossos*.

'There's great risk and effort to summon a *daemon* – or *arch-daemon* – and much blood. Those go into ships. And they require enough blood, usually, or some equal sacrifice, to near kill the summoner,' Ysmay said. 'But the small *daemons*, the *imps* we bind into lamps, into Hellfire rounds, the automatic piloting device – these are lesser creatures and need sustenance – though that's not really what it is to them – to perform whatever function the engineer has set before them.'

'How do you set them to these smaller tasks? Is there some reasoning there?' I asked.

He remained quiet for a bit and finally said, 'I cannot tell all. To do so would mean death, possibly, if the Collegium of Engineers discovered it. And I want to live.' He shook his head and looked at me. He was frightened, but there was something about his face that told me this was one line that I might try to cross, but he would not bend. Only break. Because death was the consequence. 'But I can say, as you might already know, the art – and science – of engineering is an understanding of physical forces, stressors, material strengths. The other part of it is creating covenants, and that is far more difficult, especially when dealing with creatures from beyond this world.'

'I have been told that they come from a rift between worlds, these *daemons*. One that was torn open by a sorcerer of old, looking for absolute power,' I said, thinking of Mister Ilys. He'd abstained from the use of Hellfire guns, until he had a change of heart. 'That they are simply forces of nature, and not malevolent at all.'

Ysmay shook his head. 'Some very well aren't, I'd hazard. But something doesn't have to be evil to kill you. And there's no *daemon* that won't do that. Their essence is anathema to this world. More than poison. Incendiary,' he said, noticeably uncomfortable with the conversation.

'How much maintenance does *Typhon* require?' Tenebrae asked.

'I check the wards, daily. I do whatever engraving touch-ups are needed but that is not too often. Lascars check water pressure

– two of them were rated mechanics.' He looked bewildered. 'But now it's just me.'

'Heavy maintenance?' I asked.

'Any structural repairs have to be done in port,' Ysmay said.

I stood there, looking at Typhon's warded housing. It was beautiful, in a way. Pragmatic yet intricate. I knew not the functions of the piping, and even less of the warding, but it all cascaded out in radiating concentric circles away from where I knew the *daemon* to be. When I closed my eyes – as when Beleth summoned the Crimson Man – I saw swirls of red and orange and black behind my eyelids and there was a dark figure there, pouring off heat. He loved me not.

I shivered, despite the warmth.

'All right, Mister Ysmay. Why don't you perform your inspection and maintenance now, while Mister Tenebrae and I are here.' I noticed Carnelia at the doorway. I motioned her in. 'Go on deck. Perform a visual inspection of the hull, as best you can. Let me know what you can see of the shore or our pursuit.'

'Aye, Captain,' she said, and clasped a hand to her breast and then shot it out, palm down, in the Ruman salute.

'None of that, sissy. Just go,' I said.

'I live to do your bidding, master and commander,' she said, and grinning, turned and dashed away to the main control centre.

We watched Ysmay at his inspection, and I drew Tenebrae back. 'We should be here with him, during inspections.'

'He should never, really, be alone,' Tenebrae responded. 'He's the only one who can keep us alive and the ship in working order.'

'Let's take him on deck, after this, and have the chat.'

'Agreed,' Tenebrae said.

We watched Ysmay trace the warding with his strong, very articulate fingers. A man who worked with his hands, the direct extension of his mind; they were lithe, yet possessed of a surety many hands do not possess. An artist's hands. He sank to his knees and began tracing the intaglios of engravings on the floor.

'This is where the care is needed, and around the edges of doors, where most wear takes place,' Ysmay said. 'For a while, Albinus ordered the lascars—' He fell silent.

'Albinus ordered the lascars to do what, Mister Ysmay?' I said, letting my voice crack like a whip. I wanted no omissions. I wanted no secrets.

He jumped. I will not lie: his physical response to the sound of my voice gave me a shock of something that felt very close to pleasure. But I tamped that emotion away: exploring it any more would mean I was a murderess through and through, taking pleasure from the havoc my mortal actions wreaked upon this soul. No, I could not take joy there. 'Please, sir. We are very interested in what you have to say.'

'Booties,' he said, glancing at us from where he bowed. 'Little cotton booties, like socks. He made us all wear them in here. I never saw any man of the sea come so close to mutiny as then.' He shook his head, ruefully. Maybe he was thinking about those we killed. Those men I killed. 'They just stopped coming in here, altogether. It was my domain, anyway. Typhon's Bower, they called it. I assure you, it is far from it.' He looked at his hands for a long while, considering. He shook his blond head and blinked as if waking, then he went back to inspecting the warding on the floor.

Seeing something, he crouched lower, examining it as closely as possible. 'Something I should attend to.' He stood, went to a small, metal cabinet affixed to the wall just beyond the border of the largest ward on the floor. From there he removed an awl and mallet and began some minuscule repairs on the warding. *Tap tap tap scratch scratch.* He blew on the surface, and passed his hand to clear small curls of metal away from his freshened marks. 'The *Malus* ward had grown worn in one spot. Nothing really, but best to be safe,' he murmured. A quick smile crossed his face, either at his work or his words, and then died. He stood. 'I try to keep from stepping on any of the warding but that becomes impossible.' He moved to the walls and began running his fingers over the etchings there.

In Salonica, when I visited as a girl with my mother, there had been an *angelis* fever outbreak years before, and a good number of the population – though hidden away for the most part – had been infected, husked out through whatever entity had possessed them all. Minds shattered, they would totter about the town, dressed in white gowns by their caretakers, and count stones in walls, cracks in casements. Number leaves on trees, count the sluggish warm waves lapping at shore. Ysmay's reverent examination made me fear, if but for a moment, for the integrity of his mind. What forces come into play when summoning? What other consciousnesses vie for the summoner's attention, for his or her soul?

Carnelia returned. She glanced at the engineer performing his inspections, and crossed her eyes at Tenebrae, who smiled but did not laugh at her antics. 'The hull seems fine, as far as I can tell without any experience. The front swivel is worse off, I fear, from the hasty descent. I'll say this, the guns are very cleverly constructed, with no moving parts exposed.' She held up her hand – it was black, and matched the great swath on her tunic and the smear on her chin. 'I warn you, don't touch them. They're literally caked in grease.'

'The seas will eat them away,' Ysmay said, distracted. 'Without oil. Stores of it are back there. Motor room.' He gestured toward the aft door in this chamber, where all the piping converged and disappeared.

When Ysmay seemed to come to a stopping point – though he was bemused and distracted the whole time he was in the *daemon*'s chamber – we drew him away and onto the deck. Leaving the close

confines of the ship, breathing the freshening air, tasting the salt
spray from the Occidens on my tongue, my spirit soared. I'd been
oppressed by the tightness of the ship and it was mirrored in my
body, the tenseness of my shoulders, my hands and arms. I felt as
though a great pressure had been lifted from me.

Carnelia handed Ysmay a flask of rum, and indicated he should
drink. Ysmay took it in hand, smelled it, and then made to hand
it back to Carnelia. 'I don't like strong spirits,' he said.

'You're going to make an exception, tonight,' she said, and
pushed the flask back. 'Drink, sir. Drink.' She had a way about
her, my sister. Her 'sir' sounded more threatening than any curse
or profanity she might've uttered. Ysmay blanched. He took a sip,
winced and then stood there, on deck, holding the flask in unsure
hands, looking about.

'Another few draughts will serve you well, Mister Ysmay,'
Tenebrae said, placing a hand on the man's shoulder. 'It's been a
long day.'

After he'd taken a few more swallows, Ysmay's face became
flushed. 'My first ship, she was a big brute,' he said, looking into
swells and swaying on his feet. 'Nothing like this little mackerel.'
The wind skirled across the face of the sea and made small wind-
wracked breakers at the tips of the waves. Ysmay's hair whipped
about his face and I found my own coming undone from the braids
Carnelia and I both wore.

'The *Pantalion* was massive, and kept a huge crew. I was just a
wardsman, apprenticed to the master engineer – they called us the
bloodless, since Wythys always needed more. More power, more
munitions, more heat. More blood.' He held up his arm and pulled
back the sleeve. There was a fine patina of scars there, silvery in
the light from blue stars and moon above. One single *daemonlight*
lantern hung from the main stack where the peering device from
below came to its height. 'We patrolled the Nous, the Occidens,

and later the Bay of Mageras. But nothing like when we went into the North.'

'The North?' Carnelia asked, pensive. Maybe she'd been sipping the rum as well. 'What more than the Northlands are there?'

Ysmay shook his head and laughed. The liquor had infused him with a desperate geniality. 'Oh, so much more. Beyond the wilds, we sailed. I was twenty-three then, I think.' He fell silent for a while, watching the water.

Lupina appeared on deck and brought Fiscelion to me. I pulled back my tunic and let him at my breast – in other company, they might have been offended, or scandalised. I cared not at all, at this point. The pain as he sucked was sharp but it centred me, somehow. I had taken life. I gave it. He was growing large, despite all the travails and insecurity of the past months. If infanthood imprints itself upon the person when they grow old, Fiscelion would be a traveller – it was his internal momentum from his first push of life. He came squalling into the world like a bullet fired from a gun, ripping through Kithai, the Nous, Latinum, and now the Occidens.

Ysmay went on. 'We sailed on, past countless shores, and then, once it grew cold and the sun never set, we sailed west and west again where the sun would flirt with the horizon but never kiss it. The *Pantalion* always needed blood and she stank of the burning stuff. At night, when I could give no more, Durian and I would hang our feet off the stern, pale and exhausted, and let out hooked spoons on twine until they would whip and twirl in the moon-shattered wake of the *Pantalion* and the silvergullets and yellowed pickering would snatch up the lures and we would haul them in, hands raw and bleeding.' He laughed, remembering. 'Durian was fast with a knife and always had a flask of garum about. He'd fillet the fish like drawing the simplest *pellum* ward and we'd soak the gobbets of fish in the salty garum and feast in the darkness.

We needed meat, and the silver gullet and tunny refreshed our sanguiducts of the red stuff.' He lifted the flask to his lips and took a large swallow of rum. 'Until we came to Terra Umbra.'

'Terra Umbra,' I said. The sound of my voice shocked the engineer from his reverie. 'I know of this place, from engineer Samantha Decius. She said it was where Emrys split the veil between worlds and let the *daemons* in.'

Ysmay waved his hand. 'Something like that.' He was not concerned with the legend, now. Or at all, really. What to us, the outsiders, the neophytes to his initiated knowledge, was huge and significant, to him was simply to be brushed aside.

'Tell us of Terra Umbra,' Tenebrae said.

Ysmay's eyebrows raised. 'I have heard her call you "Shadow",' he said. 'So it makes sense you would be interested.'

'The Shadowland,' I said.

'Yes,' he said. His eyes took on that far-off stare that we had seen in Typhon's Bower. 'Only one away ship went ashore, and we stayed a week before we realised that none of the party were coming back. The second mate, and his lascars, never returned.'

'What did you *see*?' Carnelia asked. She seemed quite urgent about the whole tale.

'The island itself was huge, mountainous, like it was hewn from the sea floor by vulcanic actions. But there was forest and foliage, birds wheeling in the heavens above the isle. The smell of dirt and life. The smell of land. But far off, in the centre of that dark-green isle, stood a tremendous storm, arrested except for circular motion, a maelstrom-like force, swirling upon itself. But unlike a whirlpool it was inverted. Where the sea sucks downward, this reached up. A storm that never seemed to dissipate. Tongues of flickering light, flashing about, and a column of multicoloured smoke reaching out of sight in the sky.'

'Well, that sounds like a shitstorm,' Carnelia said, rubbing her shoulder. I glanced at her and shook my head.

'Did you see anything else?' Tenebrae asked.

'When it became clear the second mate and his party weren't going to return, we took the *Pantalion* as close as we could to shore to see what we could see. All of the men stood on deck, peering westward. It was late in the day and the sun cast most of the shore into darkness but I swear—'

He fell silent, looking off into some middle distance only he could apprehend.

'What did you see?' I said, very low.

He shook his head and looked at me. 'Figures. Very tall figures on the shore. They ran along as the *Pantalion* steamed past. Impossibly fast. Leaping, jumping.'

'*Vaettir*,' I breathed.

Ysmay said, 'I have never seen an elf, but that may be what they were. But—'

'But what?' Carnelia said in a much less kind tone than we'd been taking with the engineer.

'They disappeared. Like tide flowing out of a bay, yet much faster. And then *it* appeared.'

'It?' I said.

'Yes,' Ysmay said. 'It. He.'

He tilted up the flask and drained the rest of the rum and looked away across the waves, and then his gaze travelled from wherever it was in the west all the way back to my face.

'The dragon,' he said.

'Ah!' Tenebrae broke into laughter. Carnelia followed. 'A very good jest, Mister Ysmay! Very good!'

Ysmay looked at us, puzzled.

And then he vomited up all the rum in a thunderous rush.

*

We were quiet after that. Ysmay belched an apology and sat down heavily on the deck while Carnelia found a bucket below and sluiced away the vomitus.

It grew colder the longer we stayed on deck. Ysmay would take no more rum. The wind strengthened, the seas rose, and the sky grew bruised but never really faded into blackness. A strange glow permeated the night and I was reminded of the golden fog that came to us that one night months before when the *Malphas* had drawn near Jiang. But an unease settled upon me and I knew this was not the same.

'Look,' Lupina said, speaking for the first time that night. 'Behind us. The sky is aflame.'

I turned back, looking east. The low-hanging clouds there were lit from underneath with a pulsing red glow and beyond the horizon some great fire burned. A sinking feeling came upon me then, and I looked to my companions – Carnelia, Tenebrae, Lupina, and Ysmay – and saw my own despair mirrored in their eyes.

'Rume,' Tenebrae said, and sank to his knees. 'The Immortal City burns.'

FIFTEEN

Here Is As Far As We Will Allow Rume

WE FOUND THE Dvergar silverlode and never reached the dwarven city.

Riding south, hugging the skirts of the Eldvatch, it grew moist and greener with every step. Grass – real grass, not the lashing, grasping shoal blades in the west by the Big Rill – thickened and blanketed the hillsides. We trudged over streams and through dells and over hills. We forded rivers that had names only in *dvergar* tongue, and I knew at one time, though they're lost to me now. Bess hawed and tugged at her reins, looking to forage, and at every rest found lush grass. Gynth, giving a single look to me and chucking his head at the forests covering the skirts of the gunmetal grey Smokeys, bounded off, up the slope. I assumed to hunt, but who knows what desires boiled under the surface of Gynth's calm demeanour? He was a stretcher, but unlike any stretcher I'd heard of or witnessed. A strange creature, both cruel and kind. Both fearsome and full of life. I would be lying if I said I did not love him some. And fear him some, as well.

Praeverta's dogged group kept up – the determination of my kin is remarkable, and even though Praeverta and her men were not my favourites and would win no popularity contest in Passasuego, New Damnation, or the rest of the Hardscrabble cities and towns, I admired their stamina and was proud that they kept up so well with the horses. We *dvergar* are strong, and formidable. I've always known it, and I think Fisk has too.

But it was time the world discovered how strong we are.

We passed into a valley, runnelled with a large stream that grew sooty and discoloured. A pall hung over the place, and the grasses and foliage seemed dimmed. Smoke draped the valley, and beyond, where the mountain grew, a rough stone wall half-hid a warren of timber buildings. We stopped to piss and let the horses drink before following the trail down, toward the hamlet.

Catch Hands came close. He had an anvil jaw, square shoulders. 'It's the Grenthvar, they call it. The Breadbasket.'

'What,' I said. 'This valley?'

'Yes and no. It is the valley and the mountain beyond and what they both hold between them,' he said, and cocked his head and looked at me seriously. 'You've been away from your kind too long, Ilys. Your head can only hold one idea at a time, like the advenæ, these foreigners from Rume.' He put his fist on my shoulder and mimed hammering. Not just mimed: I felt the blows, but they were given in the spirit of camaraderie and brought memories from long ago, when I was just a pup on the mountainside, grasping at my mother's apron strings. 'We contain the world, the *dvergar*, and can hold multitudes within us,' he said.

'And the Grenthvar,' I said, trying to bring the conversation back around to the subject. 'It's this region, then. It's not a word I'm familiar with.'

'It is the ore of the world, the blood of *dvergar*,' he said.

'Did your mother happen to drop you on your head as a child?' I said.

'Only a few times,' he answered, seriously. 'But the shale softened the fall.' He rubbed his skull. 'You can still feel the divots.' He grabbed my hand. 'Feel here,' he said, and brought my hand to his cranium. Sure enough, marked dents in his noggin.

'How old is this village? Grenthvar.' I could smell the cut pine on the air and hear the sound of hammer-falls and saws.

'New, very new. Last winter,' he said. He chucked his head at Fisk. 'When him and that woman came out this way with some other Rumans,' he said. 'Soon after, legionnaires showed up. They put up buildings and tried to hire workers from Dvergar,' he said, and gestured south. Dvergar, the warren city of my people, carved into the bosom of the Smokeys, lay fifteen miles to the south, close enough for this 'Grenthvar' find to be named the Dvergar silverlode. 'That didn't take,' he chuckled, and it was not a fully wholesome sound.

'The half-century of Ruman soldiers?' I said.

'Ah, well, you'll find patches of ground from here to Dvergar that are especially fertile, this year.'

As we approached the village, two figures appeared in the road. Both were familiar to me. Winfried and Neruda. Behind them gathered many dwarves, bearing Ruman gladii and home-made cudgels, scythes and spears.

'Mister Fisk! Mister Ilys! We've been waiting for you,' Winfried called. 'It seems Neruda knew you were coming long before you came into sight.'

We came closer. Winfried was different, now. There was something looser yet more focused about her. Her hair was longer and it framed her face, softening it. She'd put aside the more masculine suit she was wont to wear when I knew her before and wore leather trousers and a simple tunic and jacket – sodbuster or labourer garb. Her right arm was covered in a sling. Despite her welcoming words, her attention was fixed upon what was trussed and riding behind Fisk. Her countenance was as fierce and raptorial as ever.

'You kept the arm, then,' Fisk said. 'I thought you would have lost it.'

'It was a close thing,' the dwarf standing by Winfried said.

Neruda. He was a tight, compact man, with a wispy halo of hair over a speckled pate, a long aquiline nose, and a mouth overfilled with craggy teeth. He, too, was dressed in a workman's garb unlike the storekeeper's suit I'd first seen him in, speaking to the working class of Passasuego; now he was clad in a leather apron, patchy with stains, a belt with chisels, hammers, awls, spikes. Powder-rimmed blue trousers of thick-weave, heavy fabric, orange stitching. Knee-high workman's boots.

He was a man of halves, like me (though old Praeverta would never call him *dimidius*), and looking at him was like looking in a mirror, though I've got a little more fur up top and my teeth don't look like shattered rocks.

'I managed to stave off the blood burden and now she's regaining use of her hand,' he said. 'Every choice and turning brings us to where we are.'

'That's a whole lot of nonsense,' Fisk said. 'If you've ever been subject to powers greater than you, you might understand that.'

'I am *dvergar*,' Neruda said. 'I've eaten Ruman bread, and drunk their watered wine. I've carved their stones and raised walls while legions stood by with carbines. No breath of air, no stirring of wind, no vista, no brook, no cloud trawling over the sea can make you forget that.'

Fisk, under his breath and out of the corner of his mouth, said to me, 'I did not know when I met Ia he'd be so short in stature or so long of tongue.'

'It's good to see you, Winfried,' I said, and doffed my hat to her. 'Been a busy few months and much death and destruction has occurred during them. I was sorry to hear of your arm.'

'Buquo,' she said, simply. 'Neruda's partisans shot him out from under me and I fell, breaking it in so many places they thought they should have to amputate. But, in addition to his stoneworking and sculpture—' she gestured with her hale hand toward Neruda

'—our host is a fine mender of bones.' I saw no moment of sadness there, nor any grief at the death of her horse. She was a pragmatist to the core, and one would not find Winfried weeping for a beast of burden, even one of such stature and nobility; it was not in her character. However, she did not feel the same way about the death of her brother-mate, Wasler.

Her eyes never left the trussed form of Beleth on the back of Fisk's mount. I dismounted and unbound the engineer, and let him stand. I checked his bandages, ungagged him. Beleth swayed on his feet and promptly retched in the scrub on the side of the road. He pitched over and lay there for a long while, the moist ground and vomitus discolouring his clothes. Eventually, he sat up and looked around, his face a smeared and disjointed mess. It would be days before he felt whole again, if ever. I gave the man some water, checked his bindings once more, replaced his gag. It wouldn't do to have the engineer mouthing off now, during our first interview with Neruda.

'Our host?' Fisk said, in response to Winfried.

A voice sounded from the rear of our party. 'The *vaettir* have taken control of the Breadbasket,' Praeverta said, crowing. 'This is our land. We are of this place. Not you Rumans.'

Fisk shifted in his saddle to look at her. She strode forward, head held high, and came to stand in front of Neruda. She bowed to the man. He appeared pained at this.

'Get up, get up, Matve,' he said, and, taking her upper arms, drew her into a standing position. I had come to know the old crank better than I ever thought I would've in the last few days since meeting her in that clandestine gathering of the *vaettir* outside Harbour Town. 'Events move in the world and you are not privy to all of them.'

Winfried said, 'A Ruman emissary came and said he spoke for Marcellus, Cornelius, and Tamberlaine.'

'Who?' Fisk asked.

'His name was Flavius Vegetius Marcellus, the general's son,' she said.

'A legate. I know the man,' Fisk said. 'Not a bad fellow. He's come up through the ranks. His hands have got dirty before.'

'And what did he offer? It was an offer, was it not?' I asked, directing my question to my mirror, Neruda. In him, had all the various turnings and twists my life had taken been different, I saw a man – a leader – that I might have been: I, a speaker for the *vaettir* and *dvergar* – one just an affiliation and the other a race – and he a man dispossessed, accepted in no society, not his race, nor his employers.

'It was. He came alone to speak with me—' Neruda said.

'He was not alone,' Fisk said. 'He had a cohort behind him, at least.'

Neruda shook his head, looking at Fisk. Raising two fingers to his mouth, he gave two sharp, piercing whistles. The forests and fields around us, on the road just outside of Breadbasket, began to teem and move. Hundreds of forms appeared out of the pall and mist, their garb woolly and indistinct from the flora around them. I'd heard Reeve – Reeve who saved me from the Tempus Union – call them 'suits of *ghillie*' used for hunting and ambush in wetter climes than the Hardscrabble, where I'd spent most of my life.

Neruda said, 'He was alone, or he was by the time he started talking.'

'You killed them?' Fisk said, frowning. 'Not an auspicious way to start a negotiation.'

'No,' Neruda said. 'I am no beast of the shoals.' He grinned and many of those around him grinned as well. Even Winfried allowed a half-smile to creep up on her. 'They were stripped nude, and all of their clothing – minus their Hellfire, of course – was placed on

Frieda the Flighty, a horse of uneven temperament. She, of course, bolted at first wind of the legionnaires.'

Even I had to smile at this. It is a small thing to strip a legionnaire – most legionnaires I knew would drop trousers at the barest hesitation – but to set them chasing their clothes on a fleeing horse approached on high comedy.

But Fisk grimaced.

'Did you allow them their boots?' he said.

Neruda blinked, and glanced at Winfried. Winfried shook her head.

'Then you killed them.' He looked around at all the *dvergar* in *ghillie* suits, bearing swords and Hellfire. 'This might be the edges of Hardscrabble, but leaving someone naked and defenceless is tantamount to murder. You should've known that.'

He was right.

'And I imagine this was Winfried's idea,' Fisk said, the expression on his face becoming more grim with every moment. 'I had heard you, Mister Neruda, are a great leader of men, but no general. And so, I must think, did you come up with this idea, Winfried?'

She said nothing. The half-smile was gone.

'I'm glad you've found *something,* Winfried, since your loss. But this.' He spat. 'No blooded soldier will go into war anew without giving some respect to his enemy.'

'Yes, the Rumans are renowned for this, are they not?' Praeverta said. Neruda shushed her.

'Be silent, Matve, until you are needed,' Neruda said.

Fisk dismounted and approached Neruda and Winfried. Praeverta moved to stand behind Neruda, a glare of outrage and righteousness informing every sinew of her being.

'You're tight as ticks, I see,' Fisk said. 'That's fine. That's just fine.' A dog barked in Breadbasket; a hoarse, desperate sound. Fisk put his hand on his hip and narrowed his eyes, looking at the odd pair – the dwarf and the Malfenian woman. 'It's Ia-damned easy to wage guerrilla war when you have the whole of the Hardscrabble and its outlying regions to disappear into. But once you're fixed, once you've got a location you've got to protect, ambush and sneak attacks and these Ia-damned games you're playing cease to work.' I hadn't ever seen Fisk so outraged. 'And spending time and effort to humiliate the enemy, even if it is a company of Rume, is just wasting life.'

There was silence then. Of all of them, he was the only one who had spent time in command of men in a military capacity, and that wasn't much. Cornelius made him his legate, but none of Cornelius' legionnaires had taken to the governor's son-in-law. Fisk was a hard man, and opaque. He was a killer, as sure as any man was. He was of noble family, raised in Rume, and like any patrician boy must've studied strategy and tactics as he took watered wine and bread. He was hellacious with any Hellfire, and mean with a knife. There was very little mercy in him, for anything or anyone.

'You would do well to listen to my partner,' I said to Neruda. 'He is a man of Occidentalia and the Hardscrabble, despite his Ruman descent.'

Neruda turned his brown eyes to me. He gave a small nod.

'The Medierans did not waste time mocking us, did they?' Fisk said, ignoring my aside. 'No, they did not, though their minions might've.' He gestured to Beleth. 'This engineer you wanted so badly, this man who would give you Hellfire, he destroyed Harbour Town by sacrificing a child to the infernal. He killed thousands – thousands of Rumans, thousands of *dvergar*, thousands of settlers – under orders from Mediera.'

A hush fell over the road leading into Breadbasket, broken only by the far-off barking dogs and the squelching of the horses' hooves in the mud.

'This is how Mediera wages war! You might've defeated a

half-century of legionnaires. You might've stripped a cohort of men naked, running after their clothes. But there is silver here. And the whole world is looking at it, with hunger in their eyes. Rume is coming. Mediera is coming. The world wars on silver,' he said, pitching his voice upwards. It rang out. A flight of dark birds erupted from the treeline. 'The Medierans will find another engineer willing to sully his soul and kill an infant and lay waste to this entire valley, soon enough. Whatever evils you think Rume capable of, do you think them capable of that?'

Praeverta opened her mouth, but Neruda placed a hand on her arm, and she said nothing.

'Keep your woolly suits. Keep your ambush tactics. But if this valley isn't going to fall into the hands of mass-murdering filth with souls so heavy they will never float, it will need fortifications and an army. And only Rume can give you that.'

'The lesser evil,' Neruda said.

Fisk's face soured. 'The only way,' he said. 'They will come and take it. At least right now, you can work a deal where you keep what you think is yours.'

There was a long silence.

'Bring me a plough and horse,' Neruda said. Two *dvergar* men trotted off and returned in moments with a draught horse pulling a wagon. They unharnessed the wagon and from its bed withdrew a hand-plough and harnessed it to the horse.

'I will sow the seeds of treaty, then, and strike bargain with you, right now,' Neruda said, looking at Fisk. 'You are a legate, are you not? And high in the empire's favour?'

Fisk glanced at me. He was not well regarded by Tamberlaine at the moment, quite the opposite, but he was married to Livia, who had the ears of her father, wherever in the world she might be. And her father was, as far as I knew, still governor of Occidentalia. Fisk remained quiet.

Neruda said, 'With this furrow I will mark where Rume is welcome, and where Rume is not.'

He slapped the reins against the horse's arse and moved the plough into the field, turning over great burls of dirt to either side of the blade. Fisk came to me and said, 'You got a cigarette? We're gonna be here all day, thanks to the dramatics.'

I withdrew my tabac pouch and papers and twisted two. Fisk and I remained there, smoking and watching as Neruda ploughed the field all the way into the forest. He returned and ploughed the other side of the road, effectively walling off the valley and the Grenthvar silverlode from us, as long as we respected the furrow.

'You will supply us with Hellfire, to protect ourselves. You will write laws to protect the rights of *dvergar*, our homes and land. Will you do this?'

Fisk bowed his head. 'I will advocate for it. I am but one man.'

'It will have to be enough,' Neruda said. 'Here is as far as we will allow Rume. Come no further. Should you break your bond, we will collapse the silverlode and flee into the Eldvatch, our ancestral home in the cliffs, the bluffs and caves like warrens in the rocks.' This was no lie: I'd heard Catch Hands and Lina mention the passages to Dvergar itself, some fifteen miles distant, and beyond, east through the Smokeys to the hills by the Mammon River. He withdrew a small paring knife and cut his forearm. 'Have we an agreement?'

'The engineer stays with us, then,' Fisk said. 'He has some deeds to answer for and you'll get your Hellfire soon enough.'

'He looks only half-useful to us, anyway,' Neruda said. 'He is missing a hand?'

Fisk nodded and withdrew his own knife. He cut his arm and they clasped forearms, mingling blood. 'First thing on the morrow, I will ride to Marcellus in Fort Brust and inform him. More than likely I'll return with an army at my back.' He looked to the field.

Dvergar men and women already moved, hauling rocks and driving posts into the ground, marking the furrow.

'We have a treaty, then!' Neruda said loudly. 'Offer these men service and honour them with food. Prepare a camp for them to rest.'

Neruda walked back into the village, leaving us standing in the road. Praeverta followed him, and, after a moment, so did Winfried.

'Shifting allegiances,' I said, watching Winfried go.

'Her allegiance is the same as it's always been,' Fisk said, drawing on his cigarette and then, looking at it, tossing it onto the road. 'It is to herself.'

The *dvergar* set up a cosy camp for us, and even brought hasped pine planks and tents for dry sleeping, pots for cooking. Beleth stayed with me. Gynth returned, bearing an elk over his great shoulders. He slung the creature next to the fire and squatted on his hams, hands dangling loose in front of him. Even squatting, he was as tall as a man. Gynth remained still for the most part, but his gaze took in everything.

The rhythms of camp took me. Building the fire, inventorying food and spice. Sharpening my knives. *Dvergar* women came in procession, bringing vegetables, casks of ale, bundles of herbs. Blankets and candles. A tin of rendered grease for cooking. Old pans and cast iron skillets.

Each woman stared at Gynth for long moments before turning away. Some had expressions of wonder. Some of hatred. The old matves greeted Gynth with a bow and a murmured, '*Vrenthkin, aldven,*' which roughly means, 'You've returned, once more,' but functioned as an old greeting. A greeting one would give an acquaintance, but not one of their own family.

'What're they saying?' Fisk asked, as he slung his satchels into the tent.

'They give the old greeting,' I said, sucking on my teeth. 'An old greeting to someone you might bargain or trade with.'

'You said they used to trade,' Fisk said. 'And now this brute here. You've tamed him.'

'There's no taming *vaettir*, as there's no taming men, pard. We all follow our own natures,' I said.

'Why are their natures all so sour, then?' Fisk said.

I sighed. He could tamp it down, he could let reason prevail, but he could never put aside his hatred of the *vaettir*. How could he? It would be an abrogation of his love for his daughter, lost now so many years. It was a furrow he ploughed around himself and could never cross.

But I said, 'Remember Livia's letters? That Fantasma boy? Their natures vary, it seems. Fickle like mankind. All of it. Like *dvergar*.'

'Far as I've seen, all of their natures are bloodthirsty,' he said, frowning, looking at Gynth. 'Fantasma and this one aren't any different.'

'And ours are not?' I said, withdrawing a longknife and running it over a whetstone in preparation for butchering the elk. I didn't bother to look at Fisk; I focused on the task at hand. ' "There is no creature on earth or in heaven that is not fearful of man".'

'Don't quote *Our Heavenly War* to me, Shoe,' Fisk said. 'I'm not in the mood for literary discussion.'

It was warm enough, so I took off my jacket and rolled up my shirtsleeves to the bicep. From Bess' satchel I took my stained leather apron – much like Neruda's – and put it on. I set to butchering the elk while Gynth watched me. When Beleth stirred, moving the blood in his body, trying to ease the pain of his bindings, Gynth would shift and flex his long clawed fingers, and turn his gaze upon the engineer. Beleth would still. As the afternoon wore on, denizens of Breadbasket crossed the furrow – now a small, short stone and timber wall due to the industriousness of *dvergar* – to come and gaze upon the *vaettir*.

'He's big,' Catch Hands said, staring at Gynth. 'It's like he could hold a child in his hands.'

Fisk, unrolling his sleeping bag, said, 'Why don't you find your friends before he decides you look tasty and stop bothering us with your idiotic observations?'

Catch Hands bristled and then, before you knew it, Fisk's hand held a pistol. 'There'd be nothing I'd rather do than ventilate you,' Fisk said, and then said no more.

Catch Hands made patting gestures, palms out. 'What's your friend's problem?' he said to me in *dvergar*.

'*Vaettir* make him crotchety,' I replied, knife working on the elk. I'd run a sturdy branch through the natural grommet of bone and ankle tendon and, with some help, had hoisted the great beast up on high, rope over tree branch. I flayed away the skin carefully, preparing to open the body cavity. Catch Hands shrugged and turned away, walking back to the village. I thought he'd gone for good but he returned with a wooden trough and plopped it down beneath the elk to catch the viscera.

'I'll feed the dogs,' he said, simply.

Gynth blinked. I opened the body cavity and pulled the hot mess down into the trough. The heart – melon sized – I cut away, arms covered in blood. I tossed it to Gynth. He snatched it out of the air with a clawed hand and said, 'That's good,' in *dvergar*. He began to eat it like it was an apple.

The onlooking dwarves murmured in surprise. Gynth turned his great head (and blood-streaked mouth) to look at them. 'What?' he said. 'It's good.'

The watching dwarves scattered.

That night, after we'd eaten our fill and I'd spiced and set out the elk meat to dry in the woodsmoke, Fisk came and sat near me by the fire.

'I'm lighting out before dawn. Watch Beleth,' he said. 'I took his hand to keep his mischief to a minimum, but by morning, before it, I'll wager, Winfried will be here, sniffing around. She wants for his blood.'

'Understood,' I said. 'I will be on my guard.'

'With the deal I've struck with Neruda, he'll not want the engineer, though that old harridan Praeverta won't want us to take him out of this valley. She worked and fought us too hard to get him here.' He fell silent and lit another cigarette, and stared into the fire. I could feel the wheels turning, in there. 'Beleth is a problem,' he said. 'There'd be nothing more I'd like than to kill him. But I need him in front of one of Cornelius' or Tamberlaine's agents if I can. Satisfy the Emperor we've fulfilled his mission, maybe—'

'He'll not keep Livia from you. I hear you,' I said. 'I will keep him close.'

'Yes, that's it. For the most part,' Fisk said. 'But there's more. That trick he does. Casting himself into others. Into their bodies. Infests stretchers with demons. Wears them like a lady's frock. Sapientia and Samantha need to take him in hand, find out what they can. We're fully at war now, no half-measures.'

'Never pegged you for a patriot,' I said. It was a calculated barb. Fisk sometimes needed a few prods for him to come to what was really bothering him.

'I've seen too many children killed,' Fisk said. 'My own. Others. Before coming here, west, I was a mercenary in Ægypt, and in the Pelonesian. Too many places in the world don't care for innocence. And now that son of a bitch is turning the innocent babes into the unimaginable. Titanic weapons.'

I looked at my partner. His expression was pained. So many times had he barked orders, said gruff things, even hurtful things to those he cared not for, those he had no respect for. Those he hated. He was a man used to hate. Hate that denied the common thread of humanity. He'd killed men, and women. But, I think, none that did not mean him harm. And there, in the firelight, was Gynth, eyes glimmering. Fisk tolerated him, one of a race he'd sworn a thousand times he'd not rest until he saw the last of mouldering in the earth. So, there's a movement in the rocks and trees. The great plates of land shift. Mountain ranges are cast up like furrows and plateaus become seas. Fisk changes.

'I hear you, friend,' I said. 'If he's given this terrible knowledge to the Medierans—'

'He has. You saw how fast Neruda wanted Hellfire. The Medierans would be no different,' Fisk said, and spat out a bit of tabac that had lodged in his teeth. 'They would make no bargain with Beleth without that.'

A log in the fire popped. Fisk finished his smoke. I adjusted the elk meat over the fire.

'I'll be gone in the morning, partner,' he said. 'Remember.' He looked meaningfully at Beleth once more and then disappeared into the tent the folks of Breadbasket had set up for him.

The night grew quiet. Gynth rose, indicated he was going to wander.

'You ever sleep?' I asked in *dvergar*.

'Sleep? I have,' he nodded his great head. 'In sleep I walk in dreams. But it will be bundles of years before I sleep again.'

'What do you dream of?' I asked.

'Fire. And being buried in the earth. And blood,' Gynth said, pausing at the edge of the fire's radiance.

'None of that seems too pleasant,' I said.

Gynth shrugged and disappeared.

SIXTEEN

Thimadæl Gyre Is Greedy And Wants For Blood

RUME, THE IMMORTAL City, was no more.

We turned the *Typhon* back, once we saw the eerie light distressing the night sky, steaming into the Ostian bay, Carnelia on the remaining swivel gun, Tenebrae at the gunman's roost, broaching the great wave that came at us from shore, to witness the conflagration. There were flames, towering, lighting the underside of the clouds in streaked, garish light. As we approached the wharf, crowds of people screamed and pleaded from the shore. Men, some women, bearing children. Behind them, all of Latinum was afire, and a pillar of it – a shifting monument of flame that moved like some great old one, a titan, an old god – walked the earth. Black smoke poured off it and it had no body in the shape of man, it was wholly foreign, tendrils of fire like arms, branches of flame like legs, or children. And it grew, making a tremendous sound, a high-pitched keen matched with a bass rumble that fell away and skittered off into registers that my ears ceased to perceive yet caused my body to become as some great antenna. The air shivered and pulsed with percussion and heat, wavered with whatever strange and dark energy emanated from the conflagration. It was alive. It was awake. It bore a great malice in its heat and smote everything around it.

'My gods,' said Ysmay, coming on deck now that the engines

had begun to idle. His face was painted orange with firelight. 'The power here. Unimaginable.' He turned away. 'I can't even countenance the precium,' he said.

'The precium?' I asked, still watching the sentient pillar of fire.

'The price. Blood. Or more,' he said.

Of course. *A child. Children. Infants. Ia help us all.*

'There'll be no docking. Whatever *daemon* they called from Hell, it has remarkable integrity and won't dissipate for a long while. And if it takes notice of us...'

'I think it might be wise if you go back below decks, Mister Ysmay,' I said. 'And start the engines. We'll be leaving now.'

Ysmay scurried below, and for once I didn't have to worry about his motivation or fidelity. The engines thrummed and shivered and we put distance between ourselves and the wreckage of Rume.

I did not know what this terrible end signified, other than terrible loss.

My father was dead. People I'd loved, people I'd known all my life. All gone. The Latinum hills were scorched and wasted.

I turned my eyes north toward the dark. And west, toward Occidentalia.

It was a risk, but we took the *Typhon* into open seas. The Ruman naval fleet was in disarray – the Ostian wharf burned and those ships without *daemons* in their bellies, their sails caught fire like so much kindling, funerary candles on the face of the bay. The smell of burning pitch and wood and flesh hung with the smoke, low, like a noxious fog kissing the water's surface. We had no idea if we were still flagged as a renegade ship and no way to find out – in the captain's quarters we found a Quotidian, but it was not paired to any living person who could use it and Ysmay said it could not be reconfigured without both 'receivers' present. There was an overwhelming moment when I realised *we* might be blamed for the destruction of Rume. Our ruse at Rezzo, using Fiscelion as evidence of a plot against the state, might make us seem the monsters that did this should the men there have had any communication with Tamberlaine or his subordinates between us boarding the *Typhon* and the destruction of the immortal city.

After three days at full steam, we brought the *Typhon* to port at Narbonne. Carnelia and I had scoured wardrobes and found enough clothing in the lascars' berths that we were both accoutred as lascars – from all appearances, very young ones, of fair complexion and slim builds – and we tucked our hair underneath caps while Tenebrae wore the captain's uniform, cutting a dashing figure. We all wore Hellfire pistols.

Looking at our reflections in the mirror of the captain's berth, Carnelia announced, 'I would kiss me.' She tugged on the naval coat. Neither of us had prominent breasts, though mine were definitely larger, due to Fiscelion's feeding. But with the jackets, our sex was not immediately evident. 'I am a *very* fetching lad,' Carnelia said. Then she tugged at the crotch of the trousers. 'These britches are Ia-damned ridiculous. I don't know how you do it, especially with the nether equipment,' she said to Tenebrae, who waited outside.

'You get used to it,' Tenebrae said, shrugging. 'We've spotted the shore and Narbonne. I've instructed Ysmay to slow to half-speed.'

I nodded at Tenebrae, acknowledging the information. He wore the uniform, but ultimately, I was in command. I do not understand all the turnings and choices that had to happen to get me to this point. But there I was.

'Seems like *you* should wear the dresses and we should have trousers,' Carnelia said.

Tenebrae smiled, but it did not last long. But he said, 'That would make a pretty picture, would it not?'

When the wharf master came out in a skiff and stood on deck

in the blustery wind, he did not look at us askance, except to give news of the destruction and ask what we'd seen of it. Tenebrae described the destruction in terse, if graphic, terms.

The wharf master was a thick, genial man with a wide, flat face and ruddy cheeks. He was a tippler, no doubt, and heir to a thousand other sins, I think, though I could not be sure of that.

The man whistled, a forlorn sound, like a miniature lighthouse horn blowing into the night. 'They say that the *daemon* still burns, tromping all about, smiting left and right with great fists of fire. Thousands of hectares of land, just gone. There'll be full-on war, now,' he said. As an afterthought, he looked at our requisition request. He was not really interested in the rote performance of his job. He wanted to talk and not to listen. This was a man who loved the reverberations of his own vocal chords. 'Fuckin' beaners. Fuck 'em all to Hell. But Tamberlaine is crafty, that one, our Great Father. He suspected, after the Harbour Town incident, he did. They made a grave mistake, there, going for the tail before the head. Tamberlaine sent his generals and navarchs from Rume and all were safely away. Along with the treasury. Rume still has silver enough to war.' He looked at the *Typhon* and whistled. 'She's an evil-looking bitch, isn't she?'

Tenebrae made murmurs of assent.

'Your best choice is to hug the coast. The flotilla regroups in Beaticæ in a fortnight to keep the Medierans out of the Nous. I have standing orders here. All children under the age of ten are banned from the cities – there are villages teeming with toddlers scurrying about like rats now. A plague of children. Mass evacuations. Go to Beaticæ. You can join with the fleet there.'

Tenebrae nodded. 'Thank you, sir, for your advice. We are grateful to you for your service.'

The wharf master seemed pleased. 'Bring your ship to port, we'll top off your water and fill your requisitions. We're low on

rum, but we've gin enough and limes by the basket out of Ægypt.'
He paused and looked about. 'Proceed with provisioning, Captain
Regulus,' he said. He folded the requisition order and tucked it
inside his jacket and re-boarded the skiff.

Tenebrae walked to the bulwark near where I stood idly coiling a
piece of hemp over and over, and watched as the skiff moved away.

'She's done a fine job so far,' he said, patting the side of the
ship. 'Even when the seas have been high, she's not floundered.
And submersible!'

'I have not the experience at sea. I can't be a real judge. I've
heard tales of men sailing to the edge of the world in a simple
sailboat. I can't believe a ship that can spend time under the surface, such as the *Typhon* does, could not weather a crossing of
the Occidens,' said I.

'We are agreed,' Tenebrae said. 'Should we speak of this to
Carnelia?'

After a moment, we both looked at each other. He placed his
hand on my arm. We laughed. Harder than we had any right to.
Of course, Carnelia wouldn't give a fig. If there was a great sea
worm pacing the *Typhon*, she would try to woo him, wed him,
or behead him. No journey across the Occidens would faze her.

'What are you laughing at?' A voice came from behind us.

Turning slowly, we both came to face Carnelia.

'Nothing at all,' Tenebrae said.

'Nothing,' I agreed.

It was impossible to stop the laughter from erupting. It was
all too much. Death. Destruction. Our horrible predicament.
Fiscelion, a pawn in such a destructive game. And Secundus. Our
business precluded reflecting on my brother, whom I loved and is
gone now.

I'm sure Tenebrae felt keenly – more keenly, truly – the loss of
our brother, Secundus. To us he was dear. To Tenebrae he was

love, through and through. No man would abrogate his duties and oaths for less.

We took on water and provisions and steamed away. There was a moment when Ysmay moved to go on deck while at port, and Lupina, holding Fiscelion, slid between the engineer and the door, shaking her head and looking at him very seriously. It did not take Ysmay very long to notice the cleaver in her hand. Fiscelion cooed.

'Mister Ysmay,' I said from where I sat studying the navigational equipment – we all made a study of steering and controlling the *Typhon* for safety's sake. 'I think it would be best if you remained below deck while we're at port.'

'So I'm a prisoner,' he said.

I sighed, and turned to him. 'Would that I could have taken this boat without bloodshed. As I said before, you will not be harmed. But we cannot take the chance that you will begin telling stories to our new friends in Narbonne.'

Ysmay smiled then, an odd reaction to what I was saying. But it was not genuine. It was a pained, tight smile, twisting his face even as he made it. Some men will try to pretend they're not hurt. Or scared. Some men pretend even to themselves they are strong. But Ysmay, he was a man who was at least honest enough with himself to understand that he was out of his depth and in a bad situation, but was desperately trying to keep up his mask. It was painful to watch and made me sick to my heart that I was the cause of it.

'Mister Ysmay, please sit here with me,' I said, indicating the navigational chair.

He approached, subdued, and sat.

'Do you have family? A wife? Children?' I asked.

He remained silent, looking at me. He had large blue eyes, too big, really, for his face. 'A sister. My mother is an engineer.'

'Father?' I asked.

'No one,' he said. Engineers are a different stripe. Women rise to great stature if their skill and handiwork brings them high enough – they take themselves beyond men, beyond the reach of family and all the obligations the yoke of family brings. And men of lower class can rise high too, high as knights, high as men like Beleth, because their society is based on ability and native intelligence and even artistry, and not just relation. Or mere sex.

Here was a man who had hoped to rise high, who would have risen high, high enough for some security. High enough to have something that resembled a good life. And free.

And I took it all away.

'I would have us be friends,' I said, pulling aside the blanket that half obscured Fiscelion's face. His pink and beautiful countenance lay bare. He gave a little smile and grasped my index finger and placed it in his mouth and gnawed. I winced. His teeth were coming in. 'I would not have taken away all of your world. But I had to fight for my own,' I said. 'My son. And, sadly, our paths crossed. But now Rume is gone, and the world is changed.' I would not offer him what-ifs: no *what if we'd never come? What if you had been there in Rume?* I would offer him something better. 'You might rise high still. There will be war in Occidentalia. For silver. For land.' I looked at Ysmay. 'We need you. Rume is gone but not her people. And I *am* of Rume. We will need a man of your skills. We need you now and we need you when we arrive in the West. But what we really need is to feel that we can trust you.'

He remained silent, thinking. There was no umbrage there now. No sullenness. Just trepidation and wariness.

'You can trust me,' he said. And I believed him.

'Then you may go ashore,' I said. 'We will remain here.'

His eyes narrowed.

'I would not have you a prisoner. If we can trust you, you must be able to trust us. And so, you're free to go ashore,' I said.

163

'I have no need,' he said. 'There are things I should see to before our journey.'

I did not press him. Truly, I would rather he stayed on board. But risks are the coin of leadership. 'Will the *Typhon* weather the Occidens?' I asked. Again. This time I might rely on his answer.

He looked sheepish. But he answered. 'I don't know,' he said. 'But she's the finest craft I've ever seen. I think she will.'

Relief flooded me. To escape the hand of fate and all we had endured since Kithai, only to be drowned in a ship unfit for the open sea – I would not have my son's fortunes end in a watery grave. 'This is welcome news, Mister Ysmay. I am so pleased you think so.' I stood and brought Fiscelion to where Lupina remained watching during the course of our conversation. 'Feel free to make whatever preparations you need, we will leave on the tide,' I said. 'Er. When *is* the next high tide?'

Ysmay allowed a smile to crack his open face. 'This evening.'

'Wonderful. This evening,' I said. 'How long will it take to get to Beaticæ? We will have to run the flotilla.'

'Two days until the Gooseneck – the Strait of Algeciræ. We can make it in one, possibly, with blood.' I looked at him. 'To keep Typhon satisfied and running?' I asked.

'He'll run anyway,' Ysmay answered. 'A *daemon* combusts, always. It's part of their nature. So there's always power. But you can increase the power yield with blood.'

'And who gives it? And how?' I asked.

'I give it. You, your sister, or your servant. Mister Tenebrae. Or—' He stopped, trailed off.

'What are you implying? Why would I do such a thing?' A cold had come upon me. I looked upon Ysmay anew. And like that, my tolerance was gone. I was acutely aware of the weight of my sawn-off shotgun riding on my hip and thigh.

Seeing something in my eye, Ysmay held up his hands and

bowed his head. 'They love the blood of the young. And the pure. Please, Madame,' he said, miserable. 'Thimadæl Gyre is greedy and wants for blood—' The ship shuddered with his words. Everything shifted, and I took a step to regain my balance. His eyes grew wild, looking all about. He'd let slip the *daemon* Typhon's secret name, possibly, judging from the ship's reaction. 'I should not have . . . I am sorry, Madame! The *Typhon*, she's well-built and the *daemon* that turns the screws loves blood. The precium. If we are desperate, a thimble full—'

'Do not speak of that again,' I said. I can only imagine how awful my face was then. 'Do. Not. Or you will find my displeasure hard to bear.'

'I am sorry,' he said. It was abject. It was penitent.

This was a loss. I had made amends, gathered up the shards of the man and bound him to me, and then lost them and him once more.

'We sail for Occidentalia soon. Make yourself and the ship ready,' I said, and walked from the chamber, up on the deck to feel the wind on my face and smell land, living trees and grass and flowers, once more, before casting off.

Beaticæ was a ghost, an invisible shoreline passing by, though this was something we only knew through conversation, with Ysmay describing what he saw through the underwater seeing device. The remains of the Ruman flotilla – those that survived the destruction of the Immortal City – were disjointed and their watchmen pre-occupied. They did not notice the roving eye-stalk of the *Typhon* or the minuscule wake it made.

We passed under a cloud-wreathed moon and hazy stars, into the waters of the Occidens, swells growing. Carnelia stopped dressing in skirts and blouses and continued to wear the clothes of the lascar. 'They're comfortable and make sense,' she said, simply, 'for working on board a ship. I'm not going to cut my hair and start scratching my crotch and spitting.'

At night I dreamed of seas of blood and fire. My father framed in the door of our family villa with both of his legs, whole once more. Fiscelion cried and sucked desperately at my breast. His teeth made ruin of my nipples. Lupina did what she could to masticate food and feed it to the boy through kisses. He was growing rapidly and his shite smelled something horrible. We set him on the cabin floors and watched him crawl about, exploring, making cooing sounds, indistinct.

'Rume,' he said. It was his first word.

SEVENTEEN

I Have Weighed Your Nature.
I Have Measured Every Grain Of It

Mist rose from the Breadbasket's stream, flowing cold from the heart of the Eldvatch down through the village.

The sky was clear beyond the mists, sprayed with a multitude of stars, shining hazily onto the vaporous earth. Gynth was gone, somewhere out roaming the heights of the mountains. His natural restlessness became taut at night, stretched thin, and he prowled about, hunting, always returning red-handed and bearing meat.

In the evenings, when she came past the Pactum Wall, I supped with Lina and had long conversations about her grandmother, and mother. There was a wariness she held around me, and it hurt me that it was so impenetrable; at its heart was her knowledge of the *daemon* hand and some inkling of its power. She did not question me on it again, but her demeanour indicated she had not forgotten it.

'Lina, of all of Praeverta's group, who are the best scouts?'

'Myself, I've walked from Harbour Town to the Big Empty and no eye rested on me I did not want there,' she said, lifting her chin.

'And of the others?'

'Vrinthi is half-cougar. Seanchae is silent and swift and knows how to track and stay unseen,' she said.

'And Catch Hands?'

'He's a brawler, and good in a fight. He is no scout,' she replied.

I scratched my beard. 'How would you like a job?'

'For the Rumans? Bah,' she said.

'For us. All here. Don't you think our fates are joined? Even Neruda has come toward this reality,' I said. 'Is it just obstinacy? I already have a mule.'

Instead of irritation or anger, she laughed at this. 'What is it you'd have us do?'

'Go west, find rumour or evidence of the Medierans' movements with great haste. Return here,' I said.

She nodded. 'When?'

'Tomorrow,' I said.

She stood up from the fire and stretched her back, shook out her legs. 'I will go and tell the others.'

Lina turned to walk from the fire. I said, 'Be careful, Grand-daughter. I wouldn't have you taken from me now that I've just got you back.'

'I'm not someone to have, *Granwe*,' she said, using the *dvergar*. 'And you never had me in the first place.' She turned back, her face lit by the flickering flames. 'But I'm always careful.' She winked at me and then disappeared beyond the ring of light.

When she was gone, I stoked the fire, changed Beleth's dressing and gave him water and hard tack, helped him to shite and piss, then emptied his soil from the stinking wooden bucket inside the ramshackle shed we kept him in at night. The people of Grenthvar – Neruda's lieutenants, some men, some dwarven women, some dwarven men – had promised a cell, but their time was consumed with hollowing out the mountain and trucking the ore downhill. Great hills of the black stuff stood south of the village. To the east, rising with the mountains, teams of *dvergar* levelled ground for rails on which to run mechanised trains, as they had at the Talavera silverlode in the shadow of Brujateton, running from the mine to Passasuego. A smelt was raised quickly of the dense, near unburnable pinewood trees in the lowlands to the south. In the day, all of the Breadbasket echoed with hammer-falls and hollers, workmen's voices calling out, the rasp of saws and milling, ringing bells and the haws of mules and the nickering of draught horses and the bellowing of sweet aurochs pulling sledges full-loaded with fragrant, fresh-cut wood. No travertine here, but granite and limestone; the bones of the mountains. We remained behind the Pactum Wall, the furrow Neruda had carved around the village, honouring the treaty.

But at night, almost all was silent and a hush fell upon the valley. Sleep was precious – bodies worn out from labour demand rest. And there was the shadow of war upon us like the pall of wood fires that hung in the air, or the mist seeping from the ground. So little time. Sleep, if you could find it, was precious and no one would violate the silence of night, because they would not, if they managed to snatch slumber's raiment from the night air, want their own personal silence and slumber violated.

I checked Beleth's manacles and took off his gag so that he might have his mouth unfettered for a few hours at least. He worked his jaws and spat some blood. I had very little sympathy. There was no one around but me to talk to and his enthusiasm for dialogue had worn away; he simply looked at me in the same way he might a beast of burden or a nameless slave, his gaze passing over me as if I wasn't even there.

Leaving him, I did not immediately return to the fire where Catch Hands sat, stirring the stew. He was a passable chef, and interesting company. It was strange for me to come back to my *dvergar* roots – my kin had shunned me for so long as a Ruman auxiliary that being once more in their circle was as coming home, but finding everything is the same but foreign. It's the sinking realisation that *you* have changed and home has stayed fixed, as all motion is relative to the origin. But Catch Hands was unflappable and good company.

I walked the perimeter, up to the Pactum Wall, and around where we had made camp at the side of the road. In the mist, everything was indistinct and what sounds did reach my ears were muffled. I let my night vision come, and perked up my ears to the movements and sounds of everything around me.

A cough. A footfall.

I stilled.

Once, I abstained from Hellfire. But that was no more.

I pulled my six-gun and walked softly forward, angling back around, toward the fire.

She was at the door of Beleth's shed when I placed the muzzle of the pistol in the small of her back and thumbed back the hammer. The click of metal echoed loudly in the night air.

'And what might you be doing out at this hour, Winfried? Taking in the night air?'

She stiffened. Slowly she turned around and looked at me. 'Mister Ilys. I was—' She stopped. Shrugged.

'I'm old, Win,' I said. The situation and the pistol allowed me to be glib and over-familiar and I could give a shit if she didn't like it. 'Was born before your father's father first sucked tit. We both know why you're here. He will get what he deserves. In time. But you know better than I that he must answer questions first.'

Her gaze bored into me. She had a longknife in her belt to prick the engineer with. 'Then let us pose the questions,' she said.

'You wouldn't even know what to ask,' I said. 'But the engineers will.'

She shook her head and looked as if she wanted to spit out whatever foul taste flooded her mouth. She brushed past me, ignoring my pistol, and disappeared into the night's mist.

*

Twenty days later, Fisk returned to the Breadbasket in front of two columns of legionnaires, maybe three thousand strong. Each man, head shorn, cheeks marked with ash, expression grim, looking pissed as all Hell. The banners of the fifth and seventh Occidentalia, a rampant wolf and a bellowing bull, were clear for all to see. There were more guns than I'd ever witnessed in one place, and something I thought I would never see – a forest of pilum on the march, each one a sapling denuded of leaves. Things had changed since the *daemon* hand hung from Fisk's neck. Guns took primacy, but they had their seconds now. Two clattering, mechanical things trundled along behind the legionnaires – they appeared to be the locomotive's mechanised baggage trains, but smaller, and wearing hellaciously large cannons as jaunty caps. Neither rode on tracks, but metal treads. They were frighteningly loud, ratcheting and clanking, billowing massive clouds of soot and steam. Behind them all, the engineers' vardos and wagons being pulled by massive draught horses.

Fisk rode at the front with a regiment of cavalry. He wore his grey outrider gear – he'd not allowed himself to spend all his days in officer's garb – but his legate's eagle was pinned to his chest for all to see. It was a commonly held practice that men of high rank needed to cultivate eccentricities so that their men might love them for it, but for Fisk his outrider's garb was pure obstinacy. There were other men of rank, tribunes and praefects, but no Marcellus.

The column stopped at the Pactum Wall and began to set up camp.

Fisk looked furious when he dismounted and approached me. Gynth watched, blinking. More than a few legionnaires reached for their Hellfire or touched gladius when they saw him.

'Ia-damn it, Shoe,' Fisk said, coming near. 'The world's gone to shit.'

I waited. Now that he was here, I could see his legate's eagle clearly. It had grass laurels and three bars. He'd been promoted.

'Rume,' he said. 'It's gone. The same as Harbour Town.'

'Holy shit,' I said. It was all I could manage. 'And Tamberlaine? Cornelius?'

'Tamberlaine is alive, somehow,' he said. 'No one knows about my father-in-law. It's possible that he was in Tamberlaine's retinue that fled the city. There was some warning. Livia was involved, somehow.'

I whistled, taking it all in. 'And these men?'

'Marcellus, the whore's son,' Fisk said, spitting, 'has made me region commander – possibly under Cornelius' orders regarding his – *our* – silver interests. The thirteenth and sixth Occidentalia – they were lost at Harbour Town. Marcellus has taken the Cocks, Rams, Scorpions, and Eagles to Novorum, to protect interests there, leaving me with the fifth and seventh. The Bulls and Wolves. Neither at full strength. Neither willing to be folded into the other.' He gave a tight smile. 'Ia help the Medierans when these men take the field. Many of them are conscripts with family in Latinum. Marcellus is calling them our orphaned army.'

I remained quiet. When Fisk has the mood upon him, it's best to let him talk and wait out most of the blow of the storm.

'He took his best men. New Damnation's abandoned. Sent the tenth to do what they could to protect the Talavera silverlode. The "working silverlode", he said. And this is all he's got for Dvergar.' He looked at the Pactum Wall. 'I see Neruda's been hot to get the perimeter up. Have they started mining?'

'Yes, he's got them hauling ore. Sent rovers out for charcoal and Neruda himself has set hands to building a smelt, but he'll need engineers for that,' I said. I pointed to a copse of trees outside the wall, being felled. 'There. Beyond the curve of the Pactum, there's the mine works and smelt.'

Fisk took off his hat and wiped his brow. 'Damn, Shoe. Neruda's folk work fast,' he said.

'With good reason. There's a hostile army west of us,' I said. 'Somewhere. I've sent out some of Praeverta's group to scout. Lina, and a couple of others she vouched for.'

'Your granddaughter? Was that wise?' he said.

'She has much of her mother's disposition – she's never satis-fied with anything. And her knowing about the *daemon* hand was eating at her. I figured a job, away from the Breadbasket—'

He nodded his understanding. 'Ahh. She seemed eminently capable. Knew I could count on you.'

'I grow concerned, though. I sent her out when you went north to Fort Brust with Neruda's bargain, and she hasn't returned. I might outride some, to see if I can catch wind of her,' I said.

'Fine, but wait until the morrow. We have much to discuss.' He replaced his hat and rested a hand on my shoulder. 'I've got a passel of engineers with me, including Black Donald, who's the master munitioner. He'll need to be handled with kid gloves.'

'I sent word to Sapientia and Samantha Decius, too, that we have Beleth here. I can only hope they will come soon. He is a burden.'

'Winfried?' Fisk said.

'Like some big cat, stalking around at night, hunting her prey. Had to stick a pistol in her ribs to chase her off. Inbhir and his men erected a sort of wooden shed to lock him in at night, shackled to a boulder.' I shook my head. 'I didn't sign up to be a babysitter. Beleth's face, at this point, looks parboiled. It's rubbed raw by the muzzling.'

Fisk sniffed, uncaring.

'I need to talk with Neruda about fortifications. We have a unique opportunity – we know they'll be coming. The Medierans might be distracted now with Passasuego, but they'll turn their attention this way soon enough. We must be ready.'

I nodded and beckoned Catch Hands over to fetch Neruda.

But there was no need. He appeared on the wall, soon enough, and called out. 'So, Ruman! You have come with an army. Will it keep trust and faith in our agreement?'

Fisk turned and, finding a stump, stood upon it so all could see him. He fired his Hellfire into the air and the report of the weapon echoed across the valley. The clamour of the legionnaires establishing a camp fell away, and thousands of faces turned to look at my partner.

A moment of diminution, then, where Fisk seemed to shrink, either from the weight of all those Ruman gazes upon him, or the grass laurels and bars glittering on his chest. He shrank. And then, he did that quirk of his shoulders, as if picking up a great weight, or slinging a fallen comrade over his shoulders. He squared himself, he cast doubt and fear away. And he stood straight, head high, as if all of the Hardscrabble and Occidentalia be damned.

'Fortune plays her games,' he bellowed into the afternoon air. The sun was in the west and the shadows lengthened. Mist rose from the Grenthvar land, seeping up. Yet Fisk's voice was like a roar. 'And while I wear the grass laurels and stand before you, your captain, your legate, your commander, you do not know me.'

There was a murmur in the men, the clattering of carbines, and the whisking of cloth as hundreds shifted their weight. But he had their attention.

'So, allow me to get acquainted with you. This wall,' he yelled, pointing back at the Pactum. 'This wall is sacred. It is built on the word of Rume – Rume that is no more *except in our actions*! – and it will not be violated. Not by any son of Rume, not by any Medieran whore's son. It is inviolate! Do you understand?'

There were murmurs. There were mutters.

'I require an Ia-damned verbal assent that you men understand! So help me Ia!' Fisk's voice boomed, almost impossibly loud. Maybe it was a trick of the natural structure of the valley. Maybe it was just seeing my friend in a new light, from a new angle. He tolerates Gynth. He falls in love. He has a new family. There is room to grow, even in the most calcified hearts.

A titanic multitude of voices called out, 'Yes, sir!'

Fisk bowed his head. 'Your country, your home, your trust is there, in that stone. And should any man break that trust, he will surely die.'

Silence, then. Breathing. Fisk stared at them all. Whatever issue his optios and centurions might have with their new, jumped-up commander (and they would have many), none could deny the air of menace about Fisk, the threat of his posture. And he was known in these parts – many a soldier had heard of Fiscelion Iulii, the pistolero, the man who wed the governor's daughter. If there's one thing soldiers love more than whoring and gambling, it is camp talk. And they would have spoken of him.

Fisk holstered his pistol and stepped down from the stump. He turned to look at Neruda on the wall. Neruda met his gaze with a stern inclination of his head, then he, too, stepped down and approached. From all accounts a child of rape, mixed race, a commoner and reviled (like me) by those in power in the Hardscrabble, he'd been a simple sculptor, a craftsman, a mason, until the weight of his words tipped the balance from sculptor to statesman. He carried himself with a centred assurance that would be welcome in any command, any senate or governor's chambers. He was a man who had outgrown his beginnings and risen high.

'We have fulfilled our part, we have begun mining the silver,' Neruda said. 'No son or daughter of the mountain will break faith with you as long as you do not break faith with them.'

Fisk took off his hat and brushed his greying hair from his eyes.

His stubble had matured into a beard and it was near white now, just the barest hint of pepper in a craggy field of salt.

He held up his arm, exposing the angry but healing red mark where he'd let and mingled blood with Neruda. 'You'd have me bloodless. I swore to you before and I don't feel the need to do so again.'

Neruda shrugged. 'There are no words, no blood, no outside bond that will force a man to act against his nature, and I have weighed your nature. I have taken every grain of it. You will keep your word.'

Fisk nodded. 'It's not me you have to worry about, boss,' he said.

Neruda smiled. 'The wise can laugh. The foolish walk about always serious.'

My partner scowled. 'Can we cut the poetry? There's an army out there and we need to fortify. You have maps?'

Neruda nodded.

'Well, we're a moveable feast out here, but we killed an auroch only yesterday. We're meat-heavy and well provisioned. In a short while, the command tent will be erected, camp will be struck, and I will fete you best I may and we can discuss defence. Is that acceptable?'

Neruda smiled. 'Of course. We will break bread and bring the heart, intelligence, and wisdom this land has bestowed upon us.'

'Just bring an appetite and leave poetry beyond the wall.' Fisk stopped. 'And Winfried. I want her there. And the old bag.'

'Praeverta?' Neruda asked.

'What other old bag do you have behind that wall?' Fisk asked.

'Many,' Neruda said. 'And many of them more fearful than Matve Malve.'

'Malve?' Fisk said.

'Mother Misery,' Neruda said.

It was Fisk's turn to laugh. 'On second thought, leave her home.'

Infernal Machines

*

The legionnaires established a camp in record time, away from the Pactum Wall, among the trees wreathing the valley. The gambels and pines began to fall, rapidly, and sooty, creosote-thick smoke from fires began rising to the heavens.

Ruman soldiers are a nation on the hoof – their food, their arms, their gods, their traditions, they drag with and behind them like a comet cutting through the sky, pulling a bright tail of star stuff behind them. The war vehicles ratcheted to a stop, and the wagons and vardos with them. The lictors, priests, and engineers disembarked from their various carriages, the numerous chow bucks pulled into where the legionnaires were marking the future streets and thoroughfares in the camp that would eventually become a small town, if the future held promise. So many things we do for an uncertain future.

A great mechanised water wagon, much like the two clattering armoured wagons, chuffed up, belching smoke. Hanging all about the beast of a machine were smiths, and junior munitioners, and engineer apprentices smiling and hooting, too young for serious-ness and not under the auspices of the Bull or Wolf banners, free to be excited at the prospect of war and too inexperienced to know better.

The praetorium tent was raised like a blister on a thumb after snatching a hot iron, and just as quickly – planks laid, canvas unrolled, ash struts and poles put in place, centre spike raised, and hemp holding it down. Something that always amazed me, the efficiency of the Ruman camp.

Daemon lanterns were strewn about, as the sun had passed beyond the rim of earth. The western sky was bruised pink and purple, magnificent and sad; Harbour Town still smouldered in the west, even months later. Some *daemonfire* burns so hot even stone turns molten.

We gathered in the praetorium tent with Fisk's junior legates, younger sons of Ruman nobility left behind with Marcellus' foray east – to a boy, they all looked uncomfortable heeding his commands, though they dashed about fetching wine and bread and olives and cheese. The real work of camp orders and warfare was left to the optios and legate secretaries – most of them young men with bright minds and the patterns of correspondence and bureaucracy memorised. The main command tables were set and soon Neruda appeared with an armful of rolled maps, followed by Winfried and Praeverta and no one else.

'Hello, Winfried,' Fisk said. 'You look well. How is your arm?'
She glanced at me and back to Fisk.

I'd left Catch Hands watching Beleth with a pistol and a dagger. Gynth was nearby, waiting for me to bring him meat from the shoal auroch Fisk had mentioned but he'd said, with a shrug, 'You tarry late, I will find my own auroch.' This he said in the common tongue, which surprised me to no end and made Catch Hands laugh. *Vaettir* were quick to learn, quick to adapt. Quick in all things.

Catch Hands pointed at the *vaettir* and said, 'Could I dash about with your speed, I would accompany you.'

Gynth just looked at him blankly. 'My shoulders are broad and you are small,' Gynth had said. He added, 'But no bit or bridle will touch me. I will carry thee as my own sweet babe,' rising to the formal *dvergar*. Catch Hands laughed and hopped up, dusting his britches.

'Only after our parley with Neruda,' said I. They had both looked at me, chagrined.

Now, Winfried, for her part, gave a small bow, common to Malfenians. Hands flat on her sides, so formal. Back straight. The Ruman bow was so much silkier, so much more fluid. Maybe this is because of the Malfenian incestuous embrace. When you're fucking your sister, if there's not a great amount of formality, soon you'll be thrusting away at all your relatives. I'm ashamed to admit I've pondered the Malfenian situation more than probably is healthy.

Anyway, Winfried had found her suit, and it had been brushed smooth and removed of natty bolls, but she spared the hat and had let her hair down. She looked quite lovely.

I understood her urges, the currents that ripped at the river of her soul. Her love had died. Her brother. So many brothers lost, Livia and Carnelia's, too. Winfried wanted revenge. We all want for revenge on this monster of a world.

'I'm glad you can join us,' Fisk said, gesturing for her to find a seat. He snapped at one of his staff and a young secretary scuttled forward with a tray of wine and water. 'You've always had very keen insights, and I'm glad of your input.' He turned and gave a half-bow to Praeverta, saying, 'And you, Matve, welcome. Your experience and wisdom is a gift.'

Praeverta seemed discomposed by the kindness and flattery. She puckered her lips. 'You clean up, nice, don't you, lad,' she said, looking Fisk up and down. He'd washed his face and changed from his riding leathers and pistolero garb into the white tunic and blue trousers of the Ruman legionnaires. His grey hair was swept back from his face and the natural handsomeness of the man allowed to show. Raw-boned and rangy, but in our time together there'd been many a woman, high-born and low, who had made doe-eyes at Fisk.

'Is it possible,' Neruda said, softly, 'that Mister Fiscelion is like the Grenthvar himself, possessed of depths and hidden reserves, welcoming to all who come near, Matve?'

She sniffed. 'I've spent time with the man. It's doubtful.'

Fisk laughed. A rare thing and always an honest one. 'Praeverta strikes near the mark, I'm afraid,' Fisk said, and gestured to a table. Neruda approached and unrolled the maps. 'I have been unfettered for so long, the legate's laurels and bars are a tether I've not got used to. I am good at the killing of men. I'm ill-suited to the leading of them.'

'Earnestness is a foundation for all aspiration. If your people cannot feel your honesty, and what *you* aspire to, they cannot follow you.' He looked over Fisk. 'I do not think that will be your problem.'

'No,' Fisk said, unrolling maps. 'My problem will be Medierans.' He chose one of the larger maps and weighted down the edges with *daemonlight* lanterns. 'How accurate is this?'

'I drew it when we first heard of Rume's interest in this area,' Neruda said. 'We scouted extensively.'

'Is there access to the valley from the east? Through the Eldvatch?' Fisk asked.

'Unless they know our warrens and passages through the mines, no,' Neruda answered. 'The sons and daughters of the mountain, alone, know those ways.'

Fisk nodded, frowning. I knew him well enough that I did not need to ask to know his displeasure – already the agreement to not pass the Pactum Wall was rankling. He could not personally ascertain the reliability of his perimeter. He would have to trust to Neruda for that.

'The edges of the valley, this ridge here,' Fisk said, jabbing a finger at the map and running the length of the dark mark on the parchment. 'Is it impassable?'

'For cavalry, yes. For infantry, no,' Winfried said. 'With Neruda's permission, I have made a personal assessment of the mines, the mountains, and the valley. No Medieran will approach from the east, so we have a solid wall at which to place our backs. The West is wide open and will need to be heavily fortified. To the north and south, on those ridges, it will be very difficult to take us unaware. Should they attempt it, their losses will be heavy. If we take suitable precautions.'

Fisk looked at Winfried, with a tight smile. 'This is good. Your word is one I can trust,' he said.

'And mine is not?' Neruda responded, grinning.

'I did not—' Fisk began.

'Why was I not summoned to this parley?' A booming voice came from the tent entrance. We all turned as one to face him. A grizzled, sloppy man, barrel-chested and wearing a scorched apron over sooty clothing. He had a wide, blunt face and a mouth that could take in a draught horse's hoof, if one would be kind enough to kick him there.

No one else noticed that Fisk's hand went to his hip. But I did. It was his Hellfire he reflexively went to at the sound of the man's voice. If this was but two years ago, on the streets of Passasuego or New Damnation, Fisk might've shot him, had he been addressed in such a way. But today, Fisk (finding that he was not wearing a gun) forced himself to give a quick bow and say, 'Princeps Engineer, Donalind Vemus.' Fisk turned to Neruda. 'Lovingly referred to by the legions as "Black Donald".'

Black Donald's meaty face split open in a grin. 'That's right. And the men, they love me, do they not, Lord Commander?'

Fisk's shoulders hitched up, as if fending off a blow. After a moment, they relaxed.

'The Ruman soldier loves not words but action, Vemus,' Fisk said. 'And soldiers love Hellfire. In this way you are adored.'

'Very prettily done, upjack.' Black Donald stumped up to the table. He was built like a bull and moved like one, too. He glared at one of Fisk's staffers and bellowed, '*Wine!*' The lad looked to Fisk, who nodded, indicating the boy should fetch Black Donald his own bottle. 'And who're these lovelies?' he asked, ogling Praeverta and Winfried.

'This is Neruda, the leader of the *dvergar* indigines. To his right is Dveng Ilys—'

'Don't care about the short half-breeds,' Black Donald said. 'Just the split-tail.'

'Mister Vemus,' Fisk said. 'Are you trying to make enemies?'

Black Donald gave a double-take. 'What?' he asked, truly confused. 'No, man. But I've got priorities, Ia help me.' He sighed and nodded to Neruda and myself in turn. 'Gentlemen,' he murmured. He turned and approached Winfried and took her hand, raised it to his mouth and kissed it. He did the same to Praeverta.

'Careful with that one, sir,' I said. 'She'll gut you as soon as kiss you.'

The old woman cast me a disgusted look. 'Shut your trap, *dimidius*,' she said. 'Before you start catching flies.' To Black Donald, she said, 'A pleasure.' And damn me if she didn't smile at the burly man and let her blue-veined hand linger as he brought it to his lips.

When the munitioner was through, he clapped his hands and said, 'So, my smelt? My production area? Where are we with them and how soon will they be ready for me? I have but a single silver pig, and binding the furnace *daemon* will require at least half of that. So?' He looked around expectantly at Fisk and Neruda.

Fisk beckoned him over to the map and they began discussions. Praeverta and Winfried poured glasses of wine and joined them. I took my leave, since much of the disposition of the smelt and workshop I already knew. After checking with Catch Hands, I saddled Bess, and rode out, east toward where the Grenthvar dog-legged south and the trees fell away to grass and then scrub-brush and bramblewrack. The Hardscrabble. The far eastern edge of it. I found a vantage on a rise and rode to it while the last light of the sunset still hung above and the stars came out.

I let my eyes adjust to the growing gloom, looking for the scout outriders; Lina, Seanchae, Vrinthi. The best scouts of Praeverta's cadre.

But they were not to be seen. After a moment, I realised that Gynth was there with me, looking westward. He'd stolen up on me without my knowledge. Had it been any other *vaettir* – *Any other? Or most other? Were they all so dissimilar from Gynth?* – I might've been dead now. He looked at me and said, in common speech, 'The waiting is the hardest part.'

I laughed. Gynth blinked. Then he laughed too.

'You're an odd fellow, Gynth. We make a fine brace of outsiders, do we not?'

'Always on the outside, looking in. Always on the inside, looking out,' he said in *dvergar*. It was some sort of joke, I assumed, because he seemed especially pleased with himself for making it. Then he said, 'Look there. Riders.'

The sky had taken on the deep hues of coming night, smeared with great swatches of colour – orange and purple and pink. The clouds looked like rock salt, striated and craggy, moving like behemoths across the plains of the sky. The riders seemed tiny against the vastness of heaven, shoal plain, and horizon.

It took them a long while to come into view, but when they did, I knew it was not my *dvergar* scouts. Not Lina.

When they drew near enough, Samantha said, 'Take me to Beleth.' Sapientia, riding behind her, looked at me and raised an eyebrow.

'Now,' Samantha said.

Her face was awful.

EIGHTEEN

It Is Time We Changed The Game

FROM BEATICÆ AND beyond, the *Typhon* steamed full speed ahead. I gave blood when Ysmay asked for it, which was infrequently. Tenebrae and Carnelia spent most of whatever free time they had in the sun above, working their strange *armatura* – that peculiar martial training they had learned from Sun Huáng in Kithai. Back and forth they struck at each other, like dancers feinting. Carnelia's legs looked strong, sleek and muscular, and she laid waste to our rations. Lupina, when she separated herself from Fiscelion, ended up at the stern of the *Typhon* letting out line from a spool on a metal spike, trailing a flat, flashing metal oblong disc with a sharpened hook she called her 'spoon' and contented herself with watching the wake of our passing.

We did not take much notice of her, or her odd pastime, until she cried out and bellowed for help. Tenebrae rushed over, hooting madly, and together they wrestled with the line, winding it in, until on the deck whipped a thrashing silverfish, flashing in the sunlight, leaking blood from its many-toothed mouth. Carnelia brained it with her wooden *armatura* sword until it stopped moving. Lupina produced a knife and immediately gutted the creature and tossed the offal overboard.

That night, at least, we ate fresh. Soon, there was less *armatura*.

Tenebrae and Carnelia joined Lupina at the stern, letting out their own lines.

It was two weeks since we last sighted land and the sea began to rise while the skies grew dark. Ysmay, when he came above deck, looked worried and wan and far too thin. We'd continued plying him with rum, when we could, in hopes of increasing his appetite, but the man grew wasted, thin, and harried. He'd done what he could to repair the front deck gun, which was a loss. Without the breech cover and the bore plug, the sea water had eaten away at the internal mechanisms so much that it had become unusable. 'Wet-mount guns require grease and constant maintenance,' Ysmay had said. 'And neither was in my purview. But if the *Typhon* is to have teeth, she'll need constant care.' But he managed to make it watertight.

The rear deck gun still functioned. Tenebrae and Carnelia took it upon themselves to maintain the remaining swivel, spending hours on each, slathering the inoperable gun with grease and making sure the shrouding was tight as possible. For the working swivel, their labours included greasing treads, inspecting bore warding, and in general worshipping the more bellicose aspects of our floating world.

'I fear our first storm draws near,' Ysmay said, when I joined him in the command centre.

'It seems that way. Seas are high and the clouds nigh,' I responded. The man looked agitated, disturbed.

'It will be my first storm at open sea,' he said, blinking.

'Oh. Do not fear,' I said. 'Your vessel, though small, is as well prepared for a storm as any ship I've ever been on. Should it get bad, I think we just fasten the hatches and descend beneath the foam.'

This did not sit well with Ysmay. The idea of being submerged during a storm discomposed him. Possibly it was his mental state, in general. Possibly his fear of the great salt expanse of sea. I could not say. It was as if we had more faith in his abilities and creation than he did himself. Nonetheless, he was in high fettle and, it appeared, a great need to talk filled him.

'I must show you something, should I not make it until our journey's end,' he said.

'Please, don't say such things, Mister Ysmay. On my honour you will find no hazard from—'

'No,' he said. 'That is not it. I've always been sickly, since I was a child, and I feel—' He stopped and said no more for a long while.

I waited, silently. He would speak when he would speak and not before.

'I feel that sickness again, much to my chagrin,' he said, looking at me earnestly with liquid blue eyes. 'I hope I have shown you the operations of the *Typhon* to your satisfaction?'

'Yes! You have been a marvellous teacher. I feel as though I could steer the ship myself. I know Tenebrae and Carnelia feel the same.'

He gave a quick, insincere smile that did not reach his eyes. 'I've something else to show you. I had hoped it would not be necessary but . . .'

'But?' I asked.

'The eyes of the world are on the West, if everything you've told me is true. There is silver there, and—'

'The world wars on silver,' said I, quoting the old adage.

'And for it,' Ysmay said. 'Many times I have wished for a greater supply. The things I could have created with a workshop and a silver pig.'

'So what is it you wish to show me?'

He walked from the command and I followed him, forward, past our berths. He stopped before the end of the passage, where the lascars' berth was. Bending, he reached down to the grate and, with a heave and screech of metal, lifted it up. There were metal steps down, into a small opening covered with a hatch, which Ysmay unlocked and opened. Beyond, pitch dark.

He descended and I followed. Soon the space below was filled with *daemonlight* from unshuttered lanterns.

It was a small, cramped chamber that ended in front of us but dashed back down the length of the *Typhon,* this too with a grated floor. Yet, below the grate, in this space, was dark water. I could hear it sloshing. In it stood racks and racks of what appeared to be scaled miniatures of the *Typhon,* each one a pointed cylinder with fins and propellers, but upon closer inspection, they more resembled Hellfire rounds. Warded and deadly.

'They call them *armamare,* but the lascars just refer to them as seashots. They are *daemon*-propelled missiles that shoot forth below the waterline and follow a path one point off the port or starboard bow,' Ysmay said. He looked downtrodden, as if this was something he'd rather not be saying.

'I can understand why you would keep this from us, since you did not know our motives or affiliations,' I said.

'Bringing you here was always necessary, if only to show you the bilge,' he said. 'There's a delicate balance here, the counterweights of flotation, the ballast, and the trim tanks. Too much bilge water disrupts these systems for submersion.' At my look of confusion, Ysmay waved his hand, dismissing his previous words. 'None of these things are necessary to understand except that on occasion, the bilge must be flushed. Let me show you.'

He brought me back, toward the rear of the chamber, underneath where the command and navigational chamber was. There was a small radiant star with an eye at its centre engraved in the ceiling, marking the point where the Miraculous was, I could only assume. There was a panel where quite a few runners of piping came to meet. There were levers there, each one with an engraved icon above it: one, a long nose; the next, a bare bottom; another, a figure of a man with one haunch lifted from a bench, with a bit of smoke emerging from his arse, farting; yet another with a figure of a man vomiting.

'Why the colourful markings over the levers, Mister Ysmay?' I asked.

'Lascars. The ones that *can* read don't remain lascars long enough to have to pull levers. The others? They need colourful iconography.' He placed his hand upon the lever beneath the vomiting man and pulled it. 'If we went above, to the aft, you'd see the *Typhon* evacuating the bilge into the Occidens.'

'Thank you,' I said. 'This is good to know.'

'Let us load the *armamare*, so that you will know how to fire them,' he said.

'The shells seem even larger than the deck gun munitions,' said I.

'They are, considerably, since they have to propel themselves through water. In each munition are bound two *daemons*. One harnessed for propulsion, the other for a more, let us say, incendiary effect. Extremely deadly. However, as always, the main weapons of the *Typhon* are the deck guns. Or, the remaining one,' he said. 'And one more thing. Had I not been so discomposed when you... when you commandeered the ship... I might have remembered.'

He led me even further aft, where two racks of many deadly metal spheres lay in rows, each one intricately warded on the steel banding, with smaller parts crafted of wood and blown glass.

'*Munusculum*,' he said, giving a wan smile. 'Our little gift.' He placed a hand on one of them and looked at me. 'They are for pursuers. Both the *armamare* and *munuscula* require blood to be initialised. Cut your palm, and slap it here—' There was an evil ring of concentric silver warding and a tiny glowing hole. 'Place the orb in this,' he said, and pulling a lever on a circular port set into the wall, swung it open. He lifted a *munusculum* and placed it in the chamber, very gingerly, so as not to mar the warding. He closed the opening and pulled shut the locking mechanism. 'From here you can release it, or from the navigation "centre" above. An outer door will open and the sea will flood in the chamber and the *munusculum* will float out and into our wake, there to wait for whomever or whatever follows.' He tapped a part of the blown glass. 'If there is blood, and the glass breaks – say, from the impact of a following ship – there will be a great explosion and if the *munusculum* does not destroy the pursuers' ship, it will give them serious pause. Possibly even make them re-evaluate their motives for pursuit.' He gave a tight smile. 'Do you understand?'

'Yes,' I said. Conflicting emotions warred within me. Happiness for knowing the full extent of the *Typhon*'s armaments. Fear and awe at knowing the extent, as well. 'I have seen the destruction *daemons* can wreak on land, and at sea, Mister Ysmay.'

'The *armamare* work in the same fashion. It will take one, or even two of us to lift them, but there is a convenient mechanism – a trundle – for moving them.'

For the next hour he drilled me on the priming and usage of the *Typhon*'s hidden armaments. When we were done, he sighed and rubbed his face.

'Mister Ysmay,' I said. 'Because of our delicate relationship—' He winced at these words. I charged ahead, without thinking overmuch. 'I have abstained from issuing direct orders to you. But I have had a change of heart on that score.' I placed my hand on his shoulder and was gratified when he did not pull away from my touch. 'I order you to take two generous pours of rum and sleep for eight hours. The seas are growing higher and higher, the skies darken, and we might need you desperately and in top condition. So rest.'

He said nothing, but bowed his head. We returned to the upper world of the *Typhon* in silence.

*

The seas grew green-grey, frothed at each summit, moving mountains of brine and foam. Ysmay increased the *Typhon*'s speed, so that we cut through the water like a dolphin dancing upon waves. From the prow came huge billows of spray, rising high in the air and dousing the deck. Tenebrae and Carnelia slathered both deck guns in grease, cocooned them in oiled tarp and taut ropes, and fled for the relative dry safety of the command. We closed and fastened the hatches, tight. Our only views of the world were the prow portholes and the deck gun and command's Miraculous.

The *Typhon* felt as a toy in the hands of a mercurial and mischievous child, always shifting, inconstant. Carnelia grew green and cursed us and dashed to the head.

We had weathered storms in the *Malphas*, and were no strangers to life aboard seagoing vessels. The storms in the Nous and beyond, near Kithai, had been titanic. But there was something of this storm that dwarfed even those. I went to the front of the *Typhon*, to the berth that Lupina and I shared with Fiscelion, and peered through the thick glass porthole.

It was a view of intermittent foams and benthic gloom, then terrifying vistas of slate-grey waves and low-slung clouds, with curtains of rain. We would hang in the air, far above the trench of sea, perched on the wave summit, the *Typhon*'s engines whining, pitching upward as the screws came out of the water. Then we'd fall, the *Typhon*'s nose tilting toward the deep, and the screws would catch, the ship would surge forward, and like a needle burying itself in flesh, our ship would dive, dive deep into the Occidens, until it rose once again.

Hours upon hours we bore this, the world in constant upheaval and uncertainty. It was as if the events of the last year were distilled to their essence, and our immediate surroundings became their expression. Their art. Their culmination. Fiscelion seemed to be not bothered by it at all, though I daresay he grew tired of our storm-malaise and being prevented from crawling about above deck. At some point, I slept, though the slumber was fitful as occasionally when the ship fell, my body would rise away from the mattress and then slam back down. But with each soft impact, I would find myself in a watery dreamscape.

I did not dream of Fisk much, any more. Or the Hardscrabble. Or my father. My dreams were immediate – adrift in a skiff, wondering where my son was, straining at the oars, my back bent to the sea. Lightless sinking in a steel coffin, a soft impact and knowing I was in the deep, alone. Swimming in Salonica, surrounded by silverfish, my mother frantic on the shore. I dreamed of Albinus, and Regulus, and Ysmay; giving orders in the *Typhon*'s command, drenched in blood.

We came out of the other side of the storm to luxurious cerulean skies and calm seas.

Carnelia and Tenebrae tended the deck guns – as they did with every submersion – greasing and buffing it. Lupina caught silverfish and red tunny, sharks and grindal. We ate well and drank the ship's wine. Fiscelion crawled with assurance, not so unsteady, saying 'Rume, Rume, Rume,' and other childish babble. Finally, he said, ' 'Pina! 'Pina!' And Lupina snatched him up and kissed him all over.

Land hove into view. We spent a long time staring at the impenetrable shoreline – thick with massive trees and huddled with moss and bramble between them – inhaling the scent of land and breathing, leafy things even standing offshore. We'd had a month of salt seas and spray in the air, and nothing else. In this way, the ocean is much like the desert, devoid of life for the most part. Occidentalia is rich in trees and wildlife and we knew we were near just by scenting the air, before we saw the ink stroke of land on the horizon. As we moved north, other ships, some Ruman, some unidentifiable but definitely warlike, came into view. Ysmay, frantic, let blood for Typhon. Racing back into the command, he changed course and pressed the throttle fully forward. It took hours, but we outpaced pursuit.

When it was obvious we were not going to engage with ships or have to deal with continued pursuit, Ysmay collapsed into the helm chair, and shook. His hands would not keep still.

'Are you all right?' I asked. 'You seem unwell.'

'Nothing, ma'am,' he said. 'Just a touch of nerves.'

'You'll be right as rain with a salad and a bath,' Carnelia said, slapping his shoulder. He did not react at all to this familiarity. 'I would gut a man right now for some fresh spinach dressed in oil and vinegar. And new cheese,' she added.

'All of that soon enough, sissy. Mister Ysmay,' I said, 'I'm happy to relieve you of duty so you may rest.'

'No!' he said. 'No. I can't leave *Typhon* now—'

'Leave? I simply want you to rest,' I said.

He shook his head. 'Not yet. Not until I know she'll ... *we'll* be safe.'

'Your loyalty is commendable, Mister Ysmay. Yet, I fear you need—'

'Soon! I promise,' he said, looking at me. The look of a beggar's desperation. 'Soon.'

I nodded. The hard truth of it was Ysmay steered and manipulated the *Typhon* far better than I did, those times I had the helm. Or Carnelia or Tenebrae. He had an affinity with the ship: it was his creation, his ward, his care. He knew its secrets and foibles and peccadilloes.

A small fishing village at the mouth of a marshy river came in view late in the afternoon, and we decided to find out where we were in relation to Novorum. There, we could assess the situation in the Hardscrabble and either take a baggage-train west or remain on the *Typhon* and use it to take us to the Bay of Mageras and the western territories.

South of Sulla, at the outflow of the Weald River. The village of Okrefor offered us fresh fish, mussels, slaughtered lamb, corn-cakes, eel, carrots, onions, greens and molasses, all of which Tenebrae purchased with the considerable amount of money I had remaining from my father's safe. The stevedores, porters, and wharf master were amazed at the sleek lines and evil look of the *Typhon*, with many questions. But Tenebrae waved them off, intimating that we were on official Ruman business, which, I think, was not totally a lie. Carnelia and I were once again dressed as lascars (though she'd never stopped, really).

When Tenebrae pulled out the money bag, I couldn't help but think of my father. As a girl, asking him for treats in the Cælian streets, hand out, one sesterius, two sestersii, for shaved ice. Sometimes, out of the blue, I'm reminded, when Fiscelion is feeling ornery and non-compliant, of my father's obstinacy and drunkenness, his bright moods and his vicious humour. I feel some happiness that he left this world having at least held Fiscelion.

We took on water and sailed north without lingering, as much as we all would have loved to spend a night in beds with clean linens and eiderdown pillows. The last time we'd seen these waters, I'd been recently separated from my husband and my belly was just beginning to show, and we'd stood on the edge of the land and sea and boarded the *Malphas* that took us to Far Tchinee. Seagulls wheeled in the sky, then, and the bay was whipped high as the skiffs and jackadaws passed before us on the face of the sea.

But it was night this time. Two days hard steaming north, off the coast far enough that we'd have no dangers running aground on unknown obstacles, and we came within sight of Novorum glittering in the night, its lights reflecting off the waters of Viridi Bay. We hung a red-filtered *daemonlight* lantern up on the prow, indicating we wished to dock, and the wharf master brought a green-lit skiff out to meet us. However, when it drew near, a horn sounded, and bells began ringing, and the wharf master's ship unbanked more *daemonlights* and turned back to shore.

Tenebrae, in his captain's mummery, yelled, 'We're found out!' He raced for the gunner's roost, and the speaking device there. 'Word has travelled across the sea!' he said into the funnel.

There was no response immediately from Ysmay, below. I took the receiver from Tenebrae. 'Turn the ship, sir! Now,' I said. 'Turn and full speed.'

'*Yes, Ma'am,*' Ysmay said. But it was delayed and weak.

'Carnelia,' I said. 'Go below and make sure all is well with Ysmay,' I said. Carnelia nodded grimly and stalked off.

Lights bloomed on the bay, big mirror-backed *daemonlights*. Warships. Beyond them, there was some commotion on the wharfs, and the flickering light of fire. Klaxons beat at the air.

'Is all this just for us?' Tenebrae asked.

'I don't know, but I do not want to wait around to find out,' I said. 'Open sea. Now!' Tenebrae dashed over to the speaking horn and repeated the order. I could hear its tinny echo, faintly, as if it reverberated through the metal of the hull.

'*Understood! I've got him,*' Carnelia said, her voice buzzing through the communication device's amplification horn. '*He's preoccupied with the Miraculous and steering. Aren't you, Mister Ysmay?*' She sounded somewhat pissy, as only Carnelia could.

The *Typhon* picked up speed, throwing great spumes of water to each side of the ship. Tenebrae moved forward, removed the red *daemonlight* lantern, and banked the light. For a moment, all was quiet except for the sirens diminishing in the distance. Behind us, ships moved, but slowly. We turned our eyes to the front, hearts sinking at finding Novorum unwelcome to us.

There was a flash of light ahead, illuminating the bay like a lightning flash, revealing the waters in stark relief – silvered waves, the tongue of land lashing out from the west and ending halfway across our eye line, and the dark forms that appeared to be rocks jutting out of the water before us.

'Ships!' Tenebrae yelled. 'Ships!' The massive report of a gun echoed across the water. It was overwhelming – more than Hellfire, more than percussive waves of sound. It was engulfing, massive. I could feel the *Typhon* vibrate, and my insides felt almost as if they'd been liquefied.

The light rose on a column of ash and arced in the sky, overhead, like a great torch, revealing everything in the bay as if it was high noon. A new sun passing overhead.

Another flash of light, another incandescent rising light arced across the sky.

Tenebrae turned to me. 'I do not think it was us they were worried about, Livia,' he said.

The first light fell westward, falling like a star trapped in molasses. But as it fell, it increased in brightness and speed. And then it disappeared beyond the horizon, the buildings of the wharf, the blocks of tenements and houses of industry, the shipyards, the wharfs and warehouses. For a moment it seemed like a candle snuffed in water.

When it came, the explosion blinded me. I knew what it was to have *angelis* fever, to have one's eyes burned. An instant of terror, as the fireball grew, the sound expanding with it. Then Tenebrae's hands were on me, forcing me to the hatch, and inside the *Typhon*, as he closed and fastened the door behind us and bellowed for Ysmay to descend.

Novorum burned. We passed through the Medieran fleet, scourged to the outer banks, slinking away and hoping no one witnessed our passing. The Medieran ships, over fifty strong and mostly frigates and warships, had stationed themselves in a blockade to cordon off the coast – a net to catch any Ruman ships that weren't scuttled, while the bulk of the fleet bombarded Novorum, the seat of Ruman power in the West.

'They've been three steps ahead of us this whole time,' Carnelia said.

'They are a sea people,' Tenebrae said. 'And do not place nobles in command without having earned it.' He raised empty hands as he said it.

'It is time we changed the game,' I said. 'Mister Ysmay, take Mister Tenebrae forward and load two of the *armamare* please.'

He looked bewildered and wild-eyed. 'But— But— We can't destroy them all!'

'We do not need to,' I said. My eyes still watered. 'The biggest ship. Where the first missile emanated from,' I said. 'We target that one. And that ship only.'

'But why?' Ysmay said. 'It will only put us in more danger and do very little against the Medierans.'

'I disagree, sir,' I said. 'First, it will make them suddenly fearful. Second, it will distract them from their current occupation, namely using that Ia-forsaken artillery against Novorum.'

Ysmay blinked in the *daemonlight* of command. He put his face to the Miraculous, and turned the device about. Reaching out, he pulled back on the throttle and the thrumming of the engines diminished. 'What if they spot us?'

'They will not,' I said. I walked toward the bulkhead and placed my hand on the cold metal there. 'And I have full faith in this amazing machine, Mister Ysmay. It brought us across the sea, did it not?'

'Yes,' he said, brightening. 'Yes it did!'

'But we will fire on them not because of the ship, or for a distraction, or to make them afraid,' I said. 'We will fire on them because no one makes war upon Rume without reprisal. And *I am of Rume.*'

The words hung in the air. After a moment, Ysmay said, 'Keep this course, ma'am, keep the main Medieran warship on this point – you see it?'

'Yes,' I said, peering into the Miraculous. The glass had degrees notated. 'I understand.'

'Those two marks, make sure the *Typhon* remains on either of those. I will return soon. Mister Tenebrae?'

They went forward. All was silent, but down the hallway I could hear Fiscelion babbling, 'Rume, *Rume, Rume,* 'Pina. RUME.'

Carnelia placed her hand on my arm. 'Are you sure this is wise, sissy?'

'No,' I said. 'But I'll be damned if we slink away, toothless.'

My sister smiled. 'Good! Let us leave them shaken. They'll not burn our city without spilling some blood.'

We clasped forearms, and then realised how ridiculous this posturing was, hugged each other as we always had. I kissed her cheek and when I pulled away, I could see the tears welling in her eyes.

'I'm scared, Livia,' she said. 'Tata's dead. The world's gone to shite. What is going to happen to us?'

'We keep going, sissy. We find Fisk.' I gave a maniacal laugh. 'We are wanted by two, maybe three nations now, we have a near magical and deadly machine at our disposal, and there is war. We have a baby!' I said, and the absurdity of it crashed on me. I was hazarding my child. 'We destroy this one ship, and in the carnage and disarray, we push through to open sea. It's a solid plan. As good as running silently.'

She was silent for a long while, holding my arms and looking at me. Finally, she nodded. 'All right,' she said. 'Would that I could just have at them with my *jian*.'

197

'Circumstances have become more complicated than that,' I said.

'They shouldn't have to be.'

'No, they shouldn't have to be,' I agreed.

She looked thoughtful and drew me aside. She whispered, 'When I came down, Ysmay had abandoned his post and was going to his berth.'

'He— He what?' I said, amazed.

'I caught him there,' she said, pointing to the hatch that led to the forward half of the *Typhon*, the sleeping berths, deck gun controls, and mess. The *armamare*.

'He seemed utterly dismayed. He was weeping,' she said.

'He's under great stress,' I said. 'And hasn't rested. Do you think it was a malicious abandonment?'

'No,' Carnelia said. 'He didn't seem like he'd been caught out, when I stopped him. He just seemed – hurt? Yes, wounded, like a dog going to lick its wounds.'

'I worry about his state of mind, truly,' I said.

Tenebrae and Ysmay returned. Tenebrae wrapped his hand with a towel, having let blood to prime the sub-aquatic weapons. Ysmay took position at the navigation. I took my place at the trigger for the *armamare* – it is the duty of command to judge, sentence, and execute punishment. For better or worse, I was in command.

The engineer edged the throttle up. The *Typhon* picked up speed.

'We fire upon the warship,' I said, 'We pass through and make full speed to open sea.'

'Yes,' Ysmay said. He was pale, shaking, sweating. 'Understood. Approaching. Stand ready to fire.'

Long moments passed. The *Typhon* shuddered with speed.

'Stand ready,' he said, again.

'I am ready, Mister Ysmay,' I said.

'Fire!'

I pulled the firing mechanism.

I felt more than heard the *Typhon* shift and the *armamare* release. Ysmay stepped away from the Miraculous, and gestured that I should look. I placed my face to the glass. The night was lit with wavering light, the Medieran vessels closer now. There were aggressive-looking munitions on each ship's profile, and another flash and bloom, so bright I had to look away from the ocular and wait until the flare diminished. But this time, it was not Medieran artillery. It was Medieran destruction.

The ship erupted into expanding metallic vapour, the sea rose in anger at the grievous wound done it. It was not that the *armamare* was so deadly, it was but a match tossed onto tinder.

The warship took two other Medieran vessels with it as it quickly vacated this plane of existence. In its wake, a giant wave came rushing at us.

'Mister Ysmay,' I said, as calmly as I could. 'We should descend now as far as we can. A wave approaches.'

He looked at me, alarmed by my calm tone. He did not argue or question, he simply manipulated the controls. The nose of the *Typhon* pitched downward. My view in the Miraculous became occluded and disappeared altogether. The hull ticked and groaned.

A shudder passed through the ship. A bright metallic sound rang out, there was a explosive rush of steam into the command. Suddenly it was hot and wet and every surface beaded with moisture.

Ysmay dashed back and, pulling out a rag, began turning a valve with great haste. The steam dissipated.

He rushed back to the com, pulled more levers. The *Typhon* levelled. It rose.

In the Miraculous, the sea was once more in view. We passed among debris and wreckage. Something scraped our side in an aquatic screech.

And then all was silent. I wrenched the Miraculous around to find the other Medieran vessels. Some were capsized. Others continued to fire upon Novorum. None seemed to be in pursuit.

We were beyond the blockade.

I looked to the engineer. He remained pale and trembling. A pained expression on his face.

'Make haste to open sea, Mister Ysmay. Full speed,' I said.

By morning we were far out to sea, with no pursuit. We turned south, intent on making the southern cape, running the Medieran blockade there, and entering the Bay of Mageras. From there, we might take the *Typhon* up the Big Rill, past the ruins of Harbour Town, to New Damnation. Marcellus and his legions would be there. And, maybe, my husband and heart.

I instructed Ysmay to rest as I manned the helm. He seemed relieved and thanked me, bowing and nodding. He stumbled to his berth.

I would not set eyes upon him alive again.

A day later, we found his body in his berth, pooled in blood.

NINETEEN

My Name Was Linneus

SAMANTHA AND SAPIENTIA brought hard news. Passasuego was lost. New Damnation was lost. Mediera owned the Hardscrabble once more, as it did a century and a half ago, at least in the day. At night, stretchers came to the lowlands, raiding, killing, taking whatever they pleased. No more dreaming in their high reaches. No more slumberous days of peace and winds upon the shoals. War came, naked and bloody, and the *vaettir* came from the mountains to greet it.

I took the engineers and their retinue – consisting of seven women and men in engineer's aprons – to the tent where Fisk conferred with Neruda.

'The lode is rich, then?' Samantha asked on the way there. 'Yielding good ore?'

'It's nice seeing you again, too, Sam,' I said.

'Ah, Shoe,' Samantha said. 'I never thought you needed pleasantries.'

'I don't,' I said. 'But it *is* nice to see you.'

She'd aged, more and more. The weight of our great struggle – against Beleth, against Mediera, against the Hardscrabble and the West, and even against those that came from beyond the veil – it had weighed heavy on her. She was so thin, now, her skin hung off her. She'd been plump, once, with a great appetite, when she

201

was Beleth's assistant. Now? Her clothes hung loosely, her skin in wattles on her arms and neck. Her face was wrinkled.

'For my part, I am happy to see you, Mister Ilys,' Sapientia said, eyes merry.

'And I, you,' I said. 'Very happy.' Sapientia was a handsome woman, and formidable. Her hair was maybe a bit greyer than when I last saw her, but her supremely intelligent face was still beautiful. Had I been just a few feet taller, I might find something there in her smile. Something more. But at least her friendship was mine, and that was a treasure.

I turned back to Samantha. 'It's coughing up piles of rocks, if that's what you mean? The smelt and the rest of the mechanics of rendering silver have not been put into place, nor any munitions. But there's great heaping piles of rocks and dirt they tell me are mostly silver,' I said.

Samantha nodded, chewing her lip. 'That's good, at least. Passasuego is lost, but it's not fatal, since the lode there was petering out.'

'We'll pass the ore piles on the way to Fisk,' I said.

'Good,' Samantha said. 'I would see them.'

'And Beleth? He is contained?' Sapientia said.

I quickly told her the events of the Long Slide and our capture of him.

'*Daemon*-gripped *vaettir*,' she said. 'I thought that was a calamity. But a Beleth-gripped *vaettir*? That is the worst.'

'He'll not be doing much more gripping,' I said. 'Fisk shortened him a hand.'

Samantha snorted, as if startled, and then smiled for the first time since I'd seen her. 'Oh, my. Well that is justice for that poor girl, Isabelle. Would that she'd never met that Bantam fellow.'

'We'd all be spared this lovely war, then, Miss Samantha,' I said.

'I am no statesman, nor politician, but I think this war was coming, one way or another. I wish the girl didn't have to die. She was kind. And lovely,' Samantha said.

'Aye, she was that,' I said.

'And her hand? The *daemon* hand? Does Fisk still have it?' she asked.

'Yes,' I said. 'Locked away.'

She nodded, thoughtful. 'That has weighed on my mind more than I care to admit,' she said.

We passed the ore piles and Samantha dismounted. Her movements were stiff and fragile, as if she'd aged beyond her years. She knelt painfully near the ore.

Sapientia pulled her mount close to Bess and said to me, softly, 'She's not been well. She doesn't sleep, she eats sparingly. This happens with engineers, sometimes. The powers we work with, they can be overwhelming. Some of that—'

'Taint?' I said, thinking about a mountainside, and being naked upon it. And *vaettir* passing me by, in the darkness, because I bore no Hellfire, because I bore no silver.

'Yes, for lack of a better word. In history, it was called the summoner's gaze, this malaise. And she is affected, I think.'

'Is there a cure?' I asked.

'Of course! She needs a holiday. Drink, and sex, and food, and happiness, and the yoke of responsibility gone from her, along with all the *daemons* we bear, figuratively, and literally,' Sapientia said.

'All that sounds lovely,' I said. 'I could use a holiday myself.'

'Maybe, if we see the end of this dark endeavour, you will have one. And I hope I will, too,' she said.

Samantha turned the ore over in her hands. To me it simply looked like granite with streaks of brown and white. Had I picked up a chunk of the ore by a river bed to make a ring for a campfire, I would never have known it was precious. She walked around the perimeter of one of the heaps and then returned to us and remounted.

'It is rich,' she said. 'How long have they been mining?'

'Two weeks, give or take a day,' I said.

Samantha whistled her appreciation. Her eyes brightened. 'Let us meet Neruda, and then we have some business with my old master.'

We left the engineers' apprentices and assistants near the mess to refresh themselves and take care of the mounts. As we entered the praetorium tent, all conversation stopped. Black Donald paused in raising a cup of wine to his lips. Praeverta and Winfried looked at the newcomers, silently.

Fisk leapt up and embraced Samantha, who seemed somewhat taken aback by his overt sign of affection.

'I am glad you're here!' Fisk said. 'I trust Shoe has filled you in?'

'Yes,' she said. 'And I've inspected the ore. It looks promising.'

'Which is why I'm here,' Black Donald said, his beard bristling.

'Munitioner Vemus.' Sapientia inclined her head in greeting. Samantha followed suit.

'It's been, what? Five years?' Black Donald said.

'I haven't a clue,' Sapientia said. 'I don't mark your comings and goings on my calendar, I'm afraid.'

Black Donald barked laughter. 'What? Impossible. The ground trembles at my approach!' he said, smiling.

'Apparently it doesn't mark its calendar at your exits,' Sapientia said. 'Do you have plans for the smelt and munitions drawn?'

'I just arrived here, woman,' Black Donald said, reaching for his cup again. 'I've surveyed where they will be built. It's amazing how fast these *dvergar* are able to put up—'

Sapientia snapped her fingers. 'Thank you, Vemus,' she said.

'You are dismissed. Please have your preliminary plans to me by second hour in the morning.'

Praeverta and Winfried looked about, surprised at the turn of conversation. Fisk stilled. His eyes narrowed as he looked first at Sapientia and the bearded engineer.

Black Donald spluttered and dropped his cup. 'I'll have you know, missy, that I am Marcellus' chief munitioner—'

'And where is Marcellus? There sits the commander of the Hardscrabble legions,' Sapientia said, pointing at Fisk. 'And if you want to compare rank, sir, I am praefect and *princep primus* of the College of Engineers, here in Occidentalia,' she continued. 'You are my subordinate. I require you have plans for the smelt – including your litany, ritual, warding and precium to raise the smelt *daemon* – prepared and ready for my approval by morning. You are dismissed.'

'I have been in the service of Rume, filling their shells and casings with Hellfire, since before you were born, Madame,' Black Donald said.

Fisk turned to him. 'If you wish to remain in Rume's service, I expect you to follow the chain of command, then. Were you issued a direct order from a superior?'

Black Donald set down his cup. His face had the blank, white non-expression of fury. There is nothing as painful and fragile as a man whose pride suffers a blow, and Black Donald was no different. He stood, walked stiffly from the tent without another word.

When he was gone, Sapientia laughed and Samantha joined in.

'He's a good worker,' Sapientia said. 'But I know him of old and if you don't take him in hand quickly, he'll run roughshod all over you.'

'He'll have his plans in the morning, no doubt,' Samantha said.

'And they'll be immaculate. He's a talented engineer – a great craftsman,' Sapientia said. 'Come tomorrow, I will praise him to the heavens and he will roll over and want me to scratch his belly, tail between his legs.' She grinned again. 'It is not only the *daemons* that require rituals,' she said, and winked at me.

Fisk introduced the engineers to Neruda and Praeverta. Winfried, they were both acquainted with. He bid us all to sit and take food and for a long while, we discussed events, the great winds blowing in the larger world. The destruction of Rume, the state of Medieran troops in the West.

'Scouts, then,' Fisk said to me. 'No sign?'

'None. They were to ride to the Big Rill, split up, keep their distance. Pose as fleeing sodbusters if stopped by the Medierans.'

'And the situation in Passasuego?' Fisk asked, looking to Sapientia and Samantha. He might not even consciously be doing it, but he'd turned a reunion into a debrief quite easily.

'We fled before they took it. But it was said they had three thousand garrisoned at Hot Springs, and seven thousand now roost on the pink nest of Passasuego. The White River teemed with refugees on anything they could find that would float,' Samantha added.

'They're digging in,' Fisk said, frowning. 'They have their foothold. Now they'll move east.'

'Apparently the battle for Passasuego left the Medieran commander, Aveda, enraged and his men demoralised, but how or why was not apparent,' Samantha said. 'I can only hazard a conjecture – the city is well fortified, and well munitioned. The Medierans must have had trouble taking it.'

'There were plans to blow the mine, should the city be taken,' Sapientia said. 'Though I don't know if that occurred.'

'I hope they haven't blown it,' I said, scratching my beard. 'It'd put us in a more desperate position. They'll be looking east sooner, rather than later. And we have shitloads of work to do to be ready.'

'Our mine gives its gift of silver plentifully,' Neruda said, holding open his hands as if giving a benediction. 'But we must do three things, and do them quickly – fortify this valley and prepare for attack, construct a working smelt, and build a munitions production line. Very, very quickly,' Neruda said, softly. 'My people can assist and raise buildings in days, but we cannot raise *daemons* or etch wardings.'

'We have many junior engineers ready for work,' Samantha said. 'And Black Donald has his munitioners.'

'It appears that we each have our roles and we know what needs to be done,' Fisk said. 'Black Donald, the smelt and munitions. Neruda and your people, mining ore and construction.' He looked at the map on the table. 'That leaves fortifications. And that will fall to me and my legions.' His brow furrowed.

'Maybe not wholly, pard,' I said. Fisk looked at me. 'Sapientia reminded me of it.' I turned to the chief engineer. 'What was that great ward in the atrium of the engineers' college in Passaseugo? A *pellum*, was it called?'

Her expression brightened. 'Yes! It was,' she said.

'You said no *daemon* nor *daemon*-gripped could pass one, without being cast out,' I said. 'Is that right?'

'Yes, but what you're suggesting—'

'Is there a ward that lets them in, but doesn't let 'em leave?' I asked.

Sapientia looked at Samantha and raised an eyebrow. 'No there isn't, but—'

'I have been experimenting some, since we've had the corpse of the Grantham woman,' Samantha said. At Neruda and Praeverta's questioning looks, she explained the events that had occurred at the Pynchon. 'And it's possible that if Sapientia and I work together, we might be able to craft a new ward.' She looked thoughtful. 'And we might have help.'

Samantha looked to me.

'Beleth,' I said.

'Yes,' she said.

'Gods damn him,' I said. 'He'll do nothing but trick and try to manipulate you.'

'I know him, Shoe,' Samantha said. 'I know all his wiles.'

'Keep telling yourself that. But you don't. Every single time we've gone up against him, he's surprised us,' I said.

Fisk held up a hand. 'You think you can get useful information from him?'

'Maybe,' Samantha said. 'Can't hurt to try.'

'If you can't, then it will be time for his end,' he said. 'He must pay for his crimes. Rume is no more, Tamberlaine is out of communication though perhaps alive. Marcellus has gone east. It is my decision. Get from him what information you can. Create this new ward. We will give you all the silver and assistance you need to execute. You three shall be my agents in this and—' He snapped his fingers. A secretary scrambled up. 'I shall have orders drawn up for your authority. And Beleth's execution.'

Samantha bowed.

'I believe we're done here, then,' Fisk said. 'I need to confer with my legates, optios, and centurions regarding fortifications. Shoe, you'll take them to Beleth?'

'Yes,' I said.

'You are dismissed, then,' Fisk said, and turned back to his maps.

The engineer retinue had been assigned two empty contubernium tents and they spent an hour at ablutions and rest and preparing for their encounter with Beleth. The Grenthvar gave up its nightly mist, the sky dark, starless, the fires from the legions throwing up a yellow glow on the belly of the clouds hanging low over the valley.

When Sam and Sapientia were ready – they had washed the trail dirt from their faces and changed into clean garb – I led them to the shed where Beleth was held, holding a *daemonlight* lantern high so they wouldn't lose their footing in the dark. I'd be lying if I said that either woman was wholly calm and collected. Beleth was a force, and one to not be taken lightly.

'He is bound and gagged,' I said.

'For weeks? Do you fear that he might perish from the circumstances of his capture?' Sapientia said.

'His hand's healed up fine, and I ungag and walk him about, late at night, where he can't poison anyone with his words.' I shrugged. 'But do I care if he dies? No.'

Samantha nodded, looking at me with a taut expression on her face. Sapientia straightened her tunic and smoothed her hair.

'All right, then,' I said. 'Give me a moment to make him presentable, empty his night soil. And then we'll get you reacquainted.' I opened the door and went in.

He was awake and looking at me with bright eyes from the dirty pallet I'd made for him from old horse blankets.

'You have visitors, Mister Beleth.' Hooking him under his armpits, I hoisted him up and helped him to vacate his bowels and bladder in the bucket. I then took the bucket out and emptied it in the latrine and led the engineers inside the hut.

I removed the bit from his mouth. He worked his jaws, back and forth, and then smiled, lips cracked, broken, and bleeding.

'Pardon his smell,' I said. 'His outsides are beginning to resemble his insides.'

'The droll dwarf,' Beleth croaked. 'Ah, Samantha! You've returned to me, at last. Strike off these ropes and set me free. Together we will ride from here and create great works.'

Samantha said nothing. She squatted on her hams in front of her former master, her big hands hanging off her knees, between her legs, like a farmer inspecting his crops.

'You've withered, Sam,' Beleth said. 'You were fat and happy in my employ. Now you look as though you've got the wasting sickness.'

My wife, Illina, had died of that sickness. It was not something to bandy about. I walloped Beleth across the jaw.

'You see?' Beleth crowed. 'How the little monstrosity treats me? Cut my bonds. Let us go and have wine and discuss things over dinner, as we once did.'

Samantha remained quiet for a long while, looking closely at the bound engineer.

'Keep him bound,' she said. 'And bring him to our tent. I need more light and the table there.'

I jerked the engineer to his feet and dragged him forth. Once he was in the tent, Sapientia unshuttered many *daemonlight* lanterns, so that the tent was as bright as noon. Samantha looked at me. 'He *does* stink. Water and soap?'

In moments, I had retrieved a bucket with a cake of lye soap and some rags.

Samantha and Sapientia were tying on scorched leather aprons when I re-entered the tent. Beleth was laid upon the work table, face up.

'Had you wanted me supine, I would've done so for you, long ago. I had no idea you harboured such feelings for me, Samantha. I would have been happy to satisfy you, when you were my apprentice.' He leered at Sapientia. 'It was always rumoured that you warmed Cassius' bed, when you were his apprentice.'

Sapientia's face froze and some of the colour drained from it. Samantha withdrew a pair of shears. I jammed one of the rags halfway down Beleth's throat.

Samantha cut his clothing away, revealing his naked form. He had lost weight, too, and his flesh hung loosely off him. His skin was discoloured, deeply bruised around the bindings, and filthy from weeks without any sort of bath, except my treatment of his stump.

'Beleth,' Samantha said. 'Sadly, I do not have in my possession a torturer's board like that you used to such effect on Agrippina. Would that I did. But this table will have to suffice.'

The engineers took the bucket of water and cleaned Beleth, from toes to the top of his head, with soap, water, and rags. The water ran brown by the time they were through.

His body was a litany of pain writ in wards. Some pink and aggravated, newer, some ancient. The scarred warding began at his ankles and rose up his legs, covered his stomach and stopped at his chest.

'Look,' Sapientia said to Sam. 'None on his back, nor the backs of his arms.'

'Or what's left of his right arm at all,' I said. 'He did this all to himself.'

Samantha gave a grim smile. 'It's a good thing Fisk snipped his right arm, then,' she said. 'Otherwise, our friend might still be practising the craft.'

'No chance of that any more,' Sapientia said. 'Look here, the *corpus locus glyph* that he used to cast himself into the poor Grantham woman in Passasuego.'

Samantha dipped a rag into the soapy water and wiped at the scarring that Sapientia indicated. 'Yes,' she said. 'There's the *corpus locus glyph*, and Grantham's full name.' She continued examining the rest of him. 'He really was quite innovative in his creation of wards.'

'Look for a new one,' I said. 'Right there. He put himself in Gynth,' I said.

'Ah, your tame stretcher,' Samantha said.

'He's not tame, nor is he mine. But I would count him as a friend,' I said. 'He's saved me thrice.'

'Fascinating,' Samantha said. 'First Fisk has softened and risen high, and now you, bosom friends with a stretcher.' She shrugged, turned back to Beleth's still form. 'This ward has been marred, and marred deeply,' she said. 'It's been burned.'

'That's strange,' I said. 'I cut the glyph on Gynth to release him. Beleth rode him like a horse.'

'Can we see it?' Sapientia asked. 'Can you bring him here?'

'I can try. Give me a little bit,' I said.

Walking out, it took a little while for my eyes to adjust to the darkness. The tent behind me glowed like a paper lantern. I went to the fire outside my dwelling. In the distance, I could hear legionnaires singing songs of battle and laughing, the glow from hundreds of other fires sending sparks into the heavens in recursive paths, the scent of auroch and garum, charcoal and sweetgrass and sage on the wind. The breath and murmur of a Ruman camp at night.

Catch Hands sat near the fire and stirred a squirrel and potato stew outside my tent. 'Gynth,' I said. 'Where is he?'

'A-roamin,' Catch Hands said. 'What's he usually doin'?'

'Roaming, I guess,' I said. 'I've got a bottle for you if you could run him down before third nocturn and bring him to the new engineers' tents.'

'New engineers?'

'You haven't heard?' I asked.

'I've heard plenty. But I want to know for sure,' Catch Hands said.

'Engineers have arrived,' I said. I didn't intend to play this game. 'Content yourself with that. Go introduce yourself.'

Catch Hands jumped up, dusted off his britches, and with both hands grabbed his beard, smoothed it.

'No promises. But if I can, I will,' he said, and tromped off, to the east, up into the pines and gambels of the Eldvatch. 'Afterwards, we'll see about the introductions,' he called over his shoulder.

I returned to the engineers' tent. 'Gynth is gone roaming. But he'll be back soon.'

Samantha gave a terse nod and Sapientia ignored the interruption; she wiped at Beleth's leg with a soapy rag.

'He's been at this for a long while. Look at his legs,' she said. 'The knifework is amateurish here.' She chuckled. 'It's shite.'

Beleth grunted through the rags stuffed in his throat. He thrashed.

'It gets more refined, though,' Sapientia said. 'How much did he practise on others to develop his wardwork on himself?'

'I shudder to think,' Samantha said. 'He was expert when I became his apprentice.'

They were quiet for a while, examining his body. 'It's this one,' Sapientia said, indicating his navel. I came closer, to see what she pointed to. The skin was discoloured there, dark lines among the scarring. A larger ward, writ with a scalpel and what appeared to be ink.

'It's rough,' Samantha said. 'And dissimilar from all the others. And is that—?'

'Yes, that is a Tchinee ideogram,' Sapientia responded. They looked at each other. 'This complicates things,' she said.

'It also answers many questions.' Samantha rubbed her chin. 'And simplifies the course of action,' she said. 'We'll need a *carcere* ward for the exorcism. And for the vessel, a stoat?'

'What questions does it answer?' I asked.

'Did you ever wonder, Shoe, how Beleth might summon a *daemon* the magnitude of Belial – the one we call the Crimson Man – with such a small precium?'

'Well, no, I hadn't,' I said. 'But now you mention it...'

'He didn't have to give buckets of blood. He just had to strike a deal with a fellow *daemon*,' Samantha said.

'Oh, shit,' I said.

'Exactly,' Samantha said. 'The vessel?' She turned back to Sapientia.

'Something larger. Something closer to human,' Sapientia responded. 'A pig.'

'How appropriate,' Sam said.

'Hold up, you two,' I said. 'An exorcism? Something's in him?'

'It's a thought I had, long ago. And now, it is confirmed. Something's been riding in him for so long, the Beleth we knew might not even have any knowledge of his heinous acts,' Samantha responded. 'And we have to get it out.'

'We'll need a small smelt, charcoal, and an open, unbroken floor or space to create the warding,' Sapientia said. 'Can you help with that?'

I nodded. 'We've sourced good charcoal, and I can take you to a hanging stone. It's a near-flat rock that juts out over the last of the Hardscrabble – a lookout. A perch.'

'Good,' Sapientia said. 'And men to carry him?'

'I can do you one better,' I said, and moved out of the tent into the night.

I found Gynth coming down the mountainside with Catch Hands. At some point, Gynth had lost his trousers and was now wandering about with his privates on display, a massive feral hog slung over his shoulder. Blood from the boar ran like a cloak down his back in rivulets.

I said in *dvergar*, 'Go and clean up and put on some clothing. And quickly. I need your help. Catch Hands, take the boar.'

Gynth shrugged and tottered off, returning shortly with soaking hair, and a leather apron he had fastened around his waist like one of the kilts that Northmen were wont to wear. Blood still drenched his back – you can take the stretcher out of the Hardscrabble but you can't take the Hardscrabble out of the stretcher.

I bid him follow me and returned to the tent. The engineers were understandably overwhelmed for a few moments when a bloody, half-nude *vaettir* suddenly filled their tent – but they recovered quickly.

'Get the *draugve*,' I said, using the *dvergar* word that roughly translates as arsehole.

Gynth didn't hesitate – he knew exactly who I meant. With his big, still-bloody hands he snapped Beleth's bindings and hefted him over his shoulder. He ducked and moved outside, slick as a mink's prick.

'It's alarming how smoothly they move, despite their size,' Sapientia said out of the side of her mouth to Samantha.

'It can get a lot worse, believe me,' Samantha said.

From one of Black Donald's engineer assistants, I commandeered a small porcelain smelt and a hand bellows. From the camp provisioner, a large sack of coal. He had no pigs, but he did have a goat, which I hoped would suffice as a 'vessel'. After I had secured those things we all trudged north and west for a good piece, watching our footing, as the terrain was somewhat treacherous with loose shale, the roots of pine and gambel crumbling the stone over the years.

By the time we reached the hanging stone, the moon had risen and the stars were a milky spray across the heavens. The end of the Hardscrabble lay spread out below us; to the south, a silver ribbon of the Grenthvar trickling away from the Smokeys, winding among copses of gambel and birch. It was peaceful here on this high vantage at night. An owl hooted softly, and the high-pitched cries of coyotes and other creatures of the Hardscrabble were distant and faint.

The engineers unslung their *daemonlight* lanterns and spent the next two hours scratching and chiselling at the flat rock face with awls. 'Gods! Thank Ia this is soapstone – we'd be well and truly fucked if it was granite,' Sapientia muttered as they remained hunched over the stone, while the goat bleated merrily into night air and I built a charcoal fire. When the engineers had finished etching the warding into the rock face, they produced a small ingot of silver and melted it and then, wearing thick gloves, used a ceramic ladle with a fine mouth to outline the warding with the thinnest ribbon of silver possible. The smell of the charcoal and the burning silver made my nose itch, but they finished that task in good time and then went over it once more to make sure none of the warding was flawed or missing.

Finally, Samantha and Sapientia beckoned Gynth to bring Beleth inside the warding and lay him down. Samantha plucked the rag from Beleth's mouth. He spluttered and coughed and then went still.

'Mister Beleth,' Samantha said, 'it has come to this.'

Beleth made no response, but in the *daemonlight* his expression seemed venomous.

'Please exit the warding, sir,' Samantha said.

He made no move. 'Thank you, but I'm perfectly content here, Sam,' he said.

'I am afraid I must insist,' she responded. 'You know why.'

He began to laugh. It was a mellow sound, as if we were back in the stateroom of the *Cornelian* having whiskeys instead of out, naked beneath the stars. They were indifferent to his plight. We were not.

'Bring the goat, then,' Sapientia said to me. I led the creature inside the warding and left it, wondering how it would stay there, but something in Beleth or the intaglio of silver itself seemed to hold it in sway.

Sapientia looked expectantly to Samantha. 'And the precium? Will you let it? Or shall I?'

'It should be me. He was my master, once.' Sam drew a dagger and cut her palm, wincing. She let the blood pool there and then approached the goat and dripped it across its back. Moving to the focus of the ward, she placed her bloody palm in the centre of the stone and left it there to transfer the blood as she spoke slowly, under her breath.

Whatever incantation she might've spoken, I could not hear. Finally, she pressed her bloody hand to Beleth's navel – the tattooed ward – and stepped from the circle.

An ebony mist began seeping up, out of Beleth, out of the rock itself. As it rose, the goat bleated more frantically, desperate. Beleth writhed, his back bowed away from the hanging stone. He screamed, shouting in tongues unknown to me. I had expected great thunderous screeches and screams from the infernal realms – but no. He sounded like a man. In pain.

The dark mist filled the space, faster than I would've thought, and in a moment, it coalesced around the goat and disappeared.

'Well, that's that,' Samantha said. 'Can you hear me, Beleth?'

Beleth did not move, except for the rising and falling of his chest. His face was hidden in the cradle of his arms. His stump was bleeding again. What I thought were coughs wracked his body, soft chuffing sounds. Not coughs.

Sobs. The man wept.

'Can you hear me, Beleth?' Samantha said.

A voice, miserable and utterly lost, said, 'Yes.'

'Do you remember what you've done? Even with that thing inside you?' Samantha asked.

He did not respond for a long while. His mouth opened, lips cracked and sore. A bit of blood flecked his lips. 'Yes. Everything.'

'What did you tell the Medierans? What have you shown the Medierans?' she said.

There was a long silence. Beleth sat upright. The desolation in his features was plain. Here was a man coming to grips with his own horrors.

'Kill me,' he said. 'Please. I can't— I can't—'

'It will all be over for you eventually, Beleth. But we need answers first,' Samantha said, her voice stern.

'They had one engineer, a summoner with talent. Verdammen. I showed him . . .'

Samantha clenched and unclenched her hands. The muscles in her jaw worked as if she chewed a piece of gristle – and maybe she did, in a way. 'What did you show him?'

'Everything,' Beleth sobbed. 'The city killing. The soldiers. He knows it all.'

'Ia-damn you to perdition,' Samantha whispered, standing over him.

Tears poured from Beleth's face. 'I'm sorry. It wasn't me, it was the *daemon* inside me. So long, it's been there for so long—'

She slapped him. It was a simple thing, the movement many mothers have made to children. A cuff. But the sound of it was bright in the night air. 'How can we destroy the *daemon* hand without releasing the Crimson Man contained there? Will this work?' She gestured to the circle and the goat. The goat, which had taken on a very evil and bellicose demeanour.

'No,' Beleth said. 'No. You need a human. Or a *vaettir* or *dvergar*. You can lock it away, throw it to the bottom of the ocean, or—' He stopped, his eyes going wide.

'What?' Samantha said. 'What? Damn you!'

'You can take it to Terra Umbra,' he said. His voice was a ruin now. Between the sobbing and the long captivity, his vocal cords were torn and raw, making his voice rasp. 'The universe is worn thin, and it's the rift there – Emrys' Folly – that allows all the *daemons* through. If you took it into the breach—' He stopped again. His eyes searched the sky for something only he could see.

'What?'

'The power released would close it. Maybe. No one can know for sure,' Beleth said.

'Might it open it wider?' Sapientia asked.

'Doubtful. But possibly. The *daemon* bound in that hand is god-like in aspect. Godlike in power. And it being here is an imbalance that wants to be corrected. So bringing it to the breach . . . we just can't know. But I think it will close it. And closing the breach will end the world as we know it.'

'What did you promise him to come over with so little precium?' Samantha asked.

Beleth stilled. 'Everything.'

'Everything?' Samantha said, incredulous. 'Be more specific.'

'This world and everything in it,' he said.

'Except you,' Samantha responded.

Beleth said nothing.

'And the Emryal Rift will end it? Will stop Hellfire?'

'I believe so,' Beleth said.

'No more Hellfire,' I said. 'Holy shit.'

'The *daemons* trapped here will still be trapped here,' he said. His strength was fading. The *daemonic* goat – still held captive by the warding – gave a tremendous bleat that sounded like a man screaming. 'There'll be no new boats. No new ammunition.' He was still for a while. 'It will be a better world, though. No cities would die. No one would have *daemons* infesting themselv—'

'You did that to yourself. You went searching for power and found it. And it rode you hard. And now it's the end of your story.' She walked to the goat and cut its throat. Blood gouted from the beast's neck, all over the silver wardwork. Something dark in the body of the animal shivered and then dissipated, as if the creature's flesh were a curtain. 'This is the last time I'll ever see you,' Samantha said, and packed up her engineer's equipment. 'And for that I'm glad. The commander, Fisk, has sentenced you to die. It is wartime. There is no need for a trial, and you admit your deeds.' She looked at me. 'But I have not the stomach for it. Can I leave this to you?'

'Yes,' I said, though I did not want the task. It's a hard world, and it makes monsters of us all.

Samantha left the circle. Gynth retrieved the body of the once *daemon*-gripped goat, and Sapientia followed them away, back to the camp. I was left with Beleth, who had collapsed on the flat stone.

It was quiet for a long while, with only the sobs of the desolate man and the hooting of an owl to break the silence.

'Come out,' I called to the trees behind us. 'Come out, Winfried.'

She emerged from the trees and approached, stopping where the rock outcrop began to tower above the land below. It was early morning now, the sky lightening in the east, beyond the rim of gun-blue mountains.

'Here he is,' I said. 'And I'll not stop you from your vengeance.'

I stepped away from Beleth and she came near. In her hand was a steel longknife.

'You killed my brother-mate,' she said.

Beleth stopped crying. He sat up. 'Yes,' he said. 'I did.'

She slowly brought the knife forward and placed it on the base of his throat above his collarbone. He lifted his head. Tears streamed from his eyes. Spittle and blood flecked his mouth.

'I am sorry,' he said. 'So very sorry.'

They remained like that for a long while, Beleth on his knees, Winfried with her knife at his throat. Maybe, if he'd not been naked underneath the sky. Maybe, if he'd not wept. Maybe, if he'd not been so willing to go to death, she would've wet her blade. But she did not.

She dropped it on the stone and it clattered away, over the lip of hanging rock, to fall below. Without looking at me, she turned and began the long walk back to the Breadbasket and Neruda.

'And that leaves just you and me, now, Mister Beleth,' I said.

'Yes,' he said.

'Let us wait a while, shall we. The sunrise here is something to see,' I said. I took off my jacket and draped it over his shoulders. I rolled a cigarette, lit it, and placed it in his mouth. I rolled one for myself. His remaining hand was clumsy and dumb. His body slack.

We sat there, smoking, watching the sun's light colouring the land below us, first in blues and greys, then in tawny yellows and ochres. The lit face of the earth opened before us like a flower.

I stood. Withdrew my silver knife. It smoked in my hand. The pain was just.

'You've shown me that knife before,' Beleth said.

'Yes,' I said. 'I have.' I moved to stand behind him. 'Watch the sky, Mister Beleth. See light moving across the land?'

'Linneus,' he said. 'My name was Linneus.'

'Linneus,' I said, and drove the knife through his neck, into his skull.

Back at camp, I went to talk with Fisk. He was just washing his face in an ablution bowl when I entered his tent.

'Long night?' he asked, raising an eyebrow.

'Yep,' I said. 'And a bloody one.'

'Beleth?'

'Had a *daemon* riding him. For years. All the godsawful shit he did, the whole time there was a *daemon* on his back.'

Fisk shrugged. 'Never liked the man. But I've had a *daemon* riding around in me, if you recall. Around my neck. He could've done something.' He wiped his face with a towel. 'I fought. I could've killed myself. No, something in that man liked it and not all of his deeds were the *daemon*'s will.' He looked at me. 'And Winfried? Surely, she sniffed out the proceedings.'

'Aye, and followed us. At the end, I gave him to her. She had not the heart to do it,' I said. 'He was a pitiful sight indeed. There was remorse there.'

'And you?'

'I didn't have the heart, either. But I did it anyway,' I said. 'And we had no dogs to drag his body through the streets, as Rume likes to do to traitors, so I just tossed him from the hanging stone below. He'll be naught but bones in a fortnight.'

'Or sooner. So, that's one thing less to worry about.'

'There's a couple of new things to worry over,' I said, and filled him in on what Beleth had told us regarding the Medieran engineer, Verdammen.

'Ia-dammit,' Fisk said, through his teeth. 'Ia-damn that man. Thrown from the hanging stone was too good for him.' He sat at his command table and withdrew a machine-rolled cigarette from a pack lying there. He handed the smoke to me and took one for himself. 'The benefits of command, eh, Shoe?' he said, lighting mine from a match.

'Seems like there are very few benefits there,' I said. 'You seem like you've slept as much as I have.'

'Which is not at all,' Fisk said. 'I am ... distressed. I dream of Livia when I sleep and when I wake. The anxiety of not knowing her fate gnaws at me. I drink wine and whiskey to dull the anxiety but it just makes it worse when I wake.'

'I wish there was something I could do for you there, pard. But Livia is a force unto herself and you will be reunited, I am sure of it,' I said.

'I can only hope you're right,' he said.

'Speaking of reunions,' I began. 'My scouts have not returned, and they've been too long gone.'

'Your scouts?' he said. 'Lina.'

'Yes,' I said. 'I thought I might take Gynth and Catch Hands and outride west. See if I can pick up the scouts' trail and suss out what the Medierans are up to, all at once.'

'What do you need?' he asked, shifting into his tone of command. It was a question of resources. It was strange, now, talking to my old partner. All of the camaraderie and familiarity remained as it ever was; here was my grizzled partner, inscrutable in some ways, an open book in others. Quick to anger, deadly to his enemies, loyal to a fault to his friends. My partner. But now he was more than that. The vagaries of this monstrous world had shuffled the deck, and the hand he was dealt was one he would not have chosen for himself if he could have. But it was a good hand. And he, despite his nature, his history, his demeanour – he was suited to lead. Not because of some innate Ruman nature, but because, possibly, of his lack of it. He was a noble who had never had anything given or easy.

'A pony for Catch Hands, and extras for the scouts should I find them,' I said. 'Hellfire for Catch Hands as well. Food enough for ten days. Three to cross to the Big Rill, another two to get to the nearest town, and three to get back.'

'That's only eight days, Shoe,' Fisk said.

'Two extra for good measure,' I said.

'You'll have it,' he said and scribbled a note on a blank sheet of parchment, dropped wax from a signet candle upon it, and pressed his eagle into it. 'Talk to the provisioner. Ride safe and fast, my friend.'

I left by noon, Catch Hands bobbing along beside me on the most docile mount the stableman could find. Gynth bounded forward and circled us. In the past, that would've made me nervous, being paced by a *vaettir*, but now it was reassuring.

On occasion Gynth bounded up, smiling. Once, he said, 'How comes my little *gynth*?'

'Don't call me that,' Catch Hands said. 'Why do you have to talk like that?'

'It's your word,' Gynth said. 'I did not make it up. My tongue is—' He said something unintelligible.

'It's your name. I don't like being called "little",' Catch Hands said. 'I'm told I'm tall for a *dvergar*.'

Gynth sniffed. 'You're small to me,' he said.

'Don't get your britches in a breech,' I said. 'Everyone's small to Gynth.'

'This is true,' he said, and leapt away. In moments he had disappeared on the horizon, vaulting over gulleys and bramblewrack, like a child hopping over puddles and cracks in stone.

'Bring back supper,' I called after him.

Hardscrabble. I inhaled the dusty scent of it.

And it felt like coming home.

PART TWO

We study war so that our children might study industry. Our children will study industry so that their offspring might study art and music. Thus the world moves toward enlightenment. But, now, we must be generals.

— Neruda

TWENTY

I Stood There, Dumbly, Watching Our Death Come

Y SMAY HAD CUT his wrists to the quick. Slumped against the wall, he'd bled out, facing the door, leaving his cabin a stinking, sticky mess. From bulwark to bulkhead to berth door, the floor was puddled and sticky with blood.

I did not enter, for I did not wish to stand amidst the blood, and I was arrested by his ghastly pale face floating up in my vision like some unseemly spirit from a dark pool.

Standing there for many minutes, taking in the terrible end of the last crew member of the *Typhon*, I realised one thing: I had caused this. There was nothing I could do to brush this aside, push this away. I was the catalyst. I was the spark.

'Ia-damn,' Carnelia said, looking in after me.

'Get Tenebrae,' I said. She called out for him. 'Get him, don't yell at him. He may be above deck.'

She left and returned in moments with Tenebrae in tow.

He inhaled sharply. 'Gods, who would have thought there was that amount of blood in such a slender man.'

'He was despondent,' Carnelia said. She sniffed. 'We're all lost, at some point. But you don't withdraw just because things aren't going your way. If anything, taking your own life should have some meaning.'

I shook my head. 'The human heart doesn't work like that.

227

There are cracked vessels, broken people. Those who are hurt or moribund. Or even ill, in their mind. And they cannot help their despondency,' I said. 'And I think Ysmay was one of these people. He was possessed of a natural proclivity toward darkness, as if he was born to it.'

'He showed me how to sluice water away in rooms. There's a valve around here, somewhere,' Tenebrae said, kicking off his boots, shucking socks, and entering the berth. He walked over to the engineer's corpse as a man walking on a rocky beach – arms upraised, stepping gingerly. He tugged at Ysmay's shoulder, tilting the body forward. 'Of course, the valve is behind him. We'll need water.'

Carnelia went above deck and brought back a bucket full of sea water, which she unceremoniously dumped on the floor. Tenebrae opened the valve. The blood became a thick slurry of clotted, viscous liquid. It drained away very slowly.

'Ack,' Tenebrae said. 'Let's take his body above, and then deal with this.'

Lupina came out of the mess, dandling Fiscelion.

'It's a horror in here,' I said. 'Take him away, please.' Gods, the things that child has already endured. Either he'll be traumatised all his life or the strongest soul to ever walk the earth.

Tenebrae lifted Ysmay by the armpits and dragged him toward the door, swinging both his and the engineer's arses hallward. Once in the passageway, Carnelia, making a face, took his legs and they hauled him out and on deck. I followed them up.

The wind was brisk, and low clouds scudded across the sky.

'Should we say some words for him?' Tenebrae asked.

'Put him overboard,' I said. 'I will say words. You two can finish cleaning up his cabin.'

'That doesn't seem right,' Carnelia said.

I turned to her. 'Will your eyes well up with tears? Will you cry

228

for him, this man you didn't know? This man we tore from his life? This man whose future we took from him? Will you weep?'

She blinked in response to the fury of my words. Carnelia looked at Tenebrae. 'Over the side then, Shadow,' she said, as Tenebrae filled a sack with empty metal shell casings and tied it to his leg. They hefted his body up and over the gunwale. It fell with a very small splash. They went back below.

I walked to the ship's rail and looked over. His body had already disappeared, fathoms deep now, maybe. Food for fish, hair in a great blond swirl around his head, arms upraised, in praise of his descent.

'Whatever gods greet you at your journey's end,' I said, 'let them know I am sorry.'

I turned and went back below.

'Well, now we're truly fucked,' Carnelia said, later that day, when it became obvious we needed to adjust course.

'Ysmay has shown us all how to steer the vessel,' I said. 'We should have few problems with it as long as we don't founder.'

'Or run into any more Medierans,' Tenebrae said.

I tapped the compass on the com. 'We sail south, and west. We make sure, every day, to sight land on our starboard bow. The *Typhon* is a littoral, after all. Eventually, it will grow hot, we'll pass Fort Lucullus, and then we'll find passage into the Bay of Mageras.'

'You make it sound so simple,' Carnelia said. 'We are not lascars! You are no captain!'

'We are now!' Tenebrae laughed. The man had an inexhaustible store of laughs. Mocking, joyous, bitter, snarky, grandiose, prideful. But this one I had not witnessed from him before – it held a joyous futility that sparked a smile in return from me. Indeed, what else was there to do? Either we gave up, or we became who we pretended to be. I had not fled my family and killed my fellow man to protect my son, only to give up now.

'Yes,' I said. 'We are now. You wear a lascar's outfit. Trust me, sissy. This will work.' I placed my eyes to the Miraculous. 'Go to your *armatura*. Spend time with your nephew. I will take the first turn at helm.'

Night was the worst. I was not willing to allow us to drop anchor for sleep, so needs be we stagger our rest periods. After three days, it seemed that I was on a haunted ship, one in which the whole crew was under some magical sleep. I saw my son at meals, even more infrequently than before, and comforted myself in the paltry fact that already I spent more time with him than many Ruman matrons did with their own progeny. 'No child's company until speech and reason,' was a Ruman adage, and one that my father had adhered to.

But worse: the fear of grounding that darkness brought with it. At dusk, I made sure to set course in a more easterly direction, for fear the contours of Occidentalia would change and we go sailing, unbeknownst to whoever helmed the *Typhon*, into a spit of land jutting from the main body of the continent. This tactic meant that every morning, at first light, we must turn west, and sail full bore until we sighted land once more. In this way we zigzagged down the coast.

By turns we all gave blood to Typhon, save Fiscelion.

I do not know if that helped, but it was better to keep the *daemon* appeased than risk otherwise.

Day found night found day again. The fear of encountering other ships – Medieran warships, in particular – was worse than actually encountering them. An enormous destroyer was the first, possessed of five massive swivels; it we spotted long before they had a chance to spot us. And because, as was our wont, we kept the hatches closed while all were below, it was a simple matter for me to initiate the descent and submerge. I turned us shoreward, cut our speed, and kept the Miraculous trained on the enormous vessel. It did not notice us.

The second found us making the passage between islands into the Bay of Mageras. Not truly an ambush, but definitely a patrol of some sort.

It was day, and suddenly Carnelia was yelling for me to wake.

'Get up! A frigate fires upon us!'

I woke to bedlam. My sister's face was wild. Fiscelion screamed somewhere in the ship. The *Typhon* rocked sideways and both Carnelia and I took steps toward port to steady ourselves. Tenebrae yelled something indistinct from the command.

Seeing I was awake, Carnelia bolted back to the nav. I raced after her, my bare feet painful on the grating of the *Typhon*'s flooring. A calm settled on me and I pushed the noise and pain away. Entering the command, I saw Tenebrae peering into the Miraculous.

'They make chase. Carnelia, can you take the swivel?' he asked, his voice pitched upward, full of tension.

'We haven't taken off the gun shroud this morning!' she said.

'Do that now!' he said.

'Submerge,' she answered.

'They are right behind us. In full daylight. And it is shallow here. I fear—'

'Uncover the gun, Carnelia,' I said, taking it all in very quickly. 'Cut away the covers if you must. But do it now!'

She frowned. But she moved to obey.

'Full speed,' I said to Tenebrae.

'I am already there, Livia,' he said.

'Let me see.' I pushed him away from the Miraculous and swung the contraption about. We were in a channel, and there were different gradations of blue in the water ahead that from experience indicated to me varying depths. Without a lifetime of experience, I did not have the confidence to submerge here. There were too many unknowns.

'Vary your course, two points off port, two points off starboard,' I said. It was not much but all I could think to do. 'I will address our pursuit.'

'But—'

'No time,' I said. Reaching out, I snatched the longknife he wore at his hip and ran to the fore of the *Typhon*.

I wrenched the door to the *armamare* and *munusculum* chamber open and raced down into the cold darkness. For a moment I felt a panic threatening my strange calm, but my hand found the shutter of the *daemonlight* lantern and the space became illuminated.

Moving to the rear of the chamber, I yanked open the *munusculum* breeches, sliced my palm with Tenebrae's knife, and blooded the munitions. The infernal contraptions smoked and glowed. The stench of sulphur and the despair of the damned filled the space. With no ceremony I hefted by main strength, one by one, the pair of *munuscula* into firing position, closed their breeches and triggered their release.

From without, a great boom sounded. It was not the *Typhon*'s deck gun. It was further away, distant. Our ship shuddered and pitched over. I fell against the bulkhead.

There was a silence. The *Typhon* righted itself.

I returned to the command, breathless.

'She still follows!' Tenebrae yelled. It was quiet now; Fiscelion had ceased his wailing. So Tenebrae's voice boomed in the stillness of the chamber.

'The *munusculum* are re—'

There was another great boom. Tenebrae tensed, looking into the Miraculous.

'The mine detonated! Yet the frigate still churns the waves,' he said.

'There is another,' I said. 'Wait for it.'

Nothing.

'She slows,' Tenebrae said. 'She's become wary.'

Carnelia returned to the command, breathless. 'The gun's free. I go to my station.'

She disappeared into the rear of the ship. Soon, the ratcheting sound of the swivel moving on its trucks reverberated through the length of our vessel. Another distant boom sounded. The *Typhon* shuddered.

'We are fast, and with very little profile,' Tenebrae said. 'But she will strike us eventually if we do not outrun her, outgun her, or submerge.'

The pomp of our deck gun shivered our vessel, the despair of Hellfire washed over me. And maybe, maybe in that instant, the *daemonic* influence of munitions washing over me, I made my decision.

I found Lupina and Fiscelion in our cabin. 'Give him to me,' I said. The *dvergar* woman looked at me dubiously. 'This is not a request,' I said.

She handed him to me, reluctantly. I took him, held him close to my chest, and quickly raced out of the cabin and to the back of the ship.

In Typhon's Bower, the great engine pulsed when I entered. Its malevolence was palpable. The warding keeping the *daemon* bound emitted an evil illumination as I approached. The ship shuddered once again with Hellfire. Caught in the magnetic power of the *Typhon*'s dynamo, I could not tell if it was our guns or the Medierans'.

Fiscelion turned his eyes on the glowing wardwork, drawn to

233

the point of precium, the concentric snarls and skeins of silver threading in whorls down to a glowing mouth.

I took my son's hand and dragged the knife across it. He screamed and writhed in my grasp. From behind me, Lupina shouted, '*No!*'

I placed Fiscelion's hand on the mouth of the *Typhon*.

The engine began to smoke and shimmer. The thrumming pitched higher. The sensation of doom both increased and lessened all at once. Fiscelion's cries pitched toward unbearable. Lupina forcefully took Fiscelion from my grasp. The screaming diminished even as the sensation of speed grew.

I was alone in the room. I fell to my knees. At the edges of my awareness I could hear Tenebrae whooping and Carnelia calling out in joy and distantly felt another percussive boom of Hellfire.

I remained that way for a long while, on my knees in front of the *daemon* drive.

I did not cry.

We passed into the Bay of Mageras without further incident, having outpaced the Medieran frigate. It became procedure to stay submerged as much as possible to avoid detection from the enemy's ships in these waters.

Carnelia and I remained on edge. The remarkable speed of the *Typhon* due to the precium of Fiscelion's blood continued for days. We made amazing time, passing Aurelia and Mammon's outflow at dusk one evening, witnessing its giant cannons and thousand twinkling lights reflected on the waters and wondering if it was held by Ruman forces or Medieran. No flag flew from parapets, spires, or wharf and we dared not get closer.

Mountains appeared first as a discolouration on the horizon and disappeared in the distance, grey and framed by our wake by the end of the next day. We spotted scores of Medieran ships and spent only moments every day not submerged. The waters became deeper, there where the mountains' skirts plunged into the sea on rocky cliffs. We kept the peaks within view on our port and soon they took on the gunmetal-blued appearance I'd come to know of the Eldvatch mountains as we came around the cape. The mountains gave way to lower land, eaten away by marsh and finally, one bright morning, we passed a port with no Medieran ships and hazarded a quick exploration. It was a small coastal village, and almost every pier and wharf had half-sunken barges and derelict ships moored there. On nearing the shore, no wharf master greeted us, no gunship found us in the bay. Seagulls wheeled and banked overhead, making their lonesome cries on the heights. No bell rang, no stevedores hollered work songs. No drunken lascars sang bawdy songs.

We tied to the end of a pier, and I left Carnelia on board with the deck guns uncloaked, should any Medieran vessel surprise us – she was to fire the remaining swivel to alert us while we were ashore.

Tenebrae and I – not dressed as captain or lascar, surely, but in our civilian garb – walked to the end of the pier. A pack of wharf dogs ran away from us, yipping, as we approached. No fires sent smoke heavenward.

We went up one street, into a rough tenement neighbourhood. The seagull-threaded silence was uncanny.

'There,' Tenebrae said. He pointed. An old man sat smoking, his chair leaned back against the wall. 'Hey, old timer,' Tenebrae said, as we drew near.

'Yessir, a-yessir,' the man said. Sunken-cheeked, he gummed the end of his corncob pipe. I could not tell his exact stature, since he was in a semi-reclining position, but his oversized hands indicated he had some *dvergar* blood.

'Can you tell us where we are?' I asked. 'The wharf was empty.'

'A-yassum, a-yassum,' he said. 'That it is.'

'And this place is—?'

'Wickerware, ma'am, where the baskets come from,' he said.

'The Hardscrabble!' I said, before I could stop myself.

'A-yep, ma'am, the very arse-end of it,' he said.

'Where is everyone?' Tenebrae asked.

'Fled north, seeing as them beaners are all over Mageras and on the march now.'

'Beaners?' Tenebrae said.

'Them Medierans,' the old man said.

'And you remained? Why did you not flee with them?' I asked.

'I'm old, ma'am, and full of sleep. And rum,' he said. 'This here's my home and these hands ain't much good for digging, no more, up there at Dvergar silverlode. Don't care much for the Rumans, anyway, beg your pardon.'

'So the silverlode in the Eldvatch is now working?' I asked. If my father had lived, he would have been happy, since he had a large interest in it. He would have been displeased and petulant, however, at this current turn of events.

'If it ain't yet, it will be soon. Neruda set his teeth to it,' the old man said.

'Neruda is the leader of the *dvergar* now?' I asked. Fisk had written some of the man, back when we both had Quotidians and the blood to make them sing.

'A-yep,' he said. 'He's a real firebrand, too, that one. Sent a century of Rumans packing, crying for their mams,' he said.

'News from New Damnation?' I asked.

'Last I heard, Rume had some folks there, they'd fought off the 'Derians,' he said.

'At the fort there?' Tenebrae asked.

'A-yep,' he said, nodding.

'New Damnation is reachable by the Big Rill,' I said to Tenebrae.

'And the river there is ample deep enough for the—' I waved my hand, indicating the wharf. I did not want to say the *Typhon*'s name in this man's hearing. I probably had already said too much. I couldn't imagine that this old *dvergar* remained behind solely because of stubbornness. He would talk. And judging by Tenebrae's glance at me, he had come to the same conclusion.

'Thank you, sir,' Tenebrae said.

'How 'bout something for my troubles,' the old man said.

'Of course,' Tenebrae said, and withdrew some copper denarii. 'And let me offer you some free advice. You might be old, but you'll never get any older when you cross Rume.'

The man cocked an eye at Tenebrae. 'Been hearin' that since I was a pup. Might be true. Same could be said for the beaners.' He looked around. 'Thank you for your advice. Lemme give you a tad: this here's the Hardscrabble, son, even if it is its arsehole. And the Hardscrabble don't give two shits which way you bow. It'll eat you up, anyway.'

Tenebrae frowned. I placed a hand on his arm. 'We know where we are, now. Let us go.'

Back on board the *Typhon*, we found Carnelia breathless and stir-crazy. She only settled once the *Typhon* was away, and Wickerware distant behind us.

The next day, after sailing through the edges of stinking marsh and swampy glades, we found the ruins of Harbour Town and the outflow of the Big Rill. There were Medieran frigates in the bay, swarmed with smaller ships – troop transports by the score, skiffs, baileys, scows, trawlers plying the waters – it was a bustling but chaotic sight.

'This could be to our benefit,' Tenebrae said. 'There.' He turned the Miraculous and stepped away, beckoning me to look. 'We wait until night, use the *armamare* to perforate that big bastard, and in the firestorm and confusion, head upriver.'

'I'm worried about the *Typhon*. I know the Big Rill's deep enough for us – barges have a deeper draught – but will we be able to submerge if we come on Medieran ships?' I said.

Tenebrae thought for a moment. 'We have a very large gun. I don't think it will be an issue. We're safer there than out here, with these frigates and warships.'

Fisk was somewhere ahead of us. Up the Big Rill. If we could make it to New Damnation, and Marcellus and his legions. Or beyond, to Bear Leg – *my father's town!* – we could find him. He could meet his son. I could feel his embrace once more and the world, for a moment at least, could be right again.

I don't know if I was in my right mind, then. All the desperation distilled into an instant and I made the choice.

'Draw back, out of the bay. Out of sight. We'll rise to surface, go on deck, take air. Wait for dusk, while there's still light,' I said. 'Then we'll blow that warship and head upriver.'

I let blood to appease the avaricious *daemons* that lurked inside and loaded the *armamare* with Tenebrae's help. I did the same for the *munuscula,* should any ship follow us upriver. I said a prayer to the seven gods I knew of, to Ia, to the numen, and whatever household gods that might bless ships of the sea, despite their infernal dynamos.

We took air, and stood on the deck. Fiscelion, his hand healing well though still swaddled in gauze, toddled about and gave me kisses, my betrayal forgotten. Lupina watched me closely, as if I was a danger to my own son – but it was no use telling her that I acted for his benefit alone, not hers, not mine, not Carnelia's. That was why she was his perfect guardian. She may even have been aware of my motives, but some recalcitrant part of her could not countenance me being cruel to be kind.

I must remember never to give her unchecked access to sweets, otherwise Fiscelion will grow outward rather than up.

The sun fell toward the western horizon, colouring the vault of sky in brilliant hues. We shut the hatches, and made our descent and powered into the harbour. Tenebrae had the helm, peering into the Miraculous. Over the last weeks, he'd developed a fine hand and second sense at the controls. I stationed myself on the *armamare* and *munusculum* triggers, awaiting his command.

Carnelia was hushed and watchful. Even Fiscelion was quiet, as if sensing the coming events.

'Approaching the Medieran warship,' Tenebrae said. 'Stand by.' He wrenched back the throttle and the *Typhon* slowed. 'Barge passing to our fore.' He reversed, and our vessel slowed even more. There was a long silence broken only by our own breathing. Tenebrae depressed the throttle again, never taking his eyes from the Miraculous. 'Closing on the Medieran warship. I can see her name. *Tormenta d'Fuegae*.' He chuckled. 'I think we can arrange that.'

He turned to me. 'Fire, Livia.'

I turned the lever and felt the *armamare* release, angry missiles lancing through the foam. 'Done.'

'Turning now to the mouth of the Big Rill,' Tenebrae said.

'Full speed ahead,' I said.

'Already there,' he responded. 'Passing the ruins of Harbour Town.' Something scraped the bottom of the *Typhon*, making a long sustained screech that had a palpable physiological effect on us all.

In a moment there was a boom to our aft. Tenebrae turned his face from the Miraculous as the light from it poured out. Soon after, the concussive wave.

We were a mile upriver when the *Tormenta d'Fuegae*'s *daemon* was released and emerged into our world, wreathed in fire and clawing at the sky.

'Good,' Carnelia said. 'Damn them all to Hell.'

*

We surfaced. Carnelia and Tenebrae unshrouded the deck gun. Tenebrae manned the helm, Carnelia and I kept watch from the fore of the *Typhon* since we had no pilot's roost like the *Cornelian* had. We made slow time, navigating the river. Open sea was much faster, and I had become accustomed to the heady, wild thrumming of our ship's engines and the great salty sprays of water geysering up from the prow. I had forgotten how somnolent river travel was. The *Typhon*'s engines were banked, barely noticeable.

We passed no ships. We saw neither riders nor soldiers. What villages we passed were destroyed, either by retreating Ruman soldiers or Medieran bloodlust, I could not tell.

We reached Confluence, and found it destroyed as well, though it was not total destruction as at Harbour Town, but damage from large artillery. We took small arms fire as we approached. I could not be sure if it was Medieran soldiers, Ruman legions, or native Occidentalians. I ordered Carnelia to target the largest standing building with the swivel and fire. It was reduced to travertine and timbers.

There was no more gunfire.

We entered Lake Brunnen and found a troop transport and small Medieran littoral there. Carnelia destroyed both with our deck gun.

The reach of Rume is long.

We spent the night where once the *Cornelian* had, looking at shore, miles upriver from Lake Brunnen. There would be no more descents below; the river was too shallow now and we remained in constant fear of grounding. The wind coming from the White Mountains was chill, and every star bright and brilliant in the crystalline heavens. It was the first time I felt as though I was home. I knew this place. These waters. These mountains. We remained on deck, wrapped in blankets, watching and waiting, Hellfire not too far from hand.

We had passed riders, earlier in the day. And even now, I sensed movement from both sides of the river. I knew not if stretchers still came down raiding from the high mountains, or if the Medierans had driven them further west. There remained something ineffably different about the land. Dispossessed once more. Lost from all men, all those who would lay claim to it, to place boot on it. None could claim it without contest – this was its history. This was its legacy.

It was with these thoughts that I noticed the tall silhouette on shore.

You can see a million things in a life, and forget all of them, but you will never forget the sight of a *vaettir*.

It watched us.

'Tenebrae,' I said. 'You have your carbine ready?'

'Yes,' he said.

'Carnelia? Do you see it?' I said, hushed.

'I see it,' she said. I heard the metallic rasp of her *jian* being drawn.

'Lupina, go below, please,' I said.

'We should all go below, Livia,' Lupina said.

'And hide?' I asked. 'Where any ship might find us and fire while we cower in the dark. No. They cannot fly.' I looked to shore. The stretcher seemed to have turned his attention to the ground. He bent and lifted something. A creature. No, a man.

He struggled in his captor's grasp. Screams echoed out across the water.

'Ia-damn,' Carnelia said. 'It's got someone. Poor fucker. That thing will have it naked, skinless, and dressed to the bones in a trice.' She lifted her sword and drew her Hellfire pistol, like some pirate from a children's book.

241

'I never saw them when we were in Kithai, except the boy Fantasma. And he was so—' Tenebrae said.

'Tiny,' Carnelia said. 'A toy stretcher.'

'That one yonder, though, it chills my—' Tenebrae stopped.

The *vaettir* on shore moved, racing downstream, his doomed captive over one shoulder. He bounded up, vaulting high, clearing scrub-brush and bramblewrack. The screams grew louder. '*EEEEeeeeeeeeeeeee . . .*'

The *vaettir*'s speed was ungodly, feet moving faster than the eye could discern. Suddenly, it changed course, lancing toward where the *Typhon* stood in the slow-moving waters of the Big Rill. Like a stone skipped on a pond, it came at us.

Carnelia bleated surprise. Tenebrae fumbled at his carbine. I stood standing there, dumbly, watching our death come.

It hit the sloped side of the *Typhon* with a metallic thud and suddenly the stretcher was airborne again. Tenebrae let off a wild shot, Carnelia barked her outrage and tried to sight her pistol down her wildly swinging arm.

The great creature came down upon the deck with a meaty *twhack!* and let spill its captive, who rolled onto the deck, cursing.

'Fucking Hell, Gynth, I'm not a sack of potatoes,' Shoestring said. He stood, felt for his hat, found it missing, looked flustered. Finally, he saw me. He gave a clumsy bow. 'Howdy, Livia. Fancy meeting you here.'

TWENTY-ONE

They Will Kill Me For The Waking

W E DID NOT tarry the first night or break for camp, but rode on through, despite hazard to the horses. Some things you keep tight in the secret chambers of your heart and I did not want to admit to Fisk how much I worried for Lina.

It's one thing to have a child. It's another to find a child, unlooked for, on the wild uncaring breast of the Hardscrabble. I would make sure she lived out her days to their fullest number.

Yet, I don't know if Fisk would have made dispensations for my departure and use of resources if he thought it was purely sentimental.

Though it wasn't.

Lina knew of the *daemon* hand. Should she be taken by the Medierans, the knowledge of who possessed it and its location would pass to them, if it had not already. And if I knew anything of war or the methods of the great powers in the world, the Medierans would have a host of engineers who would know what the hand signified.

We found evidence of a small camp a half day's ride from the Big Rill, in a riven dry-creek cutting through the shoal grasses. A long-dead fire had burned itself out, and there were bones there, among the ashes. A calf auroch, from the looks of it – bones cracked, marrow sucked out. No sign of their departure. No hint of their direction.

Riding hard, we made for the Big Rill and reached it on the eastern shore of Lake Brunnen. This was a populated region, for decades relatively free of *vaettir* raids and strife, situated so close to New Damnation. There was a homestead here, with orchards of albermarle and blackcurrant bushes in neat rows, cotton fields and beans nearer the lakeshore. Sodbuster's heaven now turned to Hell. The farmhouse was just a charred husk, and no inhabitants to be seen.

'Got a decision to make,' Catch Hands said. 'North to New Damnation? Or south to Confluence?'

I shrugged. 'They'd go north. We know the Medierans have taken Passasuego, and even though Lina and her scouts did not know it, they would've seen evidence of the disposition of the Medieran forces. Maybe.'

Gynth came bounding up. He pointed toward the shore, past the house. We followed him to the shore.

It was a lovely view, despite the burned homestead. A brisk breeze whipped down from the Whites, their peaks crowned in sunlight and clouds. The lake's waves, churned by wind, broke on the rocky beach, making a dull roar that took some effort to speak over. Far from shore there moved a shadow, like some shark lost from the sea. A black needle, steaming north.

'That thing have guns?' Catch Hands said. 'Looks like an Ia-damn moccasin cutting across a pond.'

'If it's Medieran, it'll rendezvous with troops. Our best bet is to find Lina and get the information Fisk needs. Get the mounts. We're following it. Gynth, make sure it doesn't get out of sight, and once it stops, get us. We'll be on your backtrail.' Gynth nodded and dashed away, following the shore to the north. Catch Hands returned with the mounts and we followed along behind.

It was nightfall when Gynth returned, after we'd skirted the town of Lake Brunnen. What was left of it.

Catch Hands shook his head and sighed. 'Them Medierans are hard sons-a-bitches,' he said. 'A-burning every building they pass.'

'I have my doubts it was the Medierans. The Rumans, in any sort of retreat, will burn as they go so as not to leave any resources for the enemy. Ruman legions torched that town, I'm afraid.'

'Damn shame. There was a scullery maid there I quite fancied,' he said. 'And she kissed sweet.'

'I'm sure she's fine,' I said. 'And still kissing errant *dvergar*.'

Catch Hands glared at me for a moment, then smiled.

Hugging the river, we made our way north, Gynth leading us on. It was full dark by the time we'd overtaken the shadowed vessel. It was slung lower than a barge, its only telltales the guns on its deck.

We watched for a long while. Eventually figures appeared above deck to turn their faces to the moon and mountains. Undeniable faces. Faces I knew. Some, even, I loved.

I screamed. I hollered. Livia and her crew jumped, startled. I saw furtive movement, Carnelia ducking below the gunwales.

'Ia-dammit. Gynth, we spooked them. Can you—' I waved my hand at the Big Rill. 'Do your ... *waterwalking*.' This last word created wholly from *Dvergar*. Gynth's large mouth cracked in a jagged smile.

He took me in his big hands before I could protest, slung me over his shoulder, and then *moved*. My gut lurched. I felt as though I'd spew up the hardtack I'd eaten earlier. Lightning fast, the shore diminished behind me, I felt a fine spray of water and then the world turned upside down and we were in the air and tumbling head over arse. The boom of Hellfire sounded and the smell of brimstone spiced the air.

Then I was tumbling on metal. When I came to a stop, I pushed myself upright, as fast as my spinning head was able.

'Fucking Hell, Gynth, I'm not a sack of potatoes,' I said, glaring at the *vaettir*. I reached to doff my hat – it was gone, maybe lost for good down river. I gave my friend the best bow I could manage. 'Howdy, Livia. Fancy meeting you here.'

She gasped. Then, before I knew it, I was crushed to her breast and merry peals of laughter rang out – Carnelia.

'You know these two?' A man's voice.

'I know this one,' Livia said, holding me out at arm's length. 'Oh my, Mister Ilys! Never before in my life have I been happier to see someone. Anyone!'

'I imagine we can change that,' I said. 'I can take you to Fisk.'

The reaction in her was immediate. Her hands tightened on me, as if she would not let me go for fear of losing her connection to her husband.

Gynth remained still, but Carnelia stirred at the big stretcher's presence and turned to face him. 'Holy Hell,' she breathed. 'Will he—'

'This is Gynth. I believe Fisk wrote to you about him,' I said. 'He is a friend to us all.'

Carnelia looked at me and back to the *vaettir*. 'It is hard to countenance. But we met elves in Kithai, and not all of them wanted us dead, either.' She shrugged, though she did not sheathe her sword.

That one had changed, I saw immediately. No longer a winesoaked little rag. She'd put on meat, and moved like one of the big cats coming down from the mountain. It'd been more than a year, at least, and how things can change.

'Howdy, Miss Carnelia,' I said. 'Glad to see you well. I was terrible sad at the news of Secundus. He was a good lad. One of the best.'

The man standing, loosely holding the carbine, said, 'You knew Secundus?'

'Aye, sir. For my part, I counted him among my friends,' I said.

The man came forward, hand extended. We shook. 'I am Marcus Tenebrae, once of the Praetorian. It is a pleasure to make your acquaintance.'

'And I, yours,' I said. 'Your ship is quite a number.'

He chuckled and released my hand. 'It's not mine! It's Livia's,' he said.

'We're pirates now, Shoestring!' Carnelia said, voice bright.

'Much has changed,' I said. 'And things are cracking. Mediera has taken Passasuego and the Talavera silverlode. Their troops are on the move in the west. Fisk now commands this theatre for Rume.'

Livia said, 'My husband?' There was disbelief there, but some pride mixed in too, I thought.

'Yes, ma'am,' I said. 'He is as surprised as you at this turn of events. Marcellus took his best men and legions east, to protect Novorum.'

Livia sighed. 'I fear that was a mistake. The Medieran fleet firebombed Novorum – we witnessed it first-hand.'

'Are you saying that the two understrength legions at the Dvergar silverlode are all we have in the west?' I asked.

'I do not know,' she said. 'There's much for us to discuss and we have some decisions to come to before morning.' She looked at me closely. Like Carnelia, she was different too. Before, there was always merriment with Livia, like a fire banked low, simmering behind her breast. She could shift from fierce to kind, loving to wrathful, easily and by turns, but a good humour always ran underneath it all.

But no more. This world makes monsters of us all, eventually.

'But first, Shoe,' Livia said. 'Let us get you acquainted with my son, Fiscelion.'

*

The boy and I hit it off from the start. He yanked my beard and squealed, drooling, and tried to stuff my paw in his mouth. Gynth would not go inside the vessel, and I found it not much to my liking either. Livia brought the lad to me and showed no fear at the dark of night, the Whites in the distance, or the *vaettir* towering above us all.

It seemed that Lupina, Cornelius' old servant, still found very little in my visage or demeanour that pleased her. And Gynth pleased her even less.

'I must go to Fisk,' Livia said. 'I have crossed half a world to get back to him. To present him Fiscelion, his son.'

'Of course,' I said. I filled her in on the situation with Fisk and Neruda at Grenthvar, and Beleth's sorry end. She stared at me grimly as I recounted the tale and gave a single nod of approval. I also told her of Lina, and the scouts.

'That is a definite concern,' she said. 'But one that will have to wait.'

'The disposition of the Medieran troops is something we need to know,' I said. 'Fortifications of the Grenthvar have begun, but we're woefully unprepared. But Fisk needs to know of the firebombing of Novorum.' I gnawed my lip. 'It's a hard choice. I do not want to abandon Lina.'

Gynth moved to stand near me. With each of his movements, Livia, Carnelia, and the man named Tenebrae tensed. Living with *vaettir* takes getting used to.

'That one is also *gynth*,' the *vaettir* said. 'And she would not thank you for collecting her.'

'You've got a point. But I'm concerned for *her*, not her feelings,' I said.

'Are they not part of her?' he asked. 'She'll return. We are *gynth*.'

'Yeah, I got that,' I said.

'I go to find my kind,' he said in *dvergar*. 'I will bring back your hat.'

'Who?' I asked. Sometimes it was hard to tell what the big lunk was talking about, his mind moved down such strange pathways.

'Our kin. Like Neruda, I will make bargain with them,' he said.

'*Stretchers?*' I asked. 'You'll make bargain with stretchers?'

'Yes,' he responded. 'They are *gynth*. They are of this place like you, like me. And we will plough a furrow together.'

'Fuck me with a rake,' I said.

Gynth cocked his head and said in common: 'What is a rake?'

'Nothing,' I said, waving it away. 'Can you do it?' I asked.

'Nothing is written, nothing is sure,' he said, switching from *dvergar* to common and back again. 'But I will try.'

Livia and her companions watched and listened closely to me conversing with Gynth. I helped to fill in the gaps. They had seen *vaettir* in motion, their utter viciousness when attacking, their mischievousness. The disbelief was plain on their faces, even in the half-light of the stars and moon.

'Not all are—' He paused, thinking. '*Brindrelivis*,' he said, using the word for poison. 'But they do not come down often to these lands. They dream in their nests and caves,' he said. 'I will wake them. And we will cut a furrow.'

I nodded, taking it all in. The world was bigger and stranger than any of us knew.

'All right, pard,' I said to Gynth. 'So that's that. But if you see Lina, tell her to hie her arse home, will you?'

'I don't understand,' he said. 'But I will tell her to hurry.'

'This is all well and good,' Livia said. 'But the hour grows late and we've one more thing to decide.'

'What is that?' Tenebrae asked.

'The *Typhon*,' she said. 'It is a formidable ship.'

'Just today we sank a littoral *and* a troop ship,' Carnelia added. 'Would that it had been full of soldiers.'

'We could scuttle it in the lake,' Tenebrae said. 'I am desperate to be off her and on land once more, but I am loath to destroy her, as well. She's served us well.'

'And may serve us again in need,' Livia said. 'But I cannot countenance her falling into Medieran hands. Now she is a secret.'

'A secret?' I asked. 'She's sleek, I'll give you that, but—'

'Shoe, you do not understand the true nature of the *Typhon*,' Livia said. 'She is submersible.'

'You're shitting me,' I said.

'I shit you not,' Livia responded. She allowed a smile to cross her features. But I felt as though she did so only due to the niceties of our reunion.

'That is something I will have to see,' I said.

'It will be some time before that, if ever,' Livia said. 'I fully intend to leave her this very night and ride east with you. She'll either be destroyed or—'

'Or will have herself a new commander,' Tenebrae said. 'I will take her. She is too valuable to lose and I am still of Rume. I'll not let the *Typhon* fall into Medieran hands.'

'Where will you take her?' Livia asked.

'Back into the bay,' Tenebrae said. 'To Wickerware, I think. And to Covenant. I will move between them.'

'No,' Livia said. 'Rume will need the *Typhon*.'

'But the Hardscrabble is contested. The future is uncertain. You may need me and I would not see Fiscelion in want of a ship and none to be had.'

'I can't—' Livia began.

Tenebrae held up his hand. 'I will harry the Medierans by sea. I will go to Covenant or Aurelia and get lascars. But on the nones, and the ides, and seven ides, I will be in Wickerware. This is my word and warrant. It is the closest port to us not held by Mediera. If you signal, with fire, with smoke, I will see. Understood?'

There was a long silence as we all considered this. Finally, Livia nodded her head. She kissed Tenebrae and whispered, 'Secundus could have done worse.'

The blush that filled the man's face was priceless.

'Well, fuck,' Carnelia said. 'You can't run her alone. You'll need me. Running a ship with only two lascars is ... ridiculous.'

'We did it with four,' Tenebrae said. 'I'll stay beneath the waves.'

'Gynth,' I said. 'Can you fetch Catch Hands?'

The *vaettir* nodded and leapt away, legs churning faster than butterfly wings when he hit the water, leaving a moon-silvered wake behind him.

In moments Catch Hands was on deck and spluttering. 'You fuckin' gullet, manhandling me like that! I ought to—' He caught sight of Livia and Carnelia. 'Pardon me, madames. Ladies.'

'Inbhir,' I said. 'Allow me to introduce you to the crew of the *Typhon*.' I went through them one by one, without forgetting Fiscelion himself, who gurgled and laughed at Catch Hands' amazed face. 'Would you believe that this ship is submersible?' I asked.

He looked at me with a puzzled expression, very much like Gynth when confronted with a word in common he did not understand. 'What's that?'

'Submers—' I stopped. 'It means that this ship will dive under the surface of the water.'

'You're shitting me,' he said. Tenebrae laughed.

'I shit you not,' I said.

'That's something I need to see,' Catch Hands said.

'That can be arranged,' Livia said. 'Welcome to the crew of the *Typhon*, Mister Inbhir.'

'Mister? Nobody's ever called me "mister" before,' Catch Hands said. 'Everybody calls me Catch Hands.'

*

Livia embraced Carnelia and Tenebrae, giving them each a very formal Ruman farewell – a kiss on both cheeks, a hand on first her heart, then theirs. Grown stronger, that one, and colder. Full of steel, and hard-bitten. I hoped she had not become brittle with her transformation.

Lupina endured Carnelia's fawnings with some aplomb, but she frowned when she noticed me watching. Carnelia wept and covered Fiscelion's face in kisses. He squirmed and made outraged sounds. The boy was ornery. She spoke in a hushed, raw voice. I drew Catch Hands away to give them their privacy. They had circumnavigated the world, almost, by themselves in a ship they'd stolen. I could not imagine the bonds something like that forged. The three of them had a connection and their fellowship was breaking – only Livia remained dry-eyed.

To save us from swimming or the *Typhon* foundering in the shallows, Gynth ported us one by one to the shore. Except for Lupina, who refused to be separated from Fiscelion. She fashioned an infant's sling and glared at the *vaettir* as if daring him to say or do anything in response. Once ashore, the *dvergar* woman sank to her knees and kissed the dirt of the Hardscrabble and whispered, 'Home.'

The sky wore its deepest cloak of night, the moon having passed beyond the rim of the earth. Gynth looked to the White Mountains. 'I may die,' he said to me, simply, in the *dvergar* tongue.

'Are you afraid?' I asked.

'I do not know,' he said. 'I do not want to die.'

'Do you think you'll be able to make this bargain with your kin?' I said.

'Our kin,' he said. 'We are of this land.'

'Yes,' I said. 'I guess we are.'

'I think the sleeping ones will awaken, as I did,' he said. 'We

252

live long lives, and fall into nights that seem endless. But all nights end.' He looked at me and placed his hand on my shoulder. 'I will wake them and we will cut a furrow together. Or—'

'Or?'

'They will kill me for the waking.' He shrugged.

'Try not to let that happen,' I said.

'I will try,' he said.

'We are more than *gynth*.'

He cocked his head, quizzical.

'We are friends. Go with my thoughts, my prayers to the numen of stone and sky,' I said.

With a ruffle of cloth, he launched himself into the air and sped away.

We were two days on the Hardscrabble plain back to Grenthvar. In the days gone, considerable fortifications had been erected – deep trenches, the Frislandian wooden crosses that looked like many crucifixions lined up in a row and then turned on their sides, jumbled masses of stone at the edge of the killing fields, sniper towers on ridgelines and in the trees. Two score of wheeled cannons formed a line, half-obscured by the multiple iron-shod dragon's teeth littering the killing fields. Sangars and escarpments were being dug and constructed by shirtless and sweating legions who paid us no mind as we passed. The mechanised wagons with the large-bore swivelling cannons looked to the west and had good vantage over the whole mouth of the valley. The trees around the Grenthvar River had all been cut down. A sad sight to see, but they offered too much cover.

Black smoke poured toward the heavens from the Breadbasket and my *dvergar* kin – pushing one wheelbarrow after another – added to the ever-growing slag heaps on the edges of the fortification line. The sounds of industry, hammer-falls, tumbling timber, lumber being worked, the cries of workmen and legionnaires, filled the air of the valley.

A stillness had descended upon Livia, though, and even Fiscelion seemed to pick up on it. An optio, seeing us approach the praetorium tent and dismount, ducked inside.

Fisk appeared, his face stricken with disbelief. He took two measured steps toward Livia. He stopped.

Then he ran. At the end he fell to his knees before her. He clutched her to him, pressing his face into her stomach – ending their separation as it began.

Livia drew him up, and kissed him. She looked into his face for a long while and whispered something I could not hear. Then she beckoned Lupina forward and Fisk took up his son in trembling hands.

For the first time in my experience, I watched the tears well up and fall from him.

He raised his son on high with both hands and gave an exultant cry.

TWENTY-TWO

Make Them Fear The Night.
Kill Their Horses. Unman Them.

Entering the Ruman camp, I soon learned that Seanchae had returned from his scouting expedition. I found him at the mess tent, making short work of a mutton stew, spooning it into his maw with abandon and sopping it up with coarse bread.

'Lina went north, up Broken Tooth way,' he said between mouthfuls, when I asked him about my granddaughter. 'She was to push west to Sundered Rock and get a take on the Medierans at Passasuego.'

'And you?' I asked.

'Porto Caldo and Hot Springs,' he said. 'Couldn't get too close because the Medierans were thicker than ticks in a dog's ear.'

'How many do you think?' I asked.

'I reckon a thousand there, at least,' he said. 'I've made my report to the legate. Didn't seem too happy about it.'

'No,' I said. 'He wouldn't be.' I scratched my beard.

'You sweet on her, or something?' Seanchae asked. 'You're a mite long in the tooth for a woman that spry, I reckon.'

'No,' I said. 'She's my daughter's kid.'

'Ah. Well, I've scouted with Lina for nigh on a decade, and there ain't no one that can stop her when she don't want to be stopped, or find her when she don't want to be found. She'll be back soon enough,' he said.

Camp took on its final form, and I could see the town it would be someday if it continued on its current path without molestation – neat streets in a grid, brew tent, mess tent, praetorium tent billowing from the centre. At the edges, munitioners and farriers and craftsmen. Throughout, the bustle of legions fulfilling their duties.

Fisk and Livia spent the night together, of course, in the praetorium. The junior legates, messengers, secretaries, lictors, engineer liaisons, and Ruman personnel on whom the command of legions depended were, if but for a single night, exiled to the domain of the rankers, taking their stew in their own tents. There was much speculation in the general population of camp as to their commander and his newly returned wife's reunion. And their night-time exertions. But, on the whole, the legionnaires' opinion of their commander, which was tenuous at best beforehand, had swung toward pride.

Word came to me in the morning that Lina had returned. I found her heading for the Breadbasket but caught her before she passed beyond the Pactum Wall.

'Heard you went outriding, looking for me,' she said, shaking her head.

I shrugged. 'I had my reasons. You were late.'

'Shot my pony, I had to lead a passel of beaners up and down the escarpment on foot and then steal one of their horses as they slept.' She gave me an evil smile. 'Those that were still alive,' she said, hefting her carbine.

'And the dispensation of the Medieran troops?' I asked.

'Swarming around Passasuego, mad as Hell the silver's petering out.'

'Numbers?' I asked.

'Five battalions. The beaners organise their troops differently to Rumans. Three thousand. Five hundred horse. A contingent of cannoneers. Not much heavy artillery, though, we're evenly matched there,' she said. 'And few engineers, though the ones they have are guarded like virgins at Ludi Florae.' She sniffed. 'They're mobilising. Word has reached them of the fortifications here. They're cocky as Hell now that Novorum burns.' She squared her shoulders and looked at me. 'But we're far from the sea, where their strength is.'

'That's true. They're not known so much for their land forces. Livia told of some hellacious large artillery coming from their destroyers.'

'Over here, the scariest damned things they've got is a bevy of those freakish *daemon*-gripped men, and they bound about, patrolling the city now, like hounds.'

'How many?'

'No clear way to tell, but a shitload,' Lina said. She sucked her teeth. 'And they're using them as scouts.'

'That's not good,' I said.

'Hell no, it isn't. And what's worse, it all has to do with that hand that *daemon*-gripped stretcher wanted.'

'Not exactly.' I hesitated. 'You're fishing.'

'It's something, and I want to know what,' she said. 'I'm not risking my arse again for the Rumans unless I know why.'

I drew her aside. 'It's difficult to explain, but it's tied up with the engineer that started all this.'

'The one you got hogtied?' she asked.

'Not any more,' I said.

She looked at me, meaningfully.

'Harbour Town,' I said. 'That was on him. Rume. All the *daemon*-gripped. *Him*. I put the son of a bitch out of his misery.'

She shrugged. 'Nice to see you've not gone totally tame,' she said. 'But this hand he was after. You're gonna tell me what it is.'

So I did, the whole story. She looked amazed by the end of it.

'Well, that's a doozy. And I can see why they want it. Someone willing to use it would be desperate. Or insane,' she said.

'Or both,' I said.

'It's of no matter to Neruda and Praeverta now, I imagine. Your boss has got his legions around him and no one will take it from him.'

'I think he'd be fine with someone taking that yoke from him,' I said. 'I don't think he'd give up the responsibility that easily, though. Once he's got his teeth into something, he never lets go.'

'He'll either be a great commander. Or a dead one,' Lina said, and without a word turned to go.

The next day brought rumour of Medierans in force on the Hardscrabble. Fisk summoned Lina and myself to his praetorium to take breakfast. Livia attended as well, and she greeted me with much warmth, kissing me on the cheek and immediately presenting me with Fiscelion. The tightness I'd sensed about her had unclenched some, though her appearance was unaltered, but she seemed more refreshed and better rested. The child, on the other hand, was a bundle of energy.

I entertained myself with the boy, who was a sturdy little pup. He liked tugging at my mustachios and nose, and squirmed and fought to place my big, blunt fingers in his mouth.

'He's teething,' Livia said. 'And will nip your fingers off, Shoe.' Lupina watched me closely, frowning. But she couldn't squawk overloud since the boy took to me well enough and I stood high in Livia's favour.

'He's got a strong grip, that's for sure,' I said, wincing as young Fiscelion mauled my beard.

Fisk laughed and gestured for Lupina to take the boy. I was a mite disappointed – I was never the most doting of men, but the older I grow, the more I appreciate youth, the white parchment of it. The Hardscrabble is a great arena where only providence and willingness to defend your own against others, the land, the creatures that walk upon it, keeps you alive. But you never come out the other side unmarred. All the more reason to cherish the unblemished, the innocent, the young. I looked at Lina.

'More scouts have returned. Ruman outriders report that the Medierans have abandoned all secrecy and they're riding patrol in great numbers with gunmen and *daemon*-gripped throughout the shoal grasses and Hardscrabble,' Fisk said.

'Sounds about right,' Lina said, nodding. 'They can field more soldiers, so they've become brazen. No need for subterfuge.'

'This morning, I let blood for the Quotidian, the one linked with Marcellus, and much news came to me,' Fisk said, looking grave. 'The world is in shambles, even beyond Occidentalia. Rume is gone. Tamberlaine has moved his capital north, toward Gall, and ensconced himself in his northern palace where the Unsch River falls into Latinum, his forces in disarray. Mediera has formed an alliance with some Tuetons, and provides them Hellfire and support. They harry Tamberlaine unmercifully, and neither can carve out a decisive victory. An *archdaemon* still prances about in fire in the ruins of Rume. Novorum is destroyed, along with Fort Lucullus. Marcellus' forces have suffered major losses and have ventured south to Covenant and the mouth of the Mammon. From there he will attempt to mobilise and bring them west. Though there is no evidence of Mediera landing any significant forces on the east coast.' He turned to the maps scattered about the main praetorium table. 'All attention has been directed here. Because of the silver. Kithai wars with itself – and your friend the Sword of Jiang is at the centre of that, alongside his brother, as they attempt to unify the nation. Yet Mediera has set its eyes on Far Tchinee and has split its fleet. Medieran warships harbour in the Jiang bay.'

A secretary brought us boiled chicory coffee in ceramic mugs. Fisk took up his and winced after sipping. It was bitter.

' "Silver changes all fortunes," so says Willem Bless,' he said. 'Rume's has changed for the worse, and with it, all of the indigenes'.'

'Maybe,' I said. 'Seems that the *dvergar*, at least, have gained some, pard.'

Fisk frowned. 'In 2301, Pierga the Bilious of Mediera killed every native on Cephalenia – a people very much like the *dvergar* and without their *vaettir* cousins. He tore down their buildings, their temples, razed their villages, renamed the blasted isle Balearia and set up an Ia-damned duchy. The *cephalos* are gone now, all of them. The Medierans have killed whole *races*.'

'Is Rume so different?' I said.

Livia arched an eyebrow. 'You are still alive, are you not?'

'Thanks to our *vaettir* cousins, I would hazard,' I said. 'And the fact that Rume loves slaves and servants almost as much as Hellfire.'

Fisk waved his hand, dismissing the statement. 'I will not argue with you regarding Rume's oppressive tendencies. However, we have a history of democracy, though the line of Tarquins that have landed us with Tamberlaine have changed us as a nation. Yet some of that democracy still lives. We are pragmatic, to the core. Mediera has passed from pragmatism into madness.'

It was surprising to hear him refer to Rumans as 'us' since he'd spent most of his life on the outside looking in at Ruman life. The Hardscrabble changes all men, but some men's natures are indomitable.

He looked at me and his gaze shifted to Lina. 'I'll work to ensure *dvergar* rights, as I have promised Neruda. Right now, I need your help.' He beckoned us to look at the map of the Hardscrabble from the Illvatch to the Grenthvar, from the Big Empty up north to the Bay of Mageras. Fisk lifted a carved travertine figure he'd taken from a knightboard – a stone horse representing cavalry. He placed it south-east of Passasuego, in the crook between the Big Rill and the White River.

'They ride with no resistance now from Rume and we have not enough men to stop them. But we have one advantage – we know the Hardscrabble. I have some soldiers, those men born and raised here, and I have you, the *dvergar*, who can move in the hills, in the shoals, in the gulleys and through bramblewrack, and harry them. We must harry them. They cannot come to think of this place as theirs. We will disabuse them of this notion.'

Lina was nodding as he spoke, eyes bright. I could tell wheels turned behind her eyes – she had ideas.

Fisk nodded at Livia and she rose, left the praetorium tent and returned shortly with Sapientia. 'Since you've been gone, I've tasked Sapientia to our western problem.'

My friend wore dungarees and an engineer's leather apron, scorched leather gloves tucked into her belt that held knives, awls, rasps. And, in a holster, a slick-looking firearm. She had her shirtsleeves rolled up to her biceps and her arms were corded with muscle. She winked at me.

'Obviously, I have reason to want to be part of this mission, Shoe,' Sapientia said. 'I've lived most of my adult life in Passasuego and here, in the West. I would not see it die underneath Medieran hands.'

'If there's a mission, and Sapientia is a part of it, you don't even have to ask. I am invested,' I said, turning back to my old partner. I guess he wasn't my partner any more. More like boss, it seemed. Wasn't ever an even partnership, anyway. 'What's the mission, Fisk?'

'You'll pick ten of your best, along with ten legionnaires, and Sapientia, and you will make the Medierans regret they ever came to Occidentalia. We're in desperate need of time, for mining, smelting, munitions, and fortifications.' He looked at me. 'I trust you, Shoe. Harry these sons of whores. Slow them. Make them fear the night. Kill their horses. Unman them.'

'War with their minds,' I said. I nodded. 'I can do that. Lina?'

'I've already picked out my men,' she said.

'We'll have guns and horses enough?' I asked.

'Yes. You won't want for any supplies,' he said. 'The only thing you'll lack is time.'

'We're always short on time,' I said. I stood up. 'So let me meet these legionnaires. Will they have issues with me? With Lina and her men?'

'They'll not question you. I've made sure of that. You're not going to like this, Shoe,' he said. He dug in his pocket and withdrew something metal and tossed it at me. I snatched it out of the air. It was a badge with a vitis emblazoned on the front, and words praising Immortal Rume. The vitis – traditionally, the centurion's staff of office – looked uncomfortably like a phallus without the nuts.

'Centurion Ilys,' Livia said, placing a hand on my shoulder. 'Would you like some more coffee?'

'No,' I said, trying to take it all in. 'But I could use a drink.'

TWENTY-THREE

The Dogs Might Turn On Their Masters

Of Lina's men, I only knew three – Seanchae, Ringold, and the one they called the Wee Garrotte. Of the Ruman legionnaires, I knew only a man named Aemelanus Sumner who was an evocati wolf of the seventh legion – indeed, all the Rumans legionnaires to accompany us were wolves. Sumner had been one of the men escorting the *Cornelian* up the Big Rill, so long ago, when he'd faced stretchers, pistoleros, and all the beasts of the shoal. I could recall no *dvergar* hate from him, but I daresay he would rather serve a Ruman commander, though I imagine Fisk had sorted out any umbrage these men might feel at my primacy. Mediera was knocking on the Hardscrabble doors and all of his men were ready to answer them.

We rode out, fast and hard, and covered many miles the first day. The legionnaires gave Sapientia and Lina sly looks but other than that there were no overtures made by the soldiers, which was a remarkable amount of restraint for men of a legion that had not seen any rest or relaxation for over a year.

Sapientia handled herself well on horseback and outlined her thoughts regarding the anti-cavalry tactics.

'We've got to get as far west and north as we can, quickly. To find the Medieran van. We cause them enough problems,' Sapientia said, holding the reins loosely in her hands and looking west, 'they'll become incensed and reckless. They'll be happy to chase us.'

'And then we can lead them a merry chase,' I said, nodding. It was a good plan.

'One with a bloody end, for them, at least,' she said. 'I need to know possible places for ambush.'

'We convince ourselves we can hold and keep a land but, as we've learned hard, we're easily dispossessed. There are nameless and mapless miles of sun-cracked rocks, scrub, bramblewrack, ridgeline and valley that neither man, *dvergar*, nor *vaettir* hold and there's no trace of their feet passing over them. Those bits of the Hardscrabble we've had the pride – maybe hubris – to name and know are few. Sometimes the shoal grasses are an ocean, every trail a dead river.'

'I would not have known you were a poet, Shoe, simply from your appearance,' Sapientia said, smiling.

I cleared my throat. There was always something about her that made me, if not uneasy, then discomposed. Her bright intelligence and beauty could catch me off guard at the strangest of moments. 'There's the Bitter Spring and the Long Slide, but we've already used those against them, or at least their engineer and his men, and I have no idea if they discovered the bodies or know of those locations.' I rubbed my chin. 'There's thousands of gulleys and riven creek beds that end in canyons. Any one of them will do. There's Big Sugarloaf and Wee Sugarloaf.'

'Sugarloaf?' Sapientia asked.

'They've got other names. *Dvergar* like naming mountains after genitalia and anatomy,' I said.

'I don't think that practice is constrained to dwarves, Centurion Ilys,' the engineer said. Lina snorted.

'Well,' I continued, 'there's the Salt Flats south of Broken Tooth and Breentown. Rocks there jut up like sentries and there's a shit-load of hidey-holes for us to point carbines from.'

'Let me evaluate as we go. I understand the Bitter Spring is the closest.'

'Yes. Once we get eyes on the Medierans, we can make better plans. The main force will be slower than molasses, but their van, that's what I'm worried about,' I said. 'What do you have planned?'

She gestured to her pack mules. 'I've crates of caltrops, and enough silver to send *daemons* up each of their arses. And a few prototypes of some seriously vicious infernal traps.'

'I've got a couple of ideas, myself,' I said. 'You ever seen an auroch stampede?'

She smiled. 'I think this will be the beginning of a wonderful working relationship, Centurion Ilys.'

'Shoestring,' I said without thinking.

That night we bedded down in sight of the Bitter Spring. Sapientia and I rode over to inspect it. The firepit was as dead as Beleth, and it had seen no use since we'd last been there, if I am any judge of these things. And I am. At the end of the next day, we'd passed over the Long Slide – I described to Sapientia how we'd used it against them in the past – and rode until the moon was up. In five days, we caught the first sight of the Medieran van.

It was night, and they made no effort to bank their fires. We spotted the orange glow of flames and the scent of burning brush and bramblewrack a mile off. We perched on a ridgeline out of rifle range and stared down at the camp, our horses far behind us so that their nickering would not alert anyone.

'The gall of them,' Lina said. 'Proud as sin.'

'That's why we're here,' Sapientia said. 'Can we tell which direction they rode in from?'

Lina held up a finger, like a schoolmarm admonishing us to

patience. 'Wait here.' She slunk off into the darkness, blending into the shadows. We waited. She returned in an hour, breathing heavily. 'Lookouts there,' she pointed, jabbing a finger at an outcrop of rock. 'There and there.' A small rise and a far ridgeline. 'Standard amount of guards, one for every twenty or so men. I'd put their numbers at five hundred, a tenth of their main force. Rode in from the north-west.'

'So, they'll be headed south to east, I imagine,' I said.

'I don't have enough caltrops to cover all that. But let's just assume they're making a beeline toward Dvergar and put out the nasties there,' Sapientia said.

Lina tsked. 'Nope. They're going to make for there,' she said, pointing south toward a declivity between the ridgeline we occupied, and its twin to the west. 'So many on the hoof, they'll not bushwhack or try to cut some new trail. They'll go the path of least resistance. There's shoal grass beyond, and maybe a creek bed with flowing water, and they'll know it in the morning when they send out scouts. That's where we place them.'

Sound reasoning. And a surge of pride – my granddaughter knew the land and how to read it and had a mind sharp enough to etch her name into history.

So we rode into the night, south, and found shoal grasses and a trickle of water from a mineral spring. I was loath to put down the caltrops where other riders and their horses might find them, but they were lead and would eventually rust away. Until then, any rider whose mount's hoof found one would be unseated and the horse lame.

'The worst part,' Sapientia said, setting down the four-pronged metal items. She'd brought hundreds and we used at least a quarter of them, a deadly constellation of evil stars fallen to the earth. 'Is that we won't get to witness it when our Medieran friends find them.' She chuckled. 'I would pay to see that.'

'I, too,' Lina said. 'Though I hate to see the horses harmed.'

'Horses are the first to die, in war, in the Hardscrabble. Men shortly after.'

'Good thing we aren't men,' Sapientia said, and winked at Lina. Lina laughed in response.

By morning, we were miles south of them. We turned east, all of us tired. The legionnaires fell from their mounts at every rest, hobbled their horses, gave them water and oats, rubbed them down. We followed suit and took what rest we could, eating hardtack and jerked auroch. Before dark, Sapientia requested we dig a series of waist-deep holes near a fall line where striated rock met shoal. She built a charcoal fire, huffed a portable bellows on it, and melted silver. The *dvergar* she sent to find flat stones upon which to set her warding. It was a long process, and a frustrating one, for every time a legionnaire or *dvergar* approached her work, to catch a glimpse of what occupied her, she would bellow, 'The fuck, moron! Do you want to kill us all? *Daemonwork* here! Back the fuck up and stay the fuck away if you know what's good for you.'

The day dragged on, though, and I was afraid our lack of movement, in addition to the charcoal fire, would draw the Medieran van to us. I sent out Sumner and his best choice to ride scout and see what they could see on our backtrail.

'Sapientia,' I said, approaching.

'The fuck!' Her head popped up out of the hole. 'Did I not make myself clear?'

'We're sitting maids out here, waiting on suitors. How goes your...?'

'Surprises,' she said. 'I am almost through. We'll need some ground cover here, brush, or what not, to cover them up.'

'What are they?'

'Some call them *pangu*, from the Ægyptian.' She held up a thin spike. I peeked into the hole. There was a stone with intricate silverburns and warding surrounded by the spikes. 'All it takes is a bit of blood to initialise the summoning process and then—'

'Damnation,' I said, breathing. 'How big a bastard will come through?'

'Big enough to kill any nearby. Maybe more.' She sucked her teeth. 'In retrospect, it might have been a mistake to use the caltrops first. They'll be more wary.'

I sent the *dvergar* out for cover for the *pangu* and had the legionnaires prepare mats to cover the pits. Sapientia made the final placement over the devices.

She surveyed the pits. 'This looks like any other stretch of Hardscrabble. And mounted? They'll never see them.' Her hair had come loose; sweat beaded her brow and neck. Placing her hands on her hips, she smiled. 'I think we're through here.'

Sumner and his man returned, excited. 'Their scouts spotted us. One turned back to the main van and the other is on our arse, maybe ten minutes behind.'

Sapientia and I looked at each other. 'This might just work out. We want them to come here,' I said. 'Let's get this scout.'

'Do not let him get close to the *pangu*,' Sapientia said. 'Drop him before he has a chance.'

We took position. Horses behind an outcrop, men prone by boulders and a small waist-high gulley in the Hardscrabble dirt. We left the smeltfire burning but added some brush for more smoke.

The scout was skittish, but couldn't deny his own curiosity. Or his role. He rode down the fall line in the trail our horses had cut and Sumner shot his horse out from under him. The beast collapsed and the scout fell and rolled, with some considerable grace; he popped up on his feet with two six-guns pulled. *Dvergar* and legionnaire opened fire and the Medieran scout quickly found himself leaking from more holes than his body could bear.

We quickly stripped his body and dragged it, and (with some

effort) his horse, carefully around the *pangu* and arranged them in open view so that the corpses would draw the gaze of anyone approaching on horseback and away from the infernal devices waiting for them. Sapientia took the man's Hellfire. His gear and gold, I showed to Sumner (for accountability's sake) and stored on Bess to turn into the Ruman coffers, as protocol instructed. There was a day some of it might find its way into my trousers, to buy a drink or ease my body after many labours on the trail, but I was a godsdamned centurion and I didn't fancy crucifixion. Rankers and auxiliaries can pocket loot and get lashes. Centurions, with our greater pay, are held to higher standards, as I'd learned during my time in the army.

Then we rode hard, north-east, following the fall line until it disappeared into the earth and beyond.

There came a shiver, and the earth shook. Bess hawed unmercifully. The *dvergar* ponies and the legionnaires' horses nickered and whinnied. A great conflagration arose behind us. A billowing and expanding fireball, rising up, cocooning a flaming horror, full of malice.

'Well, they found the *pangu*,' Sapientia said, with grim satisfaction. 'Let's make some tracks. None of this will matter if we don't keep ahead of them.'

That night we camped near halfway up the slope of Wee Sugarloaf, in an open ledge that gave a good view of the land around and many routes to flee. We lit no fires and made sure the horses were well fed and watered. I posted five men as sentries – Seanchae, Ringold, and three legionnaires – for the first shift. Each night held four watches, and everyone, save Sapientia, took part.

'There's something moving down there,' Lina said. I stirred.

I'd been sleeping lightly, my head cradled on my hands as if looking at the stars. 'Where?' I said, rising.

Sumner rose and kicked at his men's boots. They hopped up, scrabbling for carbines and checking longknives and pistols.

I crept to where Lina sat, half-obscured by imlah brush and clumps of sage and shoal grass that wreathed the lower half of Wee Sugarloaf.

Looking out over the Hardscrabble, I let my eyes adjust to the night, the faint starlight. The moon had set beyond the far ridgeline and the earth was shadowed and grey.

'There,' she whispered, pointing. Down a gulley cut by erosion from the infrequent storms on the shoals, a dark shape moved. A loping man. Beyond it, more followed.

'Wolves?' I said.

'Bah,' Lina responded. 'Look more like stretchers.'

My gaze followed the forms, moving swiftly and then pausing, as if they were scenting the air.

'*Vaettir* rarely run on all fours,' I said, softly. Sound carries down from the heights and echoes strangely over the plains.

'I know what stretchers do, old one,' Lina said.

'*Daemon*-gripped,' I said. 'Beleth taught the Mediran engineer to fashion them from men.'

Sapientia, crouching nearby, said, 'Do you see any men? Unpossessed?'

'No,' Lina responded.

'There will be one, somewhere maybe here, maybe with the van. And he will control them, otherwise—' Sapientia said.

'They'd be rabid and turn feral,' I said.

'That's one way to say it. They would kill, indiscriminately,' she said. 'But if you can see a controller – he'll have some sort of talisman or blood connection with the *daemon*-gripped – and you kill him...'

'The dogs might turn on their masters,' Lina said.

'Ia-damn,' Lina said. 'That's some terrible shit. Thank the old gods that Beleth is dead.'

'He was glad, as well,' I said. I held up my hand. 'Wait.' The loping lead *daemon*-gripped stopped and then a shrieking sound echoed across the shoals surrounding Wee Sugarloaf. They had scented us.

The time for hiding was over. 'To arms!' I yelled, making my voice punch through the night. 'Carbines!'

The legionnaires scrambled up and onto their feet in a flash, armed and clanking over to the edge of the slope where Lina and I watched. The *daemon*-gripped moved faster than wolves might and, having seen what possession makes of men, I could not imagine what terrible wreckage their gait would make of their hands and feet. Mankind, *dvergar*, *vaettir* – we are not built to run about on all fours.

The *daemon*-gripped raced up the slope. 'Hold!' Sumner called. 'Hold until you can take a clean shot!'

Seanchae was the first to die. All of our attention was downslope.

The slavering man came from behind and bellowed, leaping. The bedevilled thing landed on the *dvergar*, driving his body to the ground with a sick, meaty impact and ripped at the dwarf's face with what appeared to be clawed hands. Behind the *daemon*-gripped, two more figures appeared.

'Behind us!' I cried. The sound of Hellfire filled the night, and brimstone billowed. Sumner's legionnaires were firing, yet dark things passed overhead in deadly arcs, leaping, like mountain lions pouncing from Illvatch heights onto unwary prey.

I had my six-gun in one hand and my silver longknife smoking painfully in the other. I fired as a dark shadow skulked past, moving terrifically fast. One of Sumner's men began gurgling, black blood spilling from his throat.

Screams came now and not all of them were from the throats

of *daemon*-gripped. Lina, turning, saw the black figure rising above Sapientia and moved only seconds before I did. 'Down!' she screamed, voice raw. Sapientia dropped and Lina fired, point-blank, into the *daemon*-gripped's chest. She must've hit his spine, because the possessed man jerked away like a marionette being pulled by its puppet master.

Ringold bellowed a war cry in *dvergar*. More shadows moved, tackling men and rolling into whipping, ferocious balls of clawed hands and biting black mouths.

'The horses!' I cried, suddenly terrified. 'On me! To the horses!'

Only Sumner and one of his men moved to join me. Another lay whining in the dark, saying, 'Mater, mater, mater,' over and over again. The *daemon*-gripped pulled back, dragging the injured legionnaire with them. The possessed's numbers were greatly reduced, but I was unable to know by how many because I never had a proper count in the first place.

Lina pulled up Sapientia and we ran toward where the horses were hobbled.

As we approached, their screams came to us, high-pitched and human-like. We increased our pace.

Two *daemon*-gripped were moving through the horses, clawing and bellowing in infernal voices. Sumner opened fire, felling the nearest man, while the other scrabbled at two mounts in particular. A shadow ripped at Sumner, and he let out a fierce bellow, firing.

'My mules!' Sapientia screeched, desperate. 'My gear!'

The mules bucked and hawed and I heard the outraged call of Bess, who wheeled about and raced toward where the *daemon*-gripped threatened her kin. Sapientia's mules bolted, their saddle-bags and burdens flopping madly as they raced off into the dark. Bess whipped around, and bucking, kicked the possessed man in the chest, sending him flying, his torso a ruined mess.

'Ia-damn it,' Sapientia said. 'My mules and gear!'

I looked back at where we had camped. 'First sortie, they find our strength and we find theirs. They'll report back to the van. I fear we're overmatched and now on the run.'

'But all of my things,' Sapientia said. 'The silver—'

'Nothing we can do about that. They'll be after us now,' I said. 'Both the *daemon*-gripped and the van. We have to run.'

Sapientia continued to curse. Lina climbed up on her pony in a trice and I was on Bess. Sumner cradled his arm from the *daemon*-gripped's attack and his remaining legionnaire helped him into the saddle and then quickly mounted himself.

'Ride,' I said. 'Make for the Bitter Spring.' I brought Bess around where I could find the reins of the dead men's horses. 'I will meet you there, if I can,' I said.

'What are you doing?' Sapientia asked.

'They have trackers just as we do. But they don't know how many of us are mounted. We'll have better luck if we split the party. I'll ride straight for Grenthvar. They'll follow me, and riderless horses.' I pulled the horses away and kicked Bess into a trot – she had no issue and balked not at the gait. She can be cantankerous, but never when there's a real threat. And she liked the *daemon*-gripped about as much as I did.

Lina kicked her horse and caught up with me. 'The Hell are you doing, old one?'

'Are you hard of hearing?' I said.

'No need to be a damned hero for the Rumans,' she said.

'It's not the Rumans or Fisk I'm worried about,' I said. I waved her away. 'Go, they'll need you and I can handle myself.'

'When we meet again, there'll be a reckoning,' she said.

'I'm sure there will be,' I said, and kicked Bess into a reluctant gallop.

TWENTY-FOUR

Will Your Eyes Leak Again?

T HE *DAEMON*-GRIPPED caught up with me the next hour, loping nearby and then leaping.

But this old soul had spent years on the Hardscrabble and faced many *vaettir*, who were at least as fearsome as possessed men. I shot the first damned man out of the air, putting a round in his eye even as he moved, as easy as Fisk might shoot out the beady eye of a sparrow on the wing.

A horse behind me whinnied violently, and turning I saw another *daemon*-gripped perched upon its saddle like the silhouette of a wild creature, hair in a crazy mess, long fingers ending in claws, clothes rippling in the wind and framed by starry sky. I could not see the man's face, but I knew he was grinning.

I twisted and fired, the boom of Hellfire making Bess twitch. But the shadow had shot up, fast, rising in the air above me to fall like an arrow, hands extended. He hit me like a hammer's blow, sending me over the neck of my mount. Bess bowled over, rolling, my gear lines ripping and all my belongings shooting away in sad arcs. Horizon and sky flashed to darkness then to sky once more as we rolled. Part of my mind pulled away from the agony being visited on my old body – the *daemonic* hands ripping at my face and shoulders, the man's bloodied knees slamming into my gut and driving all wind from me. The taste of my own blood filling my mouth. But there was sadness filling me too, along with agony. Sad because the flashing glimpse of my gear arcing away was almost the totality of my worldly possessions. Sad too because there was so little of it to see go.

We stopped rolling, dust billowing up around us, making the darkness deeper. It didn't matter. I felt lost, anyway.

The *daemon*-gripped man rose above me, blotting out the sky. His hands came down like rocks. I felt my nose give way and saw bright stars – numen of pain. His black mouth came close, blowing foetid air. A gobbling sound emanated from his throat.

I knew where to place my knife.

It entered under his chin, angled up through his mouth, through his soft palate and into his brain.

He twitched some before he keeled over.

I rose, leaking from all over. My nose was almost a ruin – I reset it and hoped I would not lose it. A *dvergar* looks exceptionally ridiculous without a nose.

A low groan came to me. I walked over to where Bess lay, neck broken. She looked up with one accusing eye as if saying, 'You got me into this, Shoe.'

'Aye, old girl,' I said. 'Yes I did.'

I drew my gun, placed the bore upon her eye, and fired. She'd been with me twelve years.

Of the decoy mounts, only two had sustained no injuries with the *daemon*-gripped attack. One was lame, and I put him down as well. The others had only suffered some nicks and scrapes and claw marks. I removed my saddle and harness from Bess's cooling body and tacked out the smaller of the two.

When I mounted, I saw the figures watching me. Three impossibly tall silhouettes.

'What is wrong with your face,' Gynth said.

'Broke my nose,' I said.

'No, not your nose,' he said. 'What is wrong with your eyes?'

'Nothing,' I said, wiping them clear. 'Why the Hell didn't you help me out?'

'You handled it well, *gynth*,' he said. 'And who is to say we did not help?' He lifted his hand. In it was a man's severed head. *Daemon*-gripped.

'Well, thanks,' I said, turning my gaze to his companions.

Vaettir take a moment to comprehend. They're fourteen feet tall from shoal grass to crown, they're sharp where mankind and *dvergar* are soft, and they're deadly as a sword blade and possibly as beautiful. But Gynth was plain in comparison to his two *vaettir* companions. The male was even taller, fifteen feet, and white as alabaster. His pate was devoid of hair, which gave him an air of statuary; or rather, he looked as though his father were a mountain and his mother the sky. He wore clothing that stank of mould, but at one time it had been very fine and it was of *dvergar* make, if I'm any judge of things. At his waist was a belt and on the belt a sword that no man could wield, it being eight feet long, at least. He watched me as a man might watch a flea. I had the ineffable sense that this *vaettir* judged me with the knowledge of thousands of *dvergar*, and knowledge of the world from before we trod these plains and made claim to them.

The female was the same height as Gynth, and had a bit more colour in her complexion than the male, which wasn't saying much. Her face was as still as stone, yet it showed, if faintly, the barest hint of amusement, in the mouth, maybe, and the eyes. She was garbed in clothing very much like the male's: intricately woven leather in pleasing patterns, but extremely old – the strands cracking without oil. Her hair wreathed her face in a white cloud shot with streaks of black, and she held a weapon that looked like a spear, but its head was as long as a standard issue Ruman gladius. Looking at her, I cringed, and imagined it in use.

'Uh, who're your friends?' I asked.

'*Gynth*,' Gynth said.

'I don't remember them at the last Ilys family reunion,' I said. Gynth looked at me blankly. 'They have names?'

'They did not say,' Gynth said in *dvergar*. 'In truth, they did not speak at all. But they listened, which is more important. I think of them as *him* and *her*.' He walked over to where Bess lay, knelt, and put his hand on her neck. 'I liked your wife. I am sorry.'

'She's not my . . .' I stopped. 'Me, too,' I said. I was quiet for a moment, my throat raw. When I could speak, I said, 'So, *Gynth* Two and *Gynth* Three.'

'No,' Gynth said. 'They are both *Gynth one*. The eldest. But if this is a naming,' he said, gesturing to the male. 'He is Illva, and she is Ellva.'

'What?' I stopped. 'Like the mountains?'

'Where do you think they got their names?' Gynth said.

'*Dvergar*,' I said.

'And where did the *dvergar* get them?' he said.

'Godsdamn it, Gynth,' I said. 'Why do you have to talk like that?'

I stood before Ellva and bowed as deeply as I could and then moved in front of Illva and bowed again. They both gave me the barest inclination of the head.

'So, where are the others?' I asked Gynth.

'The others?' he said.

'The other *vaettir*?' I said.

'There are no others,' he said.

'So, after all that, you just bring to the table two stretchers?' I said.

'I don't understand this word "stretcher". But Ellva and Illva are eldest. What need have you of anyone else?'

'I don't know,' I said. 'There's a whole cavalry regiment halfway up our arse and an army on the way.'

'That is a problem. The children, they are not numerous and care not for the events of man. Or *dvergar*.'

'I understand what you're saying, but they are only *two vaettir*. What help will they be?' I answered.

'I would recommend you cease speaking and wait to see,' Gynth said.

'I got you,' I said. In all my years – a century and more – I never thought I would be told to shut up by a stretcher. But there it is. All the roads and choosing had led me to this point where a smart-mouthed *vaettir* was the future's best hope. I sighed.

'Will your eyes leak again?' Gynth asked.

'Now, *you* should cease speaking,' I said. 'We have to go.'

'Yes,' he said. 'I hear horses approaching. Should we not address them?' Gynth said. His command of *dvergar*, now, was almost flawless. His common speech was quite good. The alacrity with which he learned both tongues was not only astounding, it was somewhat terrifying. I looked to Ellva and Illva. They had turned to stare at our backtrail.

'How many follow?' I asked.

'I cannot say. More than a sheaf, more than a bundle,' he said.

'We've got to work on your numbers,' I said. 'We've spent too much time jawing and not enough riding.'

Illva and Ellva strode up to the crest of a rise. Their movements were markedly different from Gynth, Agrippina, or Berith – the red-maned and vicious *vaettir* that had harried the *Cornelian*. They seemed as if each step was a deliberate choice, a punctuation to a thought. To say they were graceful was to lessen grace. They were mindful. The distillation of *vaettir*, the apotheosis. I followed them to the ridge and looked out on the darkened shoal plain.

My *dvergar* darksight immediately picked out the distant

riders. Three score, and riding full out. Around them, their dogs – *daemon*-gripped – bounded.

Illva and Ellva did not move and even Gynth looked a bit nervous at their stillness. I readied my carbine and checked the chamber.

At two hundred paces, the oncoming party saw us. A man raised himself in the saddle and bellowed, '*Kān! Kān!*' and gestured where we stood. I had heard those words before.

I took aim and fired. The man pitched over. The *daemon*-gripped faltered, looking about. Some stilled their forward momentum, others barrelled onward.

Illva drew his massive sword. The steel flashed, collecting starlight on the blade. Ellva raised her spear.

And then they moved.

In all my days, I have never seen the like – *vaettir* passing like white shimmering light across the shoals. At once in the air, on the ground, whirling. It was as if a storm had gathered, and released itself – instead of lightning, sword blows; instead of thunder, lashing spear strikes. Once, *vaettir* had attacked our party on an auroch hunt, leaping back and forth on the backs of the shoal beasts. But their movements – at the time so deadly and fluid – were sluggish and glacial compared to Illva and Ellva.

They lanced through the oncoming Medierans like pickpockets in a stagnant crowd, nicking heads, leaving corpses in their wake.

There was Hellfire, and confusion. Then silence.

In moments, the Medierans were dead, snatched from saddles, lying in halves in the dirt.

The horses fell out of their gallop, to a walk, and then stillness, all unharmed.

A hoot came from a *daemon*-gripped throat. Illva vaulted into the air in a low, deadly arc, his sword extended, twisting in the air, and landing feet-first on a possessed, driving him into the ground.

If there was an unbroken bone in the man's body, he would have to have been made of stone.

Ellva raced forward, feet moving too fast to see with the naked eye – it was as if her lower form, her hips, her legs, had sublimed into mist and she herself was insubstantial. Except for the strange sword/spear she wielded. She passed another *daemon*-gripped – this one a woman – and as she passed, left the possessed gouting blood and split open like a gutted fish, split neatly down the centreline. She moved on to the next, lopping off a head. The remaining *daemon*-gripped turned, loping away. But in moments, the two ancient *vaettir* had run them down.

'I see what you mean,' I said to Gynth.

'Yes,' he said. 'They are eldest.'

The *vaettir* returned to where Gynth and I stood, watching. Ellva stood in front of me and, with the haft of her spear, drew a line in the dirt of the Hardscrabble.

'They would cut a furrow,' Gynth said.

I gathered up the herd of horses, one by one, looping hemp rope through their bridles.

'Well, let's go and talk to Fisk about it,' I said.

TWENTY-FIVE

I Will Drown The World In Blood

FISK WAS DISPLEASED when we returned, three days later. But he managed to stow it long enough to take in Illva and Ellva.

'They would cut a furrow with you,' Gynth said. 'As you did here, with our *gynth*.'

'And by *gynth*, I take it you mean Neruda and the *dvergar*,' Fisk said to the *vaettir*.

'Yes,' Gynth said. 'What else would I mean?'

Fisk frowned at that. Livia stood nearby, in the clearing in front of the praetorium tent. Legionnaires and *dvergar* alike gathered around the opening.

'How many stretchers can they field?' Fisk asked.

I cleared my throat. 'Ah. Well. They only bring themselves,' I said.

Fisk scowled. 'You're wasting my time.' He turned to re-enter his command. Livia placed a hand on his arm, stopping him. 'My love, listen to them. These are *vaettir*! And they are willing to make bargain. Would you ever have thought?'

'No, I would not,' he said. He stared at them both, eyes narrowed.

'They cut down sixty horsemen in bare seconds,' I said. 'Just the two of them.'

281

Fisk cocked his eye at me. 'And for that, I am to make treaty with them in the name of Rume. Just two stretchers?'

'They are eldest,' Gynth said.

I held up a hand in front of Gynth to silence him.

'A moment?' I said, approaching. Fisk nodded, Livia beckoned me inside.

Once inside the praetorium, I said, 'I know it sounds crazy, but those two—' I took off my hat and rubbed my head. 'They move unlike anything in my ken. They're beyond *vaettir*, Fisk. It's like we're stuck in mire and they move freely through it. Time slows for them.'

Fisk waved his hands, dismissing that. 'How can they speak for all stretchers? And even if I made a bargain with them, how can I expect Tamberlaine to keep it?' he said.

'Tamberlaine would not need to know the details until the battle is won, my love,' Livia said.

'Fisk,' I said. 'Gynth led me to believe that the Illvatch and Eldvatch mountains *were named after them*. You understand? They are the mother and father of all the *vaettir* in Occidentalia, or so it appears.'

Livia said, 'Forging a treaty with them can do no harm.'

'Tamberlaine might disagree,' Fisk said. 'And disagreements with the Emperor often end in crucifixion.'

'Gynth calls them "the eldest",' I said. 'The other *vaettir* will fall in line.'

'You don't know that,' Fisk said.

'I trust Gynth,' I said.

'Ia-dammit, Shoe,' Fisk said. 'You and your strays.'

I went back out and beckoned Gynth to bring Illva and Ellva inside the praetorium. He seemed a bit surprised, and turned his scarred face to look at the two ancient *vaettir*. They followed him, in stately manner, ducking their heads to enter the tent.

'So we will make a bargain, then,' Fisk said. 'If you assist us against the Medieran army, and keep your kind from molesting our people on the Hardscrabble, I will make treaty with you.'

'Cut a furrow,' Gynth said.

Ellva, the ghost of what seemed to me a smile playing about her face, approached the command table. Between Gynth, Illva, and Ellva, the large praetorium tent seemed small and close. She placed a fingernail on a map and traced a line down the length of it. The sound of scratching filled the tent. When she was finished, she pulled half of the paper away and held it.

Livia approached the table. 'The Big Rill,' she said. 'And further west. All of it. The Illvatch. And all lands beyond.'

Fisk frowned, his face intense and dissatisfied. But in a moment, he nodded.

'Beyond the Big Rill, the Illvatch, and the lands further west will remain *vaettir* lands. We will make no forays there. We will build no more settlements. Those people that live there now must be allowed to leave and not be harmed.'

Ellva looked at Illva and then, as if coming to some silent consensus, extended her hand to Fisk. With her nail, she dug into her alabaster palm until blood welled up. Fisk withdrew a longknife and scored his hand – reopening the pink wound he'd scored in his bargain with Neruda – and drew blood.

He placed his very small hand in her very large hand and they mingled blood and made pact.

'Ia help me,' Fisk said. 'I hope I haven't sealed my doom.'

'You may have changed it,' Livia said.

Lina, Sapientia, and I were debriefed shortly after. Gynth and his *vaettir* ... parents? Ancestors? I knew not what to call them save eldest – left to roam the peaks of the Eldvatch, as Gynth was wont to do.

On the command table stood a box that I was familiar with. Samantha once held it safe. Beleth searched for it. But now it belonged solely to Fisk.

'Why is that out?' I asked.

Livia brought a cup of wine and handed it to me. 'I, myself, have asked him this many times. My husband has not given me a satisfactory answer.'

'I do not know when the Medieran army will be here, but it will be soon. Their van routed your men, and the other scouts I have riding the Hardscrabble have not returned.' He looked grim. 'There have been very few refugees.'

'They're killing everyone they come across,' I said. It was not a question.

'Mediera occupied the Hardscrabble before, under the first King Diegal, and tried to integrate his people with the *dvergar*. He warred with the *vaettir*. This time, his descendant will not be so lenient. There'll be no indigenes left, if the Medierans win. No Rumans. No settlers. A clean slate to put down Medieran seeds.'

'The *vaettir* might take issue with that,' Lina said.

Fisk shook his head. 'It is the last resort, should all else fail.'

'If the fortifications fall, and the valley is overrun, we flee into the mountains,' I said.

'We cannot pass the Pactum Wall. I will not break bargain with Neruda,' Fisk said.

Lina raised an eyebrow. 'If we're overrun, will it even matter? We do not have separate fates, now. They are joined.' She drank from her wine. 'I have spoken with Neruda about this, and he will confirm it, should you ask, but should we be routed, all bonds are broken. "It is the *dvergar* character to survive," he said. "Our stories will continue on, and you will be the tellers of them." He's got a way with words, that one,' she said.

Fisk nodded. Livia considered my granddaughter. 'You are a bright woman,' she said. 'I would like to know you better.'

Lina looked at her, askance. She was not one much for small talk. 'I—'

'Take lunch with me, ride the fortifications,' Livia said.

Lina glanced at me. 'All right,' she said. 'Though I don't know why you'd be so interested in me.'

Livia placed a fond hand on my shoulder. 'Shoestring is our closest friend,' she said. 'He is part of our family. So I would know his granddaughter.'

Lina looked at me. 'You told them.'

I shrugged.

We drank some, and they brought cheese, bread, oil, and olives.

'You can't use the *daemon* hand,' I said. 'What good will it do?'

'At Hot Springs, it stopped Hellfire. Triggers were pulled and no Hellfire released,' Fisk said.

'But the Crimson Man was riding you like a bronco. It wasn't your call. And it was *all* guns, not just the ones pointed at us,' I said. 'Once you let him out of the cage, there is no coming back. No Agrippina to snatch him away. And I want you to consider this,' I said, looking at him closely. 'Beleth and whatever was riding him wanted what is in that hand to get loose. He wouldn't have given it to you, otherwise.'

Fisk rang a bell and a junior officer entered. 'Find Engineer Samantha and bring her here. Sapientia as well.' He turned back to us. 'Let us have the engineers' thoughts.'

When Samantha and Sapientia entered, they brought with them the scorched, acrid scent of the smelt. Both wore overalls, thick leather engineers' aprons, and their tool belts, with heavy gloves tucked into them. On top of their heads, thick oculars were perched, I assumed as protective wear. They'd both cropped their hair very short.

At my stare, Sapientia shrugged and said, 'Production requires the practical, Shoe. Long hair gets in the way and is likely to catch fire.'

'I didn't say anything,' I said.

Fisk said to Samantha, 'We were discussing the *daemon* hand. What possible purpose could Beleth, and the thing inside him, have had to create it and give it to me?'

Samantha's expression stilled. Here was a woman hearing her own fears and darkness stated aloud. 'I have thought on this for a long time and have arrived at no conclusions. And that distresses me greatly. Beleth was my master, and for so long something else leered out at me through his eyes.' She sat down wearily and again I was struck at how thin she had become. Sapientia was a strong, strapping woman with powerful arms and an impressive physique – obviously needed for the rigours of the practical engineer's life. But Samantha had wasted, shrunk, the enormity of her tasks causing some diminution in her. I hoped she was not sick, that in her flesh did not lurk the same devouring sickness that took my Illina.

'First, he created the hand to fulfil the immediate task of finding Isabelle. And that it did. But it had a secondary purpose. Beleth was always concerned with vestments,' she said.

'Vestments? Clothing?' Livia asked.

'No. In summoner's terms, vestments are the containers in which we place *daemonic* energy. Every Hellfire round is a vestment. Every *daemonlight* lantern. Every engine in every ship, as well,' Samantha said.

'And every *daemon*-gripped,' Lina added.

'Yes,' Samantha said, looking to my granddaughter. 'But those are flawed vestments. An engine chamber or lantern is the perfect one, because it can be amply warded and it is almost a permanent thing without the stressor of having too much energy stored inside too small a vestment.' She raised a finger. 'However, we're talking about energy that *thinks*. *Daemonlight imps*, they have the intelligence of insects. But engine *daemons*? They are intelligent – possibly a match for ourselves, if not greater – and their anger at their enslavement is tremendous.'

'Enslavement?' Fisk said. 'Ia-damn. Rume and her slaves.'

'You are the representative of Rume, pard,' I said. 'You *are* Rume.'

'How did I get here?' Fisk said, scowling.

'A strange road with many turnings,' Livia said, touching his hair. For a moment, he pressed into her, closing his eyes, feeling the sensation of her hand there, her closeness. It was a comfortable thing, and the mindlessness of it made me happy for them. 'But we are here now.'

'Consider this,' Sapientia said. 'You make treaties for Rume and lead its men, but at this point, the fight isn't between Rume and Mediera.'

'Then who is it between?' Fisk asked.

'Us and them,' Sapientia said. 'We fight for survival, now.'

Lina bobbed her head in agreement. 'They are coming, and won't care if we're Ruman or *dvergar* or both.' This last bit she said and glanced at me. I brushed it off.

'She's right, pard,' I said.

Fisk said nothing, but looked at Livia. For a moment, some silent communication passed between them, almost the same as when Ellva and Illva had met glances before.

'The hand,' Fisk said.

'Yes. Right. *Daemonic* enslavement,' Samantha responded. 'So there is a chain of being to *daemons*. There are the *imps*, and the engine *daemons*. Then there are *daemons* of such power and intelligence that to comprehend them, one has to comprehend godhood. They outstrip mankind. And consequently are unsuited for any vestment,' Samantha said.

'And that's what Beleth stuffed into Isabelle's hand,' Livia said.

'I'm afraid so. He made some bargain with it, lured it in without copious blood. Or possibly he'd spilled blood before that in preparation. Beleth was a genius when it came to devilry,' Samantha said. She shifted in her chair uncomfortably and took a drink of heavily watered wine. 'Ultimately, he wanted that *daemon* to be free here.'

'Should it become free, what would be the consequence?' I asked. 'Another Rume? Another Harbour Town?'

Samantha shook her head. 'Possibly. Or worse.' She cocked an eyebrow at Fisk. 'You wore him around your neck, you had him riding you. What do *you* think his purpose is?'

'My memory of that time is indistinct,' Fisk said. 'But I remember glee. And hunger. All-consuming hunger.'

'That's not my favourite thing I've ever heard,' I said.

'Not the favourite thing I've ever said,' Fisk responded.

Samantha tugged at her lower lip, her eyes focused on the praetorium tent wall. The long stare, the one that saw beyond borders. 'What did it say in the caldera? When it had joined with Agrippina? It would create an army?'

' "I will drown the world in blood. I will roast your infants on spits and feast on their flesh. I will slaughter you all. I shall bathe the land in fire," ' I said. *And then she kissed me.*

Fisk sighed and took his wife's hand.

'We have two days at the most, before the Medierans are here. Their cavalry rules the Hardscrabble now and just waits for their main force.'

He picked up a cup of wine and downed it.

'Come what may,' he said, looking at us with a strange, helpless expression. One I'd never seen before on him. 'I will not use the hand.'

*

That evening – after sharing a drink with Sumner, who had clapped me on the shoulder and called me friend; we were compatriots, then, since our survival against the Hellish spawn of the Medierans on the Hardscrabble – Lina came to me as I sat near the fire with Gynth. Ellva and Illva were gone, tracing paths known only to them on the high reaches, where the gambel and pine seethed in the night wind.

In the flames, I performed my own summoning. Faces of those lost to me. Cimbri and Reeves. Secundus and Carnelia. Banty and Gnaeus. The face of Agrippina. Cornelius. Beleth. Bess.

And last, Illina. Those I'd never see again. Those I would never forget. In the praetorium tent Fisk and Livia took what comfort they could from each other, and their son, but here, underneath the stars, it was as if I were on the trail with only ghosts conjured by firelight.

'Old one,' Lina said. 'Do you have anything to drink?' She emerged from the darkness and sat opposite me, the fire casting her face in a roseate glow.

'Cacique,' I said, and unlimbered my flask. I tossed it to her and she snatched it out of the air and took a pull.

I rolled cigarettes and gave her one and we sat, smoking. Gynth rose without a word and strode off into the darkness. Dreaming untold *vaettir* dreams, eyes open. The camp stood hushed. The Grenthvar was silent – no hammer-falls filled the air, no stink of smelt, no bleat of goat, no scream of child.

'If it all goes to shite,' Lina said softly, looking at the cherry of her cigarette, 'find me.'

I remained quiet for a moment, letting that sink in. 'If it all goes to shite,' I said, 'it will be ants swarming from a boot-struck anthill.'

'This ant knows burrows other ants don't,' she said.

'I cannot leave Livia or Fisk. Or their child,' I said.

John Hornor Jacobs

'If you can collect them, come.' She rose. 'I'll wait at the far northern part of the Pactum, where the wall meets the bare rock of ridgeline. Understand?'

'Yes,' I said.

She was gone.

TWENTY-SIX

Every Man Who Makes Claim
To It Is Easily Dispossessed

THE RUMAN HOST marshalled itself in the gullet of the
Grenthvar before dawn. A cacophony of noise filled the
air: horns, bells, braying mules, nickers of horses, the chants of
soldiers, prayers of lictors and the devout, the rumbling of wheeled
cannons and munition wagons, vardos and barber jaunts. Curses.
And there was weeping. Terrified men soon bullied into silence by
other men. *Dvergar* children in the Breadbasket.

In the dim half-light before dawn, as legionnaires, lictors, *dvergar*, engineers and the breathless Ruman and dwarf host moved
into defensive positions, Fisk held high a *daemonlight* lantern and
leapt to the top of a boulder where most of the assembled men and
women could see and hear him clearly. He beckoned Neruda and
Praeverta to join him, and they took position beside him.

'Rumans! *Dvergar*! Men and women of the Hardscrabble!' Fisk
bellowed, his voice echoing across the hushed valley. 'Some of you
were born in Latinum, far away. Most of you were born here, in the
West, sons and grandsons of men who came here for fortune, for
honour. Some for duty! They held the land. For a fleeting moment.
But it is a big land, and every man who makes claim to it is easily
dispossessed! But we are here. How many of you have spilled your
blood?'

There was an undulating yawp of acknowledgement, like a

291

chorus of barking dogs – I realised it was the wolves of the Seventh Occidentalia. Then the bulls of the Fifth joined in.

'How many of you have poured your sweat into the dust?' Fisk intoned.

More response. From the *dvergar* throats, the chant of '*Vhan! Vhan! Vhan!*' came. The noise was titanic. I found myself raising a fist in the air, pumping it madly.

'In our company, *dvergar*!' Fisk yelled. 'In our company, *vaettir*!'

Praeverta gave a screeching call in imitation of an attacking stretcher. Then, from the rear of the army, it was answered by Gynth. Two more voices answered his piercing call – Illva and Ellva – the eldest. The father and mother of the West.

'We are hard-bitten! We are indomitable! We are of the Hardscrabble!'

Deafening chants ripped through the air of the valley, beating at the lightening sky.

But it was short-lived. They fell silent once more.

'Keep your heads down,' Fisk said, softer now. He had them. They all strained to hear his words. 'Mark your shot before firing. Be smart. And kill every Medieran that tries to enter this valley.' He extended his hand, outstretched toward the west, stretching out an index finger as if some augur on the steps of the Cælian temple to Ia, making a divination. 'Waste no shot.'

Silence. He bowed his head.

'We are the last of us,' Fisk said. No one other than Livia and myself would know that he was afraid. And his fear chilled me. The arc of his life – outcast, father, solitary wanderer, noble, and now leader. All the strange turnings to bring him to this place collapsed then and for a moment became overwhelming.

Fiscelion began to screech in great distemper. Legionnaires hooted, and the wolves of the Seventh howled, laughing. 'Little wolf!' a legionnaire shouted.

Fisk raised his hands. 'We fight not for Rume! We fight not for *dvergar*! Who do we fight for?'

Livia stood nearby, looking up at her husband, holding Fiscelion. Lupina hovered nearby.

'We fight for us! We fight because we are *of this place*. Remember!'

Neruda clapped, and Praeverta held a carbine in one hand and a hand-scythe in the other, exultant.

'To arms, then. And may whatever god you hold dear look over you,' Fisk said, and stepped down from his makeshift stage.

The sky was just turning blue at the edges.

Each man took his position, in every trench, every foxhole, behind every embankment. Cannoneers crouched by wagons sitting heavy on springs, full of cotton-swaddled Hellfire shells, each munition as thick as a man's thigh. On piles of slag lay legionnaires, sooty and black, prone and watchful. White-knuckled hands gripping carbines.

Gynth, Illva, and Ellva stood behind us, on the command embankment. We had a small contingent of horsemen, each armed with large-bore carbines and the strength to use them, horses champing and agitated. The killing field was open, the mist from the Grenthvar floating across it like some ghostly curtain being pulled away to reveal a bellicose performance.

An ember streaked across the sky, casting hard shadows from every standing stone, every legionnaire, each man a sundial marking the passage of time. It shone like a falling star, white-hot and angry.

All faces turned toward the heavens as it reached its apex and began to fall.

It impacted with the earth, halfway from the mouth of the

Grenthvar to the end of the valley, in the middle of the killing fields.

The *daemon* that erupted from the fireball there expanded rapidly in flame, clawing, wreathed in black smoke, taking a vaguely human form. It rushed up the killing field, a moving furnace fire, pouring heat into the air, burning off the mist of the Grenthvar. Ruman soldiers fired upon it, adding their own feeble puffs to the infernal presence. Optios screamed, 'Hold your fire, fellators! Hold your Ia-damned fire!' The *daemon* lost cohesion in its rush toward the Ruman line, becoming amorphous, indistinct, like tallow in a firepit. Soon it was just black smoke. And then nothing except a memory and soot caught on wind.

'That is not good,' one of Fisk's secretaries said.

Fisk turned to the boy, and said, 'You are relieved of duty, sir. Go to the praetorium and make yourself useful to my wife and her maid.'

The boy's face blanched and he began to quaver, until Fisk yelled, 'Now!'

He ran.

'Samantha! Donald! Sapientia!' Fisk yelled. His voice was already hoarse, and it was just the first volley. The engineers approached, hastily. 'What was that thing?'

'An *archdaemon*, I'm assuming,' Sapientia said. 'Nothing we haven't seen before. Except—'

'Except what?' Fisk demanded.

'Its permanence is distressing,' Samantha said. 'You don't see that very often. Except with Harbour Town. Or Rume, possibly.'

'Aye,' Black Donald agreed.

Up the gullet of the Grenthvar came a booming sound and then another star rose from the earth toward the sky, blinding.

'We don't have the time for mincing words. Is there a way to stop them?' Fisk said, face illuminated and his gaze on the rising missile.

'I spent last night warding stones and platforms on the battle-field,' Sapientia said. 'To protect the men from *daemon*-gripped. Those might hold against these munitions.'

'The precium,' Samantha said. 'Now we know why there were no refugees.'

'What?' Fisk asked. He turned away from the rising star.

'The blood price. The more blood, the stronger the *daemon*,' she said. 'With each missile, the Medierans are slaughtering people, sacrificing their blood. And the *daemon* summoned can remain on this plane longer.'

'Ia-damn,' Fisk said. 'Ia-damn it all to Hell. Tell the men to take cover on the wards. Any flat space you can prepare ward-ings, from here to the Eldvatch, do so now. With all haste. Do you understand?'

'But every warding takes time—' Sapientia began.

'Do it,' Fisk said.

The Medieran shell fell to earth with a titanic impact only paces from the front Ruman embankment. The fireball cast burning earth and stone into the sky in a great eruption, falling in a hard rain on the soldiers there. Bits of slag and stone and brown earth rained on us where we stood. Down range, the *daemon* raged in flame and smoke. It lurched up and forward, over the embankment to meet screaming men who suddenly found themselves aflame. Sweeping what loosely resembled an arm forward, it cast flames like a serpent spewing venom. The legionnaires in its path fell out, some burning, others firing. As the *daemon* moved, it seemed to gain strength from the death it caused.

'Yes,' Samantha said, face furious at the turn of events. She moved away, half-crouching as if any moment a *daemon* could fall on her head, bellowing at her engineering assistants. Sapientia and Black Donald followed at a hustle.

Far down the slope, bounding figures appeared, loping into the far end of the killing fields. Behind them, shadows.

'Cannons!' Fisk bellowed. 'Mark and fire!'

Percussive belches of brimstone erupted from the Ruman line of cannons – each one rolling backward from the recoil. Down range, the earth churned. Whistling sounds came from overhead – bullets cutting through the air. Men screamed. One of Fisk's attendants pitched over – a boy by the name of Marius – his jaw gone. His hands frantically pawed at the ruin of his face.

'Open fire!' Fisk screamed. 'All men, open fire!'

I raised my carbine, sighted down range, and fired.

Another thunderous crackle of explosions sounded – and slag and earth began to sizzle and cast up ejecta as if the valley was a skillet and the earth, oil. The sound of carbine-fire – ours or theirs, I could not tell – filled all perception, reeking of Hellfire and dismay and sounding like bacon crackling. I caught a glance of Sumner and two of his men huddled around Fisk, tugging at him to take cover.

Two more arcing stars lit up the morning. In their light, the Medieran host stood revealed. They carpeted the land at the opening of the Grenthvar. At their head, they had mechanised wagons with great iron-clad shields and behind them came Medieran soldiers, hiding in the lee. I fired, worked the carbine's action, fired again.

The noise was deafening, the light shifting with the falling Medieran shells as if the earth had been pitched up on end. The shock of the explosion ripped at my clothes and hair, blasting me half-way down the slag slope I'd taken cover behind. The force of the blow saved me. The heat grew unbearable. I heard a high-pitched whine – like a gear in an infernal machine about to fail – and the sound ripped and distressed the air. I scrambled back and down the slag heap, away as the *daemon* broached its peak above me.

I found my feet.

Small arms fire erupted all around, the earth pitched up to meet me as I fled backward. The *daemon* screeched and flowed toward me.

And then I was moving; moving not of my own volition, but caught up in some wild force I could not make sense of. I saw a blur of white and the earth passing below. For an instant, from on high, my eye framed the whole of the battlefield. Thousands of Medierans rushing onto the killing floor from the shelter of their iron-clad shields, like grey water being poured from a flawed bucket. Flashes of light from Hellfire, billows of smoke from muzzles. Two massive *daemons* casting about with fire and fury, one with wings, one tentacled and foreign. *Daemon*-gripped men biting and clawing at legionnaires and *dvergar*. Cannons belching flame. A blooming of cannon-fire impacts. Bodies tossed into the air like flotsam on the surf.

All things slowed (or maybe I was caught up in the glamour of the *vaettir*'s preternatural speed) and I looked up into Ellva's face like a babe held in the arms of his mother as we hung suspended in the air. Her hair caught in a clotted tangle whipped by wind. Her skin shining, flawless and white. No vein traced its way there, no pore to vent sweat and shed heat. She was almost filled with light, a pure thing, untainted by the corrupt desires of the low, mankind and *dvergar* alike.

The stretchers – *Oh why did we call them that? Why would we hang that name upon them?* – were just a stepping stone on the way to becoming this pure thing, this elemental force.

With world enough, and time, even Agrippina would have achieved this alabaster, permanent state. Incorruptible.

It was then I apprehended the *vaettir*. Not indigenes, not low things, but gods, placed here on earth as seeds to grow and war against the infernal. Maybe. As stewards of the field, and fern, and fen. Not for human or *dvergar*'s sake. Not for civilisation. But for continuity. For the earth.

Vaettir are the old gods. The numen.

'You are needed,' she said, in *dvergar*.

'*Matve*,' was all I could respond. The weight of our speed pressed me to her bosom. I felt as though I was in some powerful vice.

'A moment,' Ellva said.

We touched the earth far from the front line, among the *daemon*-gripped. Her spear flashed out, once, twice, more times than I could see and with each movement, an infernal died. She moved faster than any horse could run, any bird could fly – I had the distinct sensation that I was falling, even as we rose.

Down range she sped, holding me to her breast. Slaying all within reach, her spear moving faster than thought could travel. Her flesh was a decay running through a garden, her hands death; blood blossomed from her and spattered on my lips. It felt as a benediction. The sound of tearing flesh and gunfire, monumental. Hellfire rounds found her, pierced her incorruptible flesh, pulling a comet's tail of gore from that pure integument. Those traceries were mirrored by her: she was a comet streaking through the ranks of Medierans, pulling her tail of destruction and death with her. But the flesh closed behind, her skin became whole once more, even as we moved and her spear took Medieran life.

It was as if some immortal trawler fished the seas of men, leaving blood in its wake.

And then we were at the Pactum Wall and I was falling now, in truth, spilling out on the ground.

Fisk was there, and Sumner. Sapientia pulling a wounded Samantha away from the front.

'Black Donald?' Fisk asked, his voice full of pain.

Sapientia shook her head.

Lina said, 'Burned by *daemonfire*. Along with Ringold. And many others.'

Samantha was in a bad way – blood darkened her shirt and trousers, thick and wet. She shook with tremors and was as white as parchment. My heart fell as I looked at her. There was no coming back from that.

Screaming and smoke and the jumbled sensory impressions of war. More whistling bullets cut through the air. Junior legates and optios rallied fleeing legionnaires. Desperate pleas and curses peppered the air of the valley. The smoke of Hellfire and stench of brimstone hung over it all. A munitions wagon erupted with a sound that knocked grown men and *dvergar* alike to the ground. My mouth was full of dirt, and slag, and blood, and I could smell nothing but brimstone.

We were routed. And even still, white stars rose into the sky, making shadows shift, casting all notion of time and place into doubt.

More *daemons*. More shells falling.

'Fall back!' Fisk screamed. He bled from multiple ejecta cuts and his arm was charred where *daemonfire* had scorched him. Under his arm, he clutched the box holding the *daemon* hand.

We ran, toward camp. The sounds of dying reached my ears. I moved to help Sapientia and Samantha groaned as I slipped under her arm. Gynth bounded into view, bearing a wounded soldier.

Illva and Ellva gave Gynth a considered look, and sprang away, high into the air, and Gynth followed. He'd found a gladius to wield, and he was red from sword-tip to crown, a bloody spectre moving through the remaining trees, a crimson blur upon the face of the earth. Illva had his great sword drawn, terrible to behold. They moved downhill, faster than the eye could follow, like angels shorn of wings, wrathful and proud. Cries and screams of pain, moans of despair met their approach. In their wake, silence.

We rallied together as a group, moving as fast as possible. Camp was a shambles, all personnel in absolute disarray. Legionnaires fired at random. Tents blazed into flame. The wild whistle of bullets whipped the air. At the praetorium tent, Livia appeared, shotgun in one hand, Fiscelion in the other. 'You're hurt!' she said to Fisk.

'We'll all be hurt if we don't flee, right now,' he said.

'To the Pactum Wall,' I said. A crackle of Hellfire punctuated my words. I felt a tug at my shirt and then I was bleeding. Bright pain in the meat of my arm.

Legionnaires moved around us, firing. Lupina emerged from the praetorium, brandishing a naked cleaver in one fist and a bundle half as big as herself in the other.

'The wall!' I said. 'Lina will guide us. She's waiting!'

It was madness. My breath caught in my chest and I felt dizzy and centred all at once. I could not think, I could not reason. But running – fleeing – made sense. It was all I wanted to do. With all my soul.

There are those who age and value their own life less, as if by dint of having so much of it, the remainder is not important. But I am old and find my remaining time precious. I would not give it up easily.

We moved as a group. It was slow, and the legions around us kept up small arms fire, scenting the air with brimstone, praying loud to Mithras. At times, Fisk would give frustrated grunts, either from pain or the loss of men, I could not tell. Livia kept him moving.

'Come, we can make it,' Livia said. Her voice was like music upon my ears. Something I could focus on. 'Once we get to the wall, then beyond. Up. They will not catch us.'

At the wall, Neruda stood weeping over the body of Praeverta, who'd been charred almost beyond recognition. Only her silver hair and defiance were still recognisable.

'Come,' I said, pulling him away. 'All is lost.'

'No,' he said. 'I cannot leave her like this.'

'You must,' I said. 'Your people need you. They will destroy the mines and flee into the mountains. You must go with them.'

Winfried appeared from the smoke, coughing. She was bloodied and her arm, in the sling, seemed to have been reinjured. But there was a fierce determination in her face, and her jaw was set at a dangerous and stubborn angle.

Despite the cough and her wounds, she came forward quickly and went to her knees by Neruda and Praeverta. To the west, a chatter of Hellfire sounded and the air filled again with whistling projectiles. Sounds of wails from dying men and women threaded the smoke-filled air. The booms of guns echoed all around.

'Come, Neruda,' Winfried said. 'We must pull down the mine entrances and flee into the mountains.' She gripped his arm. 'We need you.'

'We must honour Praeverta,' he said. A tremor ran through his hands and shook his shoulders. 'Bring her body. We can't leave her here.'

'There is no time and there are living to attend to!' Winfried rose, bracing herself. 'The people of the Breadbasket gather at the mines for safety! Come!'

He tried to linger, but in the end, she forced him, pulling him upright. There was a fine mist, like oil, falling all around them. Blood. He looked at Winfried with a stricken expression, mouth open, as if trying to catch his breath. As he turned, I could see the remains of his neck, where some errant piece of shrapnel had clipped him. He fell.

A forlorn sound came from Winfried, a sharp inhalation followed by a sob. She looked around to us, her bloodied gaze passing as though she did not recognise us.

'My place is here,' she said. 'Never would I have thought my path would have led me to this place.'

Another volley of Hellfire, closer now. Fisk, Sumner, and Livia returned fire.

Winfried, in a crouch, moved away, back to the Pactum Wall. 'I must go! I have other burdens now. Go!' she cried.

She was gone, disappeared into the smoke of the burning Grenthvar.

On a spray of shoal grass, as infernal flames and Medieran soldiers came on, we left Neruda's and Praeverta's bodies. There was pursuit now. Another arcing white light in the sky. Only a few score feet away, a copse of gambel shivered in a quickly expanding fireball, casting jagged pieces of wood and branch through that space with remarkable speed and sucking all the air out. It was as if the soil and forest had been blown from the ground by an angry earth. Black smoke poured from the crater, coming in acrid billows, and within, a smothered light, choked from the world by the vapours it spewed forth. A *daemon*.

'Run!' Sumner called. 'Flee!'

Our whole party ran, upslope, toward where the Pactum Wall met the fall line of the Eldvatch ascent. My breath came in hitches, my legs burned with the exertion. Samantha grew heavier with each step. Sapientia grunted and cursed with every footfall. Pausing I turned back, looking downslope.

The fire and smoke was a living thing. Even the Medieran soldiers, now visible near its edges and firing heavily, coughed and moved away from it, for their own safety's sake. Within the smoke there were flashes of white – I might have thought it some sort of phantasm if I had not known of Illva and Ellva. What damage they could do against such infernal creatures, I did not know and could not say, other than distract it, maybe. Stop its forward momentum. But it incandesced, churning, boiling with anger. Within the smoke, a glowing movement, shifting shadows. Indescribable rage.

The *daemon*.

I found the strength to keep on, pulling Samantha forward.

At the wall, where the slopes of the Eldvatch began to soar upwards, Lina stood, beckoning frantically. It was still heavily wooded here, far from the smelt and the rest of the industrial parts of the Grenthvar, and the trees seemed to seethe with anger. A heavy wind bent their backs and whipped their tall, proud heads.

'Come on, hurry!' she cried. A barrage of gunfire sounded. Medieran soldiers bellowed in their round, tripping language. Bark flew as bullets pierced trees.

Reaching her, she led us quickly over the Pactum Wall, down a short declivity where a spring made every footfall squelch and suck at our boots, and then up a rise. The chatter and report of Hellfire fell away, momentarily. We stopped, nestled in trees and hidden by great snaggled rocks, twisted gambel and pine roots eating into the stones.

'Where do we go now? Some secondary mine entrance?' I said, breathing heavily, when we were close enough to speak.

She shook her head. 'No,' she said. 'The men from Breadbasket will be pulling down the pillars to the main entry now, if they haven't already. And all the others. It will be a long time before Mediera gets its fucking hands on that silver.'

As if in answer to her words, a crack and rumble came, shivering the earth, cutting through the din of war. To the south, only a few hundred feet away, a bloom of white smoke poured from the mountainside, powdered stone filling the air.

'And there it is. More will follow.' She surveyed the valley. We stood at the eastern end of it, where the Grenthvar River emanated from the springs of the mountain. The only way to go now was up. 'We go up there, below the treeline, and south,' she said. 'Over that ridge, yonder.' She pointed at the southern arm of the Grenthvar valley, on the far side of the village. I had never been there, though I knew legionnaires patrolled and kept watch regularly. 'Follow me, stay low, don't draw any attention to us, and we'll make it out.'

She trotted off, following a path it seemed only she could see, swiftly passing over lichen-covered rock and tree root. Over her shoulder, she called, 'Step where I step and you'll be fine.'

We followed. At first it was merely hard, clambering over lichen-drenched rocks and under deadfall. Then it became excruciating. The blood-rush of gunfire and battle gave over to exhaustion. Fisk was sorely burned, and the Medierans (or possibly even one of the fleeing Ruman soldiers) had perforated my arm with an errant shot. Just now the pain of it began to blossom. It had not stopped bleeding. And the scent of Hellfire still followed us. Bullets flicked through the forest growth, snicking through bough and branch, disconnected from any boom of gunfire.

My fear and outrage dulled. On my companions' faces, I could see the deadening of expression. Trauma and exhaustion makes mutes of all. Samantha looked near death and she felt like a sack of wet corn, lumpy and inert. As we moved her, Sapientia would look at me, eyes wide and mouth tugged down in the corner, as if she could not believe this was happening. Which, I imagine, she couldn't. Nor could I.

'We must rest!' I said, calling to Lina. 'Even if the invaders are right on top of us, we can go no further.'

'A little further!' Lina called. 'A wide cliff. Flat, with cover. Just a bit more.' She scrambled up and over a jutting stone, shooting out half-above our heads.

All I could focus on was the weight of Samantha and the cliff ahead. She had stopped moving her legs and was not responsive.

Sapientia kept saying, 'Please, Sam, please, Sam, pleasesamplease-samcomeoncomeon.'

Now, at this great remove, I cannot understand how between us we made it up to the stone. Sometimes we bury things we would not like to remember.

But what I do remember is the lifelessness of Samantha's body as we laid her down. The dull, loose expression of her face, mouth askew. The jumble of her arms and stiffness of her legs. At some point, on our climb, she had died.

I collapsed and for what seemed like a long while looked up into the sky. Letting my chest fill and collapse with air. Observing the slow-moving clouds' drift across the heavens.

The crackle of gunfire drew me from my reverie.

The sun was just breaking over the rim of the Eldvatch. I pushed myself up and looked over the edge of the cliff, into the valley below. The camp was gone, burning. Thousands of Medierans moved through the Grenthvar forests, killing indiscriminately. A thick clutch of them circled the smelt. From here, at this vantage, the Hellfire shots sounded like small rocks falling. The golden sun lit up the earth in garish colours, orange, ochre, blue, silver, red, white. The black pillars of smoke rose, hanging so close I felt as though I could reach out and touch them, push them, and topple the vault of heaven.

Below, a contingent of grey-clad soldiers moved up the incline, through the forest. An officer called to his men in *espan*, a soft, fluid string of sounds. He pointed at where we took cover above them, on the cliff. There was closer gunfire, and a hard spray of powdered rock stung my eyes. I ducked back down.

Livia set Fiscelion down on the rock face of the cliff and called to Lupina, who brought the rucksack. The *dvergar* woman took up the child, and the Ruman the bag. From it, she yanked clothing, a flask, a canteen. With just the raw strength of her hands, she ripped a tunic into strips, wetted it and began tending her husband's wound.

'They know we're here,' I said.

'We have the high ground.' Sumner worked the action on his carbine. 'Shall we dissuade them from approaching?'

Lina, who had lost her rifle in the mad rush to escape, drew both of her six-guns. She simply nodded.

I groaned and pushed myself up into a crouch.

'You're shot, Shoe,' Livia said. 'Come here.' Sapientia moved to assist her.

'It's stopped bleeding,' I said. 'And I can't let these children have all the fun.'

Taking cover behind a boulder, Sumner slipped the muzzle of his carbine over it, sighted and fired.

'The captain,' I said. 'Wait for him. Long mustachios, a little triangle of beard. A real fucking dandy.'

Sumner glanced at me, and even in our current situation, gave a tight, grim smile. 'Aye, centurion, will do.'

'I'll be back,' Lina said and slunk away, two pistols upraised and ready to fire.

'Wait!' I called, but she was gone.

I forced myself to follow. Behind me, the report of Hellfire blasted – Sumner firing again. Frantic Medieran voices sounded from below.

'Got one!' Sumner called. I liked this man. In the face of over-whelming odds, he was joyous. Not a typical Ruman trait. But then, he was from Occidentalia.

With much effort, I caught up with Lina along the rugged Eldvatch trail, before she disappeared. She moved faster than a running stream down the Eldvatch and was twice as cold, when the mood was on her.

She looked annoyed when I stopped her.

'If you must,' she said, the exasperation bubbling close to the surface, 'take cover there, behind that tree. This is the only way to take the cliff. They must go through here.'

I moved to the tree she'd pointed out. She took position behind a tumble of gambel deadfall.

The mountainside was quiet. Trees creaked around us in the breeze. I watched Lina's breath slow, and my chest relaxed in sympathy. In the distance, a crackle of far-off gunfire.

I caught a hint of movement, and I sighted down my pistol as quickly as I was able. Bark exploded near where I took cover. A storm of bullets churned the tree into splinters.

Hunching down, I heard, rather than saw, Lina's returning fire. Many shots in quick succession.

Fluid shouts in *espan*, urgent and angry. I reached around the tree and fired downslope without even looking.

Ears ringing, we waited. Silence descended upon the mountain.

There was a movement. I followed it with my eyes, but it was too fast. Illva stood over me. His sword dripped blood. In his hand, something that at first struck me as unrecognisable. But when he dropped it at my feet, I realised it was the Medieran captain's head.

Gynth appeared behind him. 'You can come out,' he said. 'The eldest have taken the intruders.'

'All of them?' I asked.

Gynth shook his head. 'In the Grenthvar, no. On this mountainside, yes.' He gestured back to the cliff. 'Come. Even Illva and Ellva cannot stop bundles and bundles of those that invade.'

'Thousands. Of invaders,' I said.

'Those as well,' Gynth said.

When we rejoined those that waited on the cliff, Sumner said, 'I have never seen the like.' He stared in open awe at Illva and Ellva.

'Nor will you ever again, most like,' Gynth said. 'We must go, and the company of the eldest will end.'

'Come on, then,' Lina said. 'Follow me and we will be underground within the hour.'

Livia and Fisk rose. He looked weak and she distressed. Lupina carried Fiscelion, who was remarkably quiet. The lad was waveborn and had been on the move most of his life. Footfalls and movement, gunfire and infernal warfare – a constant state.

I touched Ellva's hand. She turned her head to look at me like a mother would a child. Staring up at her was a strange experience – I am a man, but I remember tugging at my mother's apron, so long ago. And now, I did it once more.

'Samantha,' I said, gesturing to my friend and companion, now fallen. 'We cannot bury her.' I pointed to the peak, far above. 'Would you put her there? On high? It is the least she deserves.'

Ellva made no verbal response, but seemed to understand my request. In her great hands, she took up Samantha Decius' body. The *vaettir* gave a single nod. Then she said something in a language I could not understand.

'She says, remember the furrow,' Gynth said. 'No invader will ever rest easy here.'

The two alabaster *vaettir* turned and, gaining speed, flowed up the mountainside, out of sight.

'Did she just tell us to leave and not come back?' Fisk asked.

'That's what it sounded like, my love,' Livia said.

Fisk stood, walked to the edge of the cliff and stared down at the Grenthvar valley. Finally, he said, 'Ia-damn it all to Hell,' and walked over to where the box that held the *daemon* hand sat on a rock face. He picked it up with his unburned, good hand. Wincing.

'I think we've got something to take care of,' he said.

TWENTY-SEVEN

Don't Think Her Sex Really Fuckin'
Matters Any More, Old One

Six days underground, through winding passages and chambers nightmarish and beautiful, by turns. Much of the experience – especially the squalling of Fiscelion – I've tamped deep within me, stuffed into the unused and unvisited parts of my soul. It seems that travel suits the lad, but darkness does not.

Lina led us firmly through passages I would never have dreamed existed, the only illumination available to us a small *daemonlight* of Sapientia's that was puny against the titanic weight of the mountain's dark. But it was enough to keep us sane, at least.

Dvergar have an affinity with the stone, the mountain – we sprang from it, bursting onto the earth like seeds coming to fruition. But I am half-Ruman. And have never relished long, dim periods below ground. Gynth too withdrew into himself and seemed to shrink while underground, becoming timid and smaller. There was no demarcation of night or day, and when we rested he would sit, pull up his knees, wrap his great arms around them and cover his face, remaining absolutely still and quiet until Lina called for us to move on. Had he not responded, at the end of our rests, we might have forgotten him.

The spaces in the earth and under the mountain are never silent: whispers come to you, the metallic fall of dashing water like voices from some dim past; the clatter of rocks echoing; the susurrus of panting breath that you can't differentiate from your companion or some imagined shadowy creature pacing you. Imagination blossoms, fruits, and then rots.

Once, when I thought I might never see light again, Lina beckoned us all to climb an ancient stair carved from the living stone of the Eldvatch itself. We rose on weary legs, each step a misery. A breath of air touched our faces, full of the scents of life – sweetgrass and sage, shoal and beast. We emerged on a mountainside, under the stars and the moon as bright as a noon sun. Below us, hundreds of shifting, golden lights. They flickered like summer insects.

I found myself on my stomach, on a ledge, looking down the open face of the mountain toward the town. Lina eased herself down beside me.

'Tapestry,' she said.

'I know it well,' I said, remembering. 'Your mother was born here. I lived here for fifty years.'

'You were a wagoneer, then,' Lina said, softly. She wasn't asking. She'd had the stories from her mother – Edwina. Edwina'd been a hellion, ready to scrap at any provocation, and gave Illina and I no end of trouble. Of the seven children we'd had – Brisea, Vrinbror, Svin, Calliothir, Givae, Druin, and Edwina – it was her I thought on the most. Fast to anger, quick to love. It was as if all of the contradictions of the Hardscrabble had become distilled into the body of one *dvergar* girl.

I hoped she was still alive.

'Where is Edwina, now?' I asked.

'She married and moved out Saltlick way,' Lina said. ' "Gettin' a mite crowded 'round here, missy," she said. "There's good trapping in the Illvatch down there and I mean to take a mess of furs come winter".' Lina smiled, thoughtfully. 'That was twenty years ago.'

'I hope the *vaettir* will give them time to remove themselves,' I said.

'I think so,' Lina said. 'They are inscrutable, but I've come to think they will be fair.'

'It is all we can hope,' I said, thinking. The timbre of Lina's voice, her hands, her hair. I recalled other hands, long ago, working a shuttle, threading the course of our lives. And then those hands grew still. 'Your grandmother worked the looms.'

'Look there,' Lina said, pointing. She had nimble, yet stout fingers, my granddaughter. I could see my history there, writ in her flesh.

I looked where she pointed. Past the downward slope and in an open V where the gambels split to offer a view of the lights below, Tapestry shone. On the nearest side, in a scraggly milo field that seemed grey rather than amber in the faint light of stars, a Medieran patrol moved. Around them bounded their infernal dogs of war – *daemon*-gripped men and women. I breathed thanks to the numen and old gods that they were too far away to sense us.

'And there's smoke,' she said. I'd thought it might be issue from any town, anywhere. But Lina's eyes were sharper than my old ones. 'Tapestry burns.'

You have times of despair in your life. But hearing it in someone you love is the worst. Would that I could change it for her. But it's a monster of a world and all we can do is keep from joining its baseness, its depravity.

We went back below ground, to the darkness.

If it had not been for Sapientia and her *daemonlight*, I might have gone mad.

We all might have.

We crawled out of the earth fifteen miles north of Wickerware, like babes, blinking in the bright light of day. Lina had tried to keep us underground until nightfall, so our eyes might adjust. But

Fiscelion began crying once more, and no teat, no food, no soft words, nor rocking could stop him. He was indomitable, implacable. Outraged.

'Fuck it.' Lina shrugged. 'Let's go. We'll be blind as bats,' she said. 'Anything but this.' She looked at Livia. 'Sorry.'

The lad stopped crying in the daylight, as if shocked by the sun. Lupina clutched him tight to her breast. It was a hazy, white day, hot and windy. On the air, there was the faintest scent of salt. And rot.

We'd travelled through the guts of the Smokeys, circumventing the towns of Dvergar and Tapestry, to come almost to the end of Occidentalia.

'Wickerware,' Lupina said, with an air of familiarity. 'There are marshes around the town. They are what stink of rotten vegetables and sewage.'

'Will there be Medierans there?' Sapientia asked.

'We were there not three weeks ago,' Livia said. 'An old codger kept watch on the wharf.'

'Medieran?' I asked.

'He definitely had enough rum to drink in an empty town to make me think he had a passing acquaintance with them,' Livia said.

I nodded. 'Lina and I should go in, by night, and look around.'

'It's six ides. Tomorrow is seven. Tenebrae said he would be here then,' Livia said.

'Well, we can dick around here for a day, or go in and see what we can see,' I said. 'We start a fire, burn down a warehouse, the smoke will still be coming on the morrow.'

'And whatever Medierans that might be in the area will be coming as well,' Fisk said. His arm had healed, some, but it was awful to behold – a swamp of blisters and pustules. The skin had melted and at any moment could slough away. When it fully healed

312

– if it fully healed – it would seem as though it had been sculpted of clay by inexpert hands. I'd seen this before: smelt injuries, hotel fires, faulty *daemonlight* lanterns, misfires of six-guns where the summoned *imp* swarmed the pistolero, charring him to a crisp.

'I'll come, too,' Sapientia said. At my frown she put her hands on her waist. 'I've lost all my supplies. If this town is empty, I would see if I can find some replacements, Shoe.'

'It's dangerous—' I began.

'I raise devils, man. Don't lecture me on danger,' Sapientia said.

'And me,' Gynth said.

'We can't go in there with your titanic arse swinging all about,' I said. 'If there are any citizens remaining, they'll immediately shit themselves if they don't start shooting.'

Sapientia looked up at the *vaettir*. 'Come with us, partway,' she said. 'If we are in danger, it wouldn't hurt to have you nearby.'

'We'll all come,' Livia said. 'Stretching our party out like pearls on a string is not wise.'

'Agreed,' Fisk said. 'You three, go in. If there are Medierans there, two *dvergar* and a worker won't seem too amiss. A stretcher, a Ruman legate, Lupina toting around a squalling babe, and the rest of our motley crew might seem out of place. We'll wait at the edge of town.'

At nightfall we moved, finding the southern road into Wickerware. The land was soft here, and flatter down from the tail of the Eldvatch. Cold springs and run-off from the heights wetted the Smokeys' skirts and poured into the lowlands to stagnate into brackish marsh. The mountains were rounder here, too, worn down by the movements of the winds blowing in from the Bay of Mageras, and from a distance looked like some crocodile's tail dipping under the surface of the earth.

Wickerware was an ancient *dvergar* town, without the ordered lines of a Ruman outpost, nor the messy, sprawling disorder of a town of Medieran ancestry. *Dvergar* are fond of braids, circles. The curve of sky, the arc of a stone's throw. Wickerware – from the *dvergar*, *vrika*, for weave – was a round nest, streets in intersecting circles leading to a town market that also served as a meeting place, a forum, a heart. The village's form reflected its major product – baskets.

The town had seen some destructive force – buildings husked by fire, broken wheels and collapsed wagons in side streets and alleys. The streets were empty, no home fires cast smoke into the night sky, no lanterns glowed in the dark. A pack of wild dogs barked as we moved toward the market where all side roads led, and we took a recursive path, Lina leading, with Sapientia close on her arse. I brought up the rear.

Livia had described where they'd found the old codger when they had come ashore. I was familiar with that part of the town – indeed, there are very few places in the Hardscrabble and Occidentalia that I have not been to at least once. In this case, it was near what was once a tavern, and I must admit near such locales, I have a more fluent familiarity.

It was called Rubi's Confidence, and we approached down a narrow street marked with the signs that read 'Selvedge Ln'. Lina held up her hand in a fist to indicate we should stop. She pointed to the rooftops.

Something – or some*things* – moved there.

Shadows shifted, grew long. The dark blue sky, made milky with stars and just beginning to become obscured by clouds as rain pushed east off the Bay of Mageras, found hunched shapes running on all fours up gables and down shingled roofs.

'I am godsdamned fed up with these fucking possessed bastards,' Lina said, drawing her six-guns. Sapientia and I followed suit.

'Inside,' I said, keeping my voice low. Unlikely the *daemon*-gripped did not know we were present, but I saw no need to ring a dinner bell. We pushed inside the tavern, through the swinging doors.

Rubi's Confidence was a ruin. Tables and chairs lay in broken heaps, dark stains on the floor, a pool of oil. Sapientia unshuttered a small *daemonlight* lantern and moved its narrow band of light about the room. Overhead the roof beams creaked. Dust filtered down from the ceiling and made the *daemonlight* swim with particles.

'They're moving,' I said.

'No shit,' Lina said. 'Look.' She pointed to a crumpled heap in a corner.

There stood three casks of what appeared to be rum in the gloom, and draped across them was the body of an elderly man. Rough clothing, knobby knees and arthritic hands, stubbled grey head. Had enough blood still moved in his sanguiducts, and he been able to stand, we might've seen eye to eye. But his body was pure wreckage – lifeless. The puddle of blood around him had darkened to black.

'Fucking awful how those things always go for the face,' Lina said.

'Hate is focused on the seat of expression: the eyes. The smile,' I said, absently.

'What the Hell is that supposed to mean?' Lina said.

'You hate what you see,' I said. 'And you hate what sees you.'

More rumbling footsteps above. A darkness whipped by in the open frame of the tavern's door. I trained both barrels of my six-guns there.

Sapientia emerged from the kitchen (or back room behind the bar, I couldn't tell).

'No tools,' she said. 'But I did find this.' She held up a medium-sized amphora. She set her *daemonlight* on the bar's counter. 'Oil.'

A leering face appeared in the doorway.

I fired, the report of Hellfire massive in the enclosed space of Rubi's Confidence. It's one thing to let loose Hellfire and damnation under the Hardscrabble sky, on the plains, where the noise can float over the shoals. But inside? It becomes deafening.

The face disappeared in a welter of blood. My ears rang. It was long moments before my hearing returned, and when it did, wordless screams and guttural vocalisations came from outside the tavern. One higher pitched than the others.

'At least three more,' I said. 'A woman.'

Lina nodded grimly. 'Don't think her sex really fuckin' matters any more, old one,' she said.

'True,' I responded.

'Help me,' Sapientia said. 'The tables and chairs.' She was pulling all the wrecked furniture onto the thick wood of the bar.

'I've got the door,' I said to Lina. 'Go.'

Lina frowned but holstered her guns and helped Sapientia pile up the broken furniture. I fired once as a *daemon*-gripped passed in front of the open door of Rubi's. The roof rattled.

'They're looking for another way in,' I said.

'They'll come in through the windows, when they think of it,' Lina said.

'We'll be gone by then,' Sapientia said. She snatched up the amphora and dumped the oil in a slick rush on the bar and over the stacked ruin of wooden furniture. When the amphora was empty, she tossed it aside and set the *daemonlight* lantern on the bar in a puddle of oil. She dug in one of the many pockets of her apron and withdrew a small vial, unscrewed the cap, and poured a small amount on the lantern.

'We must go,' she said, looking at us. 'Quickly.'

'They're out there,' I said.

'Back door,' she said. 'I've got a little surprise here waiting for them.' She gestured at the lantern. The top of it began to send acrid wisps of smoke toward the ceiling. She'd used some sort of caustic, I assumed.

Looking over my shoulder, I could see shadows shifting and dancing past Rubi's storefront. They were coming.

We moved, following Sapientia's lead, guns out. As we pushed through the wooden rear entrance, a *daemon*-gripped woman dropped from above to land in front of us, crouched, bloody hands out and ready to claw, with the wicked grace of all bedevilled. Her black mouth worked, gnawing at something I did not like to think about too much. Lina, with her own deadly grace, whipped out a longknife, and as the *daemon*-gripped woman lunged forward, she grabbed her by her long hair from the back of her head, and slung her with amazing force against the brickwork of Rubi's rear kitchen wall. In a flash, Lina had sunk the longknife into the *daemon*-gripped woman's throat. She pawed at the blade's hilt and then shifted to pawing at Lina with blackened, scabrous hands. Then she stilled.

There came a soft *whoosh*, and guttural screams. Yellow light framed the rear door of Rubi's Confidence, and heat poured out onto the street – the lantern had released its *imp*, the oil had gone up in flames, and the tavern began to burn.

We paused only long enough to see black figures thrashing in the firelight. And then we moved back through the streets to circle around to the wharf.

The piers were gone, some burned away, some splintered from large-bore Hellfire shelling. Far out, on the bay, a single light.

As we watched, it disappeared and the waters went dark.

'Medieran?' Sapientia said.

'No idea,' I said. 'Possibly.'

'Probably,' Lina said.

We waited in the shadow of a warehouse. The waves rolled up

onto the flotsam-filled shore, sluggish and low. Behind us, Rubi's Confidence became a great conflagration, reflecting yellow light on the low night clouds scudding across the heavens now. The smell of burning cedar filled the air, fragrant. Smoke poured into the sky to join the blanketing whiteness above.

'Are there great wyrms in the West?' Lina asked. The way she asked, the timbre of her voice, the innocent rise and fall of it, made me think of a child asking her parent if magical creatures existed.

'Dragons?' Sapientia said, quietly. 'I'm afraid they are just a myth.'

'Not true,' I said. 'Livia has seen them, with her own eyes, when she was in Kithai. But they are very small and they call them lóng.'

'And sea serpents?' Lina asked.

'No,' Sapientia said. 'Sailors would often confuse large sea creature—'

'Look there,' Lina said, pointing at the surface of the bay. 'A serpent approaches.'

Something was moving under the water, approaching the Wickerware wharf.

The *Typhon*.

TWENTY-EIGHT

That Would Be A Bad Idea

A SHADOW UPON the water, sleek and deadly. Guns shrouded. We approached the *Typhon* on a dinghy, tossed by waves and uncomfortable in the night. Behind us, Wickerware had caught aflame – as incendiary as its namesake – and the smoke of the city filled our nostrils, caught in our hair, and only the smell of salt water washed the stink of it from us.

Sumner bent his back to the sea, tugging oars. Livia's face was devoid of all emotion as she looked back on the receding shore, her skin painted in oranges and pinks from the fires. She held Fiscelion, who looked wide-eyed at the conflagration – the dancing flames and smoke and shifting shore. He was calm, silent and entranced. Fisk sat below them, his arse in the hull water, unsteady on his feet now. His arm might have been infected, I couldn't tell.

Lina was tearless, fierce and implacable. But I found my face wet, and Sapientia, who sat next to me, put her hand on mine and squeezed as I watched my homeland become smaller and indistinct. A shifting, inconstant horizon.

When we finally reached the *Typhon*, Gynth raced across the face of the bay, his great feet churning a shining wake behind him. His foot touched the hull of the ship and he vaulted high into the air and landed with grace and terrifying agility on the deck and moved to help us on board.

Lupina leaned in close to me and said, 'Thank you.'

'Why do you thank me?'

'You wept for us both. I do not have to,' she said. 'I don't like you. I have never liked you. But we are the same.'

'Of this place,' I said.

'No longer,' she said. 'Get used to it.'

'It's like coming home,' Livia said, stepping onto the deck of the *Typhon*.

Carnelia was ecstatic. She gave Fisk a brief acknowledgement, Lupina and Livia terse hugs, and Fiscelion she covered in kisses. Tenebrae came above deck and greeted Fisk formally and offered him the captain's berth and command. Fisk, still carrying the box containing the *daemon* hand, waved off Tenebrae's formality.

'I know jack squat about ships, sir,' Fisk said. 'The command is yours, if Livia lets you keep it.'

Catch Hands was nowhere to be seen. When I asked about him, Carnelia said, 'I have never seen anyone so small vomit so much. We left him, half-dead, in Covenant.' She hid a smile. 'He was quite glad to remain on solid land, once more.'

Tenebrae hustled us below decks – it was supremely uncomfortable for Gynth, who had to literally crawl through the hatch and down the stairs into a stinking, central metal chamber that was close and pressing even for someone of my stature. I worked fields east of the Eldvatch when I was very young, those years when I wanted to see everything in Occidentalia – Rume, Fort Lucullus, the thousand-acre wood. In those years, I would pick cotton or tabac, work orchards and vegetable farms, with teams of itinerant *dvergar*, where we'd sleep in hot beds and shared bunks – groups of grown males sharing very little living space. The *Typhon* smelled the same as those flophouses.

Very quickly, berths were reorganised – Fisk with Livia and

Fiscelion were placed in the captain's, Tenebrae and Sumner in the lascar officer's bunk, Sapientia with Carnelia and Lupina in the engineer's cabin. The four lascars Tenebrae had recruited from Covenant had to string hammocks in the deck gun controls both forward and aft. This left the most spacious room (other than the command area) to Gynth and myself – the engine room, where the devil Typhon burned.

Carnelia laughingly called it Typhon's Bower and hoped Gynth and I found in it a bliss of the nuptial kind, and then she stopped. 'That was unkind, Shoe. I am sorry,' she said. 'I'm always saying things I probably shouldn't.'

'I know, ma'am. Not a problem,' I said. 'You've said worse.'

'And probably will again in the future. I am just so happy you are all safe,' she said, and then gave me a kiss on my whiskered cheek.

That one had changed. No longer the wasted wine-soaked harridan. She was robust, her arms and figure strong, her heart and demeanour full of life. With some, privilege and indolence can be cruel, hardship can be a boon, a furnace fire to smelt away all of the impurities, leaving only steel behind. I was happy to see Carnelia was one such person, even though the steel in her could be pointed. Sharp enough to draw blood.

As Gynth and I made pallets from stinking rough wool blankets and cloaks, a voice sounded through the interior of the *Typhon*. It was Mister Tenebrae.

'Attend me, attend me – debrief in the command. Debrief on the second hour in the command,' Tenebrae said. The sound of his voice was faint, coming from a small grate above the door. It was a curious sound, as if something rattled sympathetically to the sound of his voice. 'That is all.'

Gynth said, 'I will stay here.' He sat on the metal floor and stared at the pulsing glow and intricate wardwork. He drew up his knees and wrapped his arms around them as if he was back in the Eldvatch caverns and burrows on the way to Wickerware. He was shutting down.

'Anything I can do for you, pard?' I said.

'No,' he responded. 'I am too large for this place.'

'It won't be forever,' I said.

'If it is, I will just sleep,' he said, covering his face. 'I will take the long sleep.'

'The long sleep?' I asked.

He did not respond.

Fisk looked at Sapientia when we had all gathered in the command, save Gynth. 'What do you know about this Terra Umbra?'

'It holds the Emryal Rift,' she said. 'Terra Umbra, land of shadow. Where the cut between worlds occurred.'

'Its location?' Fisk said. 'I realise there is knowledge that you as a member of the College of Engineers possess that even Tamberlaine himself might not be privy to. And I will be asking you to make a sacrifice. A great one,' he said, looking at her meaningfully.

She chewed her bottom lip. Eventually she nodded. 'Yes, I know its location.'

'And will you tell us where it is?' Fisk asked. Beside him, Livia had gone still and I noticed that her hand was at her side, close to where she kept her sawn-off.

'I must think—' Sapientia said. 'I don't know if it is realistic to—'

'Allow me to say something,' Livia said. 'We have just had our whole world turned upside down and unleashed Hell upon the earth. Thousands have died.'

'The Medierans—' Sapientia said.

Livia was not having it. She held up a hand. Carnelia had changed. But so had her older sister. I loved her, as always, but

322

there was something less likeable about her now. She was fearful, and willing to do horrible things. Or maybe she had always been that way and I was just seeing it now. A beautiful contradiction. But her husband, my partner, was the same. A deadly pair they made. I do not know why I was suddenly getting finicky about my friend's willingness to use force – except that this time it was upon another of my friends.

Thankfully, Livia moved her hand away from the sawn-off and resorted to reason to persuade Sapientia.

'This use of the infernal,' Livia said, slowly. 'It will leave the world in ruins. We have in our possession, through providence, or luck, or fortune, the ability to close this rift, to stop the city killers. To end this proliferation of Hellfire. And you have reservations?'

'Of course I do!' Sapientia said. 'It's my way of life.'

'But it's the world's cancer and must be cut out.'

'I do not like being forced into anything,' Sapientia said.

'That is unfortunate. But do not feel singled out,' Livia said. 'We have *all* been forced to this.' She shifted her weight and stilled once more. It was the stillness of someone about to strike. 'Disclose the location of Terra Umbra.'

Sapientia bowed her head. I felt terrible for her – no one should be the hand that kills their own profession.

'Have you charts of the north seas? Beyond Heingistr and the Occidens?' Sapientia said.

'Yes,' Livia responded. She gestured to Tenebrae, who retrieved the chart. He spread it out on the small command table, where I imagined lascars and their commanders might take food or coffee while on duty. It was a strange vessel, this *Typhon*. Windowless yet over-lit with *daemonlights*. Offering us great freedom now, a chance for life, but prison-like. And terribly close.

We examined the map. Sapientia moved her finger to the north, between the land masses of Occidentalia in the west, and Terra

Omnia in the east, comprised of Teuton, Gall, and Latinum. The smaller Northlands, fractured states, worn as a crown.

'Mare Congelatum,' she said. 'The frozen sea, and Terra Glacies, here. There is an island off the south-west coast, thirty days' sail west and south.' She said. 'There lies Terra Umbra.'

'In the frozen north,' I said. 'How ironic.'

'It is ironic. The rift itself seethes, casting up great plumes of steam and vapours. For hundreds of miles to the east, and most of the isle itself, is wreathed in clouds and even though it is cold there, the heat issuing from the rift gives it a singularly warm and out of place climate for an island in the Mare Congelatum.' She scratched at her cheek. 'Or so legend has it. Very few alive have ever ventured there. It's rumoured that the land is guarded by devils made flesh. And the great wyrms.'

'And do you believe this to be true?' Fisk asked.

'Possibly,' she said. 'Engineers – summoners – tend to be unstable and prone to either self-debasement or grandiose summits of self-worth. Like Beleth and his folly. It goes part and parcel with the raising of devils. Most of the histories of the time of Emrys, who cut the rift, are fanciful. Also,' she said, a bit sheepishly, 'engineers are secretive and do not like sharing knowledge. So dressing up the origins of power seemed reasonable, at the time, for those early practitioners.'

'How did you gain the knowledge of Terra Umbra?' Livia asked. 'It seems that they would want to keep that for the most select few.'

'You might think so,' Sapientia said. 'But you'd be wrong. There is great secrecy in the College, but that secrecy involves summoning and the physical aspects of engineering. Trade secrets. To protect these, we make up rituals for entry into the College and for initiation into the deeper studies.' She shrugged. 'I became fascinated by the rituals and did what I could to discover their histories and origins, once I became initiated. The location of Terra Umbra . . .'

She smiled. 'When I asked them about it, they looked at me blankly. "Why do you care?" one of my professors asked.' She looked at Livia. 'And of course, I responded that I was curious.'

'Congratulations,' Livia said. 'Your curiosity will be answered.' She turned to Tenebrae. 'Set a course out of the Bay of Mageras, east. We sail for Terra Umbra.'

Gynth did not stir on the long voyage. He remained still, and seemingly a statue, and I began to understand some of how he appeared when I first met him and he rescued me from the other marauding *vaettir*. He seemed a revenant, raised from a grave, clad in mouldering garb. Illva and Ellva too had ancient clothing, as if they had just awoken from centuries-long slumber – which they had. It is just hard to countenance, even for me, a *dvergar*. I have seen a hundred-and-fifty-five seasons, but my life is but a moment to a *vaettir*.

With such long lives, there are those that turn to cruelty, mischievousness – like Berith's band that terrorised the Hardscrabble. Others deal with the immemorial passage of days to years to centuries by taking the long sleep and waking when they are ready. The progression of their soul might be the alarm to wake, or great need. Or their dreams might become dark, or whatever senses they might possess even in slumber (and I fancy these might be considerable) might sense great change moving in the world. So they stir. Or, loathing it, dive deeper into the benthic depths of slumber. But the veil of much of their nature has been pulled back and now more understanding of them comes with that unveiling – they are myriad, they are complicated, they are multitudinous.

But the *Typhon*. The same sickness that affected Catch Hands assailed Lina and me. It seems *dvergar* have an aversion to the motion of sea vessels. Or possibly it simply runs in my family, for Lupina was not affected. Lina and myself spent the first seven days at sea vomiting up all food. It was a misery. And maybe a blessed misery. Because we missed the terror of the passage from Medieran-held water.

As we passed out of the Bay of Mageras through the southernmost isle of Occidentalia, I retched up bile, Lina at my side. As we sailed north, past the ruins of Fort Lucullus (which had endured the same firebombing as Novorum) we hung listless over the bulwarks, staring into the passing waters. When we ran from Medieran ships, and exchanged gunfire, Lina and I were useless. I remember great booming, and screaming, the ship keeling this way and that. The *Typhon* itself thrummed and juddered, and these developments made my retching worse – I dribbled bile and could take no crust, not bite of fish, nor dram of liquor. I was arrested in misery, caught in a half-state, still alive and half-dead.

Then it eased. I swallowed water and it did not come back up. I was able to think once more. I was able to walk, and string words together into coherent thought and speak these thoughts to the world. I felt like an infant, born into the world.

And when I came upon the deck after those dark days, the fresh air filling my lungs, I understood how some people felt called to the sea. On the grey-green waves, tossed under the wide vaulted sky, I was strongly reminded of the shoals, in the cradle of the Hardscrabble.

Life on a ship, one as small and cramped as the *Typhon*, is a godsdamned trial, that's for sure. And sleeping in the engine room ate at me. At night, I would have bad dreams, images of being stalked by creatures in the dark. Each one thirsting for blood. Childish dreams of being chased. Horrific slumbers in which I would burn.

Waking in a sweaty nest of reeking blankets, I would turn to cast my gaze upon the glowing cage of *Typhon*. Its presence spilled out, even beyond the warded intaglio of the floor, to where Gynth and I made our berth. I spent what time I could awake, and would snatch naps where I could, on the deck, under the stars.

One day, we sighted a small village on the shore and risked port for provisions. I looked forward to disembarking.

'No, Centurion Ilys,' Tenebrae said, placing a hand on my chest. 'You must stay on board as we source food and take on water.'

'But— But—' I spluttered. The solid earth was only a short distance away.

'No,' he said. 'That is an order. You will lose your sea-legs and there is not a soul on this ship who wants to listen to you or your granddaughter vomit for days on end. Again.'

And so it was with great resignation that we remained on board as the rest of our crew disembarked. It seemed such a great cruelty to me, then. But it was mere hours until we were underway, steaming north again.

We bought food, and had gold and silver to spare, though the harbourmaster and merchants at the village asked a high price. They feared that Ruman coin would be useless now, or worth only the metal (and Ruman coins were notoriously debased) and so were exorbitant, but Tenebrae and Livia managed to strike a deal and we took on casks of home-made wine and pickled fish, garum and salt, bushels of maize and sacks of flour, crocks of butter, and two small amphorae of oil. This was all they could afford us, but most of it came in great quantities.

We fell into rhythms, we fell into trances. Maybe it was because I could hardly sleep and what I did manage was *daemon*-spiced and disjointed. Lupina, when she was not tending to the boy, got over her dislike of me enough to teach Lina and me to fish, and we spent our days letting out line, and our nights out under the stars in the shadows of shrouded guns. We had not seen any ships, Medieran or otherwise, for a long while. The days grew indistinct, shrouded and foggy. There were stretches of days where we saw no shore at all, and the waves grew high, high as a stretcher in the shoals. I worried my sickness would return but it did not.

The fish we snared were long, silver, and delicious – and vicious-looking, each mouth full of sharp teeth and their ridges with scales like daggers. Lupina, ever quick with a knife, would pluck them from the water, hauling them over the gunwale as they thrashed madly, and have them gutted in moments. So quick she was with the knife, she'd offer gobbets of meat, dipped in garum, fresh from the sea. And I could still taste the life in the flesh, as though I were one of those old Kithai *vaettir*, and the fish the snakes of the rice.

At night, I would cook – since of the crew I had the most experience – with Lupina overseeing my efforts. She was territorial when it came to fish.

The lascars found us strange, and while Sumner got along well with Tenebrae, some distance remained between the enlisted men and the former praetorian. On the whole, I quite liked Tenebrae, and there were moments he would speak or gesture and it seemed that Secundus was once more with us.

The sea, endless. The days, droning and empty, marked by fish and cups of poor home-made wine.

The days grew cold and we turned east, and north – though at this point those were just words to me, mentioned by Tenebrae and discussed at mess with the lascars and Sumner. It had no real weight, no veracity. The sun never rose or set. The white vapour that clung to us lightened and darkened and these intervals marked days. The sky was an endless expanse of white and the seas stilled. I had no sense of direction, or time. I was dispossessed, homeless. When I could sleep, I had dreams of hanging suspended in air over a circle of warding, and Fisk, Lina, and Gynth stood at the edges.

Each had their claim upon me, but none more than another. It was an agony.

We no longer hugged the coast, and we would not have been able to see it if we had. Livia assured me the *Typhon* was rugged and had made the cross-sea journey from Rume. Much of the workings of the ship were a mystery to me – the navigation, the engineering maintenance that Sapientia had taken over, the way it was able to submerge and resurface (though this rarely happened since we had sailed so far north). So I focused on things I could understand, cleaning and cooking and fishing. I found some caustic in the mess and diluted it with salt water and spent many hours cleaning the interior walls and bulwarks of the *Typhon*, polishing anything that might be polished. I lunched with Fiscelion, and dandled the boy on my knee and sang him old *dvergar* songs in my rough voice. Sometimes Lupina or Lina might accompany me, on the ones they knew. He would still, and grasp my beard and listen to the old words. They might just be noise and melody, but it brought him some enjoyment.

> *The mist grows, tall as trees*
> *Up from the seas*
> *Up from the shoals*
> *It grows, and laps at the feet of*
> *Eldvatch stones, its bones*
> *Dvergar made and dvergar home.*

On those few days when the sun cut through the fog, we would take the lad Fiscelion on deck and Fisk would hold him on high and point out the gulls wheeling and diving in our wake, or watch Lupina and Lina taking fish from the sea. He made faces at the raw fish we placed on his perfect little lips, so full of rebuke. Livia looked on, pensive and wind-tossed, and I could sense a low tension building there between husband and wife. They'd never really had time to learn to walk together, learn to be two halves of the same coin, as mates are supposed to be. 'Walk as geese,' the *dvergar* called it. Fisk, now healed from his burns, was quiet and it did not take much imagination to puzzle out the whys and wherefores. We sailed for Terra Umbra, and at the end of this journey, there was some fate that was tied to the *daemon* hand, and our world, that none of us could foresee.

The seas grew higher, and I felt as though I rode the back of some great sea beast, dipping and diving into the waves. The air became bitter cold and some mornings there was snow on the deck. Fiscelion squealed with pleasure and slid about on his arse, and the adults did the same. There was less fog, now, on the slate-grey seas and occasionally we would see great white-blue sugarloafs of ice ramping out of the surface of the sea.

We slowed to a crawl at night. By day, the *Typhon* was trepidatious, moving slowly through the waters. The ocean was calmer now in these northern climes and that helped, though we inched our way through the seas like a fat baker threading his barefoot way through his household at night, slow and tentative. The days the fog was thick, everything was still and hushed. When the sun shone, the winds would rise and the seas grow high, but, Livia told us, never as high as on the Occidens.

On the fortieth day at sea, we saw the pillar of fire, rising from the waters.

The island grew from the sea, jutting up and spanning high, wreathed in thick forests and wracked by surf. It appeared in the same slow unveiling that occurs in dreams – the mists parting at the approach, shadows of cliff and land growing and swelling, eye-sweet to one long at sea; the spiky fringe of trees becoming evident, and beyond, the swirling maelstrom in the sky – the Emryal

Rift, churning and casting off clouds and vapours, like some piece of riven invisible earth turned sideways in the sky. Smoke poured from the wound; arteries of air dragged away the rift's effluvium downwind, making it seem if there was a titanic dark wall snaking away. It was massive and claustrophobic, all at once. Those two things warred within it and on it. It was conflict as landmass.

The *Typhon* drew closer, Tenebrae steering, with some help from the lascars who spoke into voice funnels, informing him of whatever dangers lay hidden beneath the foam. We found a sheltered bay and brought the *Typhon* as close as possible, but as there were no away boats, it became obvious we would need to either swim or wake Gynth and plead for portage.

'Get your boy,' Fisk said to me, looking at the shore. 'Make a raft.'

'All right, pard,' I said. 'You're gonna hang back?'

Fisk looked at me. We'd not spent much time together on the journey. But there was no distance.

'Hang back?' he said, looking at me thoughtfully. 'I wish it was my decision, Shoe.' He shrugged. 'Livia is firm on some things and I'm not to be in the away party.'

'That's well and good, pard,' I said. 'We're able to fill in the gaps.'

'The gaps,' he said. He looked down, to the deck. 'There's likely to be some gaps.'

I went to Typhon's Bower. Gynth remained exactly as he'd been early in our journey, more than two score days before. There was mould I hadn't noticed before growing upon the hem of his trousers and his shirt. He'd been damp, I guess, when he entered this implacable slumber, and the rot took hold.

'Gynth,' I said, quietly. 'We need you, pard. Again.'

He remained still. I reached a hand toward him and he said, 'Yes.' He raised his leonine head. His eyes were unfocused for a moment, like a man coming from a dark room into brilliant light. 'Where are we?'

'Where it all begins, hoss,' I said. 'The hole all those *daemons* come from.'

He stretched out his legs, lowered his arms. Each movement, deliberate. Measured.

'Hole?'

'I think the idea is we're gonna plug it, and—' I made my hand into a fist and showed him what the Brawley folk like to call a puckered bunghole – a great insult, if made in anger; a great joke, if made in mirth. 'Stop the *daemons* from coming through.'

'As long as it is under the sky. Let us go.' He crawled toward the door and into the command chamber. It was easier than being hunched half-over.

One of the lascars presented me with an axe and hemp, and Gynth ported me over to shore. It was a rocky expanse, the countless stones worn to smoothness but piled in jumbled heaps on the shores of a large stream rushing into the sea. It rained, lightly, and our breath came in plumes, a soft rain, surely, but one that seemed it could turn to snow or ice at any moment. Beyond where we stood, looking at Terra Umbra, moss and lichen covered the larger, more removed mist-worn boulders, painting the craggy shore in yellows and ochres. Some hundred paces from the surf a forest grew, with great narrow trees like sentinels' spears piercing the air. In the distance, vaporous mountains quickly rose, blanketed in green up to snow-rimed peaks, half-occluded by clouds. And framed between mountains, up the sundered valley, the rift, churning.

The atmosphere here was charged – pregnant with possibility. And much of that possibility was frightening.

'It is sharp here, is it not?' Gynth raised his head and seemingly sniffed the air.

'Don't know about sharp, but that thing makes me nervous,' I said, gesturing toward the churning mass. 'Let's go cut some trees.'

From the great scrawls of deadfall, we took logs, those that seemed fresh enough to not be rotten, and weathered and dry enough to float. There was no lack of the stuff. I knocked off all the remaining branches and lashed a makeshift raft together within hours and began ferrying back and forth between the *Typhon* and land. The lascars remained on board, along with Lupina and Fiscelion (at least until our task at hand was complete), and Tenebrae, who for all purposes was the captain now, and the rest of us found ourselves on the shore. I know not what goodbyes were given to Fiscelion. Tearful? Earnest? Fisk's expression looked helpless and desolate after he disembarked the raft on the Terra Umbran shore. He carried the box holding the *daemon* hand.

'So,' Carnelia said. 'What next? Do we just go up to the—' she waved her hand, vaguely '—thing and toss the *daemon* hand in?'

Fisk frowned. 'I do not think that will be the way,' he said.

'No,' Sapientia said. 'I think not.'

'Whatever the case,' Livia said, placing her hands on her hips, 'we'll need to make camp. The hour grows late and no journey will be made in the dark.'

We had no tents and no kit, but we took one of the *Typhon*'s old gun-shrouds and with much hemp and Sapientia's instructions, strung up between trees a rather grease-stained pavilion with no walls and built a fire in the centre of it.

'This will work, I think,' Sapientia said, happily, hands on her hips. Here stood a woman who enjoyed problems, conquerable problems, problems she could master with her hands and her considerable wits.

'And tomorrow?' Carnelia said. She wore a sword at her hip, now, and a pistol.

'We see what we can see,' Fisk said. He placed his blankets

333

down and sat the box containing the *daemon* hand upon them. It would be a damp night, once sun set, and I was prepared for an uncomfortable rest, but anything was better than staring into the *Typhon*'s *daemonic* nether eye all night in my dreams.

'I think I will take a gander around,' I said. 'Maybe scout a bit up trail.'

'Might be wise,' Fisk said. 'Maybe I'll come along. I could use a stretch of the legs.'

'Gynth?' I said, looking to the big *vaettir*. 'How 'bout you, hoss?'

Gynth stood still, his back to the fire, sensing the air.

'That would be a bad idea,' he said. In his voice there was something I had never heard before.

'Why is that, pard?' I asked.

'Dragons,' he said. 'Many dragons.'

TWENTY-NINE

Holy Hell. I Have Never Seen The Like.

'Is that the correct word?' Gynth asked.

'Dragons?' I said. 'What are we talking about here, pard?'

Fisk, Livia, and Carnelia perked up. They moved away from the fire and approached Gynth. In most things, the Rumans either ignored Gynth, or addressed him with extreme politeness. Some flaw in their character – or possibly the inability of Ruman pride to recognise something or someone so vastly and obviously superior to them, by dint of nature, if not birth – made them hesitant and tentative around the stretcher.

'Like the *kinthi*,' he said, using the *dvergar* word for mountain lion. 'But bundles and bundles larger and covered in armour.'

'The great wyrms,' Carnelia said. 'Ah, Tata would have pissed himself in joy.'

'I might've pissed myself for other reasons,' I said. 'Gynth, how do you know this?'

'I can sense them,' Gynth said. 'They have energy that is . . . very big. Very large.'

Livia said, '*Qi*.' I remembered the curious word from her Quotidian letters to Fisk.

'There's more,' Gynth said.

'What?' I said.

'Look,' he responded.

It was growing late in the afternoon, and over the whole island of Terra Umbra a gloom hung, half from clouds and sea-mist, half from the Emryal Rift and its effluvium. I began to understand why those old engineers called it the shadowland. Our fire seemed very small and the island very large.

A group of figures emerged from the gloom. Fisk drew his sidearm, Sumner raised a carbine and worked the action. I was a bit surprised when Carnelia drew the long, elegant sword she had hung at her side. It was the sound of Carnelia's steel blade that stopped the forward motion of the shadowy figures.

'Devils seated in the flesh,' Sapientia muttered.

'No,' Lina said. 'My eyes see better than yours. Those are *vaettir*.'

They were old, and clad in armour made from what appeared to be scales of tremendous fish, viridescent and gold, but I realised in a moment they must be scales from the dragons Gynth had sensed. They wore fine cloaks of some fabric that appeared to be leather but was hard to determine, and it too shimmered like the scales. If Illva and Ellva were alabaster, these *vaettir* were the absence of all colour – or maybe the presence of all light – and seemed luminous even in the gloom and fog of Terra Umbra. Impossibly tall, they moved with a stately grace. Each wore tremendous, oversized steel blades, some curved, some straight. Two of the *vaettir* held half-spear, half-sword weapons similar to the one Ellva had wielded on the killing fields of the Grenthvar. Others held bows that no living man could draw.

Eleven, all told, and one at the head of the party approached. Looking at them, I realised how ridiculous the name stretcher was. Our mortal way of belittling something beyond our comprehension. I felt ashamed, then, that it had ever fallen from my tongue.

'Thou hast returned,' she said in an antique and formal common speech. 'It has been many years.'

Fisk said, 'We have never been here before.'

'Ah,' the *vaettir* said. It was such a human sound – a pause, vocalised. Nothing you'd expect from beings so otherworldly. 'Thou seemest so familiar,' she said.

'You have met our kind before?' Livia asked.

The *vaettir* slowly turned her head to consider Livia. 'Of course. How else would we know this rough speech?' She placed her hand slowly on the hilt of her greatsword and turned her head up and away from where we stood. For a long moment, she remained still. 'Hast thou brought us steel?'

Fisk blanched. 'Steel? We—' He paused, glanced at Sapientia.

She shrugged and mouthed *the Typhon*.

'Yes. We have brought steel and other metals,' Fisk said.

'This news is well met,' she said. She turned about, looking at the gathering gloom. 'Thou art in danger, here. Yon fire was unwise.' She smiled, then, a great crevasse appearing in her implacable white face. 'A scaled one hast sensed us and approaches.' It was an altogether strange response to the statement that something was coming. It was as if she had grown excited, a warrior called to battle. Her heart's desire.

Many of the other *vaettir* shifted their stances. A pair of them, both carrying bows, vaulted away to the nearby trees, scrabbling up to a great height in moments.

One of the *vaettir* called to the others in a sharp language that was shockingly familiar. 'One of the unripped!' he cried. 'Down from the heights, to prey upon we meagre few,' he said.

A response: 'It will find this meal full of steel and gristle.'

Swords were drawn, flashing. The long halberds brought to a ready position. The *vaettir* fanned out, bright atavistic gleams in their eyes, in crouches that were still higher than the heads of men.

We drew our guns. A cracking sounded, in the trees far away but drawing closer.

Once, when I was younger, I found myself on the Illvatch Mountains in a wood when an ice-storm occurred. I hunkered down in my shelter, knocking the freezing ice from the canvas of my tent and feeding the fire. When it was over, the world was cast in crystal and then the boughs began breaking with amazingly loud cracks and crashes. The ghostly sound of falling timber.

Whatever approached sounded the same. The echoes of falling trees resounded through the misty air.

Silence.

'Taken to the air,' one of the *vaettir* cried.

'What are they saying?' Fisk asked, looking wildly around.

'Taken to the air,' Lina said, sighting down her carbine. She glanced at me. 'Am I hearing this right? *Dvergar*?'

'Seems like,' I said, guns out and looking at the treetops. 'Strange, though. Archaic.'

A shadow passed overhead, stirring the vapours of the valley, and a wind followed with it. Something I'd never smelled before – a dense, rich scent, with hints of manure and cracked peppercorn. Tea leaves and sweetgrass. A jumbled odour. A mystery, like a stable that had housed all sorts of animals: horses, aurochs, cougars, serpents, crocodiles, bears. The scents of a thousand wild creatures mixed into one.

One of the *vaettir* gave a joyous ululating cry – a challenge and an expression of glee all at once. I'd heard that cry before, on the shoal plains, but now, to hear it in this place, gave it all new meaning. Gone was the wild harshness of it. Gone was the wicked mischievousness. Now it was exultation. The breath of rising spirits called to battle.

A shadow descended, roaring. It moved like the *vaettir* – blindingly fast, wickedly precise. The gun-shroud pavilion was ripped away and the fire exploded into a million sparks. I fell backward from the thing that had come into our camp, overwhelmed, and sensed my companions finding positions behind the bellicose *vaettir*, like children hiding behind their mother's skirts.

It looked like some strange hybrid of lion and serpent fused with wings. Powerful clawed feet churned the rocky earth, and a wedge-shaped head above a ruffled neck with gleaming, voracious eyes moved sinuously about. Leathery wings unfurled from its landing.

The dragon whipped around, lashing a spiked tail in a wicked arc. I felt myself being pulled backward and Gynth bellowing. A *vaettir* lashed forward, whipping his greatsword at the dragon's shifting head – the steel rang out and bounced off the thick scales.

Feathered shafts appeared in its neck, and the creature bellowed, releasing a trumpeting sound that would knock any strong man from his feet just from the shock of it. While it was distracted, a *vaettir* vaulted upon its back and, in a flash, brought its sword down to either side of the creature, cutting through the membranes of its wings.

The dragon went berserk, writhing, thrashing on the ground. I feared the *vaettir* on the creature's back would be crushed, but at the last moment he pushed himself away and rolled, coming up in a crouch, his sword still in hand. Grinning.

'He is torn!' he cried. 'Earthbound!'

The belch of Hellfire sounded, once, twice, and the dragon jerked. It wasn't clear if it was the impact of the bullet or the surprising *boom* of gunplay that caused the reaction. It began righting itself, levering itself up and over with its wing-arms and its tail.

The *vaettir* hooted as the dragon came to its feet and stilled. It seemed to coil in upon itself, gathering, bunching. It seemed as deadly as a drawn bow. It raised its now shredded wings – *he is torn, earthbound* – testing the damage there.

It uttered a desperate screech, and I couldn't help but think it was a realisation of the wounds on its wings.

The dragon exploded forward, ripping the earth with its great claws, propelling itself ahead with the impetus of the locomotive *Valdrossos*. It barrelled into a pair of the *vaettir*, who went flying sideways, arse over end, and disappeared into the trees with thunderous cracks and tearing sounds, moved away through the forest.

'It flees!' came the cry in ancient *dvergar* from the *vaettir*.

A male *vaettir* with a long metal spear loped away, chasing it.

'Let the scaled one flee!' another *vaettir* cried in *dvergar*. 'Yon beast will be great sport once its wits return.'

A moment of silence occurred, as the monster's retreat diminished and quieted altogether. The *vaettir* collected themselves, evaluating the states of the two who had been knocked aside, near senseless. For our part, Fisk, Livia, Carnelia, Sumner, Sapientia and I looked at each other with expressions that ranged from stunned to *Ia-damn-what-have-we-got-into*.

The leader of the *vaettir* said, 'Collect thy belongings and follow. This is no place for the short-lived.'

They made no introduction of themselves. As ancient as they were and there being so few of them – *only eleven!* – maybe they had no need of names. Maybe, having lived so long, they knew each other solely by tone of voice, or some other ethereal marker only *vaettir* could perceive. I could not tell. *Vaettir* are beyond mankind and *dvergar*'s ken, this I know now with a certainty. Here they live, in constant joyous battle with the great wyrms (though *wyrm* was an archaic term that had no true bearing on the creatures I had witnessed).

Some creatures find their bliss in struggle; reach their heaven by fulfilling their own natures. A hind falls to a wolf's teeth and that is right and just and so falling, does not mourn but goes in fullness to its blood-spiked end. The dominant wolf meets its fate at the jaws of the rising young and by falling fulfils its destiny – finding, if not joy there, then purpose.

Here the *vaettir* have found their heaven – only a dragon could be the *vaettir*'s equal.

I came to think of their leader as *Principia;* her command as such seemed unassailable. She led us away, deep within the island, and closer to the Emryal Rift. The other *vaettir* gathered up their wounded and encircled us – either to protect us from any other wayward dragons, or to keep us from wandering about the island on our own, I could not tell.

At first I thought weariness might overcome me, but a curious vigour coursed through me. We were fatigued from our long journey, it was true, but the strange wonder of the island, its unforeseen inhabitants both scaled and *vaettir*, and possibly the frisson of the churning cut between worlds casting off thick clouds and swirling vapours energised me. I felt I'd drunk whiskey and chicory, that I'd chewed cocoa leaves. A thrumming in my chest. My fingers tingling with inaction. We climbed now in full dark; dark except for the shifting light coming from the rift. It turned yellow and orange, blue then livid green and then blood-red. It pulsed like some great throat, eager for morsels to fall in and find themselves shat out into whatever infernal realms it led to.

We came to a low stone wall, older than the oldest Ruman remains on the Cælian and the Latinum shore. Older than *dvergar* warrens and high reaches. Beyond the wall, we encountered an intricately carved archway that led into the living stone mountain itself. We passed within, through winding passages and a small lightless cavern perceived only by sound, and then we rose once more, out into the thin rift light again. Another archway and we emerged onto a glade, full of grass and living things, as if we had entered the atrium of a Ruman villa. But instead, this was an open-air arbour, ringed in impassable cliff walls, hidden within and upon the mountainside. Among intricately carved pillars connected by high-spanned arches and a delightful running creek pouring out of a riven cliff wall, we found a series of stone dwellings, built to a scale suitable for *vaettir*, but not man.

The other *vaettir* dispersed, several of them tending to the ones who had been injured by the dragon. There were fires in some dwellings, which were not so much houses as round, elegant huts. Principia gestured to a large building made of carefully carved stacked stones, black as onyx. 'We have kept thy home as it was when thou left. In preparation for thy return,' she said.

'We've never—' Fisk began. Livia shook her head. 'Fine,' he said, throwing up his hands.

The *vaettir* leader entered and we followed – there were multiple rooms arrayed around a central chamber. A triclinium without any settees or chairs in the ancient fashion – basins of spring-fed water. A bust of obsidian stone depicting a revered old head of a Ruman household, the like of which you might find in any noble villa. At the base was chiselled *Myrddin*.

Sapientia ran her fingers over the rough letters there. 'So,' she said.

'It comes together,' Livia said.

Lina moved to stand before Principia. She put her hands on her waist. 'How do you speak *dvergar*?' she asked in Ruman. 'I think we can see here how you speak the common tongue. You've met us before.'

Principia said, 'Our tongue is the first tongue. What you speak must be some derivation of it.' She switched to *dvergar*. 'From where hast thou come?'

'Oof,' Lina said. 'The thees and thous give me a headache. We can stick with Ruman,' she said.

Principia nodded her acquiescence. 'In answer to your question,' she said. 'Once we were many, here. These are the arteries of energy that flow through the earth and sky. Yes?'

Sapientia said, 'Yes. The old straight track. The ethereal causeway, it is called.' At our puzzled looks she said, 'Numen, household gods, genius loci – these are all forces that tap into the old straight track. Connections of power between all things.'

'*Qi*,' Livia said. 'Sun Huáng would be happy to hear of it.' A faint smile touched her lips as she thought of her old friend. And then her face clouded with concern. No happy bower, this. No blissful end.

Principia continued: 'And from these we sprang. But over the eons, a slow dispersal. We cannot remember all that came before, nor all who have left, because of the long sleeps from which we awake new and unblemished,' she said. She turned to look at Gynth who, until then, she had seemed to ignore. 'You are but a child, are you not? And have had only one of the long slumbers. I can tell.'

Gynth nodded. But, as he inclined his head, it wasn't so much agreement as obeisance.

For the *vaettir*, life was a spiral where each sleep brought forgetfulness – a snake eating its own tail.

'Are you the oldest?' Livia asked.

'I am the first of the quickened, but not the oldest. There are those that slumber within the mountain for a thousand years.' Something about her demeanour darkened. 'Let the earth keep their slumber eternal. I dread the day when they awake.'

'I'm confused,' I said, and stomped over to a stone bench that was short enough for one of my stature. I rolled a cigarette and lit it with a match – a luxury I had not indulged in much on the *Typhon*. I drew the tabac smoke deep in my lungs and exhaled.

Principia observed me closely, head cocked. I held out the smoke, butt-first, and she took it in massive fingers. She sniffed the

343

cigarette and crinkled her nose at the acrid smoke and then took a puff. The cherry ate away the cigarette. She held in the smoke as I had and then exhaled it, a cloud of blue to hang around her head. She did not cough.

'Interesting,' she said. 'And not entirely distasteful. Do you have more of this?'

'Some,' I said. 'But let's get down to business. What you're saying is—' I waved a hand. 'That *dvergar* speak a shitty version of your language? And that all *vaettir* come from here? This island? And there are ancient ones sleeping in the mountain. And these *vaettir*—' I paused. 'These you don't want to wake up?'

'I think that's what she's saying, Shoe,' Lina said. 'Looks like you're not the old one, any more.'

'Fuck me,' I said, shaking my head. I patted my jacket, looking for my flask. I'd left it back on the *Typhon*. 'It's all too much for me.'

'Does it even matter, Shoe? We didn't come here to figure out your family tree,' Fisk said. He turned to Principia. 'The rift. You were here when Emrys made it?'

'Yes,' she said, opening her white hands as if explaining to a child. 'It was after my last awakening.'

'Can you take us there?' he asked.

'Why do you wish to go there?' she replied.

Sapientia stepped forward. 'When it was opened, it allowed certain . . .' She thought for a moment. 'Certain dark energies through. They have destroyed many lives. We would close this rift.'

'It has only been here but a short while,' Principia said. 'How many lives could it have harmed?'

'We are not as permanent as you,' Sapientia said. 'We have but short lives. Hundreds, maybe thousands, of generations have grown and died since the rift was opened.'

Principia seemed slightly amused. 'It is hard to fathom. How can you find meaning in anything, your time is so short?'

'That is a damned good question,' Fisk said.

'We do our best,' Livia added. 'We keep those we love safe and try to make their futures brighter.'

'Fascinating,' Principia said. 'It is something I will spend seasons pondering. Thank you for this. It is a novel thought and that is a great gift,' she said.

She paused for a moment. 'It is a dangerous place, the Gullet. The scaled ones make nests within the clouds it creates,' she said. 'It makes hunting them difficult.' Then an expression of grim satisfaction crossed her features. 'But worthwhile.'

'The Gullet?' Livia asked.

'The throat of the world,' Principia said.

Gynth said, 'At least it is not the arse.'

When I could stop laughing, I found all eyes on me. 'What?'

'Shoe, this is deadly serious,' Fisk said.

'Of course,' I said. 'It's always deadly serious.' I winked at Gynth. 'A good one, my friend.'

Principia looked between Gynth and myself. 'You are kindred, I can see. Closely matched, descended from the same line.'

The mirth washed from my face. I had always thought that 'gynth' was more of an expression of brotherhood, of camaraderie. But this put a whole different spin on things. I looked at my tall friend with whole new eyes.

'The Gullet,' Fisk said. 'Can you take us there?'

'Of course. But I do not think I will,' Principia said. 'You have just arrived and I would not have you die so quickly.'

'But if you accompanied us?' Fisk said. 'We could manage it? It would not have to be a long while. It would need be only moments.'

Principia looked thoughtful. 'I can imagine a possible future in which this can be done,' she said, in the odd way she had of phrasing things. Maybe her great age twisted her perception and then her use of language twisted it again, until it was just an intimation of the original thought and meaning. She continued: 'Possibly the newly torn one will be close. We can finish that chase.' She placed her hand on her sword and turned to go. She stopped at the entrance to the dwelling. 'Are you not prepared?'

'We must rest,' Sapientia said. 'Sleep. A little sleep. Not a long one. And afterwards, we will remember.'

'Ah,' Principia said again. 'I remember. You go silent for moments and then return. Echoes of dreams.'

'In the morning,' Livia asked. 'Can you take us then?'

'If my warriors are well, we will take you,' she said, and left.

We looked at each other in silence, stunned at all that had occurred.

Carnelia said, 'Well, that's a whole lot of jabbering for a stretcher.' She stretched like a cat and then bounced on her toes. 'I'm knackered but at the same time, I could spar a whole legion.'

'The proximity to the rift,' Sapientia said. 'And the ethereal causeway. This whole island is supercharged.'

'I could use an Ia-damned drink,' Fisk said.

Livia rested her hand on the back of his neck and he closed his eyes and pressed into it. The rest of us left them alone and went to find places to sleep.

In the morning, Principia and her clan had a massive haunch turning on a spit, dripping with fat and juices. It became obvious it was the remains of a dragon. All utensils were made from carved bone and claw. All plates and cups from the same, or scales. The dragonflesh had no discernible spice, but was delicious and unlike anything I'd ever tasted before. This meal was accompanied by some sort of cake made from mashed nuts and baked to hardness. To drink there was what seemed like some kind of mead. Terra

Umbra offered many plants, and what appeared to be a single harvestable creature – dragons. We drank and ate to our hearts' content and spent a long while languishing about the *vaettir*'s arbour. Carnelia went through her *armatura* and what Livia had called the Eight Silken Movements while *vaettir* watched with implacable but nonetheless interested expressions.

Eventually Fisk and Livia emerged from the chamber where they'd taken their rest. Both seemed wan, dishevelled. Whatever labours of love and grief had passed between them in the night, they had left them nearly washed away and empty.

With very little preamble or discussion other than checking our Hellfire weapons, we followed Principia out of the arbour and through passageways back onto the slope about the valley where we had made landfall. In the mist-wreathed bay, the *Typhon* sat, guns shrouded. Figures moved there and for a long while Fisk stared at the warded box containing the *daemon* hand. His face was awful. In him anger, remorse, and a desperate fate warred.

On the other hand, Carnelia was bright and cheery, bouncing all about and asking questions of Principia.

'Is your cloak made from dragons?' Carnelia asked.

Prinicipia said, 'We honour the creatures by using all they have to offer. Their scales and teeth and claws. The webbing of their wings. Their bones. Their muscles and sinew. From them we ingest their energy and grow strong.'

'But your cloak,' Carnelia said. 'It's very nice. It's what? Dragon skin?'

Lina snorted. Even Sapientia smiled.

'Yes, the webbing from wings,' Principia said.

'And your necklace. It's very lovely,' Carnelia said.

'My thanks, little one,' Principia said.

Around us, other *vaettir* moved, keeping us within their circle. Some of them seemed to be smiling, either from the incipient completion of the hunt that had begun the day before, or Carnelia's questions, I couldn't tell.

'You wouldn't have an extra cloak, would you?' Carnelia asked. 'I quite fancy one.'

Principia stopped. We had been following an ancient trail worn smooth into the rock of the mountainside by thousands of years of *vaettir* footsteps. The rift had drawn closer and at this height we could see more of Terra Umbra, what wasn't cloaked in smoke and shadowed by clouds. It was a still day, as if the rift waited for us. Instead of the vaporous spew forming a wall as it was pushed downwind by the easterly sea breeze, it rose straight up to the heavens to pool there in a whorl of slowly turning clouds. The rift itself pulsed in shifting colours, as if expecting us.

The *vaettir* unhooked the intricately wrought bone brooch at her throat and unslung the cloak, passing it to Carnelia. Carnelia thanked Principia, gravely, and bowed. Then she brightened once more.

'I have just the thing!' Carnelia cried. From her small rucksack, she withdrew some scissors and busily began cutting at the dragon cloak. We took this opportunity to drink water and rest. In moments Carnelia had risen from the rock face where she worked and stood, twirling the cloak onto her back. 'How do I look?' she asked.

Fisk turned away, brooding. Livia, though, smiled and said, 'You look lovely, sissy.'

'Thank you, Livia,' Carnelia said. And then, impishly, she dashed forward and gave her sister a kiss. 'I love you.'

Livia laughed, holding her sister out at arm's length, and looking at her with a puzzled expression. 'What has got into you?'

'I am just happy!' Carnelia said. 'I can't explain it.'

'Well, let us focus on the task at hand,' Livia said. 'Now is not the time for such exuberance.'

Carnelia bobbed her head up and down in acknowledgement. 'Of course, sissy. I can see I'm irritating—' She mouthed *you-know-who* and pointed at Fisk. Livia frowned, shaking her head.

But Carnelia had moved on. To Principia, she said, 'Do you make all your own jewellery?'

By midday, we had risen high. Behind us, deep green forest climbed the mountains of Terra Umbra. We stood on a cliff above a wide stone canyon, as large as the Plaza del Monstruo in Passasuego or even the whole of the Breadbasket village. At its centre, the heart of the Emryal Rift.

'The cloak of vapour is not as thick today, so we must be wary,' Principia said. 'I can sense at least one of the scaled ones moving below. It is possible there are more.' She inclined her head, sensing. 'This close to the Gullet, energies become confused.' She grinned. 'It is very exciting. The newly torn one will be outraged and want to exact revenge.'

'They're that intelligent?' Lina asked, resting her carbine over her shoulder and cocking her hip. It was such a pose of the Hardscrabble, I felt an intense longing to be back home.

'Of course,' Principia said. 'Why would we waste our energies with anything less?'

'Good point,' Sapientia said. 'There's something to be said for that.'

'Let's not get to moralising,' Carnelia said. 'That's my least favourite thing, ever.'

We threaded our way down a switchback trail, doing our best to keep our feet. On the canyon floor, the *vaettir* spread out. Principia gestured to one of her group who wore a bow, and the archer dashed off across the canyon floor and up the other side, scurrying up and out to disappear in the undergrowth there. Another took a position halfway up the switchback we had descended.

Off in the distance, muffled by rift-smoke, a screech came. Angry.

'The torn one. It knows we're here,' Principia said.

'You've called them torn before,' Carnelia said to the *vaettir*, whom it seemed she considered a bosom friend from her tone. 'Why?'

'Once their wings are cut, they cannot fly,' Principia said.

'Would they be more challenging to hunt if they flew?' Carnelia said.

A puzzled expression crossed Principia's wide, noble features. Illva and Ellva had seemed very distant. Principia's immediacy was refreshing. I had to wonder if it was the constant, eternal struggle here between *vaettir* and dragon. Maybe that was why the *vaettir* in the Hardscrabble were so vicious and mischievous. They had no opponent to constantly test their worth and, through conflict, calm and centre them. As if that was a fundamental flaw in their character – the need for conflict.

In that, they are not so different from man.

Principia said, 'It is part of the hunt. They must be torn, so they can then be harvested.'

The walls of the canyon were wet and gleaming, and a palpable thrumming travelled through the stone of the floor up my legs to my torso. The rift light from the Gullet came in pulses. The screech of the dragon grew closer.

Fisk, his voice strained, said, 'Come on. Closer.'

He pressed forward, into the heart of the canyon, nearer the rift.

A whistling came from overhead – an arrow – and it pinged off something behind us. We turned, startled. Panting, pluming great gouts of hot breath, the great wyrm gripped the side of the canyon wall, coiled. Another whizzing, and an arrow pinged off the rock face where the dragon had just been.

Now, in the light of day and the rift, the dragon's movements could be seen. It flowed over rocks as a snake might flat land. It travelled as mercury, flashing iridescent and blue. It was down the canyon face in a flash and moving toward us.

Principia's warriors moved into action. A swordsman leapt skyward, a full thirty feet in the air as the dragon passed where he had just stood. Another vaulted into a low arc, passing over the creature's shoulders and lashing out with her sword; it echoed with a bright ringing *clang!* but did no visible damage.

The dragon whipped about and its gaze settled on us. It opened its great maw and for a moment I was overwhelmed by the size of the opening and the concentric rings of teeth all pointing down its throat. Gullet indeed.

Fisk had his carbine up and firing, billowing Hellfire. Levering round after round.

The dragon, suddenly experiencing disorienting pain and overwhelming noise, gave a startled grunt and refocused on Fisk. Its neck curled in on itself, it crouched low, ready to strike. It dashed forward. But Fisk moved, blindingly fast, though not of his own volition. Gynth had leapt up, snagging his arm, and pulled him out of the way of the dragon's strike.

With its attention on Fisk, it did not witness Livia, Sumner, and Sapientia fanning out to its flanks. They let loose a barrage of Hellfire that surprised even me. I had both my six-guns out and firing.

The dragon wheeled about, like a maddened dog looking for its tormentors. Round upon round of Hellfire filled the air with brimstone and despair. The *vaettir*, overcome by the noise, had paused. But now, seeing their prey's discomposure, they leapt into action.

One of the *vaettir*, wielding a poleaxe, whipped it across the dragon's face, splitting the scales there and penetrating the skin, opening up a great gash that exposed the muscles and flesh beneath. Blood came in a heavy flow, spattering everything as the creature turned in an arc.

Feathered fletching sprouted like blossoms on the dragon's back and haunch, and it cast its head up to screech and bellow at the sky.

That was a mistake.

Principia, her greatsword in both hands, launched herself forward, catching the great beast on his neck with her blade, cutting deep. She passed through the reach of the wyrm's grasping claws, twisting her body so that it turned in the air and came down on her feet, ten paces beyond, unscratched. She lanced forward once more, moving blindingly fast and, leaping, left her sword quivering deep in the body of the dragon as she passed.

But that was not enough. The beast had strength still. We poured the rest of our Hellfire on it, and more arrows found their homes in its flesh. It became slower. Blood and drool spilled from its open mouth. It pawed feebly at us.

Finally, Principia leapt onto its back, her hand finding the hilt of her sword. It flashed out and fell again, once, twice. The dragon lay still.

'Holy Hell,' Sumner whispered. 'I have never seen the like.' He was a normally taciturn man and hoarded his words. This was exceptional.

'Yes,' Sapientia said. 'And I doubt you ever see its like again.'

Principia instructed her warriors to begin breaking down the dragon, harvesting all of it, every part. One dashed into the forest above the canyon and returned with massive leaves with which they wrapped the heart and tongue and liver of the beast. Other *vaettir* made short work taking the fabric of the wings and used them to bind other bits. For any man or *dvergar*, most of the cuts and cutlets they removed from the dragon would be too much to lift – but for *vaettir*, it was a simple chore.

A silent joy fell upon them and they worked, all humming a tune that wove in and out, each *vaettir* with a different melody, forming a musical braided chain. It was a celebration, it was an exultation. For this breathless hanging moment, all of creation was focused here, on this fallen creature, on this movement of knife and flesh. Tomorrow they would rise again and find a wyrm and begin a hunt, as they were meant to do. But today, they found happiness. To rise and fall and rise again.

Our party watched in silence. Gynth stood silently, torn between worlds. It was a dreamlike reverie, the *vaettir*'s. The Emryal Rift beyond, pulsing and churning, casting off smoke.

Sapientia turned to Fisk. 'We have come to the end, then.'

Fisk looked at her. He seemed smaller now. With every league, every mile, every step – for him, a diminution. The world had grown large and he had not grown to meet it. Livia took his hand.

'I will not argue with you any more, my love,' Livia said. There was pain in her tone and the words came with the thickness of great emotion held in check. 'This is your fate,' she said. 'You were marked by Beleth and bore the Crimson Man and now it has come to this. The last reckoning.' She came close and pressed her hands to either side of his face and kissed him through the tears that were now beginning to flow. 'But come back to me, if at all possible. Take it into the rift and be done with it and return to me.'

'You know that is not possible,' Fisk said. 'Once he rides me, he will not stop until he rides the world.'

'You don't know that!' Livia's voice cracked. 'You don't know!'

'I do, my love,' he said. 'Remember me.'

There was a moment then when it seemed Livia would falter, that she would fall to her knees and weep uncontrollably, tear her hair and clothes. But she did not. She squared her shoulders like some beast of burden resigned to a yoke being settled upon its back. She wiped her eyes and then kissed him once more.

'Go to your fate, then, my love,' she said. 'I will bear witness. We shall all bear witness.'

The *vaettir* pulled away, some of them already moving up and out of the canyon. Fisk fell to his knees in front of the warded box that contained the *daemon* hand. The hand of Isabelle Diegal, the daughter of a king who destroyed cities.

From around his neck, he withdrew a key on a chain and unlocked the box. He looked at it for a long while, his face abject and devoid of hope.

He opened the box.

It was empty.

THIRTY

I've Always Had A Terrible Habit
Of Getting Into Things I Shouldn't Have.

L IVIA GAVE A low cry. Fisk looked like an axe-struck shoal
auroch led to slaughter on Ia Terminalia, drunk and wreathed
in laurels. He searched the box as if the hand was hidden there,
and he simply could not perceive it.

From behind him, Carnelia said, 'I've always had a terrible habit
of getting into things I shouldn't have.'

Fisk rose to his feet in a flash, turning. Livia lurched forward,
as if she couldn't operate her body properly.

Carnelia stood holding the *daemon* hand by its silver chain.
It turned slowly on its hasp. Her face was flushed, but a sly grin
was plainly visible. Her new dragoncloak billowed out around her,
and her other hand rested on the *jian* given to her by Sun Huáng.
Behind her, the rift shifted colour to a deep crimson. Vapours
poured off it, some smelling of elements and spices from unknown
and impenetrable worlds.

'Sissy, what are you—' Livia began.

'No!' Carnelia said. 'Don't even start. All this idiotic talk of
fate and destiny. It would've driven Tata mad. It almost did me.'

'Carnelia,' Fisk said, taking a step forward. 'Stop. You don't
know what you're doing.'

'Yes, I do,' Carnelia said, raising the *daemon* hand. 'I'm choosing my own fate. And I'm choosing *yours*.'

The chain slipped over her head and the hand fell to end up on her chest. From the rift, light and energy poured out. A gleeful and malicious grin spread like oil upon the surface of her face. Her eyes became dark and smoke began to pour from them, deep holes to some inner furnace. Shimmering air all around her, warping. Above her a crown appeared, distending, conjured from the air and fashioned of noxious fumes. In her left hand, a seething amalgam of darkness. A sceptre.

Her right hand fell on the hilt of her sword. She drew it with a slow motion. It seemed two blades at once – the *jian* and a blade of smoke. She raised it on high. In my mind's eye, I recalled Agrippina smiting the earth of the caldera and promising to drown the world in blood. That time was nigh.

But then, the Crimson Man paused, and he looked at his hand, the one that held real steel, and not just phantoms and conjured smoke.

The crown lost cohesion. The sceptre disappeared.

For an instant, Carnelia stood before us, once more.

'Oh, fucking Hell,' she said.

She turned and strode into the mouth of the rift.

A percussive wave of air pushed us backward from the Emryal Rift, rocking us on our feet. Streamers of light issued from the opening as we backed away, toward the canyon wall. The cut between worlds – all worlds, maybe – throbbed, swelling. Its whorls and substance turned like some terrible whirlwind, shifting around an inconstant axis, its centre fluctuating. *Vaettir* screeched. Howls came down from the mountains around us – the dragons sensing some great change come upon their world.

It was a gargantuan shadowplay, swelling. In the swirling mists stood a crimson figure with a crown and sword, radiating malice and outraged impotence. Facing him, a small figure, but growing larger, rising up to meet him.

His sword fell, and the glee with which he swung was hideous to behold. Here was a thing of infinite cruelty, here was a thing of titanic desires. And now, it was caught in the throat of the world and there was but one way to vent its rage.

Carnelia.

She moved, dancing. Her motions silken. And it was hard to discern that they were even motions at all, as within the rift there was no real space. It was the nexus of all spaces, and indifferent to physical form. It was as if what occurred there, in the cut, my mind perceived somehow and made it understandable, comprehensible. Because the horrors contained within would consume the world. Snuff out my conscience like a candle.

But Carnelia! She moved. With every blow the Crimson Man made, she flowed around it. It was joyous, it was merry – and in some ways, it was more *vaettir* than *vaettir*, more graceful and centred than I could imagine Sun Huáng ever being. She yielded to every offence, recursive and rebounding.

They swelled and grew. Shadows moving back and forth. The crimson rift light turned white and blinding.

And then it was gone.

We stood blinking in the smoking ruins of the canyon, a great smear of dragon's blood before us. Wind coursed through the canyon, dragging away the smoke and revealing the crumbling rock wall beyond that had once been occluded by vapours. And beyond, the mountains rising up into the sky. A wedge of blue there, above. The jagged trees outlining a ridge. Snarls of deadfall, ferns and brush. Snow on the peaks.

Where the rift had been, there was still *something*. A line, churning in the air, like some volcanic seam releasing gas. But it was small now, the size of a *vaettir*. What poured off it was minuscule compared to what had been before.

'There's no way to totally seal it,' Sapientia said. 'It is but scar tissue the universe will not let heal.'

'Truly?' Lina said.

'I don't know,' Sapientia said, giving a rueful smile. 'Maybe.'

Livia and Fisk walked arm and arm, faces empty. It would take them a long while to come to grips with what had happened here. But, I think, in that moment when Carnelia wrested Fisk's fate from him to herself, they apprehended the nature of her greatness, which had been, up until then, so easy to miss. She cloaked herself in frivolity, to hide her true nature.

We spent weeks giving Principia and her people all the steel and metal we could spare from the *Typhon*. Our main concern on returning to it was seeing if it would still run. But Sapientia's prediction held true – *daemons* bound here remained bound here, even after the rift was closed. We had devalued silver and increased the value of *daemonbound* in one fell swoop.

Livia and Fisk closeted themselves with Fiscelion. Tenebrae wept openly at the news of Carnelia's demise.

Sapientia, Lina, and I spent our time drinking rum and home-brew wine.

'What became of Carnelia, do you think?' Lina asked. 'You know, when she went over to the other side.'

Sapientia leaned back against the gun shroud – after reclaiming the greasy canvas we had used to make the tent – and looked up at the sky. Now the rift was gone, Terra Umbra was no more. The clouds had dissipated and land that had been in darkness for thousands of years suddenly saw the light of day.

She drank deep from her cup and then gestured me to pour some more. I tilted up the pitcher and gave her good measure.

'I don't know,' Sapientia said. 'But we know what happens on this end, when *daemons* come through. A massive release of energy.'

'Are you saying she would be a *daemon* there?' Lina asked.

'Maybe. It's possible, when she came into that world, whatever it was, she would expand into a titanic fireball.' She drank some more. 'She'd become a great explosion.'

'She was a great explosion on this side,' I said.

We bid farewell to Principia, who seemed bemused at the idea of goodbyes.

'I look forward to your return,' she said.

'It is likely we will never journey back here. Our world is out there,' Livia said. Her sombreness had faded. As had Fisk's. And they had begun the truly hard work of raising a son.

'You will return, eventually.' We did not argue.

Gynth came to me. 'You will never return, will you?'

'No, hoss,' I said, looking up at the big bastard. 'I don't think we will.'

'I would have you stay,' he said. '*Gynth*.'

'Pard,' I said, 'you've got a good deal here. This is where you belong. Spending your days chasing those scaled sons-a-bitches and doing exactly what *vaettir* are supposed to do.'

'Yes, I know,' he said. 'But I will miss you all the same.'

'And I you, hoss,' I said. 'Come.'

I motioned and he fell to his knees and for the first and last time in this life, I gave a *vaettir* a hug.

Tamberlaine was dead, killed in a *daemonic* attack on his new Gallish capital. Another city killer. And Rume was destroyed for eternity, nothing left except slag and stone.

But Novorum was being rebuilt. Marcellus had rallied the

remains of the legions there and, in some pitched battles, had turned the tide. Mediera held the Hardscrabble but were being pressed hard by guerilla *dvergar* forces. And *vaettir*.

Engineers and the military were stunned. No more Hellfire. Munitions became precious, those that were left.

The legions had retreated through time three hundred years to gladius, pilum, and shield. And no one fought better than Rumans with these.

We were greeted, at the harbour, by Senator Gaius Cornelius Ursus. Flanked by praetorians in gleaming phalerae and lictors hefting fasces, he stomped to the end of the pier where the *Typhon* was moored, his silver bear's leg clearly visible. Along with its flask.

'You're back!' he cried. 'I never thought you'd come back!' The smell of whiskey pouring off him was quite strong.

'Tata, we thought you were dead!' Livia said.

'Dead?' Cornelius said. 'Preposterous. After your escape, I fled to the country, because crucifixion doesn't sit well with my complexion. Then everything went up in fucking literal flames. There wasn't a senator left alive, practically. So, when I went back to Tamberlaine, hat in hand, he reappointed me governor here.' He sniffed. 'There was a lack of qualified men.'

Cornelius looked around. His gaze fell upon Lupina, who held Fiscelion.

'There he is!' Cornelius crowed. 'There he is!' He came forward, his hands making grabbing motions.

Lupina turned the child over to Cornelius, reluctantly. He lifted him up on high.

'Where is Carnelia?' Cornelius asked, absent-mindedly. 'Isn't it just like her to be late greeting her father?'

'Tata, I have something to tell you,' Livia said, eyes welling.

'Me first. I have some good news and bad news,' he said. 'The bad news is that I was not able to get Tamberlaine to rescind his order of divorce for you and my legate, Fisk. Sadly, you two are no longer man and wife.'

Fisk and Livia said nothing.

Cornelius went on: 'Nor could I get him to rescind his adoption of you. He was distracted, maybe, with all the death and destruction.' He sighed. 'You are no longer Cornelians.'

'All right, Father,' Livia said. 'Is there any good news?'

'Somewhat,' he said. And then a grin spread across his face. 'It seems that Tamberlaine's heir Marcus perished with him in Gall.' He turned the infant Fiscelion this way and that, looking into the child's beaming face.

'So,' Cornelius said, his expression exultant, 'may I introduce you to Fiscelion Hieronymous Iulii Tamberlaine the Second, Emperor of Rume.'

After a moment of enduring our stunned silence, Cornelius harrumphed.

'Where is Carnelia?' he said, craning his neck and looking over the *Typhon*'s deck. 'Is she hiding?'

THE END